Faith and Beauty

JANE THYNNE

SIMON &
SCHUSTER

London · New York · Sydney · Toronto · New Delhi

A CBS COMPANY

First published in Great Britain by Simon & Schuster UK Ltd, 2015
This paperback edition published by Simon & Schuster UK Ltd, 2016
A CBS COMPANY
Copyright © Thynker Ltd 2015

1 3 5 7 9 10 8 6 4 2

Simon & Schuster UK Ltd
1st Floor
222 Gray's Inn Road
London WC1X 8HB

www.simonandschuster.co.uk

Simon & Schuster Australia, Sydney
Simon & Schuster India, New Delhi

A CIP catalogue record for this book is available from the British Library

PB ISBN: 978-1-4711-3194-3
Ebook ISBN: 978-1-4711-3195-0

Typeset in Bembo by Hewert Text UK Ltd, Edinburgh
Printed and bound in Great Britain by CPI (UK) Ltd, Croydon CR0 4YY

'We want girls who believe unreservedly in Germany and the Führer, and will instil that faith into the hearts of their children. Then National Socialism and thus Germany itself will last for ever.'

Dr Jutta Rüdiger, head of
the Faith and Beauty Society

'In the peoples of Germany there has been given to the world a race unmixed by intermarriage with other races, a peculiar people and pure, like no one but themselves.'

Tacitus, Germania

'Who will ever ask in three or five hundred years' time, whether a Fräulein Muller or Schulze was unhappy?'

Heinrich Himmler

For John Carey

Berlin, April 1939

It is cold in the dense woods of the Grunewald at seven o'clock on an April morning. Even though Spring has dotted the moss with bluebells and wild daffodils and filled the tops of the pines with nesting birds, the temperature is still enough to goose-pimple the arms and cause the hardiest hiker to shiver. It's gloomy, too, even in the glades, where the early sun filtering through the boughs gives only a greenish, watery light and leaves most of the tangled ferns and mulch in darkness. The mist hangs low between the closely packed trees, confusing any traveller unwise enough to stray from the path. The mix of wood here – pine, oak and birch – has remained unchanged for thousands of years, and wild boar forage for beech mast in the undergrowth as they have always done. Hunters search for deer and pig along dirt tracks that have been trodden since the Middle Ages. Though the city is only a few miles away to the west, the forest could be the same primaeval place it was in the Ice Age, when melt water first created the lakes surrounding Berlin's flat sandy plain and the early German tribes emerged from the boggy swamps.

In the Grunewald, history slips by like a leaf falling to the forest floor.

★   ★   ★

Hedwig Holz squinted down the barrel of the Walther PPK
pistol, released the safety lever, cocked the hammer, took aim,
shut her eyes tightly, and squeezed.

Nothing happened.

She dropped the pistol with a sigh, aligned it again, keeping
two fingers wrapped around the grip and a little finger curled
beneath the magazine the way she had been shown, and aimed
again. Despite the freezing air, she could feel a trail of sweat
running down her brow and a maddening itch from her woollen
vest just below her arm that she longed to scratch. What was
more, in her hurry to dress that morning she had chosen the
tighter of her two skirts and the waistband was now digging in
uncomfortably. Yet she had to stop these trivial bodily sensations
from distracting her, just as she must ignore the thrushes flitting
between their nests in the high pines, the squirrels scrambling
among the branches, and the whole awakening Grunewald
around her. She must concentrate. Straighten her arm, feel the
cold metal of the pistol burn against her palm, find the target and
shoot. Even without her glasses, how hard could that be?

She aimed, shut her eyes again and fired, but although the gun
worked this time, the shot veered wildly off course, ricocheting
around the tranquil woods and provoking a chorus of screeches
from the crows overhead. Hedwig flinched, brushed the sweaty
trails of hair from her brow with the back of her sleeve and aimed
again. The rustling in the trees above had broken her concentration, and her next shot went even wider, sending a flutter of
birds up into the sky and provoking muffled laughs from the
gaggle of girls behind her.

They had been there for an hour now, a group of twenty
young women, all startlingly alike from a distance, with blue
eyes, plaits of various shades of gold pinned up on their heads and
white smocks with neckties over a navy serge pinafore, ankle
socks and clumpy black boots. They made a curious sight as they
threaded their way along the woodland path behind their leader

– an Amazonian figure called Fräulein von Essen, who wore a leather jerkin and carried a satchel of ammunition and a target which she established a hundred metres away from the firing site. They could expect to be there for another hour at least, Hedwig thought despondently, until Fräulein von Essen was satisfied that every girl among them could shoot a man at a hundred paces.

Shooting was the last activity Hedwig expected when she joined the Faith and Beauty Society. Far from shooting a man, all most girls wanted was to capture one. The Glaube und Schönheit Society was, after all, the Third Reich's elite finishing school for young women. Its girls were the pearls of the Reich and the plan was to equip them with the poise, polish and talent required to marry into the top ranks of the Nazi hierarchy.

To this end, every weekend, and several evenings in the week, a select group of girls would gather at the Faith and Beauty community house in the picturesque woods outside Neu-Babelsberg to be educated in the finer points of civilization: history, the arts, music, dancing and dinner party conversation. How to discuss Beethoven intelligently and dazzle a man with knowledge of the Franco-Prussian War. How to make tapestries and play chamber music. How to waltz, sketch a head and paint a decent landscape in watercolours. Any old Bride School or Mother Class could teach a girl to cook a herring, the wisdom went, but some German girls should be setting their sights on higher things. That was why Reichsjugendführer Baldur von Schirach, head of all Nazi youth groups, had hit on the idea of a society for the cream of the nation's young women. Those who passed the selection procedure were the Third Reich's Vestal Virgins, according to the introductory talk – a comparison that made Hedwig blush profusely when she heard it for the first time.

Every girl applying to the Faith and Beauty Society must be blonde and blue-eyed – the precise colour was measured against an eye chart containing sixty different shades – but there was no actual stipulation that they must also be beautiful, which was fortunate for Hedwig, whose moon-like face was earnest, rather than exquisite, and whose mousy hair could only be called blonde by a vivid stretch of the imagination. She was tall and bosomy, a born worrier with a perpetually anxious air that vanished only when a good-natured smile lit up her face, exposing her wonky teeth.

Hedwig's appearance was in stark contrast to her only friend in the society, Lotti Franke, a slender beauty with thick, honey-gold hair, a bold gaze and full mouth. Lotti looked like a girl in a Renaissance portrait, with eyes as blue as gas flames and skin like whipped cream. Although Faith and Beauty girls were encouraged to acquire a suntan, Lotti maintained that sunlight caused wrinkles and insisted on coating herself with Nivea and remaining as pale as wax.

Despite their physical differences, the two had been close since they met on the very first day of school, with their satchels on their backs and the traditional cone of sweets in their hands. Frau Mann, the Faith and Beauty principal, never lost a chance to boast that the two girls proved the egalitarian nature of the society. In the Third Reich, elites weren't just for the rich. The other girls might come from middle-class homes with pianos and maids, but Hedwig and Lotti were unambiguously from the wrong side of the tracks. Hedwig and her five brothers inhabited a cramped apartment in Moabit – four rooms with a cuckoo clock in the parlour, a pervasive aroma of pork fat and a bathroom they shared with another family. Lotti's family was even poorer than Hedwig's. It had been a great sacrifice for the Frankes to find the fees, but Lotti was an only child, and generally Lotti got what Lotti wanted. And what she really wanted was a ticket to a better life. To meet all the right people and leave working-class Berlin behind for ever.

Lotti was passionate about fashion, and as part of her Faith and Beauty course she had chosen to study costume design at the nearby Ufa film studios in Babelsberg. She had met any number of film stars – Lilian Harvey, Willy Fritsch, Brigitte Horney and Marika Rökk – and she was full of snippets of celebrity gossip. Which actor was sleeping with someone else's wife, who had undergone cosmetic surgery, what girl had caught Reichsminister Goebbels' eye. All the Faith and Beauty girls crowded round her. Lotti was the type who knew secrets, and even though she probably made most of them up, hearing about a film star's drug habit was infinitely more diverting than a lecture on Napoleon's Retreat from Moscow.

Hedwig braced herself, focused and took aim again. The gun was heavy – half a kilo of iron that had to be aimed with a straightened right arm. Her next shot went even wider, provoking unrestrained shrieks of laughter from her fellow students. Damn pistol shooting. And archery. What on earth was it for? Fräulein von Essen told them archery would reawaken their sense of the mediaeval, but Hedwig had a nine-to-five job as a librarian. She had never had a sense of the mediaeval and didn't want one now. When would she ever need to handle a bow and arrow? Let alone a gun?

As if reading her thoughts, Fräulein von Essen stared at her, flint-eyed, and signalled, with an infinitesimal incline of the head, that she should try again. Hedwig needn't think that mere ineptitude would reprieve her from pistol practice. They could stay there all day, as far as Fräulein von Essen was concerned. Didn't Hedwig remember taking that oath to the Führer about loyalty, sacrifice and achievement?

Hedwig was distracted – that was the problem – and it was Lotti who was distracting her. She had not turned up for pistol practice that morning, nor had Hedwig seen her at their previous community meeting. She was out during the day, of course, but everyone was supposed to congregate at the community house at six for dinner and evening instruction and Lotti had already missed a two-part talk on Mediaeval Tapestries.

Hedwig knew what the problem was, of course. Lotti was in love. When Hedwig asked her who the lucky man was, she had turned secretive, so Hedwig assumed he must be unsuitable. She had no idea who it could be, but Lotti had been making endless outings over recent weeks and refused to tell Hedwig where she had been. God forbid she had eloped. The thought of what that would do to Herr and Frau Franke, who worshipped their clever daughter and had gladly donated their savings for her Faith and Beauty training, made Hedwig wince.

When her next shot veered even further from the target, prompting a further burst of hilarity from the others, Fräulein von Essen put an unexpected stop to Hedwig's misery by ordering her to give someone else a try, so she moved gratefully to the back of the group, leant against the trunk of a tree and miserably surveyed the dank, mushroomy woods around her.

She knew she was supposed to like the forest. They were constantly sent on hikes with a knapsack and compass, the branches whipping in their face and the undergrowth threatening to trip them up, and besides, true Germans belonged in the woods. They had learnt that in the weekly Race Ancestry lessons; according to the Roman author Tacitus, the German race had originated in the forest before giving birth to the whole of human civilization. The original Germans were blue-eyed with golden hair and vigorous bodies, and life in the forest had made them a tough, warrior race.

But the silence unnerved her. Berlin was a cacophony of noise, yet here were only pigeons rustling and cooing, the occasional sound of a deer crashing through the undergrowth and the sporadic crack of the girls' guns.

That morning though, the silence had been shattered by a bevy of construction workers who had begun work a few hundred metres away, building an air-raid shelter. Because of the warmongering of the British, the whole of Berlin was digging air-raid shelters now. Wherever you went in town the rattle of drills and clang of spades could be heard in the background, preparing for the day that British bombers appeared in the skies. Everyone was talking about war but Hedwig didn't believe it for a second. As far as she was concerned, the chances of any actual fighting were as remote as those ancient battles between the rival tribes of Europe that Tacitus wrote about. No foreign country had stood in the Führer's way before, and there was really no reason to suppose they would now.

On the way back Fräulein von Essen couldn't resist a dig at Hedwig's hopeless aim.

'Back again tomorrow, ladies. And perhaps this time Hedwig Holz will be able to manage just a single shot on target.'

Chapter One

Berlin, in April 1939, was partying like there was no tomorrow.

The Führer was fifty and the whole of Germany was in a frenzy. The 20th itself had been declared a National Holiday and the largest military parade ever held – five hours' worth of stormtroopers, hurricane troopers, tornado troopers and every other type of trooper – was proceeding along the new East-West axis, the great triumphal boulevard that ran all the way from Unter den Linden to the Olympic stadium. Guns and tanks glittered in the morning air as the boots of fifty thousand soldiers thudded rhythmically into the ground. Heinkel bombers, Messerschmitt fighters and Stuka dive bombers performed fly pasts at five-minute intervals, leaving lightning flashes of vapour in the sky. Deputations of the Hitler Youth and the League of German Girls had arrived from all over Germany. There were armoured cars, cannons, Howitzers and anti-aircraft guns. And more than a million spectators, most of them carrying black bread sandwiches, bottles of beer and swastika flags.

Clara Vine shuffled her feet and looked down at her glossy Ferragamo leather pumps. They were hand-stitched in Florence, had cost the earth and they hurt like hell.

Why on earth had she not worn comfortable shoes?

She was hungry and thirsty and longing to sit down. She had been there since nine that morning, but had only managed to secure a place three deep opposite the Führer's saluting podium on the Charlottenburger Chaussee. The view to her right was obscured by a large woman with a squashed felt hat, accompanied by two boys of around six and seven. To begin with Clara had pitied the children, doomed to spend the morning fenced in by a forest of legs, but after hours of their relentless wails, enquiring when exactly the Führer was coming and how much longer would he be, her sympathy was wearing thin. To her left was a war veteran, medals pinned proudly to his chest, saluting frenetically like someone with uncontrollable muscle spasms. He had come all the way from Saxony and he was not the only one. Thousands of visitors had poured into the city. The stations were teeming and every hotel from the Adlon down was block-booked. People who couldn't afford anywhere else had pitched their tents in the parks.

Like all birthdays, Hitler's special day had begun with presents, but that was where the ordinariness ended. Vast marble tables had been assembled in the Reich Chancellery to display Meissen porcelain, silver candlesticks and Titian paintings, alongside rather more modest gifts from ordinary people, largely made up of swastika cakes and cushions. The Pope, the King of England and Henry Ford had sent telegrams. The engineer Ferdinand Porsche had presented Hitler with a shiny black convertible VW beetle. Rudolf Hess had acquired a collection of priceless letters written by the Führer's hero, Frederick the Great, and Albert Speer had given him an entire scale model of the Welthauptstadt, the new world capital, with buildings made out of balsa wood and glass and a thirteen-foot model of the proposed triumphal arch. This was, without doubt, Hitler's favourite present and he pored over it like a boy with a train set until he could be persuaded to tear himself away.

On the face of it, Berlin was putting on a magnificent show. Gigantic white pillars had sprouted all the way along major thoroughfares. The newsstands groaned with souvenir birthday issues. Swastikas waved from every conceivable surface. Spring was a riot of colour in Berlin, so long as the colours were red and black.

Beneath the birthday bunting, however, everything was a little shabbier in Germany's capital. The tablecloths in the restaurants were spotted because there was no detergent, the bread was sawdust and the Ersatz coffee undrinkable. People looked the other way on the trams because there was no tooth-paste, precious few razor blades or shaving foam, and the sour odour of humanity and unwashed clothes hung in the U-Bahn. Even high-class nightclubs like Ciro's stank of low-grade cigarettes and taxis home were non-existent because of the petrol shortage.

After the previous year's Anschluss, when Germany annexed Austria, followed by the bloodless seizure of Czechoslovakia that March, most of Europe guessed a war was on the way. When it happened, it would be Poland's fault, according to the Ministry of Propaganda and Enlightenment, which ensured that newspapers were black with seventy-two-point headlines screaming belligerent revenge on the Poles for their atrocities against Germans in the disputed 'Polish corridor'. *Poland, Look Out!* There had been murderous attacks on Germans in Danzig. God help any country that stood in Germany's way.

Looking around her, Clara guessed that despite the marching and the machines, no one in this great big birthday pageant really wanted war. The ghost of the last war was still behind their eyes and the thought of what another would do haunted all but the very young. Only the little boys beside her, who now had squeezed between the legs of the stormtroopers guarding the route, saw anything thrilling in the inexorable wall of men and tanks rolling past. Everyone else was getting by on an edgy cock-tail of hope and denial. Everywhere you went, nerves flashed and shorted, like violet sparks above the tramlines. Tempers frayed.

The whole city was as pumped and jittery as a dog being forced to fight.

Above their heads, loudspeakers strung along the street barked out radio broadcasts of Joseph Goebbels between bursts of military music. Goebbels was cheerleading the nation as though the Führer's birthday was synonymous with facing up to the Poles. Enthusiasm for both was compulsory.

'*No German at home or anywhere else in the world can fail to take the deepest and heartiest pleasure in participation.*'

Clara winced. The voice of the short, club-footed Minister for Propaganda and Enlightenment still got under her skin like shards of glass. Even now, after six years in Germany, hearing it daily on the radio and at the Babelsberg film studios where she worked, Joseph Goebbels' wheedling tones could make her flinch like chalk on a blackboard.

Clara was only there because of a solemn promise she had made to her godson Erich Schmidt, who at sixteen had been chosen to lead his battalion of Hitler Youth in the parade. It was a great honour, Erich had impressed on her several times. Only from where she was standing there seemed little chance of even glimpsing Erich, let alone of him registering her loyal presence.

It didn't have to be that way. As an actress contracted to the Ufa studios, Clara had qualified for a place in the VIP enclosure, alongside prominent personalities in their finery and portly Party dignitaries trussed up in field grey. The viewing stand, garlanded with golden laurels and tented drapes like a marquee at a country wedding, offered a far better view and a gilt chair to sit on. That was why she had risked the Ferragamo shoes, as well as the skirt suit and the tip-tilted hat, which now looked far too smart amid the stolid burghers of the Berlin crowd. Only, when she reached the gates of the VIP enclosure, she realized she couldn't face it. She spent enough of her life in close confines with Nazi officials, without wanting to join them behind a velvet rope with no chance of escape.

A frisson of excitement ran through the crowd. A posse of steel-helmeted, black-jacketed SS officers had appeared and were elbowing their way through, glancing from left to right. Joseph Goebbels, who was filming this extravaganza for posterity, was controlling every aspect down to the last detail. No one was allowed to take their own photographs and police were deputed to arrest anyone in the crowd who wielded a camera or failed to perform the Nazi salute. As the SS men barged past, Clara saw an elderly couple at the back of the crowd, the man a teacher or a pastor perhaps, and his grey-haired wife beside him, being hustled off to a side street and lined up against a wall to await the police wagon.

Mirror periscopes swivelled like reeds in the wind and the screams around her intensified, rising into a wall of sound. Shouts swelled and clashed in the air like brass. The cordon of SA and SS officers linked arms to prevent the surge of sightseers spilling into the road.

'He's coming!'

The excitement of the moment caused the stolid woman beside Clara to burst into a cry of joy.

First came a fleet of motorcycle outriders, then Hitler himself, upright at the helm of his seven-litre Mercedes Tourer with his arm raised in the trademark salute he could apparently hold for two hours straight. His peculiar, impersonal stare travelled like a searchlight across the crowds as his head swivelled intermittently right and left, seemingly seeking out individual faces. Flowers were hurled through the air, hitting the sides of the Mercedes with soft thuds. Surprisingly, only two members of the Adolf Hitler Leibstandarte bodyguard were at his side. The usual car of followers was absent.

How vulnerable he was. All it would take was a single shot and the leader of all Germany, the object of all this adulation, would be extinguished like a light bulb, along with the fears of an entire continent. Clara wondered if she was the only person in the crowd who had such a thought. German civilians were never told about attempts on the Führer's life but Clara had heard that in Munich several years ago, during a parade like this, a pistol had been found in a newsreel camera mounted on the roof of a car, the barrel of the gun pointed down the lens. A couple of other attempts had been averted at the last minute. Each lucky escape only served to convince Hitler more firmly of his deepest belief: Destiny was on his side.

As he came parallel a shaft of sun lanced through a rent in the clouds, and a finger of light pointed down towards his car. Hitler's bright blue gaze swivelled in Clara's direction and seemed to penetrate right to where she was standing.

Clara ducked her head, turned sharply and pushed her way back through the crowd. She had a long day ahead of her and a party to attend that evening. And today of all days she had chosen to move house.

Chapter Two

Stepping over the bags she had dumped in the hallway, and shrugging off her coat, Clara looked around her new home.

For an actress working in the Babelsberg studios, just a short distance away through the Berlin forest, this place couldn't be more perfect. It was set in a colony of houses built in the nineteenth century by rich Berliners, seeking respite from the city on the bucolic shores of the Griebnitzsee. The villas around the lake, all of them designed by up-and-coming architects, boasted a variety of styles – sweet, gabled cottages in the early nineteenth-century Germanic domestic fashion, turreted mock baronial places, alongside modernist constructions with clean lines and open-plan spaces. Since the 1920s, the original owners – the bankers and industrialists – had given way to film stars and now the little group of houses was known locally as the Artists' Colony. It was Berlin's version of the Hollywood Hills – an oasis of luxury just a short drive from the city centre for those who could afford privacy and architectural distinction.

Not a category that included Clara Vine.

Although her acting contract with Ufa kept her in regular film work, she was far from the heights of stardom that promised a place in the Artists' Colony. It might have been her half-English heritage, or the rebellious twist to her smile, that prevented directors from casting her in leading roles. Or perhaps it was merely that the preferred template for a Reich film star was blonde and buxom – a pattern fitted perfectly by her friend Ursula Schilling, who had been one of Ufa's top actresses until the previous year, when she joined stars like Marlene Dietrich and Billy Wilder in the sanctuary of Hollywood. This was Ursula's house and Clara was only here until Ursula decided when, or if, it was safe to return.

If she didn't know better, Clara might have wondered how Ursula could bear to leave it. Though small, the house was exquisite in every detail. It had been designed by Mies van der Rohe, with a steep gabled, red-tiled roof, vanilla-painted façade and teal-blue shutters on the windows. Beech, oak and pine trees grew all around, shielding each house from any sight of its neighbour, and giving each dwelling a sense of total, rural isolation.

The front door opened directly into a panelled, open-plan drawing room running the entire length of the house, furnished with bookshelves, and a piano. Expensive rugs covered the polished wooden floor and there was an armchair soft enough to sink in and never get up.

Ursula had been gone for months now, but the way she had left the house, you would think she had taken a shopping trip to the Kurfürstendamm rather than an ocean liner across the Atlantic. Everything was still there – cushions, lampshades, curtains. The rubble of lotions, stubby kohl pencils and cratered powders on the dressing table. She had abandoned all her books and furniture, not to mention crockery in the sink and withered rosebuds in a dry vase. Even Ursula's clothes were still in the bedroom, draped carelessly across chairs, falling out of drawers and hanging in scented layers of silk and satin like gleaming ghosts.

Fortunately Clara didn't have much luggage of her own. She had always travelled light, ever since her days in repertory theatre in England. All she had with her was a few changes of clothes, her leather jewellery box, Max Factor make-up, a book of Rilke's poetry with a duck-egg blue cover, and the sheaf of mail she had grabbed from her apartment just before she left.

Wandering into the kitchen she set down a bag containing black rye bread, eggs, potatoes and an onion. She had stood in line for the eggs and onion and had every intention of enjoying them in an omelette as soon as she had unpacked. As she ran a tap to fill the kettle, she opened a cupboard to rummage for a cup and discovered, with the delight of an archaeologist making an antique find, a jar of real Melitta coffee, almost untouched. The only coffee to be found in Berlin right now, Kaffee-Ersatz, was a gritty concoction of chicory, oats and roasted barley mixed with chemicals from coal, oil and tar; so a jar like this was real treasure. Unscrewing the lid, she inhaled deeply. Everyone in Germany obsessed about food now. They dreamed of potatoes fried in butter, crispy chicken and fragrant roast meat. Of real coffee and cream. Being half English, Clara dreamed of thick wedges of Fuller's walnut cake and solid chunks of Cadbury's chocolate, which were even more impossible to find.

Cradling her fragrant, smoky-flavoured coffee – black, no milk – Clara went over to the far window, from where a long sliver of the lake was visible, its hard silver surface marbled by high clouds, and a dark fringe of woods beyond. A narrow jetty protruded into the water, a duck standing upon it frisking a rainbow of water across its back. Shielding her eyes against the dazzle of light, she opened the French windows and stepped outside. She had not had a garden since childhood, when nine acres of Surrey at the foot of the north Downs had formed the limits of her world and where she, her elder sister Angela and brother Kenneth had raced snails, collected tadpoles and played French cricket.

Resting against the sun-warmed brick she breathed deeply, inhaling the scent of narcissus and sweet woodsmoke from a bonfire, letting the smell of nettles and grass float through her. In the city a hundred different noises made up silence, like the colours that together constitute white light; the rumble of traffic, the bang of a shop door, the jangle of a milk cart, the whine of a wireless; but out here the silence had a different texture. It was a deep, ancient quiet, the kind you never found in the city. Thick and tangible, oppressive almost. Clara could see why no one bothered locking their doors. The only sounds were the distant chug of a steam cruiser, squabbling squirrels in the high branches of the pines and her own breathing.

But it was no good. Whenever Clara relaxed, her mind would return to the same matter. The matter that she tried to keep buried, but became increasingly urgent as time passed.

Leo Quinn.

Leo was the British passport control officer who had first suggested her other – and what felt increasingly like her real – role. At his urging, Clara had begun to feed details of the gossip and feuds of the senior Nazi women to British Intelligence. Moving, as she did, in the regime's high society, Clara had become a spy on the private life of the Third Reich. For years she had formed a link in the shadowy chain that stretched across Europe, passing news of the Nazis to her contacts in Britain's Secret Intelligence Service, learning from Leo the tradecraft and secrets of a spy's life.

And in the process she had fallen in love with him.

At the thought of Leo, sadness swelled and images of their last two weeks together flared in her brain. They had spent the time enveloped in each other, taking a borrowed car out to the lakes and plunging into the crisp water, slippery fronds beneath their feet. Making love in a bedroom, the morning light spangled across his face. Walking in the forest, beneath the shifting leaves. Talking about the future, and Leo's urging that she should leave Berlin for the safety of England. She thought of his fingertips tracing her face as though committing it to memory. Holding her so tightly she could feel the blood pulse through him, his mouth on hers and his arms encircling her as though he would never let her go.

And yet he had let her go. Without a second's hesitation.

It happened quite abruptly one morning. He had received a message the previous night, requesting that he return to work in London without delay. Clara didn't even know what Leo's job entailed – only that it was something to do with encrypted communications and that he was based in a London office block, somewhere near Oxford Street, but also made frequent sorties abroad. Yet as soon as he had told her his orders, he was knotting his tie and glancing at his watch. Then he pulled on his jacket, gave one last look back, and headed out of the door.

That was six long months ago and she had not heard a word from him since. Not so much as a postcard.

Where are you, Leo?

The questions ran through her head like beads on a rosary.

Most evenings after she had finished at the film studios, she would have a solitary supper and bury herself in the latest novel her sister had sent out from Hatchards bookshop in London. Occasionally she would be dragged out by friends, and other times she took Erich to the cinema or for a meal. At night she might stretch out a hand across the satin counterpane to where Leo had been, but more often she fell asleep the moment she climbed into bed, exhausted by the constant busyness she had adopted to keep thoughts of him at bay.

Yet increasingly a mutinous anxiety arose in her, that she tried and failed to suppress. Why had Leo not been in touch? For someone whose work involved communication, it was ironic that he had failed entirely to communicate with her. Agents learned to compress their words into codes, but what code did silence contain?

On one side of the room a gigantic, rococo mirror was angled to reflect a photograph of Ursula on the opposite wall, an icy peroxide fantasy swathed in fur. Gazing into the mirror, Clara tried to see what Leo saw.

He had always said she had a face that was easily able to conceal her feelings, or to project other emotions entirely. The glossy dark hair with its russet streaks had been cut short for her current film role, and the effect was to frame her face more closely, emphasizing the widely spaced blue eyes with the brows high and thinly plucked, in the current fashion. Her sleek dress, flatteringly nipped in at the waist, gave her an air of self-assurance, even if it was worn in patches and the cuff was starting to fray.

Yet that self-assurance, like her identity itself, was a construct. The document she carried in her bag at all times, certifying that Clara Helene Vine was a full member of the Aryan race, disguised the fact that she was, in Nazi terms, a 'Mischling', with a Jewish mother and grandmother, who under the strict race laws now in place could not marry a gentile, work for one or even sleep with one without the threat of imprisonment.

At the thought of it, she pulled out her Max Factor compact, dabbed her nose a little, ran a layer of Elizabeth Arden's Velvet Red round her lips and gave a defiant smile. If she was going to present a false face to the world, it might as well be an immaculate one.

She turned to her bags, began unpacking and placed three photographs above the fireplace. One of a smiling six-year-old and another of the same boy ten years later, grown dark-eyed and sombre. Her godson, Erich, who was even now burning to join the Luftwaffe and perhaps would soon get his chance. The third photograph was of her mother Helene, throwing her head back in laughter to reveal perfect white teeth. Acting a part, as she had been from the day she arrived as a new bride in England at the age of twenty-two, leaving Germany behind and with it any mention of her Jewish heritage. There was no picture of Leo.

Though Ursula's house was far more luxurious than anything else Clara had known, that had nothing to do with the actual reason for her move. In recent weeks Clara had been increasingly convinced that her apartment in Winterfeldtstrasse was being watched. Far too frequently there were men around to clean the windows of the block opposite, or to paste new advertisements on the hoarding outside. Clara carried out all her usual precautions. She placed a dish of water for the cat just inside her front door. She didn't have a cat, but anyone entering the apartment surreptitiously would knock the dish and make a damp mark on the carpet. She left a tube of lipstick balanced on the casement window latch which would be easily upset if the window was opened. Although she was certain there had been no actual intrusion, the previous week she had dashed home in an unexpected shower and almost collided with an unfamiliar figure in the lobby.

'Can I help you?'

He was a sinewy young man with a lean, evasive face.

'Just sheltering from the rain.'

But he was bone dry. No pearls of water clung to the fabric of his umbrella or dripped from its spokes, nor was there any drop on his coat, dampening his felt hat or soaking his scuffed leather shoes. He carried a bulky case, and avoided her eye when she addressed him.

That was the moment she decided. Clara was experienced enough to distinguish between the instinctive feeling of being observed – that constant prickle of self-awareness all actresses develop – and the insidious lick of nerves prompted by Gestapo surveillance. She had learned to trust her instincts and at that second they told her it was time to switch locations without delay. She had no desire to check the face of every street sweeper or sneak a glance into every idling car on the kerb. Fortunately, she remembered Ursula's offer of house-sitting. Out in Griebnitzsee there was very little chance of passing strangers. It was almost too isolated. But then, she might not be spending too much time at home.

She propped an invitation on the mantelpiece. It had arrived two weeks ago at the Babelsberg studios, with no covering note. It was printed on stiff, heavy, ivory card with shiny, engraved lettering and gold edges – the kind that Angela ordered from Smythson's in Bond Street for her cocktail parties and At Homes. Just the feel of it gave Clara a jolt of nostalgia for Angela's smart society gatherings, the Mayfair ballrooms filled with actors and politicians, the theatre people and poets. She pressed it to her nose and inhaled the faintest trace of cigarette smoke.

Captain Miles Fitzalan
requests the pleasure of the company of
Miss Clara Vine
At a ball at the St Ermin's Hotel
Victoria
London SW
Champagne and carriages at 1am

The only difference about this invitation was, Clara did not know any Miles Fitzalan and nor had she heard of the St Ermin's Hotel. And she guessed, whatever this meeting was about, it would certainly be no party.

Chapter Three

Being seduced by Joseph Goebbels was every starlet's worst nightmare but for foreign journalists it was a rather pleasanter experience. The Press Club he had established at a cost of half a million marks on Leipziger Platz was a comfortable mansion of gleaming wood and chrome, superbly fitted out with ornate restaurant, reading room, library and bar where journalists were encouraged to congregate in the clubby armchairs and write their stories in luxurious ease. The restaurant served the type of white-fleshed schnitzel, buttery vegetables and rich, flaky pastries that were no longer available elsewhere in Berlin, accompanied by fine wines and the holy grail of Viennese coffee. All the international newspapers were available, a Tannoy system was in place, and journalists could obtain anything from reduced-rate opera tickets to special red identification cards for procuring taxis. They could also write their copy on the typewriters there and have it cabled directly back to their own newspapers, if they didn't mind the censors crawling over every word.

The club was practically in earshot of the Propaganda Ministry in Wilhelmplatz, but that was irrelevant because beneath every plush leather banquette was a listening device to collate conversations, and anything missed was scooped up by the superbly attentive waiters who doubled as Goebbels' spies. All the journalists knew the Press Club was an eavesdroppers' paradise, but the quality of the food and the prices at the bar made it a popular destination, just so long as you didn't mind your thoughts being shared by a wider audience, which journalists by their very nature generally didn't. The level of comfort encouraged harmonious conversation and the only permanent disagreements came from the three clocks on the wall, telling the time in Paris, London and Tokyo.

Clara made her way towards Leipziger Platz with some difficulty. Battling the throng of people who had spent all day at the birthday parade was like wading through a drunken river upstream. It was as though every one of Berlin's five million souls had turned out to see the Führer. Whole family groups walked several abreast on the pavement, the fathers lugging picnic baskets and the mothers folding seats. Clara breasted the flow, passing bars belching beer breath through open doors and navigating crash barriers, skirting the boozy crowds and dodging the sharp sticks of flags trailed by exhausted children who had been up before dawn.

Eventually she escaped up the porticoed steps of the Press Club, edging around a twenty-five-foot portrait of the Führer in the lobby proclaiming 'Our Loyalty: Our Thanks' and entered the party.

Like everywhere else in Germany, the Press Club was celebrating with unrestrained joy. Goebbels had allocated a large quantity of Sekt to assist the celebrations and despite the fact that the drinks came accompanied by a liberal sprinkling of bureaucrats from the Reich Press Chamber, the foreign correspondents had decided en masse to take full advantage of it. Clara looked round for the plump, sandy-haired figure of Mary Harker, the journalist she had met when she first arrived in Germany and who was now a close friend. Mary, with her passionate concern for the underdog and her deep sense of justice, had been reporting from Europe for the *New York Evening Post* since 1933.

Having someone good-hearted, wholly on her side and who, most importantly, had an inkling of her secret role, meant that Mary was the only person with whom Clara could genuinely relax.

Mary's hearty laugh and distinctive New Jersey accent were instantly recognizable from the far side of the room. She had barely changed since they first met six years ago. She still had the same mordant sense of humour, the same favourite old black dress, her hair was a corn-coloured tangle and her lively eyes were hidden behind heavy-rimmed black spectacles. As usual she was at the centre of a throng, and loudly enjoying herself.

'Clara, let me introduce Bill Shirer, from CBS, and Louis Lochner, head of the Berlin bureau of the Associated Press.' She indicated a short man with a moustache, waving a pipe, and his balding colleague. 'And Sigrid Schultz of the *Chicago Tribune*,' she gestured at a tiny, china-complexioned woman with a fierce stare. 'Guys, meet Clara Vine. A star of the Ufa studios, as I expect you know.'

The group nodded politely. American correspondents were thick on the ground in Berlin. There must have been at least fifty, staffing the wire services, broadcast stations and newspapers, but you rarely saw so many together.

'Quite a turn-out,' said Clara.

'We're congregating for safety,' laughed Shirer. 'Roosevelt has refused to send Hitler a birthday card, so we Americans aren't flavour of the month any more.'

'At least you remember what it's like to be popular,' came a voice from behind. 'We British haven't been popular for years.'

Clara didn't know the voice, yet in another way, she recognized it instantly. It was the kind of voice that echoed across public school playing fields and down the corridors of the British civil service in Whitehall. The same voice that belonged to friends of her brother back in England: precise, understated and slightly mocking. A tone that said most things should not be taken very seriously and very little should be taken seriously at all. Clara turned to see two men, one tall and lanky in a three-piece suit of Harris tweed and another, shorter figure with a shock of blond hair, a freckled face and alert blue eyes, his old school tie secured with a tiepin.

'Clara, meet Charles Cavendish and Hugh Lindsey. Your fellow Brits,' said Mary, eliciting a look of pure puzzlement on the men's faces.

'Clara's half English, didn't you know? She's the daughter of Sir Ronald Vine.'

'The Ronald Vine?' asked Cavendish, with the look of disdainful astonishment which always accompanied any mention of Clara's father's name. Almost immediately he concealed it with a polite smile and stuck out a hand, but not before Clara had noticed.

'The same.'

To be known as the daughter of one of England's most prominent Nazi sympathizers had been invaluable in gaining the trust of senior members of the regime. Her father's loyalties had been Clara's ticket into the inner circles of the Third Reich. Yet still, it was an uncomfortable façade to maintain, especially with the British.

Somehow, the other journalist, Hugh Lindsey, appeared to understand. His eyes travelled over her with intuitive sympathy. He had an easy laugh and an expansive manner that seemed to put people at their ease.

'None of the Nazis love us Brits any more. Despite the Duke of Windsor's best efforts.'

'Hugh's just arrived from London,' Mary explained.

There was a rapid turnover of foreign journalists in Berlin. Reporters were constantly having their visas withdrawn for overstepping Goebbels' mark, or allowing criticism of the regime to creep into their stories.

'He's Rupert's replacement,' added Mary.

'Not that Rupert could ever be replaced,' said Hugh, gallantly.

Clara gave Mary a quick, private glance. At one time Mary had been half in love with Rupert Allingham, the aristocratic head of the *Daily Chronicle*'s Berlin bureau. Eventually his increasing frustration with the regime, combined with his increasing drinking, had the predictable results and when his friends gathered at the Lehrter Station to wave him off, they agreed that however much they were going to miss him, Rupert's expulsion from Germany had been an accident waiting to happen.

'You have big shoes to fill,' she told Hugh.

'Big beer glasses too,' he replied lightly.

'Rupert's well out of it,' Charles Cavendish remarked. 'There won't be any war. I've heard Chamberlain is having a nervous breakdown. Whenever people try to talk to him, he just stands feeding pigeons through the Downing Street window.'

'You wonder how the Nazis would even have the time for war,' added Bill Shirer. 'They're so busy being at war with each other. Von Ribbentrop and Goering aren't even on speaking terms, I hear, and Goebbels can't stand either of them.'

'I'll be able to update you on that,' said Mary. 'I've been granted an interview with Goering tomorrow. My new minder just told me.'

'Your minder?' said Clara.

'Sure. Over there.' Mary jerked her Martini glass to indicate a group of officials towering over Goebbels' five foot six frame. They were vigorous, hard-faced men, mostly in uniform, and those in civilian dress wore the Party emblem in their buttonhole.

'We have one each. Mine's the one with the face like Babe Ruth and the charm of Al Capone. They've been appointed to keep an eye on us.'

'Don't they have enough spies?' complained Shirer.

Every newspaper office in Berlin had its quota of government informers, from the translators to the secretaries, following them like wasps at a picnic and keeping a watch on their contacts.

'Goebbels says Germany's message needs to be better controlled than ever. The minders have to note every word we write and every place we go. Mine's going to be spending a lot of time at the Adlon bar.'

'Mine too,' laughed Hugh.

Clara glanced again at the group of men clustered around Goebbels and as she looked, one man caught her gaze and returned it. He was a haughty figure in a closely pressed uniform, with a hawkish nose and cheekbones as sharp as an SS dagger. Even from across the room she felt his eye travel over the contours of her silk cocktail dress, down her body then up again to her face. As their eyes met a brief smile lifted the corners of his mouth. He nodded and raised his glass very slightly in her direction.

'Did you see all those presents being taken into the Chancellery this morning?' said Cavendish. 'Weren't we always told it was frightfully spoiling to have too many presents? What's wrong with cake and champagne?'

'You can forget the champagne,' said Mary. 'I asked. The Propaganda Ministry informed me that the birthday dinner consisted of asparagus tips and artichoke hearts in cream sauce. And the only alcohol on offer was beer at one per cent proof. I'd love to see the guests' faces when that was served up.'

'I heard our host gave Hitler a hundred and twenty feature films,' said Hugh Lindsey. 'But then what do you give the man who has everything?'

'Poland, probably,' said Mary.

Clara glanced again at the tall figure who had caught her eye. In her time she had evolved many tricks for remembering faces, and one of them was to think of which animal she was reminded of. This man would be a large, powerful creature, a panther perhaps, with his dark colouring, black livery and sleek, muscular demeanour. There was an impatience about the flare of his nostrils and the brief glance he cast towards the door which said that as far as he was concerned, the party couldn't end soon enough. As she looked their eyes met again and he gave a smile that suggested amusement at some private joke only they shared. Immediately she looked away.

She wandered over to the window to watch streams of people returning from the parade, their flags turning the street below into a shimmering sea of swastikas. Having spent all day offering rigid salutes at every opportunity, they were relaxed now, drunkenly loud, singing off key. Overhead, the last squadrons were passing, their drone fading into the distance. The crash barriers were being folded away and litter collectors were busy picking up the odd abandoned flag and empty cardboard Wurst carton. More than any city on earth, Berlin liked order. On the surface at least.

'It's an historic occasion.'

Clara turned. The man who had been surveying her from across the room had come up behind her. At closer quarters, he was more than merely good-looking – there was a kind of perfection to his features. His eyes were grey as pewter, his silver-flecked hair swept precisely from the kind of face Clara had seen on statues in the British Museum – haughty, aristocratic, chiselled by generations of breeding, and a nose that in relief would fit perfectly on an ancient Roman. The only unambiguously German thing about him was the four silver pips and stripe on his collar badge that marked his rank as an SS-Obersturmbannführer.

'I suppose. We have an awful lot of historic occasions nowadays. Sometimes one longs for a simple, unhistoric day.'

The Obersturmbannführer raised a dark eyebrow.

'Aren't you enjoying the holiday?'

'I'm not a great one for holidays. I'd rather get back to work.'

Close up he smelled of fresh leather. No one, except soldiers, smelled of that any more: the rest of the leather in Berlin was worn, scuffed and long overdue for replacement.

'Personally I'm finding it a welcome respite. But perhaps that's to do with my current occupation.' He rocked backwards on his heels and followed her gaze down at the street.

Clara didn't ask him to elaborate so he continued.

'Herr Doktor Goebbels has suggested I acquaint myself with all aspects of the Reich Chamber of Culture. I can cope with the concerts, but the Minister thought I should watch as many films as possible and frankly, I'm finding it a formidable job. He's provided me with a list of movies and I'm having them screened as often as I can bear it.'

'Tiresome for you.'

'Indeed.' He drained his glass. 'I'm managing two per evening.'

'Almost as many as the Führer, and he watches movies for pleasure.'

'Well it wouldn't do to compete with the Führer,' he replied smoothly. 'Though watching these films does rot the brain, don't you find?'

'Considering I spend my time acting in them, I suppose not.'

If the Obersturmbannführer was abashed by his obvious faux pas, he didn't show it. A small sardonic smile danced on his lips.

'So you're an actress! That's the work you're so keen to get back to. And what are you acting in at present?'

'A romantic comedy.'

'Tell me about it.'

Clara kept her eyes concentrated pointedly on the street below.

'Not much to tell. It's nearly finished,' she replied tersely, hoping he was not going to ask what her current project was called.

'And what's it called? Just so that I can look out for it?'

There was a sarcastic composure about him. It was clear he enjoyed prising the information out of her. Turning, she met his gaze full on and said, 'It's called *Love Strictly Forbidden*.'

His smile broadened slightly.

'Very stirring. And is it your character who is forbidden to love?'

'You could say so.'

Liebe Streng Verboten was a romantic comedy of the most frivolous kind. It was set in occupied Vienna and Clara played a ditsy girl who fell for a local hotelier. Although the movie was sure to be a cast-iron success, secretly Clara understood the officer's disdain. *Love Strictly Forbidden* had as much in common with cinematic art as Kaffee-Ersatz had with a rich blend of Ethiopian Arabica. It would take no more than a couple of weeks to film and the result would be the same as ninety per cent of the Ufa output – frothy romance, as light and forgettable as a Haribo marshmallow candy. But although she knew this, Clara was not about to sympathize with this man's patronizing remarks. She wondered exactly who he was. He must be fairly secure if he was prepared to disrespect Goebbels so airily. She inclined her head.

'It's not often you meet someone who never visits the cinema. Presumably you never see the newsreels either. You must feel awfully out of touch.'

'Sometimes I think it's the only way to live at the moment,' he murmured, then the supercilious expression returned, and he said, 'But you're right. The cinema is important and I'm attempting to embrace it.'

'Which films have you embraced recently?'

'I tried watching *Dance on a Volcano*.' He paused, with a soupçon of scorn, his lips curled. 'It was billed as an historical drama, though I'm still trying to work out what it had in common with History. But then, perhaps History is whatever Doktor Goebbels says it is.'

'A word means what I choose it to mean, neither more nor less,' murmured Clara.

'*Alice Through the Looking Glass*,' the officer replied in English. 'Lewis Carroll is a much underrated philosopher.'

Startled, both by his comment and his flawless English, she stared. 'Have you read it?'

'I spent two years living in England. I was an aide to Von Ribbentrop when he was ambassador there. So yes, I've read it. But I've omitted to introduce myself.' He clicked his heels and bent to kiss Clara's hand. His mouth was softer than seemed possible from such chiselled perfection.

'My name is Conrad Adler. And you are Fräulein . . .'

'Vine.'

'Vine?'

'That's right.'

Could it be a mistake or did a transitory frown cross those perfect features, like a shadow momentarily darkening the sun? Clara was used to her name provoking an immediate reaction. Often it caused people to widen their eyes, or refer at once to her films, but the expression that flitted across Adler's face seemed more puzzlement than recognition. Almost as soon as she had noticed it, however, it was gone, to be replaced with a courteous smile.

She retrieved her hand. 'Clara Vine.'

'Clara Vine.' He repeated her name experimentally, as though tasting it in his mouth like a fine wine. 'Yes. That's a good name for an actress.'

The smooth smile was back in place.

'So if you work for Von Ribbentrop, what are you doing here?'

'I've been seconded to another task for three months.'

'Can I ask why?'

'I'm afraid not. I'm on loan,' he shrugged. 'Like a painting in a museum.'

A gale of laughter reached them from across the room and Clara glanced instinctively over at the Propaganda Ministry bureaucrats, gathered tightly around Goebbels and guffawing unctuously at his remarks.

Adler followed her gaze.

'My guess would be that you're English . . .'

'Half English.'

'Yet you choose to live in Berlin? Why?'

Could he tell that this was the question she most often asked herself?

'It's an interesting time. Germany is changing fast.'

'I agree with that. To think ten years ago there were soup kitchens and people standing on the streets with boards around their necks and camps for the unemployed outside the city. And now this.'

He nodded towards the street, from where faint strains of the Horst Wessel Song, the informal Nazi anthem, floated up.

'No unemployment. Autobahns everywhere. Germany is great again. And all without a shot being fired.'

'I saw some pretty large guns in the parade this morning.'

A glimmer of amusement flickered behind his well-sculpted countenance.

'Ah. We must never forget there's a narrow boundary that separates the savage from the civilized. So, Fräulein Vine . . .' Still that teasing, probing smile. 'At first glance you could be pure German. You have Aryan features, yet there's indeed something distinctly English about you too. A certain look you have – the one you're giving me now. It's like fire behind ice.'

He held her gaze deliberately, provocatively, and for a moment it was as though he was seeing through her, to the Clara Vine who hid behind the carefully composed surface. The heat entered her face, the sounds of the room fell away and a silent connection sparked between them. It was an unspoken understanding, a charge of sheer energy between a man and a woman. His gaze swept over her body like a physical touch, and Clara found herself speechless.

'Perhaps,' Adler murmured, moving closer. His uniform exuded an aroma of starched linen and some sharp, citrus-scented pomade. 'You might like to help me in my research.'

'How exactly would I do that?'

'As you're evidently the expert on these things you could accompany me to the cinema.'

'I'm a little busy right now.'

'Busy filming *Love Strictly Forbidden*. Of course.' Amusement flickered in his eyes like candlelight. 'All the same, let me give you my card.'

He slipped a card into her hand and she transferred it to her bag.

'You could tell me if I'm watching high-quality art or low-grade trash.'

Instantly Clara regained possession of her senses. The presumption, the arrogance of the man, took her breath away. She had told him she was an actress, yet still he was intent on disdaining her profession. She was about to issue a curt riposte when Hugh Lindsey appeared, inserted himself bodily between Adler and Clara, and thrust a glass of sparkling Sekt into her hand.

'Got you another drink, Clara. Oh, sorry. Was I interrupting?'

'Not at all,' said Adler, his mouth tightening slightly.

'Only we're making plans to go to Erich Carow's cabaret next Wednesday. Have you heard of it?'

'Fräulein Vine is already acquainted with my deficiencies as regards popular culture.'

'Mary says it's unmissable.' Hugh turned to Clara. 'There's a whole group of us going. Care to come along?'

'I'd love to,' said Clara.

'Excuse me, Fräulein. I should leave.'

Adler clicked his heels, nodded at her and melted away.

'Thought you needed rescuing,' grinned Hugh. 'Who was that?'

'Probably another of Goebbels' lackeys,' said Mary, coming to join them. 'They never leave Clara alone because they've seen her on screen.'

'Actually, he works for the Foreign Ministry. And he'd never heard of me,' said Clara. She finished her drink and checked her watch. 'You know, I'd better be getting back. The S-Bahn will be crammed.'

Mary's face creased in concern.

'Be careful, after the news.'

'What news?'

'It just came through on the ticker tape.'

The ticker tape of the DNB, the German news agency, was stationed in a corner of the Press Club, from where it spewed out important information at all times of the day and night. Generally this important information concerned improved crop yields and record steel production numbers, but occasionally some actual newsworthy incidents seeped through.

'Everyone's talking about it. A girl's body was discovered by some construction workers close to the studios. They were building an air-raid shelter for the Artists' Colony. And that's where you're living, isn't it?'

'A body?' said Clara.

'In a shallow grave, apparently. Barely even covered. It was one of the Faith and Beauty girls.'

'Faith and Beauty?' said Charles Cavendish. 'What on earth is that?'

'It's the Nazi's finishing school for young women. Hitler's ideal women. They join at seventeen and they're groomed as consorts for senior Nazi men. They have a community building near there.'

'Extraordinary,' said Hugh, taking out a notebook as though he was about to begin a news report there and then. 'They're groomed, you say?'

'What about this girl then,' interrupted Cavendish. 'Could it have been an accident?'

'No. She was strangled apparently.' Mary checked the piece of paper in her hand. 'Lotti Franke, aged twenty.'

Until then, Clara had been silent but the girl's name went through her like an electric jolt and she tore the paper from Mary's hand.

'It can't be!'

She stared at it but the name was there in stark type. Lotti Franke.

'Oh Clara, did you know her?' asked Mary, gently.

'Lotti's my student. She was assigned to me from the Faith and Beauty Society to study costume design. I was looking after her. She's such a talented girl. It has to be a mistake.'

Mary put a hand on her arm.

'I hope so too, Clara. But I can't see why it would be. The Criminal Police have announced it. They think the killer took advantage of the Führer's birthday because he knew everyone would be in town. What was she like, this girl Lotti?'

'She's ... was ...' Clara paused, and conjured up Lotti's exquisite face with its wide cheekbones, ivory skin and pale blue eyes. The slender, feline grace. 'She was beautiful, but very intelligent too. And free-thinking. When I showed her round the studio she knew all sorts of detail about the sets of *Metropolis* and *Nosferatu* and she was terrifically knowledgeable about photographic technique. Hardly any young people in Germany know that kind of detail about Expressionist film any more. I thought it was pretty daring of her even to talk about it.'

'Liking Expressionist film may not be encouraged, but it's not enough to get you killed,' said Mary sombrely. 'The police are telling women to be careful in isolated areas. There's a dangerous man on the loose.'

'Will you be okay going back on your own?' said Hugh, laying a solicitous hand on her arm.

'Of course. But thank you.'

Mary looked doubtful.

'Remember what I said, Clara. Be careful.'

Clara left the club and walked north, allowing herself to be carried in the flow of the straggling crowds all the way to the

S-Bahn at Friedrichstrasse. The news about Lotti Franke had obliterated all traces of Herr Conrad Adler and their conversation from her mind. As the cool air played on her flushed cheeks, her head filled with images of the girl she had known for just a few weeks, the flaxen hair cropped in a Bubikopf – the short bob frowned upon in these more conventional times – striding along the corridors of Ufa as if on a catwalk, impervious to admiring glances. Lotti had been unusually beautiful, yet her beauty was matched by an exceptional intelligence. Though Clara was supposed to answer Lotti's questions and show her around, quite often Lotti had been the one to provide information about Ufa's past, and the films she had seen. What a waste of a life. Clara tried not to imagine that slender figure sullied with earth, the perfect limbs crumpled and askew in a shallow grave.

At Friedrichstrasse the station was predictably packed but the crowds that surged onto the trains were different from the normal commuting throng, more jovial and less truculent. Wedged in one of the steamy carriages jammed with jubilant day trippers, Clara looked out at the darkness flashing past, the necklace of lamps strung like pearls along the track and the chill Spring night fizzing with neon. Everyone on the train was tired and content. The Führer's fiftieth birthday had been a moment of excitement, a firework flash against an ever-darkening horizon. Yet for one family, the day would always be marked by loss. Clara had no idea where the Franke family lived, but she knew the Faith and Beauty building was nearby in Neu-Babelsberg and at that moment she resolved to call there the following day and ask for Lotti's address. The least she could do was to visit her parents as soon as possible to commiserate.

Chapter Four

Lotti Franke's parents lived in Schulzendorfer Strasse in Wedding, an industrial area of cavernous grey streets and barrack-style five-storey tenement blocks grouped around dank courtyards. The blocks were more than six apartments deep, accessed from the street by a grimy archway and cramming together individual apartments with workshops, shared kitchens and communal privies. All around, iron-framed chimneys belched smoke and men with cloth caps and collarless shirts trudged by, carrying bags holding Wurst and sandwiches for lunch.

As she climbed off the tram, Clara was immediately assailed by the yeasty stink of malted barley, wheat and fermenting hops. It seemed to permeate everything from the bricks of the buildings to the paving stones beneath her feet. It issued from the local Schulzendorf brewery that provided jobs for hundreds of local workers and barrels of cloudy, sour Weissbier for their relaxation afterwards. Consumption of the traditional Berlin brew had soared in the past few years and not even the new craze for Coca-Cola could begin to rival it.

Five floors up a stone stairwell reeking of urine and cooking, Marlene and Udo Franke's apartment was three cramped and dingy rooms. Lotti's father was moored on a sofa, his face devoid of animation and his eyes red-rimmed and pouchy from lack of sleep. A day's growth of stubble shadowed his chin. Marlene Franke was, by contrast, seized by a frenetic activity, rushing in and out to fetch photographs of Lotti and asking repeatedly how Clara took her coffee. It was clear to see where the daughter's good looks had come from, though Marlene's blonde hair was tied in a lank bundle and her startling blue eyes were crazily bright.

Everything about the apartment testified to an ardent faith in the Führer. The regulation picture of Hitler hung above the stove in a cheap gilt frame, the lurid colouring giving him a somewhat consumptive air, and set out on a veneer table dressed with a lace doily was the Führer corner. These shrines were everywhere now – in shops and offices, cafés and restaurants, as well as family homes. People thought they brought good luck. Mostly they featured a picture of Hitler and a candle, but the Frankes' shrine was an elaborate affair, with a copy of the *Jubiläumsausgabe*, the anniversary issue of *Mein Kampf*, in honour of Hitler's birthday, and, flanking Hitler, headshots of Goebbels and Goering, like the two criminals at some devilish crucifixion.

Marlene Franke backed into the room with a tray of trembling crockery, set it down and sat next to her husband, rocking slightly.

'Lotti was a wonderful daughter. I don't know how we're going to cope without her,' she said, twisting a damp rag of handkerchief between her fingers. 'She had such promise, didn't she, Udo?'

With a twitch of shaggy eyebrows, Udo Franke assented.

'She wanted to be a costume designer. She saw all the movies.'

'I was impressed by how much she knew about film, when she came round the studio with me,' said Clara. 'She was very intelligent.'

'And artistic,' said her mother, with a nod at the wall. 'She modelled all her own designs. She had even been photographed by the fashion photographer Yva. Have you heard of her?'

Everyone had. Yva was one of the most celebrated fashion photographers in Berlin. Her pictures were in all the glossy magazines – *Die Dame*, *Elegante Welt*, even *Life* magazine.

'We kept them all.'

Every wall in the room was plastered with photographs of Lotti wearing dramatic, elongated costumes in shapes that were plainly inspired by Expressionist film.

'My daughter said fashion was Art,' said her mother, with a touch of defiance. 'And Art couldn't be categorized into acceptable and unacceptable. There's only good and bad Art. I'm sure we're not meant to think that – it's not what the Führer says, is it? – but you couldn't tell Lotti what to think. The most you could do was tell her not to say such things out loud. Now I'm tormenting myself thinking it was ideas like that which got her in trouble.'

'I can't imagine her views on Art could have led to her death,' said Clara gently. 'Have the police anything to say about the investigation?'

'Nothing. They've just left. A Kriminal-Inspektor Herz and some other rank. They said everyone was out of town. The Führer's birthday, you see. No one saw anything strange. They asked if our girl had a boyfriend, but I said there was no one.'

Her face darkened with misery. 'So much for that Faith and Beauty Society,' she said, savagely.

Clara couldn't help but agree. When she had called at the Faith and Beauty community home earlier that day, the grim-faced principal, Frau Mann, had met Clara's enquiries with a transparent lack of sympathy. It was as though Lotti had corrupted the whole idea of Faith and Beauty. If Faith and Beauty girls had to die, it should be gloriously for the Fatherland, not sordidly at the hands of an unknown murderer.

'They're supposed to look after the girls. Instead they filled her head with ideas about getting away. They took her to London, did you know?'

'To London?' Clara looked up, surprised.

'A couple of months ago.'

'What were they doing there?'

'It was a deputation.' Marlene Franke began to scrabble in a drawer. 'I kept the invitation. It was so beautiful.' She handed Clara a piece of card – precisely the same kind of stiff, high-quality invitation with embossed black italics as rested on the mantelpiece at Ursula's house.

The British Women's League of Health and Beauty
At Home
Claridge's Hotel

Clara had heard of the British Women's League of Health and Beauty. It was an organization dedicated to improving the well-being of Britain's young women and it regularly held outdoor galas where groups of trim girls in navy gym shorts performed synchronized athletics. Photographs of these events frequently appeared in the press, not always for the reasons the organizers imagined.

'Do you know Claridge's Hotel?' asked Udo Franke. 'It's very grand. As big as the Paris Ritz and almost the equal of the Adlon. Marble everywhere, Lotti said. And beautiful food, much better than you expect English food to be.'

'The people were charming,' added Marlene. 'The dinner was given by something called the Anglo-German Fellowship. That sounds like a nice group of people.'

'I've heard of it.'

Clara had more than heard of it. Her father, Sir Ronald Vine, and her elder sister, Angela, were two of its most trenchant supporters. It was the last outpost in England of sympathy for the Nazi regime. With a jolt she realized that if the Fellowship had organized the dinner, there was every chance that Angela would have been there. Angela might even have met Lotti, without knowing that her own sister knew her too. Clara felt the tectonic plates of her life shifting beneath her, the two parts of her life clashing unawares.

'They said a visit to London would be valuable for her education. She would meet civilised people, and converse with them about high-minded subjects. London!' The way Marlene spat the word out, the city might have been a sink of unimaginable depravity. 'It must be a dreadful place. I wouldn't be surprised if she met the madman there.'

She burst into a torrent of sobs and buried her face in the sodden handkerchief.

'Now then, Marlene.' Udo Franke roused himself from his trance and placed a hand on his wife's juddering arm. 'You're imagining things. Nothing happened in London. Lotti loved that trip. It was a big opportunity for her. How many girls get to visit London?'

'So much promise, and a few months later she's dead.'

Udo Franke trained his weary gaze on Clara.

'Fräulein Vine. My wife and I are touched by your visit. It's a great comfort to hear how talented our daughter was and we would like to hear more. But I implore you, if you hear anything which could help us find the monster who killed her – anything, no matter how small – you will come back and let us know.'

Clara took his large, moist hand. She knew there was no possibility that she would be privy to any information that could help catch Lotti's killer, yet she also knew how unbearable she would find the grief if anything befell her godson Erich, and he was not even her flesh and blood. Could people ever be truly happy again after the death of a child?

'I promise I will.'

On the way to the door, her attention was caught by a small, framed photograph of Lotti.

'It's special, that one,' said Udo Franke. 'It's from the dinner in London. It's only a snap, but it's the last one we have of our little girl, which is why we put it by the door.'

The picture was entirely different from the artfully posed and backlit studio portraits on the other walls. In it, Lotti sat beaming at the camera across a snowy tabletop, a picture of composure between the crystal decanters and silver bread baskets, surrounded by a gaggle of Faith and Beauty girls. Although it was a group photograph, the eye was instantly drawn to Lotti, the candlelight forming a dazzling halo that accentuated her flawless complexion and the perfect proportions of her face. Next to her, leaning into the picture, was a much plainer girl, with a ruddy-cheeked round face and unbecoming plaits.

'Who's that next to Lotti?'

'That's her best friend, Hedwig. They knew each other since they were tiny,' said Marlene Franke. 'Hedwig looked up to our daughter because Lotti was so good at everything, and so much prettier, of course. But Hedwig's a nice girl. Very upset too.'

Clara stared at the picture for some minutes, far longer than she needed. It was full of the terrible poignancy that freights photographs of the past. Those smiling faces, so joyful in the present, so optimistic for the future, and so innocent of what was to come. A sadness washed over her as she realized she was really searching for another image – the face of her own sister, Angela.

She didn't find it.

Opposite the tram stop outside the Frankes' block, as if in direct mockery of the commuters shuffling their aching feet, was a poster featuring a gleaming new Volkswagen people's car with the slogan: '*Save five marks a week and you will drive your own car.*' Most people in the queue looked as likely to buy a rocket to the stars as a Volkswagen. Erich's grandmother, Frau Schmidt, a nurse at Berlin's biggest hospital, the Charité, was saving from

her meagre salary and had worked out it would take her five
years before she could afford one. After another few minutes
shuffling alongside the others in the queue, Clara decided to
walk.

Berlin was changing. It still looked like Berlin, but every day
it was a little different, as subtle as fashion that shifts from one
season to the next, raising hemlines, adjusting shoulder pads and
tightening waists. It even smelt different. People used to talk
about the famous Berliner Luft, the fresh air that blew into the
city from the Grunewald, but now the city reeked of sour breath,
bitter cigarettes and stale, unwashed bodies. The only soap available was gritty and impossible to lather because there was no fat
in it. People had taken to carrying their own soap around with
them, if they had any, because to leave it lying unattended risked
finding it missing.

Clara's mind went back to the photograph of Lotti Franke,
and the certainty that Angela would have been at the same event.
Yet again she regretted the estrangement from her sister. She
thought of the last time they were truly close, when she was
sixteen and their mother had died. Standing in a ragged group
around the graveside, and Angela's hissed reminder: *Dig your nails
into your hands to stop yourself crying.* Repressing emotion was an
article of faith for Angela. Concealment was more than courtesy,
it was a way of life.

Behaving properly. Being properly British. That was Angela's
code. Yet surely the quick, intelligent sister she knew was still
there – buried beneath the visits to Harrods and bridge nights
and society teas. Angela's letters tended to focus on the inter-
minable round of charity events that she conducted, the death
of relations and the relentless progress of her husband's political
career. *Gerald is in line for a big promotion. Chamberlain is so
impressed with him.* Clara responded with a dutiful list of parties,
premieres and work reports. Nothing intimate. Nothing political. Nothing real.

Right then she resolved that she would write to Angela very soon, and attempt something they had not managed for ten years. Communication.

Clara passed a loudspeaker lashed to the side of a building, blaring out 'Deutschland über Alles' and obliging everyone to give a perfunctory right-armed salute. She generally avoided giving the Führergruss by ensuring she was carrying something in both hands, but that day, distracted by thoughts of Lotti, she failed to comply.

A hand on her shoulder made her jump like a coiled spring. A man was standing in her path.

'Documents please.'

He had a complexion the colour of concrete and an expression that epitomized the *Berliner Schnauze*, the direct, graceless, sceptical manner so many of the city's inhabitants had perfected. He flicked the lapel of his jacket to reveal the aluminium disc marking him out as Gestapo.

Clara handed over her ID and watched the stupidity and aggression warring in his face as he scrutinized it. Although the small piece of card was beginning to fray at the edges, she never had any doubts about the quality of her identity documents; such was the skill of their forgery. All the same, even if papers were in order, a policeman or Gestapo official could still confiscate them if he didn't like you. Clara wondered what this man saw in her. The usual Berliner, cowed in the face of authority and determined to keep a low profile? How much did her face give away? Into her head floated the remark of Conrad Adler.

Like fire behind ice.

'Alles in Ordnung.'

Gracelessly, the man returned her identity card and she stuffed it back in her bag.

She carried on, remembering Mary Harker's warning. *They're intensifying their surveillance. Goebbels has assigned a minder to each of us*. Might that apply not only to foreign journalists but actresses too? She thought again of the man in the lobby of her apartment block; the lean, expressionless face, the trench coat belted loosely, the way he avoided her eye.

In the fortnight before he had disappeared, Leo had talked a lot about the techniques of espionage. One afternoon he had told her about a list that all agents were being trained to memorize, if they believed they were being followed.

Number One: look out for the unobtrusive. A shadow could be anyone. The young woman who clicked her painted fingernails on the counter beside you in a shop. The newspaper seller who slipped you a friendly remark each day with your change. The runner at the studio, or the car park attendant who joked about how he would always save the best space for you. Or a head-scarfed Frau, like the one a few steps behind, grey-skinned and footsore, weighed down by a kilo of potatoes in her shopping basket.

Number Two: watch for anyone walking at a steady pace. A shadow would neither be nonchalant, nor too purposeful, though as far as vehicles went, the opposite applied.

Number Three: listen for a car that moves either too fast or too slow.

If surveillance was suspected, there was *Number Four: change your appearance*. Find a fresh coat, ditch your jacket, remove a hat. The slightest change could help to evade detection.

But whereas it was easy to put on a headscarf or abandon a briefcase, it was far harder to shave off a moustache or disguise hair colour in the course of pursuit. *Thus Number Five: check for distinguishing features*. A shadow rarely had time to change their shoes. There was also *Number Six: listen for what you don't hear*. And if surveillance was certain, there was *Number Seven: stick to public places*. In case of arrest or capture there was *Number Eight: stay calm. Don't react instinctively*.

There were a couple of other points on the list and Leo had made Clara commit them to memory and recite it back to him.

'That list will keep you safe, Clara. It'll be more use to you than any creed.'

That was one relief about the trip she was to make the next day. In London, there was no chance of being followed. And it would not be the Gestapo she had to worry about, but Captain Miles Fitzalan, whoever he might turn out to be.

Chapter Five

Of all the beautiful places in Berlin, could there be any lovelier than the sunlit drawing room of the Faith and Beauty community building, with its marzipan-yellow walls, charming meringues of plaster on the cornices and tall windows propped open to allow a freshening waft of pine from the woods beyond? Outside, a flock of hens pecked in the shade of the orchard and horses were being saddled up for riding lessons. A group of rowers were preparing for an outing to the lake, and on the lawn, two girls in face masks were taking instruction from the fencing master, their bodies as quick and flexible as the sleek silver foils they wielded. The quiet of the morning was punctuated by the solid, comforting clunk of the grandfather clock, and the faint scrape of a violin issued from the music room on the other side of the house. It was impossible to imagine that near this idyllic place just a few days earlier, a crumpled body had been found beneath a heap of leaves.

When Hedwig Holz first saw the Faith and Beauty home she was open-mouthed with amazement. She had grown up in a drab apartment, with nothing but a window box to tend and a dank cobblestone courtyard below. Even though their apartment was slightly better than their neighbours' on account of her father's managerial job, it had still taken weeks to accustom herself to such refinement. When she told her parents about the classes in Art, home décor, fashion design, needlework, flower arranging and conversation, her mother could barely contain her amazement. *Conversation!* Who needed classes in that?

Hedwig felt much the same about Art. Sitting in front of her easel she sighed, squinted at the life model, made some further experimental cross-hatching, then rubbed out the face she had drawn. Already a murky patch testified to the number of times the sketch had been erased – the model was beginning to look like something from one of those old horror films, *The Cabinet of Doctor Caligari*, starring Conrad Veidt, with nothing but a shadowy void where her features should be. Hedwig dreaded the moment Herr Fritzl, the art master, turned up to linger at her easel, twirling his moustache while he tried to think of something constructive to say. Their portraits were supposed to mirror the correct proportions of the Nordic form – every figure must have broad shoulders, a long body, and slender hands – but Hedwig's sketch could have been straight out of Grimm's fairy tales.

The Saturday life drawing class had been Lotti's idea. Hedwig didn't have an artistic bone in her body and would gladly have signed up for skiing, rowing, even high board diving rather than humiliate herself with Art. Hedwig's father, a stolid production line manager at the AEG engineering works, thought art training, like everything else on the Faith and Beauty curriculum, was a lot of effete nonsense, but he deferred to her mother, who had ambitions for her only daughter. Privately Herr Holz told Hedwig to concentrate on her job and think about her promotion prospects. If indeed she had time for promotion, before marriage and motherhood came along and put an end to all that.

Hedwig agreed. She had never imagined getting a job as a librarian and she loved it. Although her most taxing duty involved looking interested while doing very little, she enjoyed sitting at her desk, greeting visitors and being the only female in the building. She could think of a thousand better ways of spending her weekends than attending Faith and Beauty art classes, but Lotti had set her heart on it.

It was agonizing to think that Lotti had sat in this class only two weeks ago, sketching costumes, her bold, confident lines delineating impossibly glamorous women, their outfits carefully annotated in her flowing handwriting. Hedwig could picture her now, high eyebrows arched above aquamarine eyes, chin jutted forward as if she was born to it. As if, indeed, it was all slightly beneath her.

Hedwig knew Lotti only wanted company, yet where Lotti was concerned she could never say no. Faith and Beauty girls were encouraged to think of themselves as a spiritual sisterhood, but to her Lotti was more like an ordinary sister. As children their two families had sometimes taken holidays in the countryside outside Berlin together and Hedwig and Lotti shared a room. She recalled Lotti's grave face, reciting German poetry, or expanding on her ambitions for life, requiring only that Hedwig be a devoted listener. And when Hedwig had confided her most precious memory, of the first time a man kissed her, Lotti had burst into peals of mocking, sisterly laughter.

Sister or not, she was dead now, and Hedwig felt an utter desolation.

The murder had sent shockwaves through the Faith and Beauty community, but although no one could talk of anything else, they were forbidden to talk about it at all. That was useless when it was all over the newspapers and a pair of steel-helmeted soldiers were shuffling their feet on permanent guard outside the front gate. A hasty set of new regulations had been formulated for the girls. Shooting was curtailed so long as the killer was at large and replaced with rowing. No girl was permitted to walk alone the short distance from the Griebnitzsee S-Bahn through the forest, though that was quite unnecessary advice because being alone was frowned on. The Party disapproved of solitude on the grounds that faithful citizens would always prefer communal life and privacy in all its forms was strongly proscribed for Faith and Beauty girls.

Hedwig stared out of the window and wondered if her mother would agree to her leaving now. Etta Holz adored the idea of her only daughter being here. Faith and Beauty training gave German girls such an advantage. No going to the Nuremberg rally and getting pregnant by the first Hitler Youth you encountered. Hedwig would be invited to parties with senior Party members. She would be cultivated and polished and pass into the top echelons of society with ease. 'Once you've finished you'll hold dinner parties for all the top SS men and you'll be able to talk about . . .' Here Frau Holz paused, having no idea what top SS men might possibly talk about. *The Merry Widow*, she finished lamely, recalling the Führer's favourite operetta. 'It will pay for itself, you'll see.'

But the real reason that her mother favoured the Faith and Beauty Society was that it meant her daughter would grow out of Jochen Falke.

Jochen did not have the kind of looks deemed handsome among Hedwig's friends. His high, Slavic cheekbones and skinny frame were far from the muscular athletes modelled by the Führer's favourite sculptor, Arno Breker. But he had quick, hazel eyes which always seemed to flicker with amusement and a swagger about him that reflected his inner confidence.

He was an artist too – in a way. He worked at an art manufacturing plant in Kreuzberg, a humdrum place that carried out all forms of printing and publishing, as well as commercial artwork, signs and advertising. But the real money-spinner was merchandizing the Führer. Hitler souvenirs were big business. Birthday figurines, postcards, ashtrays, medallions, posters, cocktail forks and bottle stoppers. There was a whole variety of jewellery, and cameo brooches were especially popular because everyone wanted their Führer close to their heart. Jochen's speciality was pictures. On a good day he could reproduce Adolf Hitler a hundred times over.

'What takes the Fräulein's fancy?' he would laugh, parodying an unctuous shop assistant. 'We have Hitler in a gilt frame, Hitler with children, Hitler at the Berghof, Hitler with Bismarck, or would Fräulein prefer the Führer's hands alone?'

He worked with a photograph in front of him, softening the nose and making the eyes larger, adding a tint to the cheeks. 'Just doing a little cosmetic surgery.' He brought one back for Hedwig's mother, who hung it proudly opposite her bed. Hedwig thought seeing the Führer's scowl like that last thing at night would give her nightmares, but her parents seemed to like it.

She looked up to see Herr Fritzl approaching. He was bound to say something uncomplimentary about her efforts. Last time he claimed Hedwig's approach smacked dangerously of Degenerate Art, which was tantamount to accusing her of treason. Apparently in the Weimar period Berlin had been a hell-pit of sexual depravity, and obscene nudes by Degenerate painters like Otto Dix corrupted the morals of an entire nation.

The thought of Otto Dix's nudes only reminded her of Lotti, her graceful gymnast's limbs askew in the clumsy crush of death. She pictured the diaphanous wings of flies glittering like cut coal in the air above her body. What had Lotti ever done to deserve that fate?

Hedwig picked up her charcoal stick and turned back to the horror on her easel, but found she could no longer see it because of the tears slipping down her face.

Chapter Six

On London's King's Road there was a queue to collect gas masks from Chelsea Town Hall. Whole families were waiting, the children jumping up and down, wriggling with excitement, the parents, anxiety etched on their faces, keeping up appearances because they were lining up alongside their cooks and housemaids. One little boy was singing, 'There's going to be a war!' until he was abruptly hushed by his father. Those who were leaving, already issued with masks, were rather more subdued. Having had their first taste of the acrid rubber contraptions with their bleary glass panels at the front and straps fastened behind the head, perhaps the dangers of the future seemed suddenly more real.

Watching from the top deck of the number 11 bus, however, Clara was transported to the past. She had a vision of herself on this same bus with her mother, sitting in exactly the same spot – front row of the top deck – Helene Vine upright and proper, handbag balanced on her knee, and Clara herself, a small simulacrum, pressed warmly against her mother's side. Angela, meanwhile, sat aloof across the aisle. Clara had always been her mother's daughter – the only one of them named for a distant German ancestor rather than a resolutely English relation – and the only child who resembled her too. Angela, with her honey-blonde

hair and long gangling legs, was already exhibiting the first colt-
ish inklings of the glamorous model she would become.

Now Clara was alone, in a mac and a printed silk scarf and a
copy of *Picture Post* unread on her knee. *Miss Penelope Dudley-
Ward, the English heroine of the London-Paris-New York hit, French
Without Tears, wears a rose, turquoise and gold brocaded lamé jacket
and a full satin skirt in a deep rosy red.*

The bus halted before a group of men hauling sheets of corru-
gated iron for bomb shelters. Clara wondered if Angela had a
shelter of her own, and if she did, whether she would ever need
to use it. It was hard to imagine the elegant Angela shivering in
a damp construction of earth and sheet metal that flooded when
it rained, or cramped in a basement, with a torch and a book.
Angela liked a pink gin and a rubber of bridge in the evenings.
Listening to Cole Porter at the Café de Paris or visiting the cellar
of the Embassy Club in Bond Street, where until recently the
Prince of Wales and Wallis Simpson had danced the quickstep on
the tiny dance floor.

Clara had a sudden, fervent desire to get off the bus and visit her
sister, but she knew the prospect was impossible. How would she
explain this flying visit to London? What cover could she credibly
construct that Angela would not instantly penetrate? Despite her
long practice in controlling impulsive urges, it still took an almost
physical strength for Clara to stay in her seat and not dash down
the winding stairs and jump off the back platform of the bus.

After six years away, she scanned London's familiar surroundings as though hunting for changes in the face of a long lost
friend. There were the same advertisements for Wrigley's
Spearmint Gum, Ovaltine and Eno's Fruit Salts, and Peter Jones
had changed its Victorian redbrick frontage to a sleekly modern-
ized tower of glass and steel. But now its windows were pasted
with criss-crossed strips of brown paper to protect against potential bomb blast, the kerbstones had been painted white and sandbags, exuding a smell of damp jute, were shored against the side

of every building. A giant recruitment advertisement for the RAF, *Salute to Adventure!,* towered beside Sloane Square tube and a group of young men, subjects of the first wave of conscription, sailed past in a National Service truck. Other details, too, Clara could not help noticing. Women wore little hats tipped slightly forward and to one side. Jackets were more boxy and defined, coats had puffed shoulders, shoes were tightly laced and the whole female silhouette had become harder and more definite, as though Fashion itself was braced for what was to come.

Disembarking at Westminster she made her way across Parliament Square, past Methodist Central Hall and along the Georgian terraces of Queen Anne's Gate. Bright, luminous bursts of laburnum and wisteria blossom hung over sun-warmed walls. Through the pellucid blue sky the bells of Westminster Abbey marked four o'clock. The Abbey's bone-white frontage of pleated stone was draped with a veil of soot and placards along the railings announced that it was now open day and night as part of a 'Vigil for Peace'. Passing a film poster for *The Spy In Black*, Clara was startled to see it starred Conrad Veidt. Just a few months ago she had passed the venerable German actor in the corridors of the Ufa studios. Now he was established in a new life and a new career in England.

It could happen to her too.

As she walked, she felt her body tense and her shoulders knot in the familiar brace. It was impossible to shake the tension which clenched her stomach. She thought for a moment it might be the dizzy rush of nostalgia, set off by everything from the pillar boxes and the plane trees to the pennies with the King's head on them. Even the newspaper seller outside St James's Park underground station, advertising the first sight of the new pandas at London Zoo, prompted a yearning for the city she had not realized she missed so much. In reality, though, she knew it was only nervous anticipation of what this meeting would bring.

*   *   *

The St Ermin's Hotel was a shabby, late-Victorian redbrick mansion block in Caxton Street, set back from the road and only a few hundred yards from 54, Broadway, where the headquarters of the Secret Intelligence Service was based. On a weekday afternoon it was the last place on earth one would associate with espionage. The lobby, all tartan-trimmed upholstery and dusty carpet, was hushed and gloomy. Watercolours of the Lake District hung alongside a painting of the King, and the smell of congealed vegetables and floor polish exuded a distilled essence of Englishness. A couple of ladies in hats and fur capes taking tea at a side table were the only sign of life.

Clara hesitated. It had not occurred to her until then how exactly she would make contact with the mysterious Captain Miles Fitzalan who had invited her to his fictitious ball. She approached a girl reading a copy of *Woman's Weekly* behind the mahogany reception.

'Is there a Captain Fitzalan staying here?'

The girl gave an insultingly perfunctory smile.

'Can I ask who wants him?'

'Miss Clara Vine.'

Putting down *Woman's Weekly* the receptionist reached wearily for the telephone.

'They're fifth floor.'

'Thank you.'

'The lifts only go up to fourth, but if you press the button to the left, it'll take you all the way up.'

Clara emerged from the lift to find a long, dingy office partitioned by panes of frosted glass and plywood, filled with men in pinstriped suits lounging and chatting at desks. A fug of cigarette smoke hung in the air, lit by broad shafts of sunlight penetrating the murky windows. Though she was dressed quietly enough, in a skirt of hounds-tooth check, a blouse with scalloped collar and a small pearl necklace, curious eyes swivelled immediately towards her. A louche man, with rumpled hair and tie at half mast, one ear pressed to the telephone, gave her a wink but Clara barely had time to look around her before an imposing figure with a scarlet carnation in his buttonhole approached.

'Miss Vine. So pleased you could come. What do you think of our offices? None too decorative, but very handy for clubs and so on.' Pumping her hand, he detected her incomprehension and added, 'I'm sorry. You don't know me from Adam. I'm Major Grand. Lawrence Grand.'

'Clara Vine.'

'Precisely. Please follow me.'

Anyone who did not know that Lawrence Grand had recently been seconded from the Army could have detected it instantly from the ramrod bearing, tanned complexion and the military exactitude of his pencil moustache. Clara recognized his type immediately. He wore his politeness like a uniform, buttoned up against the possibility of revealing the merest snippet of extraneous information.

Striding ahead, he led the way to a corner office with a view of budding plane trees and a line of pigeons shuffling along the soot-dappled rooftops of Westminster.

'Do sit down. Smoke?'

'Thank you.' She took the proffered Senior Service, and he slid across his desk a cut-glass ashtray studded with ochre stains like pollen in a lily.

'Who are all those people?'

'Ah.' Major Grand fired up her cigarette and assessed her, head on one side. 'That, Miss Vine, is a question I can't possibly answer. Not only would it endanger my people if I identified them to you, but it could put you at risk too. Let's just say we have all sorts from all walks of life. Often the very last sort you would expect.'

'Of course. I'm sorry.'

'On the other hand, seeing as you've been so good as to come all the way here, you're entitled to ask a few questions. You'll probably want to know what we're about.'

Clara guessed this was her cue.

'Can I ask who you are, for a start?'

'Certainly. The fact is, we're a bit of a fledgling venture. We're called Section D. Connected to the Secret Intelligence Service. Physically connected, in fact – there's a tunnel that runs under this building all the way to Broadway, not that anyone I know has used it. We've been up and running for a few months – ever since SIS concluded in the wake of the Czech invasion that war is unavoidable – our intention being to establish agents in those countries which face being overrun by the Wehrmacht.'

For Clara it was still a shock to hear, uttered so casually, the idea that war was 'unavoidable'. Every fibre of her hoped that wasn't true. She dreaded what would happen to her friends, to Leo, and most of all to Erich, if it happened.

'We've already placed officers in Sweden, Norway, Holland and Spain, not to mention Austria of course, but infiltrating people into Germany, let alone being able to do anything useful once they're there, is a very different challenge. Which is why, Miss Vine, your name has come up.'

'You want me to apply?'

Grand bent his head to the complex task of extracting another Senior Service from his jacket pocket and fitting it into an ebony cigarette holder, then rose and strode over to the window.

'People don't apply for us, because we don't officially exist. We approach those we think might be valuable. You've been in Berlin now, what, five years?'

'Six.'

'Quite so. They've just been celebrating the Führer's birthday, I hear. What was that like?'

'Not exactly understated.'

He laughed drily.

'So I understand. As a matter of fact, Noel Mason-MacFarlane, our military attaché in Berlin, offered to shoot Herr Hitler during the parade. He has a sixth-floor flat on the Charlottenburger Chaussee with a clear line of sight to the saluting podium and he said it would be easier than bagging a stag at a hundred yards to pick the beggar off. This chap's an excellent shot so we put the plan forward to the Prime Minister.'

He stared down at the street below as though Hitler was saluting right there on the pavement below him.

'If you can believe, the PM overruled it as unsportsmanlike.'

Clara could barely contain her astonishment. So she had not been the only person to contemplate the idea. Hitler might have been assassinated, while the eyes of the world were on him. What would the Ufa newsreel have made of that?

'Unsportsmanlike?' she echoed incredulously.

Grand tucked his hands in his waistcoat pocket.

'That was his precise word.'

'I'm surprised.'

'Good.'

He wheeled round, all jocularity replaced by an expression of intense seriousness.

'Our feeling here is that even at this late hour Mr Chamberlain badly underestimates the danger of Herr Hitler. I hope if you were ever in the same room as him, you would have no qualms. If the opportunity arose, we would not want you, Miss Vine, to be hindered by fears of "unsportsmanlike" behaviour.'

Her heart bucked with fear, but she replied calmly.

'I can't imagine the opportunity would arise.'

'Perhaps not.'

He sat and crossed one leg over the other, stroking his trousered calf and scrutinizing her, as if trying to decide something.

'I'm aware that life in Berlin is not a bed of roses. But it's going to get much worse now that war is on the horizon. We all have decisions to make, but yours is especially acute.'

Clara bent her head and smoothed the skirt on her knees, as though the mere action would help straighten out the questions in her mind. She had guessed that this summons would be a request from the British Intelligence Service – those shadowy men in Whitehall who had over the years been the ultimate recipients of all the gossip and information she relayed. She knew too that, just like Conrad Veidt and a host of other actors, if she chose to return to England she could make a fresh start in the British film industry. Yet mentally she had shied away from the question facing her. That same question which, beneath the penetrating gaze of Major Lawrence Grand, she knew she must now face.

'We need to know, when hostilities arise, whether you intend to stay in Germany. It's going to get a lot more dangerous.'

Something about Grand's bland assurance suddenly rankled. Who was this man in his smart suit and comfortable office to talk of danger? What could he know of what she went through on a daily basis?

'You forget I've already been arrested and interrogated by the Gestapo, Major Grand. I've had plenty of opportunity to understand how dangerous Berlin can be. I'm not even living in my own apartment because I think I'm being watched.'

An apologetic smile transformed his face and she could see a glimpse of the kindly man beneath the gruff exterior.

'Forgive me. So I take it you have decided to stay?'

Clara quailed at the direct question. The twists and turns that had determined her life had always been impulsive ones. The decision to leave England for Berlin in 1933 had come after a chance meeting at a party. The agreement to spy for British Intelligence came about because of an episode of Nazi brutality she had witnessed in the street. None of the decisive events in her life had ever been premeditated. Ultimatums made her nervous. She remembered how she had shied away from Leo Quinn's proposal of marriage because he insisted that she leave Germany. Perhaps avoiding decisions was her own personal form of cowardice.

'Actually, I haven't quite made up my mind.'

'I see.' Grand was plainly taken aback. 'Your prerogative, of course. But there was a specific task I had in mind . . .'

'Which is?'

Suddenly Major Grand sprang to his feet, eyes on the door. Clara registered the clatter of china and the next moment, with a perfunctory rap, a large woman in a floral apron backed in, pulling a tea trolley behind her containing a large steel urn and a stack of pale green civil service crockery, as well as a plate of Rich Tea biscuits.

'Milk and two, Major Grand?'

'You know me so well, Mrs Fairclough,' said Grand, helping himself to a biscuit, snapping it mathematically in half and dabbing up the crumbs with a forefinger. 'And for my guest?'

'Just milk please.'

The sight of the malty, copper stream of British tea splashing into the cups prompted another jolt of nostalgia. Although Clara's time in Germany had introduced her to the pleasure of coffee, no one else in Europe made tea the English way, well brewed, refreshing in all weathers and the answer to all crises.

After Mrs Fairclough had dispensed the tea, plunked in the sugar lumps and manoeuvred the trolley out of the door, Grand perched on the desk in front of Clara and fixed her more intently.

'To answer your question, this is a task of the utmost delicacy. One that goes to the heart of the future peace of Europe. I don't mind saying it will determine whether those gas masks we've all been given will ever get used. There are rumours going round Intelligence circles that a Nazi–Soviet pact is in the offing.'

Clara looked up from her tea with a frown. 'A pact with the Bolsheviks? Surely not?'

'A marriage of convenience is I think what they call it.'

'But the Nazis and the Bolsheviks are ideological enemies. It could never happen.'

'My feelings precisely,' said Grand. 'I would have thought hell would freeze over first. However. If the rumours are true, there would be very grave repercussions for the rest of us. From what we hear the idea of a pact is being propelled by von Ribbentrop. He has a pathological loathing for the British so he's presumably working on the basis that "My enemy's enemy is my friend".'

'Even so, it's so unlikely.'

'Personally I agree. It's arrant nonsense. Besides, our own people are negotiating with Comrade Stalin right now. But we need more solid intelligence. Something concrete. We need an inside track to the Foreign Ministry and that's where you come in.'

Into Clara's mind came the impatient, chiselled face of Conrad Adler. *I'm on loan from the Foreign Ministry. Like a painting in a museum.*

'Von Ribbentrop is a stupid man,' said Grand. 'Vain and foolish. His wife however is another matter. And I think you know her.'

Grand pulled a newspaper photograph out of a manila file on his desk and, craning across, Clara saw with astonishment that it was a yellowing page from the *BZ am Mittag* showing herself talking to Annelies von Ribbentrop at the launch of the Reich Fashion Bureau in 1933. The passage of six years had done nothing to soften the rigid composure of the Foreign Minister's wife, the iron set of her jaw, nor the dyspeptic smile that could so easily be mistaken for a grimace.

'What do you make of her?'

Clara thought back to the first time she met Frau von Ribbentrop, just after the regime came to power. Then she was an arriviste, desperate to impress with dinner parties at her Dahlem home, and now she was half of one of the most powerful couples in Europe. Kings, presidents and prime ministers came to her parties. She was a far more ardent Nazi than her husband, yet their marriage could not be more different from the marital catfight the Goebbels waged. The Von Ribbentrops were said to share everything, especially political plans.

'She's a formidable woman.'

'Indeed. A couple of chaps here met her when von Ribbentrop was ambassador to Great Britain, and they were frankly terrified. She was always cornering them to complain about the weather – as though they could do anything about it – and insanely jealous about her husband's behaviour with the ladies. He was said to send a daily bunch of red carnations to Wallis Simpson and she couldn't tolerate it. She was a bit of a laughing stock actually. She brought a marching squad of SS guards over who created the most frightful atmosphere and above all she had the most dreadful *nouveau riche* taste. Decked out the whole of Carlton House Terrace in marble cladding. It looks like a public lavatory. It's going to take years to unpick.'

Clara finished her tea and returned the saucer to the table.

'I take it it's not her artistic tastes you're concerned about here.'

'Precisely. More her knowledge of diplomatic manoeuvres. To what extent she influences the husband's decisions.'

'Goebbels always says von Ribbentrop bought his title, married his money and got all his political views from his wife. They say even Hitler is wary of her.'

A flicker of a smile. 'I suppose that's the thing about marriage – one can never tell what goes on inside. Do you see much of her?'

'Hardly. Last year she tried to have me arrested as a spy.'

Clara hesitated. Something Mary Harker had mentioned came to mind.

'But she is holding a press reception to show off the refurbishment of the new Foreign Ministry building. The Reich Chamber of Culture always likes actresses to attend these events if possible.'

'To supply a touch of glamour.'

'That's the idea. But even if I went, I can't imagine she would give me the time of day, let alone confide any military secrets.'

'I'm sure she'll come round,' continued Grand, as though Clara's objections were negligible. 'Find a way to get closer to her. From what we've heard, Frau von Ribbentrop frequently formulates political policy, which is later passed off as her husband's.'

'She's not like him though. Not the kind to be easily taken in.'

'Then you'll need to find another way in. If the German Foreign Ministry is contemplating a marriage of convenience with the Soviet Union it's vital we know as soon as possible.'

Grand paced across the room, thumbs tucked into his waist-coat pocket.

'The Soviet Union is the key to everything. It's a complicated dance. If Germany attacked Poland and the Red Army joined in on Poland's side, and Britain and France came to her aid, then Germany would be in a parlous position. They would never choose to fight on two fronts. But if the Nazis are making advances to the Russians, it's essential that we uncover every piece of information that we can. And we only have a matter of months to do it.'

'Months? How can you be so sure?'

'If Hitler's set on war, he won't attack before harvest time. But he'll want to make a move before winter. It's a tight window.'

He slid his cuffs and checked his watch, as though setting a deadline.

'If you decide to stay in Germany we'll need to brief you. We'll set up another meeting. Shall we say a fortnight's time? In Paris?'

Clara laughed.

'That's impossible. I already had to plead a family emergency to come to London. I couldn't make a trip to Paris without Goebbels finding out.'

'Tell him then.'

'I don't think you understand,' she said, as patiently as she could. 'Travel is severely restricted for members of the Reich

Chamber of Culture. You need permission to go abroad and nowadays it's not often given. Certainly not without a plausible explanation.'

For a second, Grand steepled his fingers in thought, then he aimed them towards her in the shape of a gun.

'How about if you were to feature in French *Vogue*?'

'*Vogue*?'

'You know, the fashion magazine.'

'I know what *Vogue* is, Major Grand. But why would they want to feature me?'

'Well, it's not a magazine I'm intensely familiar with, *Horse and Hound* is about my limit where periodicals are concerned, but we have a friend who works as a photographer there and I daresay a spread on European cinema might be the kind of thing he does. My sources tell me you've done some modelling in the past.'

Clara nodded, realizing precisely how much detail about her lay in that manila file in front of him. In 1933, shortly after her arrival in Berlin, she had been invited to model outfits for the Reich Fashion Bureau, an establishment set up by Hitler. That was how she had come into contact with Magda Goebbels, Emmy Goering and the other senior Nazi wives.

'Excellent then. Our friend's name is Thomas Epstein. He occupies apartment four, number eleven Rue Léopold-Robert in the fourteenth arrondissement of Paris. Can you remember that?'

'Of course.'

'I'll tell him to expect you. Shall we say two weeks today? And we'll need to have whatever information you can obtain by July.'

'July! But, you see, I don't actually think . . .'

'I hope I did impress on you, Miss Vine, that time is very much of the essence.'

Grand walked briskly to the door, as though Clara's objections, let alone any further pleasantries, were a dangerous waste of time. Suddenly she sensed her chance slipping away. She couldn't leave without asking the question that was tearing her apart.

'Major Grand, do you know Leo Quinn?'

Outwardly, his genial expression remained intact, but minute study of his face revealed that her question had disturbed him. A muscle flickered in his jaw and he gave the barest nod of assent.

'Would you have any idea where I could contact him?'

'Contact Mr Quinn? Now why would you want to do that?'

Clara hesitated, wondering if Grand knew the truth. He knew so much else about her, there was every reason he would. Every reason except Leo's careful, meticulous attempts to keep their love affair secret.

'He's an old friend of mine. He's the one who got me into all this in the first place when he was a passport control officer in Berlin.'

Grand paused with his hand on the doorknob.

'If I were you, my dear, I should forget Mr Quinn.'

It took everything Clara had to prevent the alarm that rose in her showing on her face. Blindly she trained her eyes Major Grand's moustache and gripped the cotton handkerchief inside her pocket.

'Forget him? What do you mean by that?'

'Just what I say.'

'Is it bad news?'

'Need-to-know basis, I'm afraid.'

'But I do need to know.' She clenched her teeth. 'Has something happened to him?'

Grand gave another businesslike smile but his voice was softer.

'I don't like telling you this, my dear. I *shouldn't* be telling you this, frankly. But our networks in Europe have taken a bad hit. We lost a couple of agents in Austria and Mr Quinn was involved. Our network there was blown.'

'In Austria? I thought . . .' What did she think? She had no idea what Leo did, where he went or what his job really was.

Grand stared beyond her, a pained expression on his face, his mouth grim as though fighting to contain emotion.

'There's a break in the chain somewhere. An informer on the continent. I can't be any more precise than that but it behoves all our people to be doubly, triply cautious about who they trust.'

'But Leo. You don't know what's happened to him? Not for sure?'

Grand touched a hand to her shoulder.

'I'm sorry. Your friend was a brave man, my dear. You should be proud of him.'

'He *was*?'

He imprisoned her hand momentarily in a tight clasp.

'Thanks once again for coming. Can I take it you remember the way to the lift?'

Numbly, Clara retraced her steps along the corridor. Tears welled in her eyes, blurring the partitioned offices and the men on telephones. She was barely aware of the clack of typewriters and the chatter of secretaries carrying files clipping alongside her. A tall, tawny-haired man with a narrow, toothbrush moustache glanced at her quizzically, as though about to enquire if she was all right. As their eyes met she noticed that he had irises of two different colours, one blue and one brown, and the irrelevant thought went through her head that such a distinguishing feature would make undercover work impossible; this agent must be office based. Ducking her head, she walked swiftly to the lift.

She did not look back. If she had, she would have seen Major Grand poised at the entrance to his office, an unusually sympathetic look replacing his rigid military demeanour.

In Caxton Street a brisk wind had got up, rustling the leaves on the plane trees and causing women at the bus stop opposite to clutch onto their hats. In a breeze like that, it was unsurprising that anyone should have tears in their eyes and no one gave Clara the slightest attention apart from a grinning bus conductor, sailing past on the platform of his bus, who called, 'Penny for your thoughts, darling!'

She walked like someone dazed by an explosion, the exterior world locked off behind an invisible wall. The bomb that had gone off inside her had caused everything around to resettle in unrecognizable disarray.

She progressed blindly, wondering what to do in the hours before making for Liverpool Street station and the boat train. Suddenly, the shock she had received overcame her instincts and, turning on her heel, she caught up with the bus that had just passed and jumped aboard, heading for Elizabeth Street.

She sat numbly on the lurching bus. *If I were you, my dear, I should forget Mr Quinn.* It was as though all the ballast was knocked out of her and she might simply collapse without the coarse red and blue backing of the seat beneath her. All she could think of was knocking on Angela's door and feeling her elder sister's sinewy arms enfolding her in a stiff but heartfelt embrace. She was aching to breathe in Angela's trademark perfume and bury her face in soft, sensible cashmere. She had not seen her sister for two years. They might disagree politically; they might have avoided any intimate exchanges for a decade, but Angela was, after all, her only sister. And at a time when she felt desolately alone, Clara yearned for the visceral comfort of flesh and blood.

She had never visited Angela's home in Belgravia but it was exactly as she expected. Wedding-cake white stucco, window boxes trimmed with box and ivy, expensive cars parked outside and a black door so polished you could see your face in it. It was hard to believe her sister had come so far. In her mind's eye Clara still saw her in an Aertex shirt, cotton skirt and white leather T-bar shoes, standing in the garden of their Surrey home, arguing over a tennis racquet.

Her heart was thumping as she waited on the step and raised the lion's-head knocker, but it was a while before the door opened, and then it was only an indifferent maid who peered out and did not invite her in. Her cap was askew, as if she had only hurriedly fixed it on, and her hair badly pinned beneath.

'Mrs Mortimer is out. Mr Mortimer is at the House of Commons.'

'It's Angela I want. When will she be back?'

'I can't say, I'm sure. The mistress left instructions that she's away.'

'Away? Away where?' Emotion made Clara abrupt but she didn't care.

The maid hesitated, as if deciding whether she needed to elaborate for the sake of this insistent stranger, then resolving that to be on the safe side, she did. She poked a strand of hair defensively beneath her cap.

'She's visiting her sister. She's been gone for days. Would you like to leave a message?'

Visiting her sister? What was that supposed to mean? Angela only had one sister, and she, Clara, was standing right there on the doorstep. She knew for a fact that Gerald had no sisters. Yet it was inconceivable that Angela could have embarked on a trip to Berlin unannounced; her normal travelling requirements made the Queen of Sheba look casual. Angela was the last person to turn up in a foreign country without the most complicated advance arrangements about luggage and hotels, which usually changed several times. She liked to be met at the airport and lunched in the appropriate restaurants, which in Berlin meant the Esplanade and the Kaiserhof, before attending both the theatre and the opera. Unlike Clara, Angela never did anything on impulse, so it was unthinkable that she should have packed a suitcase and slipped away to Berlin without a word, as Clara had done all those years ago.

Yet a second before she opened her mouth to protest, some deep, acquired caution prevented Clara from blurting out these objections and she divined a possible explanation. Angela's excuse must have been dreamed up to cover some less innocent activity. The only explanation was that she was indulging in an illicit affair. Yet further questions would only give this maid something to gossip about.

'Shall I tell her who called, miss?' enquired the maid, offhandedly.

'No. Thank you. It doesn't matter.'

Clara turned and made her way along Elizabeth Street, skirting around the workmen who were removing a set of wrought-iron railings, presumably for aeroplane manufacture. As she went, she tried to see her sister from this new, surprising perspective. Glamorous Angela, modelling Jean Patou in her brief dalliance as a fashion mannequin, had always been elegant and unflappable. She was a Vine to the ends of her racehorse-long legs and when their mother died, Angela was seamlessly co-opted into the circle of their father's sister, Lady Laura Vine, and an endless round of society parties, tennis matches and charity events. She enthusiastically participated in their father's Anglo-German Fellowship, and from everything Clara knew, was still fundraising for closer ties between Germany and England.

In every respect Angela's life could not be more different from Clara's own, except one. Neither of them had got around to having children. Perhaps that was the reason. Maybe Angela was engaged in an affair because her marriage to Gerald Mortimer MP was already crumbling. If so it was sad, but given her brick-faced brother-in-law's manner, not entirely surprising.

Clara progressed up to Knightsbridge, past Harrods and along Piccadilly until, eventually, her steps took her to a Lyons Corner House on the Strand, where she drank two cups of tea and ate a bun pocked with currants and smeared with a dab of oily margarine. Then she retraced her route, skirted the soot-stained lions of Trafalgar Square and found herself outside the National Gallery.

It was only when she was sitting on one of the leather benches, surrounded by glimmering gilt frames and blankly studying a painting in front of her, that she gave into her feelings. Major Grand believed that Leo had died and that Clara should consign his memory to the past. *I should forget Mr Quinn.* But how did anyone forget? In one way, it was treacherously easy. She thought of Leo's face fading, like a photograph left out in the sun, until no image remained. If it blanked out entirely, she would have nothing but his words to resurrect him; just the letters he had written to her and the book of Rilke's poetry that he gave her. Yet how could Leo be dead when her body still held the memory of him, pressed into every muscle and tendon? A wave of stubborn denial engulfed her. Why should she believe it? Just because someone told you something, didn't mean it was true.

When at last her focus cleared, she saw the painting she had been staring at was Jan van Eyck's *Arnolfini Marriage*. The Bruges merchant in wide-brimmed hat and sable-lined robes clasping hands with his young bride in her sage-green gown. Crystalline daylight streamed through the window and glanced off the oranges on the window ledge. The bride, with her little dog at her feet, seemed frozen in reflection, poised at the threshold between concentration and distraction. What was she thinking? Was she happy to be betrothed to this older, wealthy merchant, or was the ornately opulent room merely a gilded cage? Was the marriage a love match, or an aristocratic contract, so appropriate to the times? *That's the thing about marriage – one can never tell what goes on inside.*

Major Grand's request rose in her mind. Might von Ribbentrop really be attempting a pact with the Soviets? *A marriage of convenience,* Grand called it. It seemed unthinkable, yet so much of what seemed unthinkable had come to pass in Germany in the last six years.

Suddenly, Clara's focus was razor sharp and she was no longer looking at the tranquil Belgian interior with its subdued and pensive bride, but through it, to a garishly refurbished German Foreign Ministry and the steely, square-jawed grimace of Frau Annelies von Ribbentrop.

Chapter Seven

Fifty young women, outfitted in thigh-skimming white dresses and matching knickers, their hair in coronets of radiant blonde plaits, filed into the Faith and Beauty canteen for lunch after gymnastic practice. An aroma of sweat mingled with clouds of steam rising from trays of meat, potato and overcooked cabbage as the girls, in their pristine ankle socks, formed a line every bit as precise as a stormtroopers' honour guard.

Above them, Hitler hung, brooding eyes inclined downwards to the tanned legs and heaving breasts, and a slogan beneath him reading *Future German mothers! Your body belongs to the Führer!* Three passing policemen, part of the investigation into Lotti's death, pointed to the picture and made a ribald remark. Hedwig couldn't hear what they said, but she had a good guess.

The Faith and Beauty girls had been practising for a 'special event'. No one knew what it was yet, only that it was on the Führer's command, and that the eyes of the world would be on them. Hedwig assumed it would be something complicated involving hoops. Hoops always made her nervous, because of having to throw them in the air and catch them and the terrifying possibility that one's hoop would escape and roll away to the eternal shame of herself, her family, the community and ultimately the Fatherland itself.

Gym was compulsory here. On their first day the leader of National Socialist Youth, Baldur von Schirach, had turned up in person to address them and told them gymnastics focused 'the harmonic cultivation of body, mind and spirit'. Privately Hedwig wondered what the point was of learning social graces that expressed their individuality, when gymnastic displays made everyone look the same.

Everyone, that was, except Lotti. She had been the star gymnast of them all, lithe and acrobatic, her lissom physique curling obligingly into extreme poses with no apparent effort. She claimed gymnasts had better sex because they were more in tune with their bodies. That was the kind of thing Lotti said and Hedwig had long got used to it.

She rubbed the place beneath her armpits where her outfit chafed and left angry marks on her skin. Being tall meant that from the moment she joined the Jungmädel at ten, followed by the BDM at fourteen, the regulation uniforms had never quite fitted. Lotti was as graceful as a cat and could make the frumpiest outfit look like something from *Elegante Welt* but Hedwig's body was always awkward. She sprawled on a chair like a disjointed puppet and stooped to make herself less tall. Watching her one day, wrestling with a blouse, Lotti joked it was not the clothes, but Hedwig herself who didn't fit. It was a light remark, but secretly it terrified her. It was something Hedwig had always feared about herself – that she was different from the others. That everything the Fatherland wanted from a woman – obedience, enthusiasm, and utter loyalty to the Führer – was somehow missing in her. And one day it would be found out.

In a way, it had been found out already.

Jochen was the only son of Eastern immigrants who came over in the years after the war and settled among the grim tenements of Prenzlauer Berg. He was as tough as any Hitler Youth but his strength came from digging vegetables, rather than paramilitary exercises. They had met through a chance encounter at the

Botanical Gardens and if ever she felt in Jochen's pockets Hedwig would find dried seeds in mysterious leathery pods that he was planning to plant in his allotment. When they went walking he could pick out the least significant plant by the side of the path and make it sound special by telling her its Latin name. Despite the fact that he spent all day manufacturing Nazi memorabilia, he had never joined the Party or talked excitedly about army service, or the chances of war. On the Führer's birthday he had taken the train out to the borders of the city and spent all day harvesting asparagus, while everyone else travelled in the opposite direction.

It was inevitable that when Hedwig's parents met Jochen the encounter would be a disaster. In their cramped parlour, with its dark brown paint and sooty stove, Jochen had sat dumbly, making monosyllabic comments, eyes fixed resolutely on the tabletop. Hedwig felt her mother wince when he fetched out a rag of a handkerchief to wipe his face and saw her father frown every time he heard Jochen's rough Berliner accent. Herr Holz had fired off questions to Jochen as though conducting one of the questionnaires that every German now completed in the workplace. *What were his interests?* Botany. *What was his ancestry?* Polish. *What was his Party membership?* Non-existent. The answers could not be more disappointing, and as Jochen wolfed down the sausage stew as though it might be taken away from him, and wiped his plate round with a piece of bread, Hedwig could read the verdict in her parents' eyes. He had failed the test. This boy was not what their daughter had joined the Faith and Beauty Society for. Precisely the opposite, in fact. What was she thinking of?

Afterwards, there had been a row. Frau Holz claimed Jochen would never amount to anything and if Hedwig stuck with him, the only house she could hope for was a greenhouse. Herr Holz went further, demanding she end the relationship there and then. Hedwig knew that from then on her assignations with Jochen would have to remain secret. Which was why, perversely, staying in the Faith and Beauty Society suited everyone. Her parents wanted her there so she would not see Jochen, and she wanted to be there so that she could.

After lunch that day there was Dinner Etiquette, focusing on how to lay the correct knives and forks, fold napkins into swastikas and clever ways with sugar icing. The entire topic was fiendishly complex. There were guidelines for which flowers went with different dishes. Roses with beef. Orchids with fish. The Führer's favourite, Edelweiss, if you could find it, with anything.

Everything was about rules now. The girls had each been given a Rule Book to mark down everything they learned. How to talk, how to look, how to conduct yourself correctly. Girls should wait for the men to pick up cutlery and start eating first. Hedwig studiously noted everything she learned, but in truth, it was like taking life lessons from a fairy tale. No one in Berlin would be holding five-course dinners in the near future. You couldn't get sugar icing and the chances of finding a side of beef were about as likely as the Führer himself dropping by to eat it.

Gloomily she selected a hunk of rye bread to accompany the thin gravy. Today's lunch was sauerkraut, bread soup and fake meat. Everything was fake now; not just the coffee, but the rice cooked in mutton fat moulded to make artificial chops, rice mixed with onions and oil which was called fake fish, the nettles in soup and the horse chestnuts in bread. It reminded her of a joke Lotti had told. *What's the difference between India and Germany? In India one man, Gandhi, starves on behalf of millions. In Germany, millions starve on behalf of one man.*

Lotti was the only woman who dared tell jokes in public, with a rich, full-throated, gurgling laugh. That was also against the rules, of course. Laughing was inelegant for women, according to the principal, Frau Mann. It implied criticism and did not befit a German woman. Smiling was a different matter – indeed Faith and Beauty girls should always smile when a man addressed them

– but laughing, well, the way Frau Mann talked, it was as though a healthy dose of female laughter could bring the whole edifice of the National Socialist Party crashing down.

'Are you eating that?'

Hilde Ziegler was eyeing her slice of rye bread and Hedwig shrugged. She used to be hungry all the time. A hunger that filled her dreams with fat pork chops, chocolate and cake with real cream and pastries made with butter, but since Lotti's death, her appetite had disappeared.

She glanced out of the window to the woods at the far end of the garden. At the place Lotti was found, the police had erected arc lights, the kind you saw in film studios, bathing the area in a dazzling phosphorescent glow. But there was one secret that no amount of police spotlights were going to uncover.

Everyone in Germany kept a place in their mind, like a cellar in a house or an attic concealed by a study door, that nobody knew about. A place where they thought their own thoughts and examined their true feelings. And when Hedwig retreated to this place and shut the door behind her, what she mainly felt was guilt.

Chapter Eight

Even though he was standing in the shadows, Clara could feel his eyes on her. Calculating, malign, dangerous. Attempting, with the precision of an interrogator, to dissect her performance and separate pretence from reality. Analysing every minute facial movement, every glance and gesture, to pounce on falsity and drag the truth from where she had concealed it.

Despite the heat of the arc lights, she shivered.

She was wearing a flimsy pink silk dress and spectacles and standing next to Heinz Rühmann on stage five of the Ufa studio – the very same sound stage on which Marlene Dietrich had only a decade earlier filmed *The Blue Angel* and Fritz Lang made *Metropolis*. Now, in contrast to those cinematic masterpieces, stage five was playing host to the final scene of *Liebe Streng Verboten*. *Love Strictly Forbidden* was pure, high-octane candyfloss for the eyes. The plot revolved around an ambitious mother who wanted to marry her daughter to the lord of the manor, while the daughter was in love with a lowly hotelier. It was a farcical procession of mistakes and confusions with a satisfyingly happy ending and just the kind of escapism Herr Doktor Goebbels prescribed to soothe a nation's frazzled nerves.

In truth, Clara was glad that the film required the minimum of effort. Her visit to London and the news of Leo occupied all her thinking space. She felt stunned, as though she had left part of herself in England, and *Love Strictly Forbidden*, which had all the depth and sophistication of a Wurst carton, was the ideal vehicle to occupy her. The lovelorn secretary was a popular role in German cinema and she had played it a number of times over the last few years, so it was easy to go through the motions. It helped that Heinz Rühmann, one of the biggest blond heartthrobs of the German screen, was an old friend, so kissing him was no great hardship.

Yet even the most intimate of love scenes required an army of people in the studio; director, assistant director, crew, clapper-board loader, piano player. Continuity girl, props manager, cameraman and gaffer, and a make-up artist with brushes and palette primed for a last-minute touch-up. Boys with belts of tools hung from the cranes, and in distant glass cubicles sound engineers fiddled with knobs and microphones. All morning everyone's attention had been focused on the small pool of light occupied by Clara and Rühmann, but when the Minister for Propaganda entered, suddenly no one was watching the actors any more.

As soon as Clara saw Goebbels take shape in the shadows, assistants fluttering around him and the violet haze of his ciga-rette smoke coiling upwards into the studio roof, she knew there was no point going on. The man in charge of all film-making in the Third Reich was not the type to linger respectfully in the shadows. Once he registered that she had seen him, he gave an infinitesimal nod and Clara, with a quick apologetic smile to the director, threaded her way through the camera cables and followed Goebbels as he hobbled in his built-up patent leather boots along the corridor to his office.

The Propaganda Minister's limp was the first thing everyone noticed about him and the last thing they dared mention. In the early days of the regime, the Society for the Aid of Cripples had brought out a pamphlet celebrating Goebbels as the supreme example of mental powers triumphing over physical disabilities. The charity got a taste of those mental powers shortly afterwards, when their pamphlet was burned and the society closed down.

Reaching his office, Goebbels flung open the door.

The office was a symphony of gleaming light, polished oak and pale leather furniture. Chrome lamps graced a desk of immaculate walnut and stills from Ufa's greatest hits were displayed in tasteful black frames on the walls. Pride of place was devoted to an enormous, close-up picture of Goebbels' own face, cadaverous, hollow-eyed and exuding all the gravitas of a wanted poster. The office also came fitted with the standard accoutrements of any minister of the Third Reich – microphones concealed in the walls, lamps and picture frames – invalidating the need to close the door quite so firmly as he gestured Clara to a seat.

Goebbels stalked across to his desk and flung himself down. Generally, his charm was as polished as his own furniture, but that day his bony visage was grimly set and his pomaded hair greying visibly. Despite the immaculate Hugo Boss herringbone suit and shimmering silk tie, he looked more wretched than Clara had ever seen him. A twitch flickered the corner of his left eye. Something serious was plainly troubling him and though there was no shortage of troubles that might concern a senior member of the Nazi government in the Spring of 1939, Clara guessed Goebbels' misery had nothing to do with the prospect of European war.

She wondered if it was the stomach complaint that had forced him into hospital recently, or the fact that Lída Baarová, the Czech actress he had been besotted with, had been banished from Germany on Hitler's orders. Yet instinct told her it was the same old story – the ongoing marital war with his wife Magda, who according to studio gossip had taken revenge for her long humiliation by initiating an affair with Karl Hanke, her husband's aide, and was now disporting herself in an unseemly manner around the city's nightclubs. On Goebbels' desk Magda stared out from a silver picture frame with a look that could freeze blood. Clara wondered how he managed to stop himself turning it to the wall.

He eyed her coldly.

'You look totally unrecognizable with those spectacles. You don't need them, do you?'

'Not yet.'

'Good. They're hideous. Take them off. Spectacles on women are worse than trousers. They lend a dreadfully academic air and I loathe academic women. Besides, it makes it harder to tell what you're thinking.'

Unbidden, Conrad Adler's phrase floated once again into Clara's head. *Like fire behind ice.*

'Actresses are supposed to project their feelings, not suppress them. It doesn't do to look sly. Especially . . .'

He broke off to reach for the silver cigarette box, a gift from Hitler himself, and extracted one, tossing it carelessly in Clara's direction and offering a light. Having savoured this pause, he resumed.

'Especially when you're about to appear in the most ambitious film that Germany has ever seen.'

'*Love Strictly Forbidden?*'

Goebbels cast his eyes to the ceiling, as though beseeching divine help, and tapped a finger on his patent leather boot.

'Don't be ridiculous, woman. *Love Strictly Forbidden* is a piece of nonsense designed for brainless secretaries on a night out whose highest ambition is to seduce their employer and entrap the poor sap into marriage. I'm talking about something of immense artistic importance.' He exhaled a weary stream of smoke, as though the woes of the world had settled on his narrow shoulders.

'You, Fräulein Vine, have been plucked from – well, perhaps not obscurity,' he gave a sardonic wince, 'but very far from stardom, to feature in a documentary film about the making of Germania.'

'But I . . .'

'Don't interrupt. It's the inspiration of the Führer himself. He feels the time is right for a full-length film about the triumphs of our nation and a celebration of our cultural conquests abroad.'

What exactly could Goebbels be referring to? The re-militarization of the Rhineland? The annexation of Austria? The seizure of Czechoslovakia?

'Which cultural conquests did you have in mind?'

Goebbels' eyes narrowed to check for insubordination, then he said, 'I take it you've heard of the Ahnenerbe?'

'I'm not sure I . . .'

'Herr Reichsführer Himmler's hobby.'

The mention of the sinister, moon-faced SS chief was like an ice cube down the spine. Himmler had that effect on most people. Generally his hobbies involved building new concentration camps and expanding the Gestapo's state-of-the-art surveillance system, but no one, as yet, had suggested making a film about them.

Goebbels crossed his skinny legs and sighed.

'I can see I'm going to have to explain. You must have seen newsreels about the trip to Tibet?'

'Oh yes,' she said quickly. 'That.'

The weekly newsreel was shown before every feature film. Clara had dozed through one just the other evening when she visited the Ufa Palast with Erich. Vaguely she recalled footage of scientists disembarking from a plane at Tempelhof airport. From what she could recall, the expedition had been dedicated to proving one of Himmler's most cherished notions – that the Aryan race was pre-eminent on earth. They had been examining Tibetan natives for evidence.

'Himmler's full of these obsessions,' grunted Goebbels. 'If it's not the Ahnenerbe, it's that place down in Wewelsburg.'

Sensing that he had imparted a little too much information, he drew himself together, rose and clasped his hands behind his back.

'Anyway. The Ahnenerbe is a scientific institute established to research the cultural history of the German race and whatever our private thoughts about the SS-Reichsführer's – *enthusiasms* – its work will be the centrepiece of this film. It's got foreign locations, history, adventure.' A little, dismissive wave. 'Everything people love.'

'It sounds very ambitious.' Clara made a mental note to grill Erich about the Ahnenerbe as soon as possible. As an ardent member of the Hitler Youth he always knew about these things.

'It is. As the Führer sees it, the Ahnenerbe is at the very heart of our work as National Socialists. It seeks to propagate the eternal values of the Germanic races. Etcetera, etcetera,' Goebbels waved his hand to signify the kind of officialese beloved of his own newsreels and newspapers.

'I'm giving you the broad-brush details here, but you're going to need to familiarize yourself fairly swiftly because from what I hear Himmler is taking a close interest in this film and he's perfectly liable to turn up on the set without warning.'

Goebbels' face twisted with distaste at the thought. The prospect of another senior Nazi intruding on his own department was plainly a huge irritant. He strode over to the window to look out on a small square of lawn in the style of a mediaeval cloister, where actresses and secretaries liked to relax between takes, gossiping and catching the sun and, all too often, the minister's eye. Although his gaze travelled automatically over the tanned legs and golden figures on display, his mind was plainly elsewhere.

'I would have thought, Fräulein Vine, you would be flattered to be involved.'

'I am. Very. Who's the director?'

He swung round, his expression, if possible, even more dyspeptic.

'I was coming to that. *Germania* is to be directed by Fräulein Riefenstahl.'

Leni Riefenstahl.

Leni Riefenstahl was, without doubt, the most famous female director alive. Her film about the 1934 Nazi Party rally, *The Triumph of The Will*, had seduced not just Germany, but many around the world. Her documentary about the 1936 Berlin Olympic Games had just won Best Film at the Venice Film Festival. If *Germania* was anything like Leni Riefenstahl's previous epics, it would make all Clara's previous films look like home movies.

'I'm honoured, Herr Doktor. I really am. But . . .' For a moment Clara's habitual composure had deserted her. 'I don't understand why I should have been given the privilege of presenting something quite so . . . high profile.'

'That makes two of us,' said Goebbels gracelessly. He rubbed a hand over a cheek silvered with stubble. His complexion was dull with fatigue.

'It's the obvious question, and the first thing I asked too, but Fräulein Riefenstahl has not deigned to honour me with an explanation. She just said the Führer had given her a free hand and you were what she wanted. She's irrational like that.'

He drummed his beautifully manicured fingernails on the desk and regarded Clara with disdain.

'You seem very cool, considering the honour that's being handed to you. You're invited to star in a movie made by the world's most famous female film director about the most powerful country on earth. I can't imagine you've received many more significant propositions recently. Or perhaps you're too busy? Possibly you have too much on your plate?'

'Of course not. It's a huge honour. And I'm very grateful.'

If he was mollified, he didn't show it.

'Good. Well there's a tight deadline so you'll need to start straight away. I'll have Fräulein Riefenstahl get in touch. Where are you living now? Winterfeldtstrasse, wasn't it?'

'Not any more. I'm very near here actually. At the Artists'
Colony by the Griebnitzsee.'

'Griebnitzsee?'

She had surprised him. No doubt he assumed he knew everything about her movements, so his surprise provided a crucial
piece of information.

Whoever had ordered surveillance on her apartment, it wasn't Joseph Goebbels.

'Strange choice. I've never seen you as the country type.'

He was more accurate than he knew. Already Clara wished
she was back in Winterfeldtstrasse, watchers or not. She'd never
realized how much she loved the comforting racket of the city
around her, the clank of the trams and trains on Nollendorfplatz
a few blocks away, which started early in the morning and didn't
end until late at night, the rattle of shopkeepers rolling up their
blinds, the shouts of the newspaper men and the crash of bottles
from the local bars. She even missed her unglamorous view, the
walls with pipes snaking down them, the uneven rooftops and
unsought access to other people's windows. Some things you
never knew you loved until they were gone.

There was a knock on the door and a secretary's head craned
around.

'Your sitting, Herr Reichsminister.'

'Already? Show him in then!'

His face brightened and he sprang to his feet.

'Another official portrait, I'm afraid. I'm not a vain man. I
don't like the idea of ministers flaunting themselves, but the
Ministry will insist. It has to do with official prestige.'

A shock-headed figure with an easel had edged into the room
and was standing uncomfortably by the door.

'Herr Messel! Come in! You have precisely twenty minutes of
my time.'

He moved to the window, so that the light sliced onto his
cadaverous cheekbones, fixed his gaze on the sunbathing girls
outside and assumed a philosophical air.

'At least Herr Messel is a decent German artist. My fellow ministers have not been so scrupulous. Von Ribbentrop actually asked André Derain to come from France and the chap turned him down. Extraordinary, don't you think?'

Clara was saved from replying by a clatter and a soft exclamation of dismay. Beneath nervously fumbling fingers, Herr Messel's easel had collapsed.

'For God's sake, man!'

Goebbels gave Clara a brusque wave and she realized that if she didn't act now, she might not have another chance.

'As it happens, Herr Doktor, I have a request. It's another kind of cultural expansion really. *Vogue* magazine in France have asked to photograph me. In Paris.'

She might as well have proposed flying to the moon.

'*Vogue?* You? Why?'

'They first suggested it when I was there last year,' she lied.

'Why not Brigitte Horney or Marika Rökk?' Goebbels protested, cruelly citing two better-known actresses. 'Or Lilian Harvey?'

Clara shrugged. 'It's a feature called Cinema and Fashion. Apparently the article's a tribute to German cinema. Under the aegis of the Reich Chamber of Film,' she added politely.

The idea prompted an explosion of vicious laughter from Goebbels, long, hacking guffaws culminating in a spluttering cough, like a chainsaw refusing to start. He bent his heaving shoulders over to recover.

'I shouldn't laugh. I can see how desperate they are to curry favour. But it'll take more than that.'

'I'm sorry?'

'Nothing. Just thinking ahead.'

'I was hoping you would give your permission for a few days' travel.'

He was certain to refuse. Why, after all, should he grant permission for such an insignificant jaunt? Nazi Germany had never been interested in accommodating the French – precisely the opposite. Many more powerful artists had had requests for foreign travel turned down. Since Marlene Dietrich's defection to Hollywood, Goebbels lived in eternal suspicion that his stars were about to jump ship and thumb their noses at the Nazis from the safety of America or Britain.

She tried valiantly to remain unruffled beneath his sceptical gaze until Goebbels spread his hands in mock surrender and said, 'Go, if you want to. But I can't spare you for more than forty-eight hours. I'm all for the cultural conquest of Europe but this film is far too pressing to be held up for some trifling magazine piece. Particularly if it's French.'

Chapter Nine

If there was one occupation that offered true job security in the Third Reich, it was manufacturing uniforms. From the field grey of the Wehrmacht to SS black, from the attractive slate blue of the Luftwaffe right down to the dark brown overalls of the Reich Labour Service, uniforms were the only product that was never in short supply. And amidst the plethora of uniforms lay numerous fine degrees of difference. A universe of trimming, braid, buttons, silver oak leaves, daggers, insignia and gleaming death's heads existed, all of it signifying specific titles and ranks and requiring meticulous attention to detail. Contracts to dress the armed forces sparked fierce competition among tailors, and those who were lucky enough to win business were keen to advertise their skills. To this end, twin lifesize mannequins in black SS Death's Head uniform had been erected in the window of Fromm's tailor shop, in a small street just off the Königsallee, scaring late-night drunks and terrifying children on their way to school.

Clara averted her gaze from the mannequins and checked the address again. It was hard to imagine a less appropriate workplace for a Jewish seamstress, but this was where she had been led to find her old friend, Steffi Schaeffer.

The bell clanged behind her as she entered the shop and looked around. It was a hushed, deep-carpeted space, perfumed by a tangy mixture of polish, leather and expensive pomade. Bolts of cloth were stacked at every level, dull grey, blue, pinstripe and herringbone, rolled up and reverently folded like vellum manuscripts in a mediaeval library. Against one wall a dresser of gleaming mahogany with ivory-handled drawers was stacked with containers of braids and buttons, tortoiseshell, horn and bone, visible through the glass compartments.

On the opposite wall was a gallery of Fromm's more famous clientele. First came the ordinary stars, the actors Gustav Fröhlich, Hans Albers and the boxer Max Schmeling sporting immaculately cut dinner suits, and above them, at eye-level, hung the true celebrities of modern Germany: Heinrich Himmler, with his trademark wide grey breeches and clinical grimace, mad-eyed Rudolf Hess, and Reinhard Heydrich, head of the SD security service, as skeletal and expressionless as any catwalk model.

From the interior gloom a stooped figure emerged with a measuring tape around his neck, peering at Clara through a pair of pince nez. She guessed this must be Herr Fromm. He nodded towards Himmler's photograph.

'We are honoured to have the SS-Reichsführer as a regular customer.'

'So I see.'

'And Herr Reichsminister Goering is also a most rewarding client,' he added unctuously, plaiting his fingers.

'I can imagine.'

Anyone who loved dressing up as much as Goering did would keep a team of tailors in full-time occupation. Clara peered at a picture of Hitler's second-in-command cavorting in the bejewelled guise of a Roman emperor, in toga and fur-trimmed slippers, with hair freshly permed and ruby rings on his pudgy fingers. He was clearly wearing full eye shadow and lipstick. German women might be constantly informed that make-up was degenerate but different standards applied to German men, it seemed. Senior ones, at least.

'We turn our hand to all varieties of costumes,' continued Herr Fromm smoothly, as Clara examined another shot of Goering looking absurd in an orange suede jerkin and green Tyrolean hat with an animal tail sticking out of it.

'That's his uniform as Reichsjägermeister. It required the most exquisite stitching, but here at Fromm's we pride ourselves on attention to detail. Hugo Boss, of course makes uniforms for everyone – the Sturmabteilung, Hitler Youth, National Socialist Motor Corps . . .' He waved his hand in a faint gesture of deprecation. 'But his are made in factories. Discriminating gentlemen prefer bespoke uniforms and ours, of course, are entirely handmade.'

He halted the advertisement enquiringly.

'But may I ask how I can help? Is it concerning a uniform for your husband, perhaps? Or something for yourself?'

Although there was no one else in the shop, Clara lowered her voice.

'I'm looking for Steffi Schaeffer.'

The poker-straight demeanour did not change, but there was a flicker of scrutiny behind Herr Fromm's shuttered eyes.

'We're old friends,' she added.

'Please,' he gestured towards the back of the shop and ushered Clara through a velvet drape into an even gloomier room where volumes of swatches were distributed like open books and a slender blonde woman was measuring out lengths of field-grey serge. Steffi Schaeffer.

The other woman jumped up and embraced Clara, then, keeping hold of her hands, she stood back and looked her up and down.

'How on earth did you find me?'

It was hard to equate the figure before her with the poised and beautiful woman Clara had first met in the Ufa costume department six years before. Steffi Schaeffer still had an air of elegance, but her caramel-blonde hair was now liberally threaded with grey and hollows of worry shadowed her face. The lines bracketing her mouth might have been carved there with a knife. The hand that held Clara's was still soft enough to accomplish the most delicate stitching, but her eyes had hardened. Steffi Schaeffer was no longer a costume designer, nor a seamstress with her own premises and a list of private clients. She was not even a German. All Steffi Schaeffer could call herself now was a Jew, and like all the other Jews who made up ninety-five per cent of Germany's textile trade, she relied on people like Herr Fromm to make use of her skills. She was lucky, probably, that Herr Fromm had been prepared to take her on.

Instinctively Clara waited until the tailor had melted from view.

'Don't worry about him,' said Steffi. 'He's been a godsend. I've lost all my customers, but he gives me what work he can. If anyone important arrives at the shop he shouts, "Get on with that jacket, Elsa!" through the curtain. It's our code. How did you find me?'

'I went to your old studio. Several times. It was only by chance the Blockwart saw me and said you might be here.' She looked around the minuscule room. 'What happened?'

'What happened?' There was bitter acid in Steffi's voice that had not been there before. 'Kristallnacht happened.'

The night the previous November when synagogues were burned, Jewish homes and shops demolished, and thousands of Jews arrested all over Germany. The carpet of broken glass had spawned its own sinister, poetic coining, known the world over. *Kristallnacht*. The Night of Broken Glass.

'The authorities demanded that we repay the cost of repairing shop fronts. Then there was the new law – the Exclusion of Jews from German Economic Life – that meant I couldn't run a business. It was the same for all of us seamstresses. Until a few years ago almost every seamstress in Germany was Jewish. Now, can you believe it, they claim all Jewish influence has been eradicated from the German clothing industry. Who do they think makes the clothes? The Nazis are very demanding; they want the best and that only comes from Jewish tailors.'

'Is Herr Fromm taking a risk, employing you?'

'Of course he is. Officially I need a permit to be here. We're banned from almost everything now. Swimming, going to the cinema, walking in the park. Any sentence with a verb in it, that's what we're banned from. They'd probably ban us from breathing if it were possible.'

Steffi hesitated, as if she was still, after all these years, calculating how far Clara could be trusted.

'You asked if Herr Fromm is taking a risk employing me. He is. But he's taking an even bigger risk than that. My dressmaking business may not be flourishing, but my other business is.'

Clara understood at once what she meant.

After she lost her job at the Ufa studios, Steffi had found another, more urgent line of work, assisting a network of underground resistance workers who helped Jews disappear. Steffi's network provided clothes, food and disguises for those who needed to vanish fast, helping them to move from safe house to safe house as they kept one jump ahead of the Gestapo's net.

'In fact, there's something you should see. Come with me.'

Steffi led the way up two flights of worn wooden stairs and into an upper room divided in two by a floral curtain.

It was a stark contrast to the polished leather and gleaming mahogany cabinets below. The window shutters were three quarters closed, casting a dim shadow across the battered sofa and cheap chest of drawers. There was a pungent smell of compressed humanity, stuffy and fetid. In the midst of the room a young girl sat at a Singer sewing machine, bent over a pile of blue gauze.

'This is Esther Goldblatt.'

The girl raised a pair of inscrutable almond eyes in brief acknowledgement. She had a haunting gaze, level and unblinking. She could be no more than fifteen, with jet-black hair bundled up in a bun and a slight, resentful twist to her mouth.

'Everyone's learning something now; infant care, mending, glove-making, millinery,' said Steffi brightly. 'So I suggested Esther train as a seamstress. She's a very promising pupil.'

'Frau Schaeffer is exaggerating,' said Esther, tersely.

'Not at all. You'll pick it up in no time. You're artistic, after all.'

Steffi turned away, and as she did, subtly but distinctly, the girl rolled her eyes. It was the gesture of teenagers the world over, the one that expressed an utter disconnect between the world of adults and adolescents, and Clara was instantly reminded of Erich.

'How long have you been here?'

Clearly the girl's presence in the stuffy attic had nothing to do with dressmaking lessons.

'A whole week.'

It showed. Her skin was pale from lack of sunlight and her hair was lank.

'She sleeps on the sofa bed and if anyone comes,' Steffi tilted at the cushions, 'she can hide in the bedframe. It lifts up and I've fixed the catchment so it looks as if it's broken. I've tacked material on the underside and drilled holes for air. A friend who runs a restaurant on the Ku'damm brings us food.'

'But . . .' Clara hesitated. 'Why?'

Steffi lowered her voice, as though hoping in vain that Esther would not hear. 'The police want to question her about one of her school books.'

'I don't understand.'

'It was a drawing book, but I made it look like a school book,' explained Esther, refusing to be excluded from the conversation. 'I covered all my sketch books with blue waxed paper and stuck labels on them from school, with titles like *Algebra* and *Racial Theory*, and hid my pictures inside.'

'What did you draw?'

'People being arrested,' she said tonelessly. 'I did some of the day when they lined us all up against the garden wall and forced us to watch while they smashed our possessions. They threw a hammer at the mirror and they tore all the keys out of the grand piano. Then I did drawings of the Gestapo men on the day they took our father away. I draw everything. Here. I did another one today.' She passed a piece of paper to Clara, who took a quick look.

'It's only people's faces.' The girl's voice was deliberately blank, as though challenging Clara to protest. 'Steffi can't complain about that.'

Esther was right. It was nothing but a panorama of faces. Ordinary Berliners' faces. Grinning, interested, indifferent, heartless. Clara had seen those faces a hundred times, when people were being arrested or loaded into trucks. Or an old man was hauled off by a policeman from a station platform while onlookers stood by. Yet still she was stunned by the skill with which Esther had captured them.

'Father said I should draw what I liked.'

'Well your father's not here now, is he?' snapped Steffi.

'So what happened?'

'The police came and said our house had been requisitioned by a high-ranking SS officer and our family would have to move. They started combing through all our rooms. They'd already taken our jewellery, but then they found my books.'

Clara imagined the hulking forms of the policemen crammed into the apartment, guns at their hips, eyes flitting everywhere, rough hands reaching into drawers.

'Once they looked inside her books they came back for her the same night,' added Steffi. 'Fortunately her mother had already brought her to me, and she and the older sister are in hiding too.'

Esther's eyes dropped, as if acknowledging for the first time the gravity of her predicament.

'I hate it here,' she burst out. 'There's nothing to do. I can't even wash because there's no soap.'

'Have you seen your mother?'

'She came yesterday, just for an hour. The worst thing is, I miss my cat. What's going to happen to him? Who will look after him while we're gone?'

It might have seemed strange that the girl should expend her anxiety on a cat, rather than her mother and sister, or her father, imprisoned in a camp, but Clara was not so easily fooled. Esther was focusing all her anxieties on one, easily identified treasure. It had been the same for Clara when her mother died. She recalled the obsession she had with her horse Inkerman and his lame leg. She remembered burying her face in his glossy pelt, and inhaling leather and straw and sweat.

'You mustn't worry about him,' she said gently. 'He'll be fine.'

'He's only a kitten.'

'Cats are good at looking after themselves.'

'My mother kept saying nothing would happen. My father won the Iron Cross in the war. He didn't believe in running away, my uncle came back from Palestine because it was too dirty, and then in the Olympics he said no city on earth could compare with Berlin. Father said Jews always thrive under pressure. He said pressure turns coal dust into diamonds.'

Suddenly the vulnerability of Esther Goldblatt, with her narrow shoulders and solemn, mistrustful eyes, touched something deep within Clara – a protective urge that was both mysterious and utterly familiar.

'How old are you?'

'Fifteen in July.'

'Fourteen!' She turned to Steffi. 'She's a child still. How can they be looking for a child?'

'She's a young woman in their eyes and she has disseminated subversive material,' said Steffi.

'It's not material!' Esther jerked her chin proudly. 'It's Art!'

'If your drawings were passed around they could influence other people,' Steffi retorted. There was a harshness about her that had not existed in the early days of their friendship. It was born of exhaustion and worry, no doubt, but Clara felt for the girl on the receiving end.

'Now get on with that hem, Esther, while I have a word with Fräulein Vine.'

Steffi descended one of the flights of stairs and stared out of the window to the street below.

'Poor kid,' said Clara.

Steffi shrugged. 'She doesn't make it easy. Perhaps it's harder for her than others because she came from a wealthy background and the family sheltered her from what was going on. They had a large apartment in Charlottenburg and her father owned several factories. Nothing was too good for those girls. But she tries my nerves, Clara. I'm at my wits' end and she complains about being shut up in an attic and not having enough to eat. What does she think this is? The Hotel Adlon?'

She gripped the banisters with clenched hands.

'Esther's situation is not hopeless. The father may be in Sachsenhausen but the mother and sister are safe and they have an uncle in America who has given them an affidavit to move there. But Esther's quota number is very far down the list and it will take years before it comes up. The only country that gives transit visas to people with American quota numbers is England, so Esther needs someone in England to act as guarantee for her because she's too young to earn a living there. She would have to be adopted by a British citizen.'

'Officially adopted?'

'Only until the age of eighteen. But that's not all. The person in England must deposit a large sum of money to sponsor a refugee.'

The complexity of the situation dimmed Steffi's countenance, and her face creased again into a lattice of lines.

'We can supply most things. We have a doctor who brings medicine and a young man who produces passports and identity papers for us. He turns his hand to anything. Work permits, release papers, travel permits. Tickets for buses and trains. His work is superb, but he can't magic up an English sponsor. And on top of that, Esther can't stay here for long. Herr Fromm has been very good but he generally only takes Jews in for one night at a time. The other day Heydrich came in and Herr Fromm said measuring the inside leg of the top man in the SD with Esther two floors above was enough to give him a heart attack. His nerves are in shreds.'

'What will you do?'

'If we could just find some way to get her to England . . .'

'You're asking me to help.'

'I'm sorry. You don't have to get involved in this. You can't have expected this when you came today. I wouldn't blame you if . . .'

'No, of course. I'll do everything I can.'

A clatter on the street below caused them to turn, but when they looked down they saw only several large rolls of black cloth being unloaded from a van and carried inside.

'Herr Fromm got his orders in early,' said Steffi quietly. 'There's going to be a boom in black. Black crepe, black cotton. Black serge to cover windows in a blackout. Black felt to conceal the car headlights. Black voile.'

'Why voile?'

'War means widows. And there'll be clothing cards too, so materials will be rationed. Herr Fromm is wise to stockpile early.'

She reached out a hand.

'I forgot. I have something for you.'

She went over to her bag and brought out a velvet pouch, from which she withdrew a box containing a three-stranded string of pearls. The pearls were old, Clara could see, and of the highest quality, with an intricate gold clasp and a soft gleam that seemed to hover around them as they nestled on their bed of crimson velvet. She looked on in astonishment as Steffi fastened them around her neck.

'What's this?'

'It's not a gift, I'm afraid. More a loan. I've sewed hundreds of necklaces and rings into the linings of women's dresses, but the Gestapo are getting wise to our scheme now and they routinely rip up people's clothes, so I thought of a better hiding place. These pearls are valuable. They belonged to my grandmother, and you know the thing about pearls – they come from the sea and they need moisture to keep their lustre. They must be worn and I can think of no one better to wear them for me.'

Clara touched the necklace and smiled.

'I'd be honoured. But only until you need them again.'

'I don't need them. In fact, I want you to sell them.'

'Are you sure?'

'Next time you go to England, sell them and keep the money there. That way if Esther manages to leave, we can have something to pay her sponsor.'

Steffi stood back and studied the necklace with an approving smile.

'In the meantime, pearls suit your skin. They have a way of lighting up the face, don't you think? But my necklace does show up that dress you're wearing. Look at this rent in the sleeve. Let me darn it while you wait.'

Clara felt ashamed. That had been the original purpose of her visit.

'For heaven's sake, Steffi. You have more important things to do than darn dresses.'

A hint of the seamstress's old self returned as she examined the sleeve critically, assessing its texture and precise shade.

'Allow me. It's relaxing. And besides, you are, almost certainly, the only customer I have left.'

Chapter Ten

Albert Speer looked more like a man touring the stations of the cross than someone inspecting his own, recently completed refurbishment of the Foreign Ministry in Wilhelmstrasse. The Führer's favourite architect was a good decade younger than most of the Nazi élite and it showed; his chestnut hair was lustrous, his muscular frame filled a finely cut suit and Hitler's fondness for him was said to border on the homoerotic. True, by the standards of the Nazi élite – the obese Goering, mad Hess and crippled Goebbels – Speer was practically an Adonis, but as he toured the room on the queenly arm of Annelies von Ribbentrop, the architect's handsome face was not a happy one. Indeed behind the bland, professional composure it was possible to detect outright dismay at the sight of the journalists, celebrities and actresses gathered to toast the new décor at 73, Wilhelmstrasse.

Perhaps because the end result was far from what he had planned. Speer, whose own style was cool, severe and neoclassical, favouring shimmering colonnades of pristine marble, must have winced at the grandiose swags of cerise velvet that now gussied up each window, the silk wallpaper and mounds of soft furnishings. Opulent chandeliers had been fitted and the walls were plastered with old Masters in handsome gilded frames, Rembrandts and Goyas hanging in tiers three and four high, displayed in order of expense. Every pillared hall, every marbled vista, every gleaming polished wall now bore the flamboyant personal stamp of Joachim von Ribbentrop. Or to be more accurate, his wife.

Clara stood amid a group of journalists at the far side of the room, Major Grand's words resounding in her head. *From what we've heard, Frau von Ribbentrop frequently formulates political policy, which is later passed off as her husband's.* It was true, the Foreign Minister's wife was very different from those of other senior men. Magda Goebbels was too depressed to care about politics and Eva Braun, the Führer's girlfriend, probably couldn't spell Czechoslovakia. The only international affairs Frau Goering cared about were holidays on the Italian Riviera. Annelies von Ribbentrop, by contrast, was highly educated and politically motivated. She dominated her husband and insisted he discuss every decision with her. She knew more, and would impart far less. How could Clara possibly find a way into her mind?

That day the châtelaine of the new Foreign Ministry was wearing a suit of hairy mauve, a pussy-bow blouse, emerald earrings and a welter of pearls at her throat. Powder settled into the lines round her eyes like wrinkles on old paint and her hair was set like concrete. Her delight at parading Albert Speer was all the greater because of the hot competition for his services. He had already redecorated Goebbels' Propaganda Ministry with lacquered walnut fittings and installed a home cinema in the Minister's townhouse. He had renovated 11, Leipzigerplatz, the grandiose, turreted monstrosity that was home to the Goerings, and in January he had signed off on the brand-new Reich Chancellery, on which eight thousand workers toiled night and day. Now he was starting his most ambitious commission to date – rebuilding Berlin as the world capital of a continental empire. Speer would be the man responsible for turning the Führer's dreams into stone. No wonder he seemed anxious to get away from the von Ribbentrop's soft furnishings.

'Poor Speer,' said Hugh Lindsey, who was standing at Clara's side. 'He's the only one who seems remotely modest, and he has the least to be modest about. Some of his buildings are genuinely exciting.'

'Not so exciting for the Jews whose homes are being razed to make way for them,' commented Mary.

'You've heard about his next commission?' said Hugh, helping himself to a canapé proffered by a waiter in silk stockings. 'Hitler wants Speer to build a Führermuseum in Linz. His home town. It's going to house his collection.'

'What collection is that?' asked Clara.

'Clara, you must be the only person in Germany who hasn't heard. The Führer's planning to create the greatest art gallery ever seen.'

'The only problem is,' added Mary conspiratorially, 'so is Goering. When I had my interview with him the other day I thought it was going to be about the Luftwaffe, but it was all about art. He says his country villa, Carinhall, will house the biggest private collection in the world.'

'Makes sense,' said Hugh. 'Nothing about Goering would be small.'

'Goering told me his collection will be far more important than Hitler's. He wants to track down all valuable art of Germanic origin, whatever that might be, and return it to the Reich. It's quite a spat. Apparently, Speer's calling it "the picture war".'

'Thank heavens I've found you, Clara.'

The voice that broke into their conversation was the kind of theatrical whisper designed to reach the back row of the upper circle.

'What do you make of it? Not exactly cosy, is it?'

Emmy Goering, the wife of Hitler's second-in-command, sailed unopposed through the goggling throng. Frau Goering had been an actress herself before fate decreed that Hermann Goering, on a rare outing to Weimar, should catch sight of her and fall in love on the spot. Now her fortunes were transformed – she was married with a child, and universally known as the First Lady of the Reich. Yet despite having accumulated more wealth than she could have dreamt of, Emmy Goering had also accumulated enemies, and none more potent or bitter than Annelies von Ribbentrop. As Mary and Hugh melted discreetly into the background, Clara recalled Major Grand's motto.

My enemy's enemy is my friend.

'Poor Annelies,' continued Emmy, watching acidly as the Foreign Minister's wife shepherded Speer around the room. 'All that money and no taste whatsoever. You know she's announced that all German embassies should be redecorated as precise replicas of the Reich Chancellery? Can you imagine the expense? Now she has a whole ministry to play with, her extravagance knows no bounds. She doesn't understand restraint.'

It was hard to know how to respond to this. The Goerings' own palatial villa would make a Borgia feel at home. Besides the gem-encrusted gold chairs and mosaic floors inlaid with lapis lazuli swastikas, it was a temple to taxidermy. You could barely move for stags' antlers protruding from the walls, and cases containing pheasants, vultures and eagles. The first artefact to greet visitors in the hall was a stuffed giant panda, a gift from the King and Queen of England.

Frau Goering steered Clara into an alcove, away from the throng.

'Thank God the Winter Relief drive is over. We had to spend an entire morning with the von Ribbentrops rattling collecting boxes in Wittenbergplatz.'

The annual Winter Relief charity was always crowned with the appearance of Party VIPs on street corners jovially touting lapel pins and coin boxes.

'It took everything Hermann had to keep smiling, but now everything's much worse. Something terrible has happened. You'll never guess.'

She paused dramatically and Clara tilted her head, awaiting the bombshell.

'The Italians have gone and awarded von Ribbentrop the Collar of the Annunziata.'

'What on earth is that?'

'You mean you've never heard of it? I wish I hadn't. It's Italy's greatest chivalric order. It's a gorgeous piece, solid gold, and studded with diamonds. The holder becomes the honorary cousin of the Italian king. Hermann has wanted it for so long. When he heard that von Ribbentrop was to have it he was almost physically sick. You know he adores jewels.'

Clara recalled the photograph of Goering in Herr Fromm's shop, adorned with gold dagger and blue diamonds in the persona of a Roman emperor.

'That's why he admired your Duke of Windsor and his American duchess. All their jewellery! Hermann couldn't stop talking about the Duke's art deco cufflinks and the Duchess's Cartier diamonds. He says you can tell a lot about a person from their taste in jewels.'

'I bet you can,' said Clara, recalling Wallis Simpson, studded all over with pearls the size of pigeon eggs.

'Jewels are an absolute obsession with Hermann. I fret about him. It's an addiction.'

There was every reason why Frau Goering should worry about her husband's predilection. His addiction to morphine tablets – originally prescribed for war wounds – was part of the reason for his monstrous size, which led to his nickname Der Dicke – Fatso.

As if on cue, a waiter materialized with a tray of smoked salmon sandwiches and Emmy popped a couple in her mouth.

'You should try not to worry.'

'That's easy for you to say,' Emmy replied through a mouth of crumbs. She sighed and patted the corn-coloured hair wound round her ears in thick plaits. 'It's driving him crazy. But it's not just that. It's something else.' She frowned in genuine perplexity. 'We're just back from a rest cure in San Remo – in fact I wish we were still there – but all the time he's been in the most terrible mood. He's preoccupied with something, but he won't tell me what it is.'

Clara wondered if she should point out the obvious.

'Could it be the international situation?'

'That? Oh no. Don't be silly. Hermann assures me there will be no war. We need another three or four years of peace. The English – with respect – are terrible warmongers, but the future of Danzig can hardly concern them. And besides, the Führer won't want to see all his new buildings bombed. No.' She paused, as though trying to solve some incomprehensible puzzle. 'All I know is, it's definitely to do with a jewel.'

'This golden collar, you mean?'

'No. Another jewel. Hermann's been cheated out of it. That's all I can get out of him. He said it again at breakfast this morning. He's been cheated out of a jewel. He's looking for it high and low and God help anyone who gets in his way.'

'It's hard to imagine anyone cheating your husband.'

This remark prompted a peal of laughter from Emmy.

'Don't you believe it! Von Ribbentrop spends his life trying to cheat him.' Belatedly realizing the consequences of being overheard, she lowered her voice.

'Only yesterday Hermann told me von Ribbentrop is cosying up to the Russians.'

The Russians? Suddenly all Clara's nerves were on alert. Could it be possible that her questions were to be answered this easily?

'Well, one Russian in particular. I think you know her. Frau Olga Chekhova. Annelies's new best friend.'

The letdown was instant. Clara had acted with Olga Chekhova many times over the years. Although she was Russian by birth and a niece by marriage of the great Anton Chekhov, she had lived in Berlin for decades and had even been given the honorary title of Staatsschauspielerin, State Actress. However skilful the acting talents of the kindly Olga Chekhova, one role she was surely not playing was that of spy. She was a motherly woman behind the silk and pearls, and the last person one could imagine meddling in the murky waters of Stalin's henchmen.

'Olga Chekhova's a huge supporter of the Führer. I don't think there's anything suspicious about her.'

'Oh don't you?' said Emmy, with a distinct air of affront. 'Well just between us, Hermann has heard some very unsettling things about La Chekhova. Her brother is a senior official with the NKVD.'

The NKVD was Stalin's secret intelligence service. As cunning and brutal as the Gestapo themselves, they formed a fearsome network of ruthless agents stretching across Europe. Yet while this revelation surprised Clara, she had no doubts about her friend.

'You think it's strange that a woman whose face is on every billboard in Berlin could be working in the shadows? That an actress could also be a spy?'

Was it detectable, the frisson of alarm that tightened Clara's throat and widened her eyes?

'I do.'

'Trust me, these times bring out the strangest behaviour in people.'

Frau Goering paused primly.

'So what are you doing at the moment?'

'I'm about to start a film about the Ahnenerbe.'

The Minister's wife rolled her eyes.

'Ugh. Heini Himmler's little passion. All that archaeology and measuring skulls. If men must have obsessions, give me Hermann's jewellery craze any day. Why on earth do we need a film about the Ahnenerbe?'

'Herr Doktor Goebbels said the Führer was attaching the highest importance to it.'

Her eyes gleamed with mischief. She pounced on this information.

'So you've seen Goebbels? How was he?'

Clara hesitated. It was always risky to give Emmy Goering too much detail unless you wanted it to reappear at some future date with your name attached.

'I thought he looked strained.'

'Doesn't he! The man's a bag of nerves. He's just been in hospital with kidney pains but I'm sure it's all down to Magda. You have no idea of the stories I've been hearing.'

Clara guessed she was about to find out.

'Are they having troubles again?'

'Troubles! You have no idea. Far be it from me to feel sorry for the Herr Doktor, but I think it behoves a wife of a senior man to behave in a certain way and the way Magda is carrying on would try the patience of a saint, which, as we all know, the Herr Doktor most certainly is not. Fortunately my Hermann is in the pink of health. He was up to two hundred and eighty pounds – he seeks comfort in food, you see – but he lost forty pounds on his diet. I know because he was trying on his outfit just this morning. Oh, but of course . . .'

Her face brightened.

'That's why I was looking for you, Clara. We're holding a reception for Prince Paul of Yugoslavia. It's a state visit. There are eight days of celebrations, but our party will be the high point. You must come. It's at the Schloss Bellevue. We've had to invite the von Ribbentrops unfortunately but it should still be great fun. As a matter of fact we're having a deputation of those Faith and Beauty girls to the ball.'

She gave a grimace. 'We had no choice. It's Himmler's wish. They're being trained up to take their place in polite society. We have to let them loose on diplomatic guests so that they can prac-tise their conversational skills. God help us, but at least they'll look decorative.'

'Thank you. It sounds very glamorous.'

'Don't thank me. It was Hermann's brother who wanted you to come actually. It was his particular request.'

'His brother?'

'Albert's in the film business but he's fearfully shy. You'd never believe the pair of them could be brothers. Quite Hermann's opposite.'

Clara was astonished. In the world of celebrity, the family of Germany's second most powerful man could hardly remain low profile yet she had never heard of Goering having a brother, let alone one in the film business.

'I had no idea the Minister even had a brother.'

'Nobody does. He works for Tobis-Sascha, so we don't see much of him.'

The film company Tobis-Sascha was based in Vienna.

'He comes to Berlin from time to time to keep in touch. They're devoted to each other, but Albert is nothing like Hermann. He's just an ordinary little chap, and he hates these grand affairs. You can keep him company. Stop him being overawed.'

She gave a small, indulgent smile.

'We want it to be really special. The Goebbels are laying on something for the royal couple at Schwanenwerder – the usual gemütlich picnic-on-the-lawn affair – but we thought international visitors deserved something a little classier.'

Between Goering and Goebbels, competition to entertain foreign dignitaries was fierce. As the visit of Prince Paul was part of Hitler's plan to pressure Yugoslavia into supporting his moves in Europe, not an inch of red carpet would be spared in the wooing.

'Prince Paul's practically English, as you know. He's a great friend of the British royal family, and our dear Duke of Windsor of course, so it will be nice to have some English people to greet them. Anyway, I'll say goodbye now.'

Emmy Goering turned rapidly on her heel and Clara turned to find the reason. Annelies von Ribbentrop was heading in her direction. She aimed a speculative glare in Clara's direction and, as she passed, a smile parted her mouth, thin as a chink of light through metal shutters.

'Lipstick, Fräulein Vine? Better hope the Führer doesn't see you wearing that.'

'Better hope Goering doesn't see either,' murmured Mary, sidling up from behind. 'I hear Elizabeth Arden's Velvet Red is his absolute favourite.'

Chapter Eleven

'What you need to understand about Hitler is that he regards himself as first and foremost an artist. His ultimate desire is to sit in the Berghof and paint mountains for the rest of his life.'

Leni Riefenstahl leant back, crossed her legs and blew a plume of cigarette smoke into the middle distance. At the age of thirty-six she was the most famous female film director in the world and, with her deep-set eyes, cascading curls, and full mouth, certainly the best-looking. Her form was encased in that season's Chanel wide-legged trousers teamed with an open-necked silk shirt and chunky amber beads nestling at her throat. Her voice was like gravel dipped in treacle. Leaning back on a pelt of bear fur she seemed for all the world like some rare and endangered creature herself, svelte and powerful and wild. The Führer's very own femme fatale.

She paused for a sip of coffee before adding, 'If you want to know how I know what Herr Hitler thinks, it's because only a few weeks ago he was sitting exactly where you are now.'

Clara suppressed the urge to leap out of the seat immediately.

'The Führer comes to your home? That's quite an honour.'

Leni gave a slight, leonine toss of her head.

'He likes to confide in me. He says this house is one of the few places he can properly relax.'

Leni Riefenstahl's villa at 30, Heydenstrasse was a modish, low-built white-faced house in Dahlem, a neighbourhood popular with Nazi bureaucrats, high-ranking Party members and industrialists. Towering hedges screened a succession of handsome villas with stucco detail and mansard roofs and the leafy peace was punctuated only by the occasional dog's bark and the low growl of a lawn mower. Owning a villa like this was a testament to Leni Riefenstahl's success, and lest anyone forget it, a gigantic self-portrait of the director herself, holding a Leica camera, hung on the drawing-room wall, alongside a framed cover of the previous year's *Time* magazine, on which she posed as seductively as possible on a pair of skis. It was all a long way from her origins as the daughter of a Berlin heating engineer, yet while Leni Riefenstahl might have made her name in the German craze for films about mountain climbing, social climbing was just as much her forte.

'Here. I bought Linzer Torte in his honour.'

She drew a tray towards her, fingers glimmering with opal and moonstone rings, and cut a fat slice of the tart for Clara. Linzer Torte was named after Hitler's birthplace but despite its unfortunate associations Clara could not stop her mouth from watering at the crumbly pastry with lemon zest and ground nuts filled with plum butter and a lattice of pastry on top. Gratefully she took a piece and bit into it. Leni ate nothing but fished out a packet of Rothmans in a battered gold case and lit another cigarette.

'How did you first meet the Führer?' Clara enquired.

'I read *Mein Kampf* cover to cover on a train journey and it changed my life. I wrote to him at once and to my astonishment he invited me to spend the afternoon with him. He told me he had seen all my films and the one he loved best was *The Holy Mountain*. He said my dance on the shore was the most beautiful thing he had seen in his life.'

Clara remembered the footage of Leni capering on the beach in a barely-there scrap of gauze. This in itself said a lot about Hitler's taste in films.

'He told me once he came to power I would be the person to chronicle his Third Reich. It was a huge honour.'

'Which you have certainly repaid.'

She gave a gracious toss of her head.

'I can't deny it. Josef von Sternberg, the director you know, was in love with me. He asked me to go to Hollywood with him in the twenties. I could have gone but I sacrificed myself. I felt it my duty to stay and support the Führer.'

'That must have been a difficult decision.'

And an ill-judged one. Yet Leni seemed pleased by this idea. She ran a hand through her lustrous mane, flicking and stroking it like an expensive pet.

'It's true. Loyalty is my weakness. Unfortunately, because I am loyal and the Führer loves me, the Party hierarchy hates me. I'm not one of their drab little hausfraus or neurotic wives. I like Frau Hess, but the rest of them I could take or leave. For Magda Goebbels I feel nothing but pity, I despise Frau von Ribbentrop and as for that jumped-up actress, Emmy Goering, well, the less said the better. You see, Fräulein Vine, I'm not the kind Goebbels can push around. I'm my own woman. If I have any problems I go straight to Hitler himself.'

Springing to her feet she crossed to the wall, which alongside the portraits was festooned with advertisements for her work.

'Tell me, Fräulein Vine, or Clara as I'm going to call you, have you seen all my films?'

'I'm a great admirer.'

'Good. I knew I was right to choose you.'

Leni spun around and beamed at her.

'I like the fact that you're half English. I've been to England. I spoke at Oxford and Cambridge. They loved me. How is it you're living in Berlin?'

Clara thought of Leo, his green-eyed gaze and the reddish tint in his hair. The day six years ago that she had gone to him in the

British passport control office and taken up his offer to spy for the Secret Intelligence Service. The weeks of patient schooling in the arts of espionage, surveillance and evasion. Then the love affair, which had never been part of the plan.

'I fell in love.'

'With Berlin?'

'No,' she laughed. 'With a man.'

'Anyone I know?'

'I shouldn't think so. Besides, he left in '33.'

Leni nodded sagely. She would assume that Clara's lover was Jewish – an actor or director from the film studios perhaps. The day Hitler came to power an exodus of Babelsberg's greatest talent – Billy Wilder, Fritz Lang, Peter Lorre – had taken the first train across the border.

'I know how it feels. I'll probably always be single, even though so many men have been desperately in love with me. My life often feels like a movie itself. They're always trying to make a film about me. When I was in Hollywood they wanted Marlene Dietrich to play me. I soon put a stop to that.'

'I wondered, Fräulein Riefenstahl. Leni. Could you explain a little more about my role?'

The director's attention snapped back to the present.

'I'm glad you asked. You see – and please don't take this the wrong way, Clara – your face has a useful quality. It's a blank canvas. It's like I can project anything I want on it.' Her eyes misted, as though the entire storyboard already existed in her mind. 'You will be the anonymous German woman who accompanies us from the forests of Berlin, where the original Germans lived, to today's Berlin, and the new world capital as created by Herr Speer. We begin with an aerial shot of Berlin, and as the plane comes closer we find you, the nameless woman, standing by the Brandenburg Gate.'

'And the script?'

Breaking out of her reverie, she gave a slight, dismissive shrug.

'There is no script. You don't need one. You will project no distinct identity. Basically, you are the soul of Germany. Just like the French have their Marianne. You will be the spirit of *Germania*.'

The spirit of *Germania*? No wonder Goebbels had been incredulous at the choice of Clara for the part.

'Herr Doktor Goebbels did wonder . . .'

'Don't talk to me about Goebbels.'

Leni Riefenstahl flared her nostrils like a thoroughbred racehorse, came to sit beside Clara and placed one hand on her knee. Her voice lowered to a husky whisper.

'You know he's infatuated with me.'

'I had no idea.'

'My dear, from our very first acquaintance, when he invited me to the opera and shoved his clumsy paw up my gown, he has never let up. In fact he has virtually stalked me. I've tried so many ways to put him off, endless chats about Magda, talks about my boyfriends. I once spent an entire evening recalling what a wonderful time I had at his wedding. None of it worked. When I rejected his advances he did everything he could to sabotage my career.'

'That didn't work.'

'Thankfully, not. But he banned any reports about me in the press for an entire year. He lied to the Führer about me. My advice is, don't believe a word he says. I've never met a man who lies like him. He was determined to ruin me but I was bold enough to stand up to him and the Führer backed me. In fact, that's one reason I wanted you presenting the film.'

'Because . . .?'

'I knew Goebbels would want some buxom Nordic blonde to present it. Probably some little party he was screwing. There's no end of them, as you well know. So I decided to choose the precise opposite. Which was you.'

Clara could not help smiling at this display of wilfulness. However manipulative and deceptive Leni Riefenstahl might be, it was refreshing to find a woman so different from the down-trodden Nazi wife. That was, no doubt, what Goebbels found attractive too.

'There was another reason, of course.'

'Really? What's that?'

Leni sprang skittishly to her feet again.

'Oh, never mind. You don't need to know. Besides, I liked the look of you. I'd seen a couple of your films and I thought we would work well together. Did Goebbels brief you at all? We have a scene at the Ahnenerbe, Himmler's institute. It's a couple of streets from here.'

Was it visible, the shiver of apprehension that ran down Clara's spine?

'Is Herr Himmler often there?'

'Whenever he gets the chance. He's terrifically proud of it. But mostly the place is full of fusty scientists. I've arranged for one of them – Herr Doktor Kraus – to show you around the day after tomorrow. I've asked him to give you a feel for their work. It's all rather eccentric, but Himmler has decided that no stone should be left unturned. In fact, he's just agreed to give this film an unprecedented honour. His most precious project in the entire world is going to be opened up for the purposes of the movie.'

'What's the project?'

'His castle. You must have heard of it. Wewelsburg in Westphalia. It's marvellously photogenic. Fearfully gloomy and impressive.'

She yawned like a cat and began flicking through a diary.

'So we'll need to discuss the shooting schedule. Pre-production is well advanced; my location managers have been working over-time. I've already hired all the crew and set up the camera posi-tions. We're on a tight deadline. The Führer wants *Germania* to be ready for this year's Nuremberg rally.'

'Five months! For an entire film? That's impossible!'

Leni Riefenstahl, sniffed, fished in her bag and extracted a blue glass perfume atomiser encased in gold net and pumped a fine sheen of perfume around her.

'That's what I said. But the Führer told me we aren't the only ones. He said the whole world's on deadline now.'

'The problem is . . .' Clara hesitated. 'I have go to Paris for a couple of days.'

'Paris? What on earth are you doing there?'

Clara calculated that now she had told Goebbels she might as well establish her cover story as solidly as possible.

'I'm to be photographed for *Vogue*. For the September issue. They have a feature on European actresses.'

A slow smile lit Leni Riefenstahl's lovely face, then she burst into peals of laughter.

'The September issue? That's ambitious. Who knows what will be happening by September! Let's hope they're still keen on German actresses by then.'

Making her way home Clara passed a news kiosk and her eye was caught by the face of Lotti Franke peering out of the front page of the *Berliner Zeitung*. The newspapers had seized on Lotti's death with a kind of ferocious delight. Beside the political complexities of Danzig and Poland, the murder of a single German girl was somehow more outrageous and far easier to contemplate. There was a salacious edge, too, to their interest. The Faith and Beauty girls were supposed to be a cut above the ordinary. They were the élite of German woman-hood, being groomed as consorts for the top men. Yet what did that grooming entail? Who knew what went on in these places? Were the morals there any different from the Bund Deutscher Mädel, which everyone nicknamed the League of German Mattresses? Despite everything Himmler said about producing more babies for the Reich, the promiscuity of the German girls' associations still shocked the more stolid citizens of Berlin. Who was to say the Faith and Beauty Society was any different?

Clara hated to think of the ponderous, devastated Udo Franke and his distraught wife, anxiously awaiting news, hoping for some fragment of intelligence that could explain the inexplicable murder of their only daughter. She was already regretting telling the Frankes that she would find out what she could. It was a thought-less comment, uttered in a moment of emotion, yet it was plain that there was little to tell. There was nothing Clara could uncover about Lotti's death and no chance that she would discover anything more than any other regular newspaper reader. No man had been caught. No details of the murder itself had been given out. No lines of enquiry had proved fruitful. All the police were saying was that women should be careful around the Grunewald at night.

As she exited the pretty redbrick station at Griebnitzsee she noticed that two policemen had been freshly stationed there, stamping their feet, studying the commuters as they straggled out of the station tunnel. The man who killed Lotti Franke was still at large. What if he returned?

Clara's uneasiness lasted all evening. She made a simple meal of sausage and bread and tried to relax with a novel. She picked up *Jane Eyre* and put it down again. It might be her favourite novel but recently she had found herself craving detective stories – a world where problems arose, then were solved and the world put right. She hunted out her old copy of *The Thirty-Nine Steps* and took it to bed.

It was hard to sleep. At one point she jolted up, her heart racing, all her nerves alert at some strange noise, a distant creak in the house. She sat, her mouth dry, and gazed round, disorien-tated in the unfamiliar room lit by a wash of bright moonlight creeping through the curtains.

She was convinced that someone had entered downstairs, only to conclude that it was the wind in the distance banging the gate.

Yet she always made sure to latch the gate. A few moments later, she heard it again. A faint creak. And from outside a sound like the crunch of the gravel on the drive. Her heartbeat quickened, but when she drew the curtains there was nothing there but the rain-pitted Griebnitzsee and beyond it the black emptiness of the forest.

She lay down, regretting again that she had sought refuge so far from the city, wishing herself back in Winterfeldtstrasse in the busy heart of Berlin, with the comforting presence of millions of fellow citizens slumbering nearby. She missed everything about her old apartment. Her beloved blue and white china, her comfortable red velvet armchair with its stack of novels along-side, and her chic little mirrored bathroom. The tree-lined cobbled streets with the old-fashioned green water pump oper-ated by its dolphin handle. Even her unlovely view of cluttered rooftops patrolled by pigeons, the pipes extending down the backs of houses and the washing cobwebbing the narrow alleys below.

Eventually, her thoughts turned to the other issue – the issue which was crowding out every other concern in her mind. Major Grand's request. How was it possible to gain any insight into von Ribbentrop's mind? The idea of a casual gossipy chat, the kind she could have with Emmy Goering, was an impossibility with the Foreign Minister's wife. Yet how else would she discover if the Nazi regime was genuinely contemplating an alliance with their old enemy?

It was an hour before she dropped asleep and when she finally did, Leni Riefenstahl's parting remark echoed in her mind.

The September issue! That's ambitious. Who knows what will be happening when September comes?

Chapter Twelve

If the marriage of Joseph and Magda Goebbels really was one long screaming match, then their children had inherited their tendencies, judging by their shrieks as they tore around the back garden of the Propaganda Minister's residence. The window of Mary Harker's room in the back wing of the Adlon Hotel had a clear view of the Goebbels' garden, which was located on a street that had been, to the Propaganda Minister's great irritation, freshly renamed Hermann-Goering-Strasse. As Clara waited for her friend to finish typing a dispatch, she gazed in fascination at the antics of the little blond Goebbels children. They had arrived in yearly instalments as regular as any Volkswagen production line and they were given names beginning with 'H' in homage to the man whom both parents loved more than each other. The eldest, Helga, in a white smocked dress, was chasing Helmut, the only boy, rumoured to be slow and a great disappointment to his father, while Hilde, a ringleted five-year-old, was pushing two-year-old Holde around the paths on a wheeled wooden horse. All the while the latest addition, Hedda, slumbered in the shade of a lime tree in a baby carriage. Of their mother there was no sign. Perhaps it was true, what everyone said about Magda Goebbels; that she was too busy engaging in an affair in bitter retribution for the way her husband had humiliated her.

'See what you think of this.'

Behind her Mary Harker sat back from her Remington, removed a sheet of paper and read aloud:

'*A few years ago Adolf Hitler declared war. It was war on "degenerate" art – which to him means any work in a modernist style, or colours "not found in Nature" and, most of all, any work by Jewish artists. George Grosz, with his emaciated prostitutes and bloated plutocrats, was declared cultural Bolshevik number one. To comply with the Führer's wishes, Propaganda Minister Joseph Goebbels instigated the seizure of thousands of artworks from the Reich's museums by modernists like Picasso, Dali, Léger, Miro and Van Gogh. German Jewish artists have fled; Max Beckmann to Amsterdam, Max Ernst to America, and Paul Klee to Switzerland. Others live in internal exile, forbidden to paint, or even buy paintbrushes. Some of them carry on secretly by the most ingenious of means. One of them has switched to watercolours, so his neighbours will not notice the smell of oil paint. But now the war against degenerate art has been taken to new levels.*'

'So what's happened?'

'As a matter of fact,' Mary leaned forward, 'it's something rather shocking. Even by the standards of the Nazis, and they do know how to shock. My editor, Frank Nussbaum, wants it on the front page. Last month a fresh stash of confiscated artwork from Austria arrived in Berlin. There's meant to be a system. They store the art in a warehouse in Kopernikusstrasse and a dealer called Hildebrand Gurlitt has been appointed to separate the so-called "degenerate" pieces from the rest. Then they sell them, supposedly so that they can make money out of what they call garbage. But Goebbels has done something drastic. He held a symbolic bonfire.'

'You're not going to tell me he burned all those artworks?'

'A thousand paintings and sculptures, nearly four thousand drawings and watercolours. All burnt to ashes in the courtyard of the Berlin Fire Department.'

'Just like he burned the books on Opernplatz in 1933. I can hardly believe it.'

'They're saying Goebbels did it deliberately to spite Goering because Goering was desperate to have some of those paintings for himself. I suppose it makes sense. They're at each other's throats all the time.'

Clara sat in contemplation, trying to puzzle out something in her head. Slowly she said, 'I heard something else about Goering. I don't know if it's significant but he's very upset about a jewel.'

'A jewel?'

'You saw me talking to his wife at the Foreign Ministry, remember? Frau Goering told me he had been cheated out of this jewel and it was obsessing him.'

'Who cares?' said Mary. 'It wouldn't be his jewellery anyway, would it? It probably belongs to some poor Jew. Everything they touch is stolen.'

'So how did you discover about the bonfire?'

'Hugh Lindsey discovered it. He had a contact down at the warehouse, who told him everything that had happened and Hugh told me.'

'Nice of him to share a scoop like that.'

'Well Hugh is nice, as I'm sure you've noticed.'

'I have. He seems charming.'

'So . . . what are you saying?'

Mary snatched off her glasses and theatrically narrowed her eyes.

Clara laughed. 'I'm saying he's charming! I think he's very good-looking, but I'm not interested.'

'Good, because I rather like him myself. There's something about him that reminds me of Rupert.'

Clara could see that. The humour, the laconic English drawl, the underlying implication that there was nothing in life that could not be solved by a dry sherry and a quiet chat between gentlemen. A way of talking that made the other person feel the wittiest, most amusing person in the room.

'He's such a contrast to his friend,' said Clara. 'Charles Cavendish is so patronizing. He's the worst kind of Englishman. I wonder how Hugh can bear him.'

Mary's face lit up.

'The one thing I've discovered about Hugh in the short time I've known him is that he's utterly loyal to his friends. Even the objectionable ones.'

Clara smiled. She dearly hoped a romance might flourish for her friend. Mary was popular with the male reporters, but too often her dry humour, quick wit and raging interest in politics ensured that she was treated as a colleague first and a woman second. Perhaps this time, Clara could do a little matchmaking of her own to help it along.

As these thoughts went through her head, Mary was scrutinizing her with a forensic attention.

'How about you, Clara? I have the feeling there's someone in the picture. I hope it's not that Nazi we met the other night at the Press Club.'

'What do you take me for?'

Clara had never told Mary that Leo Quinn had returned to Berlin the year before, or that their love affair had resumed. So, however much she longed to, she now could not share the anxiety that was tearing her apart.

'Well if there's no one keeping you here, you need to think about the future.'

Mary was giving Clara one of her direct looks, the kind that brooked no evasion. That quality must be what made her such a fine journalist. She never shied away from asking the important question, and she never let tact, delicacy or embarrassment hinder her pursuit of the truth.

'Your two countries are on the brink of war. You don't have journalistic protection, like me.'

'I have my identity documents. I'm a member of the Reich Chamber of Culture.'

'They're pieces of paper, Clara! The Nazis never let pieces of paper get in their way. If they decide that your loyalties are divided, it will get very difficult for you. Let alone if . . .'

Mary fell silent and raised her eyes to the light fitting. Both women knew that rooms in the Adlon allocated to foreign journalists came accessorized not just with tea-making equipment, telephones and soda siphons, but high-quality listening devices, monitored and changed as regularly as the bed linen.

'Don't say anything you wouldn't like to see on the front page of *Der Angriff*.'

Der Angriff was Goebbels' own paper, full of the worst kind of accusations and propaganda.

But Mary didn't need to say any more. Her face said everything. Despite a passionate concern for her friend, she knew Clara's existence in Berlin was not as straightforward as it seemed.

'As it happens, I *am* thinking about the future. I'm off to Paris in a couple of days.'

'Paris!' Mary's eyes lit up. 'How did you swing that? What wouldn't I do to be in La Coupole right now, drinking with Hemingway, or living at the Hotel Scribe and having cocktails at the Crillon. And the food! Foie gras sautéed with grapes. Blanquette de veau. What are you going for?'

'A magazine shoot.'

Despite her friend's delight, Clara wondered what Mary must truly think. What would anyone think of a woman who tripped off to model the latest fashions when the only outfit on everyone's mind was an army uniform and the colour of the season was field grey?

Mary sighed.

'Just thinking about Paris makes me want a vodka Martini. Let's get to the bar.'

From the tinkle of a piano to the soft patter of the famous elephant fountain and the murmur of moneyed voices, everything about the Adlon said that, despite all circumstances, it was still the social epicentre of Berlin. It was far too grand to display signs reading 'No Jews or Dogs', which graced less smart establishments, although a discreet placard next to the lifts announced that they were barred for non-Aryan use. Yet while superficially the Adlon was the same, there were signs that all was not well. The hotel was crowded, but that was because people thought there was no point holding on to their money. The same three-piece orchestra played in the lobby, the same women in satin evening gowns congregated for parties and the famous grill room and bar was still the central meeting point for foreign journalists mingling with diplomats, military attachés and businessmen in fur-collared coats. But now their conversations were more guarded. Everyone wanted to know what was going on but no one wanted to be the person imparting privileged information. Gossip was less likely to concern marital indiscretions than military manoeuvres. Scraps of information would be pounced on and passed around. The Adlon was one of the few places in Berlin where foreign newspapers were available, and hotel staff could be seen in the corridors leafing quickly through the papers before delivering them to guests.

Hugh Lindsey was standing with Charles Cavendish and Bill Shirer at the bar, reading aloud from the classified advertisement section of that day's *BZ am Mittag*.

'Listen to this! *Two vital, lusty, race-conscious Brunhildes with family trees certified back to 1700 desiring to serve their Fatherland in the form most ennobling to women, would like to meet two similarly inclined Siegfrieds. Marriage not of essential importance. Soldiers on leave also acceptable.* Who said romance was dead?'

'*Desiring to serve their Fatherland*? Does that mean what I think it means?' asked Mary.

'It certainly does. Fidelity and chastity are out of fashion, didn't you know? And not just for race-conscious Brunhildes. The whole of the top echelon of the Party are at it. Heydrich is a regular womanizer. Rumour has it he's established his own brothel up in the West End called Salon Kitty's. He's wired the place throughout so he can spy on his own men. And we all know about Goebbels, not to mention the gossip about his wife.'

'One wonders how she finds the time,' drawled Cavendish. 'Frau Goebbels is in and out of clinics like a cuckoo from a clock.'

Mary took the newspaper from Hugh and turned it over. It was folded into a rectangle, and the other side bore a large photograph of Lotti Franke. She gave Clara a sympathetic glance.

'Still no news on your Faith and Beauty girl?'

Clara looked, but a quick scan confirmed that nothing had changed in the investigation. The press was merely taking the opportunity to run another picture of a photogenic young woman to drive its circulation. Death had given Lotti the celebrity that life had never offered.

'The way they're reporting it, they're treating it like a national tragedy,' complained Charles Cavendish, loftily. Clara felt a stab of dislike. Everything about his reaction reminded her of the snobbish young men of Angela's set, who would only talk to women as a last resort, and then only those whose fathers or brothers they knew.

'Presumably it feels like that to people who knew her,' glared Mary.

'Ah yes,' said Cavendish, with a light apologetic shrug. 'Sorry. How's work, Clara?'

'Busy, thank you. I've been cast in Leni Riefenstahl's latest film.'

He raised a laconic eyebrow.

'That's quite an honour, isn't it? The Führer's favourite film director. Goebbels says Leni Riefenstahl is the only woman in Germany who truly understands what the Party is about.'

'I'm a woman and I have a pretty good idea of what they're about,' interjected Mary.

Their talk drifted on to other subjects – the bonfire at the art warehouse, their forthcoming trip to the cabaret, the endlessly engaging rumours about the Goebbels. But as they talked, Clara's eye was caught by a stately figure progressing along the far side of the gleaming marble lobby, beyond the palm court and its celebrated elephant fountain, towards the revolving doors.

Erect and dignified, she seemed to glide rather than walk, and lurching in her wake were two burly men in ill-fitting dark suits, like a pair of tugs accompanying a ship in full rig. As she passed, a momentary hush descended on the matrons taking coffee and cake and the Party members quaffing cognac at the bar. The Adlon might be the epicentre of glamour in the Third Reich but it was not every day one had a close-up sight of the biggest star of German cinema, the beloved Grande Dame, Olga Chekhova.

Everything about Chekhova emphasized her star status, from the ropes of pearls to the beautifully cut dress and mink stole, strong Slavonic face and high cheekbones. Her immaculate complexion glowed as though lit by an internal lightbulb. She had the star's innate charisma, an invisible forcefield of energy that rippled through the space around her, causing heads to swivel magnetically and voices to hush. Impulsively Clara called out.

'Olga!'

Hearing her name the actress looked over and a flash of recognition passed between them, yet almost immediately she turned again without replying and carried on.

Clara was stunned. Olga Chekhova had cut her dead.

She was baffled as much as hurt. She had worked with Olga on several films and had been invited to numerous dinners at her smart Kaiserdamm apartment, hung with icons and Fabergé enamel frames and thronged with White Russian emigrés in astrakhan coats. The evenings were long and sentimental, filled with anecdotes about Olga's Moscow childhood and fuelled by red caviar and blinis, borscht, poppy seed strudel and delicious Russian vodka. Despite her fame, Olga had always taken a keen interest in Clara's career and treated her more like a daughter than a rival actress. So why, when it was patently obvious that she had seen Clara just yards away, should she choose to ignore her?

Clara had a sudden, devastating flash of intuition. It must be to do with the two business-suited men; swarthy, anonymous types whom she could not place. They didn't look like film industry figures. They didn't even look German. Was it possible that Olga did not want Clara to see who she was with? Although the incident had lasted a matter of seconds Clara had a sense of sinking dread. Perhaps it was true, what Emmy Goering said. That as well as being Hitler's favourite actress and the greatest star of Third Reich cinema, Olga Chekhova, the sister of an NKVD operative, was herself a Soviet spy.

Chapter Thirteen

The headquarters of the Ancestral Heritage Research and Teaching organization – the Ahnenerbe for short – was situated in a handsome building in one of the most upmarket areas of the city, 19 Pücklerstrasse, Dahlem, just a few doors down from Martin Bormann's town house. Its vine-covered walls and gleaming, stained-glass windows projected a hallowed air of academic respectability, as though this centre of German heritage combined a sacred chapel and a university in one. The strongest impression, however, was that everything about the building, from its ivory sandstone façade, to the new model Cabriolet parked on the gravel drive, reeked of money. Whoever was funding Germany's search for its own cultural identity wasn't short of a few Reichmarks.

Crunching across a half-moon of pristine gravel, Clara stood for a second at the door, summoning her courage, before entering and looking around the expensive wood-panelled hall. The place seemed deserted. Ranks of display cases lined the walls, filled with stone carvings and wooden figures. There was a tortoiseshell – a vibrant swirl of orange and black – a papery snakeskin and a glass-eyed fox. There were photographs of cave drawings and eerily lifelike plaster casts of human faces momentarily reminding her of visits to the Natural History Museum in

London during the long school holidays of childhood. But that was where the resemblance ended. Approaching the first cabinet she saw with a shudder that it contained a selection of human skulls alongside a series of instruments that resembled callipers. On inspection she saw that they were steel measuring implements, designed to record the size of noses, cheekbones and jaws. Alongside each skull was a note about the previous owner's racial characteristics.

Dalic: high stature, robust and heavily built, rosy skin, blond hair, light eyes, brachycephalic cranium, big mouth and thin lips.

East Baltic: medium to low stature, fair skin, strong build, brachycephalic, light hair and eyes.

Dinaric: wedge-shaped profile, receding forehead, large nose, weak receding chin.

Nordic: dolichocephalic. Forehead and chin scarcely receding. The Nordic people are the spine of the human race.

A clatter of boots behind her alerted Clara to a man trotting down the gleaming staircase. His face, with its full complement of blond hair, blue eyes, flawlessly symmetrical features and long horse's nose, might have been torn straight out of the textbook illustrating the final race in the display case, the Nordic. He also possessed an immaculate SS uniform and a penetrating aquiline stare.

'Admiring our Untermenschen? We use them as teaching aids to instruct students in racial typing. We can tell so much from skull form, size of brain and so on. Compare the features of Nordic dolichocephalism – lofty brow, narrow temples, large eyes, aquiline nose – with this Slav – see his round facial structure and small nose? Our founder, the SS-Reichsführer, believes a man's entire character can be told from anatomy alone.' He clicked his heels. 'Herr Doktor Kraus.'

Clara gave him her hand and felt his eyes flicker speculatively over her face, reading the shape of her forehead and the spacing of her eyes as if mentally pigeonholing her personality.

'And you, I take it, are Fräulein Vine. Was no one here to meet you? That useless girl.' His eyes roved across to an empty desk in the corner of the hall. 'I told her to expect you. Are you aware of our work? I would give you a copy of our magazine if our young librarian had not deserted her post.'

As if on cue a tall, pink-cheeked girl dashed into the hall, almost invisible beneath a towering stack of magazines which she proceeded to drop on the floor by the desk.

'I'm sorry, Herr Doktor. I was just getting these.'

'Don't worry,' Clara said, directing a consoling smile at the girl who was scrabbling around collecting the litter of papers. 'I've seen the latest copy already.'

Clara had found the Ahnenerbe's magazine on a newsstand the previous day and spent several dispiriting minutes flicking through it. From what she could find out, there were forty separate research projects in subjects ranging from musicology, astrology, linguistics and Sanskrit to Runes, all devoted to proving the existence of the lost Aryan master race.

'Perhaps you'd like to see some of our exhibits,' said Kraus, directing a savage stare at the flustered young woman.

He stalked along a corridor flanked by more glass cases into a grand drawing room lined with shelves crowded with books, paintings, pottery, and tiny, primitive figurines. African fertility sculptures and tribal masks rubbed up against turquoise Egyptian shabti figures. Thighbones rested casually alongside pan pipes. Long curved yellow teeth grinned beside flint spear tips. They had the dusty, jumbled, abandoned air of holiday souvenirs assembled by an especially undiscriminating tourist.

'The Herr Reichsführer is an avid collector,' commented Kraus. He drew her over to a series of photographs of orientals.

'The élites of Asia – the Brahmin priests, the Mongolian chiefs, and the Japanese Samurai – are all descended from Aryan invaders. Take these chaps ...' He indicated a row of Tibetan tribesmen in shawls, clustered like scouts around a camp fire and gazing at their SS guests with a mixture of hostility and bewilderment. 'Even the most casual observer can see at once that the higher Tibetan classes possess Nordic characteristics. Note the long heads, narrow faces, receding cheekbones. They are quite clearly descended from the same race as us Germans. It's an added pleasure that the swastika should also be an ancient Tibetan symbol.'

'Fascinating,' said Clara, neutrally.

'Isn't it?' He removed his glasses and polished them with a handkerchief before replacing them. The tiny rimless spectacles almost vanished in the folds of his face.

'The same measurements of skulls allowed us to prove that the Antarctic was once inhabited by Germanic peoples. Physiognomy is destiny. We can tell any number of qualities – intelligence, honesty, propensity to criminality – simply from a person's racial characteristics.'

'It must take a lot of training to recognize all that just by looking at a person.'

If he detected her sarcasm, he did not flicker.

'You're quite right. It does. It's a whole new specialism, the discipline of Criminal Biology. And I flatter myself that I am at the forefront of it. Of course, I was already something of an expert on Race Science. Are you familiar with that?'

'Very.'

Race Science was one of the biggest growth sectors in Nazi Germany. Universities were hastily establishing new lecturing posts in the subject, and schools held twice weekly lessons in it. At Erich's school it had now entirely replaced Biology. Clara had recently helped him with his homework and waded with horror through a pyramid diagram of racial hierarchy, which placed the Master Race at the top, Goths, Franks, Vandals and Normans beneath, and 'sub-human' Russians, Romani, Serbs, Poles and Jews on the bottom row.

'We have aural displays too,' continued Kraus. 'The Ahnenerbe has recorded folk dances in Finland. I would have the equipment set up for you but . . .'

'Honestly, it's fine.'

'In that case, you should see our library.' He flung open a further door. 'We keep a complete archive of ancestral Germany history.'

Clara stepped in with relief. Somehow, no amount of books could be as depressing as the contents of the previous room. The library was a soft gleam of dark, polished leather, with volumes stacked floor to ceiling, shimmering with gilt tooling. None of them looked like they had been disturbed since they were placed there. The girl she had seen before, wearing an owlish pair of spectacles, was bending over a manuscript.

Kraus hovered as Clara surveyed the shelves.

'An early copy of the *Bhagavad Gita*. A Sanskrit epic. It tells how thousands of years ago a pure Aryan race invaded India. The SS-Reichsführer finds its teachings inspirational. He carries a copy wherever he goes.'

He was hovering uncomfortably close. To escape him, Clara moved towards a glass display case where a piece of text was framed.

'*The peoples of Germany have never contaminated themselves by intermarriage with foreigners but remain of pure blood, distinct and unlike any other nation.*'

'Magnificent, isn't it?' said Kraus. 'It's from the *Germania*. Written by Cornelius Tacitus in 98 AD. One of the greatest historians and prose stylists who ever wrote in Latin. You know it, of course?'

'I don't think so,' said Clara, racking her brain for any fragment of knowledge that might linger from Miss Herbert's classical civilization lessons, conducted in a stuffy classroom in Kensington a lifetime ago.

'Really? All German schoolchildren are taught him from the age of six. Tacitus was the first historian to study the early

Germanic clans. And what he discovered is very pleasing for us. As far back as when they wore the skin of wild beasts, Germans had a natural nobility, inured to corruption or servility. They scorned luxury and prized military courage above all things.'

He sighed, reverently. 'The *Germania* is a precious work for us. In many ways it's a blueprint for the National Socialist revolution.'

'So which one is it?' asked Clara, her eyes roving round the library shelves.

Kraus gave a short, bitter laugh at this question.

'Oh, but we don't have it.'

'Would it not be good to have?'

'My dear Fräulein, I don't think you understand. There is only one copy of the *Germania* in existence. The Codex Aesinas. And that's in Italy. Herr Mussolini was aware just how much we National Socialists revered that book and three years ago he promised Herr Hitler that he would make a gift of it.' His expression stiffened. 'Unfortunately the Duce went back on his word.'

'That must have been frustrating for the Führer.'

'You have no idea.' Kraus allowed himself a small smile. 'However, we have the typed texts and most of us have learned the important passages by heart. Rather like mediaeval monks learned the Bible.'

The story of Mussolini's treachery seemed to put a dampener on the tour. Kraus paused and checked his watch.

'I trust I've answered all your questions, Fräulein Vine. Though it is of course an honour for our work to be immortalized in film, today does happen to be especially busy. I have the SS-Reichsführer arriving shortly. I'm not sure . . . would you like to meet him too?'

Clara managed to prevent herself recoiling in horror.

'No. I mean . . . No, thank you. I must leave.'

She looked across to where the librarian was sitting. The girl had clearly been listening to their conversation. Even though she was pretending to flick through a pile of papers on her desk, the tips of her ears had gone pink and there was a high flush on the apple of her cheeks. As Kraus clicked his heels and left the room, she said softly, 'Excuse me, Fräulein Vine?'

Clara turned.

'Your magazines?'

'It's okay, thank you. I don't think I'll be needing them. I've seen enough for one day.'

Clara left the building and set off down the gravel path, but as she did she heard footsteps pattering rapidly behind her and turned to see the librarian heaving breathlessly into view.

'I'm sorry, Fräulein. I mean, I wonder . . .' She hesitated, then cast her eyes down again. 'I'm sorry. I shouldn't interfere.'

'What did you want?'

'It's just. I know who you are.'

Clara was used to being recognized, and direct approaches from strangers usually involved an autograph. Automatically she pasted a friendly smile on her face and reached for the pen in her bag, as the girl before her continued.

'You're the actress, aren't you?'

'That's right.'

Though she was flushed with agitation, the girl had a sweet smile and soft, heavy-lidded eyes.

'No. You see, I'm a member of the Faith and Beauty community. Where the girl was killed.'

'Lotti Franke?'

'She was my best friend.'

She uttered this sentence with an air of incomprehension, as though even now she was trying to understand the desolation of death.

'I'm Hedwig. Hedwig Holz.'

Instantly she came into focus. The girl from the photograph in the Franke family apartment. Large and clumsy in her regulation uniform, an awkward foil to Lotti's eye-catching beauty.

'I'm so sorry.'

Hedwig hesitated, twisting her hands on the edge of her unbecoming tweed skirt.

'The thing is . . . Maybe it doesn't matter, but . . .'

Clara recognized the first rule of her training. When a door is ajar, push it open.

'Of course it matters. Whatever you have to say, if you were a friend of Lotti's, I'd love to talk. You must be very affected by what happened. Would you like some lunch?'

Hedwig's eyes lit up and then dipped again, like a dog denied a treat.

'I can't. I need to be at my desk when SS-Reichsführer Himmler arrives.'

'Why don't we take a short walk? Just round the block. We're bound to see the official car when it passes. And if Herr Doktor Kraus is angry, I'll tell him I asked you.'

'Would you?'

'Of course.'

With a reluctant look behind her, Hedwig Holz slipped through the gate and they proceeded down the road.

'I shouldn't complain. Herr Doktor Kraus has been very kind to me. It was he who offered me this job actually, right after his lecture on Mate Selection.'

'Mate selection? What on earth is that?'

Distractedly she said, 'Oh, we have to select genetically suitable mates according to the Nordic–Greek ideal.'

Select mates? What kind of young women referred to their boyfriends like this? Come to that, what kind of girl talked of love and marriage in terms of their genetic suitability? Almost as soon as she had asked herself, Clara knew the answer. Girls in Nazi Germany.

'We have these social evenings. We Faith and Beauty girls have been specially selected by Herr Himmler as suitable mates for his future warriors, so there are dances and dinners with SS officers. I hate them, to be honest, but one of our group is already engaged to a man she met. They're getting married in a few weeks. The trouble is,' her face clouded and she shot a quick glance at Clara as if calculating whether she could trust her, 'I already have one. A boyfriend, I mean. That's why I'm in the Faith and Beauty Society.'

Clara frowned.

'But if . . .?'

'My mother hopes I'll meet a handsome SS officer and forget Jochen altogether.'

'And might you?'

'Not a chance.' She smiled softly. 'Especially if they see me dancing. Fräulein von Essen, she's our instructor, says I dance like a pantomime cow. There's a ball next month and I'm terrified.'

Clara laughed.

'They have something like that where I grew up. In England. They were called debutante balls.'

Angela had done the Season. It began in May with presentation to the King at court, followed by a series of dances packed with aristocratic young men, the weak-chinned, the graceless and the brutish, who steered the girls around the dance floor while their chaperones, a formidable jury of matrons perched on gilt chairs, scrutinized from the sidelines. Every deb had their own dance – Angela's had been held at their aunt's home in Piccadilly – but high society husband-hunting horrified Clara. She didn't want to learn any old-fashioned etiquette. She remembered Angela's lofty incomprehension.

But how will you ever know how to behave?

The Faith and Beauty girls were Hitler's debutantes – groomed to take their place in the ranks of Nazi aristocracy. Only as well as learning what fork to use at dinner and how to arrange roses, Hitler's debs were drilled in the last detail of National Socialist ideology.

'You'd understand then,' said Hedwig. 'We're supposed to learn all the social graces because we guard the spiritual health of the nation.'

'That's asking a lot.'

'That's what Lotti used to say.' Her face fell. 'Lotti was always full of you, Fräulein Vine. She said you were the only one who showed real interest in her ideas. You said she had a bright future.'

'She did.'

'She worked as a photographer's model sometimes. At a studio in Schlüterstrasse. They paid her.'

'She had real talent. I'm so sorry you've lost her.'

'She told me you were half-English. We went to London.'

'I heard. Did you like it?'

For a moment, Hedwig's face glowed as if all the lamps in Claridge's Hotel had lit it from within.

'I loved it. We both did. It was the last time I saw Lotti really happy.'

They came to a bench and sat down and Hedwig began to unburden all the anxiety and pain of the last few weeks in a torrent of words that Clara only occasionally interrupted.

'Lotti wasn't what people thought she was. I mean, she had another side that people here didn't see. A different side.'

'In what way different?'

Hedwig knitted her fingers and gazed around her for inspiration.

'She wasn't this perfect specimen of Aryan womanhood that the principal always says we are. Lotti was very . . . ambitious.'

'That's good, isn't it?'

'Yes,' agreed Hedwig hesitantly. 'What I mean is, she knew what she wanted. She liked talking about people like Marx and Engels. Sometimes I had to tell her to keep her voice down but she didn't care what people thought. And . . .' With a quick desperate glance at Clara, she lowered her voice. 'Men liked her very much.'

'I'm not surprised. She was very beautiful.'

Clara recalled the slight, defiant lift of Lotti's head when men's eyes flicked over her and stuck to her all the way down the corridor.

'She was a magnet for them. They followed her like dogs. It didn't matter if they were married or single. You could see their eyes glaze over when they looked at her, as if they were imagining things, you know? Like they were picturing her with no clothes on.'

'Did she like them too?'

Hedwig blushed, despite herself. She was twisting her hair and gazing sightlessly into the middle distance. There were layers of shadow in her voice, of things that remained unspoken.

'She slept around – even when we were over in London. She slipped away a couple of nights and made me promise to cover for her. I tried to talk to her about it, but she said what was wrong with that? She wasn't married or anything. She didn't feel at all guilty. She couldn't get hold of condoms any more, no one can, but she carried a bottle of vinegar with her and used it as a douche. It works perfectly,' she blushed more profusely, 'apparently.'

'Did she have a regular boyfriend?'

Hedwig pushed away the hanks of mousy hair which had escaped her plaits. There were beads of sweat in her hairline, Clara noticed, and her gaze flicked around as though someone might be watching.

'That's just it. When the principal, Frau Mann, asked me, I said no. But now I've been feeling so guilty about it. I think I should have told the truth.'

'Which is?'

'Lotti *had* met someone. She wouldn't tell me who. Usually she'd talk for hours about her boyfriends.' A shy sideways glance. 'I'm sorry, Fräulein, but she liked boasting about what they did in bed. Only this time it was different. She was infatuated with this man, but she wouldn't even tell me his name. She just said he was very interesting. An artistic type. And he had a secret.'

The chill breeze sent a fragile confetti of petals spiralling down from an apple tree, and a petal stuck to Hedwig's cheek. Clara reached across to brush it away.

'What sort of secret?'

'She wouldn't say. He was on her mind all the time. But this man didn't make her happy. I think perhaps he saw other women. One of the last times I saw her, Lotti said that she had had enough. She would show him he couldn't play around with her. She had something on him. But at the same time . . .'

The roar of a passing car caused Hedwig to startle, and turning back to Clara she lowered her voice.

'The fact was, she was really frightened of him.'

Clara wanted her to keep talking, but she could see it was no use. The girl was as nervous as a kitten.

'Why should she be frightened of this man if she was in love with him?'

'I don't know.'

Clara noticed a café across the road.

'Would you like to have a cup of coffee with me?'

Hedwig sniffed and squeezed the bridge of her nose to hold back the tears.

'That's kind, but I'd better get back. Herr Doktor Kraus will have noticed by now, and God help me if the SS-Reichsführer has already arrived.' She paused. 'If you hear anything about . . . about Lotti, would you tell me? I need to know. She was a dear friend and I would do anything I could to find who killed her.'

'I feel the same.'

Clara took out a tan leather Smythson's notebook and scribbled her address and telephone number in it with her silver pen.

'Take this. And if you remember anything else, just call me. It might be useful.'

She tore the page out and pressed it into Hedwig's hand.

'Thank you, Fräulein Vine. And please be careful. If that man is still out there, all of us women need to watch ourselves until he's caught.'

Chapter Fourteen

'So were you really there? I didn't see you.'

Erich regarded Clara suspiciously, his dark brows knitted above sceptical eyes.

'I told you. Right opposite the Führer's saluting podium.'

'And you definitely saw me?'

Goebbels was fond of saying that for a lie to be believed, it had to be a big one, but Clara thought that at certain moments, a little lie was a better choice.

'I was very proud of you.'

It was Saturday, and they had just finished one of their regular weekend pursuits. A swim at the Charlottenburg public swimming baths. It was a lovely old building – the pride of the district – decorated with porcelain dolphins, the high glass ceiling with its turquoise blue struts echoing with the shouts of parents and children.

Clara loved these weekend meetings with Erich. She found herself looking forward to them throughout the week – a moment of sunny respite from the darkening political scene. Children lived so much more in the moment. She liked hearing about his friends, their fights and feuds, and talking about books, films and her own childhood. Erich especially liked to hear about his dead mother, Helga, who had befriended Clara when she first moved to Berlin. Although he had only come into Clara's life six years ago, some of her happiest times had been with Erich. Rowing on the Wannsee, the sun bouncing off the clear water of the lake as Erich learned to handle the oars, or his enthralled face beside hers in the silvery glimmer of the cinema as they sat through innumerable war films.

Clara knew very little about teenage boys and had no more expected to find herself entrusted with one than she might an elephant or a giant panda, but had come to love Erich as if he were her own.

The best part of the swimming mornings came afterwards when, exuding the tang of chlorine and the virtuous flush of exercise, they would wander a couple of streets along to the vast Rogacki market hall and sate their appetites. Despite the food shortages, the market always gave an impression of plenty, and the café she and Erich liked best was famous for its generous portions. Over the years Erich had grown almost visibly before her eyes as he devoured mountains of Spätzel and Wurst and cakes and ice cream.

That day Clara had ordered Pflaumenkuchen, sweet doughy plum cake topped with cinnamon sugar and a dollop of whipped cream, while Erich, more like a boy playing chess than choosing cake, deliberated lengthily before selecting Pfannkuchen, a type of jam doughnut. To Clara's secret pleasure he also ordered Himbeersaft, the sugary raspberry juice so loved by children in Berlin. It consoled her that perhaps he was not growing up quite as fast as she feared, despite the fact that he outgrew every shirt she bought for him within a matter of months.

'Anyway,' Erich seemed mollified by Clara's admiration. 'You can watch me march again if you like.'

'So soon?' said Clara, trying hard to inject some enthusiasm into her voice.

'In the cinema. It's a movie already. *Hitler's Fiftieth Birthday*. We've watched it twice in the HJ film hour.'

'That's great.'

He shrugged.

'I suppose.'

He pulled out a packet of cigarettes but at the sight of Clara's face put it away again.

'Anyway, I've got better news than that. I've been appointed to the HJ-Streifendienst.'

Clara beamed at him lovingly. She had no idea what it was, but any achievement of Erich's gave her a lift. She gave a little shake of his arm.

'Darling, that's wonderful! Clever you. What is it?'

'It's the Patrol Force. We keep order at meetings and watch out for troublemakers. We make a note of anyone criticizing the Party, you know, disrespecting the Führer, or displaying anti-Party sentiments, and we put that in a regular report to our divisional office. It's a way of keeping the HJ strong and united.'

'Oh.' Clara couldn't help the disappointment seeping into her voice and Erich flared with annoyance as if she had rubbed a raw wound.

'I knew you'd be like that! You should be pleased. Anyone else would be. It's a privilege. A position of responsibility. If you get into the Streifendienst you're on track for recruitment to the SS and sometimes you go directly to SS officer training school. You can't believe what an honour it is.' He had a high flush on his cheeks. 'But you're never pleased when I have good news.'

'That's not fair,' she said gently. 'But all this talk of the SS is quite new. I thought you wanted to join the Luftwaffe.' He had been talking about it for years and his bedroom at home was plastered with pictures of famous pilots – Ernst Udet, Werner Mölders, Adolf Galland. 'You've spent so much time building gliders and taking rides in fighter bombers.'

'I know.' Erich frowned and fiddled with his glass. Clara had hit on the heart of his dilemma, as she so often did, but that didn't mean he was ready to forgive her. He felt the familiar stab of self-pity. His mother would have been prouder of him, if she had lived. Even Oma, his grandmother, had made his favourite supper as a reward.

'It's true. I did want to join the Luftwaffe. I do. But when someone gives you a chance like this. The SS, Clara! All the others were green with envy. It means I've been singled out for leadership.'

Clara forced a smile. The HJ was all about spotting future leaders. Once a likely candidate had been identified, they were plucked by the leadership schools, in Vogelsang and Crossinsee and Pomerania, and trained in political science and administration as well as obedience, zeal and mental fitness for the struggles they would face deploying the Führer's wishes.

'You just don't understand.'

'I suppose I don't. I'm sorry.'

'It's all right.' Erich never sulked for long and besides, it was Saturday, and the Pfannkuchen, glistening with sugar, had just landed on his plate.

'Everything will change if we go to war with Poland, anyway, and that's only a few months away.'

'You seem very sure.'

'I am,' he said, through a mouthful of sweet dough. 'We're not supposed to say, but our battalion has already been issued with luminous paint for painting the kerbstones. So people can see their way in a blackout when the Poles begin their aerial bombardment.'

The news gave Clara a chill. Everyone knew Goering had laid elaborate plans to defend Berlin in case of bombing, and the HJ were endlessly practising air-raid precautions, but the idea that these plans were now being put into action made the threat of war seem even more real.

Erich licked his sugar moustache. 'It's quite exciting. They're saying we'll be pushed to fight over Danzig by the autumn. The Poles are refusing to see reason.'

'There's *nothing* exciting about war.' There was steel in Clara's voice but she couldn't help it. 'Don't ever make that mistake.'

Erich shrugged and returned to his glass of Himbeersaft. Men were better judges of these things than women. Male reasoning powers were scientifically superior to women's and the woman should never presume to argue with the man. He had learned that at the HJ, where they were taught that even the highest BDM leader in the land could not issue orders to the lowest HJ boy. Yet somehow, it was hard to point this out to Clara. His godmother could get quite sardonic when he explained ideas to her. He decided on this occasion to humour her. He was going to be away for several weeks and besides, he had a favour to ask.

Clara reached a hand across to Erich and patted his arm.

'Why don't we talk about something else?'

She hated talking politics with Erich. Subjected to weekly political conditioning at the HJ, and gifted with a naturally quick, analytic mind, he loved to pursue political debates. The exhaustion of having to maintain a façade with the boy she so loved, while dreading what might happen to him in a war, was draining. Erich's argumentative nature would have made him a good barrister but instead he was probably destined to become cannon fodder in Hitler's deluded war. She looked at his face, still puppyishly rounded, and his eyes shining with a sense of absolute rightness, the clarity of conviction so common in the young and dangerous in the old.

'Have something else to eat. It's a treat, remember.'

It was a treat because Erich was to leave the next day for a three-week Hitler Youth camp, north of Berlin. Clara had first taken him there when he entered the senior Hitler Jugend and acquired his short brown trousers, black boots and belt with its iron eagle buckle. Above the camp entrance was a banner with the slogan '*We were born to die for Germany*' and Clara's sarcastic comment had caused a predictable squabble between them. But it was soon forgotten. Even though the marching, bayonet drill, grenade throwing and pistol shooting went against Erich's naturally studious nature, and he was often so tired that he would fall asleep in class, he embraced the HJ with emotional fervour, like the parent he no longer had.

'What's this favour you wanted to ask?' asked Clara, wrenching her mind back to the present. She had already guessed that the answer lay in the wicker basket that Erich had tucked beneath the table.

'It's only for a couple of weeks. Just while I'm away.'

He lifted the basket's front grille to show Clara its tiny, trembling cargo; a pair of young rabbits huddled together. Erich and his grandmother, like a vast number of Berlin citizens, had taken to breeding rabbits for meat and the animals were kept in a hutch on the balcony. As Erich was off to camp his grandmother had suggested that she wring their necks to save herself some work, but instead he had brought them to Clara.

'They're only young. It's far too early to kill them. You will look after them, won't you? Just while I'm at camp.'

Clara poked a finger through the grille and felt their impossibly silky fur. Beady eyes blinked at her and soft noses twitched, too young even to fear a predator.

'I would, darling, but I'm going to be in Paris for a couple of days.'

'Leave them some cabbage leaves and water. They'll be okay. Better off than if they stay with Oma, anyway. Please.'

He opened the basket, took one rabbit onto his lap and stroked it. The tiny creature remained motionless, ears flattened, nose still quivering.

'All right.'

She felt a pang of tenderness. Even now, with all his Hitler Youth bluster, his cigarette smoking and adolescent edginess, the child in Erich still surfaced. She remembered their trips to the zoo, in the early days after Helga had died, and of Erich's fury that wild animals should be caged.

The thought of exotic animals brought yesterday's trip to the Ahnenerbe back.

'I meant to ask. Have you ever heard of the Ahnenerbe?'

He rolled his eyes.

'Everyone's heard of it. *You've* heard of it, Clara. We saw a newsreel about the latest expedition, remember?'

'I wasn't concentrating.'

'It's very interesting. They're scouring the world for the origins of the German race.'

'You would have thought the German race originated in Germany.'

He frowned.

'It did, I think. But the Ahnenerbe has discovered that the Aryan race used to rule all sorts of places. That's exactly why our soldiers must fight to reclaim our original lands.'

So that was what Erich and his friends had been told.

They parted at the S-Bahn and she kissed his cheek fleetingly, because he hated public displays of affection. Then she sat on the platform, with the basket of rabbits alongside her, waiting for the train. On the next bench was a mother with two children – a little girl of around a year old, thumb in mouth and dark-lashed eyes fluttering shut, and her older brother, who was hanging off the handle of the pushchair impatiently, longing for the train to arrive. As he caught sight of Clara's rabbits and stared with fascination, his mother reached down a hand and ran it idly through his shock of hair.

The gesture, so ordinary, sent a shaft of longing and loss through Clara. It was something she remembered from when she first knew Erich, at the age of ten. How casually, fondly, she had run her fingers through his dense, springy tuft of hair. And now such gestures were forever out of bounds. Never again could she ruffle his hair or pass a proprietorial hand across his face. It was only a tiny, incidental loss when set against the scale of losses that faced everyone just then, but she felt it, and it ached.

Erich had been damaged by the Nazis too. Nowhere near so much as Esther Goldblatt, in silent hiding, lying awake every night in fear of footsteps coming up the stairs, yet the wounds Hitler's regime had inflicted on him were lasting and real. His mother had been murdered by the Nazis when he was ten years old. He had lost all his security and was left with only a grand-mother and Clara herself. No wonder he reserved his ardour for dreams of heroism. No wonder he poured all his passion and loyalty into that other family, the Hitler Youth – the family that never left him with a second to himself.

If she went back to England for good it would mean leaving Erich and she didn't want that, even if, sometimes, Erich did everything in his power to make himself easy to leave.

A voice jerked her back to the present.

'Fräulein?'

It was a lottery seller, coming along the platform with a tray-load of orange sealed tickets. The Reichslotterie, the German state lottery, was all the rage. Everyone played – except Jews, who were banned from buying tickets – and the money supposedly went to a variety of noble causes: job creation, Winter Relief, mother and child. Whether the odds were entirely as pure as mathematics would suggest, or rigged to minimize payouts, was another matter. Some people said the Party ensured winning tickets were very thin on the ground. Despite that, everyone had their favourite numbers, and in a vote for improbability and as a protest against her own, mathematical brain, Clara always selected primes. Now she handed over the requisite fifty pfennigs, the ticket seller saluted and she picked five numbered orange envelopes. Only each one she opened had a blue ticket with the single word *Nicht* written on it.

She might have seen it as an omen, had she not long since learned to disregard them.

Chapter Fifteen

'Why did you want to meet here?'

Hedwig sneaked a quick look around her and frowned. They never went to restaurants, let alone ones like this. They couldn't possibly afford it. The 'Alois' restaurant, at 3, Wittenbergplatz, just across from the ritzy KaDeWe department store, was a pretty smart place. The building had belonged to a Jewish family, until it came under the uncomfortable scrutiny of a tavern proprietor whose influence was out of all proportion to his pale, sweaty, unprepossessing form. For the bespectacled Alois, who had set his sights on the Jewish family's home and subsequently had them beaten up and evicted, was not just a former Bavarian waiter and petty criminal, but the half-brother of the Führer himself. Even though relations between the two men were not what anyone would call brotherly, no one in the Third Reich felt like questioning the strength of that particular sibling bond.

'It's amazing what a powerful brother can do for you,' said Jochen under his breath as he surveyed the menu and selected a dish of liver dumplings. 'From a petty thief and drunken waiter to owning a classy joint like this.'

'The Führer's brother's a thief? That can't be true.'

'He served a couple of prison sentences in Austria before he fled to Britain to start a new life. Then he married another woman without bothering to divorce the first. He's a family disgrace. His brother even made him resign from the Party.'

'That may be,' Hedwig said softly, trying to avert her eyes from a group of rowdy stormtroopers leering in her direction. 'But I don't see why that would make you want to come here.'

'I thought I'd give it a try,' he said, briefly, rolling a cigarette with one hand. 'If it's good enough for the SS. And aren't you supposed to be mixing with SS men now? I thought that was what the Faith and Beauty Society was all about. Moving in the right circles.'

'Jochen, please.' She placed a hand on his arm. She knew he was jealous, seeing his girlfriend being primped and groomed as a consort to senior Nazi men, and it hurt her to think it. 'I told you I'd never be interested in any man but you.'

He managed a smile, a quick flicker that transformed his face, and, just for a second, erased all the worry lines.

'Any news about Lotti?' he asked more gently. 'Are the police still searching? Have they found anything yet?'

'Nothing. They were there again this morning. They kept asking if we had seen anyone.'

In a matter of a few weeks, the Faith and Beauty home had transformed into a full-blown crime scene. Kripo cars cluttered the driveway and the corridors were full of detectives, their male boots ringing unnaturally loud on the polished parquet floor. Police tape fluttered across the lawn like ribbons on a maypole. Why would a girl like Lotti go into the woods? That was the question they all asked. Faith and Beauty girls were not the sort to make unlikely assignations in the Grunewald, unless someone had forced them. It tormented Hedwig too. Lying awake at night, she tried to imagine the man who had killed Lotti, yet she couldn't conjure any features. Only a face that seemed to compress into it all the horrors of the night.

'I'm surprised they haven't questioned me more, but no one wants to know. It's as though no one really cares.'

'Of course they care.'

'They don't. Or if they do, it's only because it's in the news-papers, and it might look bad if they don't arrest someone soon. I miss her, Jochen.'

'I know.'

'Do you think I should ask the police if I can help them more?'

'No.' He was firm about this. 'Don't do that. If they need anything they'll tell you.'

He lit two cigarettes and gave her one.

'How's that other friend of yours? Irna? She's getting married, isn't she?'

It was true. Irna Wolter had scored the greatest triumph of them all – the jackpot of the Faith and Beauty lottery. She had won the heart of an Obersturmbannführer and was to wed him later that month. She was currently at the Reich Bride School on Schwanenwerder Island, studying for the certificate she needed to qualify for marriage into the SS.

'She's at Bride School now. Getting ready for the wedding.'

'Are you invited?'

'I wish I was but it's not in Berlin. It's at a special SS training school. A castle, can you believe it, in Westphalia. Women aren't allowed in.'

'Some wedding. Is that the kind you want then?'

'Don't be silly. You know I don't want anything special. Besides, there's only one man I want to marry and he doesn't have much time for castles.'

Jochen looked down at his fingers, which were yellow and nicotine-stained. Usually they had traces of ink on them too, from work. It was always this way when the subject of marriage came up. He would immediately clam up and avert his gaze. Hedwig felt the familiar, agonizing tear at her heart. She tried not to talk about weddings, but it was he who had brought the subject up. If he couldn't bear the idea of a future with her, then why didn't he come right out and say so? Lotti had always said she should put it to Jochen straight, but Hedwig feared that if she tried that, Jochen would back away and she would be left without the only man she had ever loved.

Being with Jochen was like being with a dog that had been ill-treated and had never lost the distrust in its eyes. Sometimes she wondered if he would ever form a commitment, at least to her, but at other times she thought she should be patient and loving and not push too far. Perhaps it was still too early, or maybe Jochen cared more than he showed about her parents' entrenched hostility. Often she found herself scanning his face like a cryptologist, trying to divine a hidden meaning in his silence. Usually she would cover up any pauses by saying all the things that she didn't mean, rather than saying what she did, but this time she stayed quiet, and unwelcome tears welled in her eyes. Since Lotti's death she found herself crying at the slightest provocation.

'At last.'

Their Leberknödel arrived, and though the dumplings turned out to contain far more breadcrumbs than liver, maybe that was for the best. Hedwig always felt guilty eating meat now. More and more people were turning vegetarian because they wanted to follow the Führer's example, and they had been told that even the top men in the Party, like Hess and Himmler and Goebbels, regularly enjoyed vegetarian meals, though Jochen said this was all made up. It was important to be thrifty too. The newspapers were full of recipes about how to make cakes without fat or eggs. They had been told that bread, sugar and coffee were in short supply because the Führer wanted to increase the racial fitness of the nation. Just as Hitler was preparing for war by building tanks so his people must prepare their bodies for war through frugal eating. Only the other day on the radio Doktor Goebbels had condemned Berliners who complained about the coffee shortage as 'cosmopolitan', which was as good as calling them Jews. If people really wanted to please the Führer they should become vegetarians, like him.

'We were learning about the Führer's love of animals,' she said, for the sake of conversation.

Apparently, the Führer had decided some animals were never acceptable to eat. Snails were all right, though just the idea of their little eyes on tiny grey stalks made Hedwig nauseous, but lobster and frogs' legs were out. That hardly mattered as Hedwig couldn't afford lobster and she was scarcely likely to encounter frogs' legs any time soon.

'He's banning scientific research on animals. And there are to be new regulations on the care of horses. Hitler says all Germans love horses.'

'Preferably in a stew,' said Jochen, shortly.

'Germany is the first country in Europe to make laws to protect animals.'

'Tell that to the bombers,' he replied, forking a dumpling into his mouth. 'Nothing's going to protect animals if a war starts. And it will.'

He gave a quick glance behind him and leaned closer.

'At work they're already printing rationing coupons. Colour-coded ones – white for sugar, blue for meat, purple for fruit and nuts, yellow for dairy and green for eggs.'

'Rationing?' She was wide-eyed.

'Sure. Twenty-four hundred grams of bread a week, five hundred grams of meat, two hundred and seventy grams of fat, whole milk for children and invalids only. If you go into a diner or a café you'll need to provide a coupon for fat or a coupon for meat, else you won't get a meal. It's serious, Hedy. The authorities are making preparations.' He looked up at her, inscrutably. 'As it happens, I am too. I've joined the RLB.'

The Reichsluftschutzbund, the Reich Air Protection League, was busily organizing blackout provisions and shelters in event of war.

'I had my first outing yesterday inspecting cellars. All blocks have to convert their cellars, and in some streets all the cellars will interconnect, in case escape routes get blocked. You wouldn't believe what there is underneath your feet, Hedy. There's a whole network of underground canals, tunnels and shelters already constructed. You'd be astonished.'

She was bewildered at this initiative. 'That's not like you.'

'Why not?'

'You hate thinking about war, or the Führer's attempts to protect Germany.'

'Perhaps I've changed my mind.'

A terrible thought seized her.

'Does that mean you're going to enlist?'

'Your parents would like that, wouldn't they?'

So her suspicions were correct. Her parents' hostility bothered Jochen far more than he showed.

'Of course they wouldn't. They just need time . . .'

'Then I could go off and get killed and not bother their dear daughter again.'

Her eyes filled with tears.

'Please stop talking like that. You know I hate it. It tears me apart.'

The savage look fell instantly from his face and he reached out a hand towards her.

'Don't cry,' he whispered. 'I'm a cruel beast, but I don't mean it.'

He wiped away a tear that was dripping off the bottom of her spectacles.

'I thought you'd be pleased that I'm spending my evenings in cellars rather than nightclubs or bars.'

'There are plenty of nightclubs in cellars,' she joked with a brave sniff. Any quarrel with Jochen engulfed her in alarm, but being Hedwig, she didn't stay miserable for long. Jochen was the only person in the world to call her Hedy. She hated her name. Her parents had named her after St Hedwig's, Berlin's Catholic cathedral, an uninspiring place whose pediment was lined by ranks of stone saints surveying all comers like police officers inspecting the faithful. There were no glamorous Hedwigs in history, or literature, or any kind of culture. Even the Viennese movie actress Hedwig Kiesler had moved to Hollywood and changed her name to Hedy Lamarr.

'Anyhow. How's work?' she enquired, pulling herself together.

'Busier than ever. You can tell your father, our company's supporting the Reich just as much as any soldier. Our products make millions for the Party. The Führer makes a pretty packet out of it too. He charges for the use of his image. He makes a pfennig every time his face appears on a postage stamp.'

'I'm sure he gives it to the Winterhilfswerk. The Führer wouldn't want any money for himself.'

'Wouldn't he? That makes him different from the rest of them then. I heard old Joey Goebbels was making money selling all those degenerate paintings they took down from the museums.'

'That's only Jewish art, though, isn't it?'

His eyes sparked dangerous fire.

'What does that mean exactly?'

'I mean,' Hedwig laboured on, trying to remember what Herr Fritzl had told them. 'It's disgusting, isn't it? Not like your kind of art.'

'Not like my kind of art?' he repeated in a tone that seemed slightly menacing. Hedwig knew she had said something wrong, or obtuse, but she didn't know how to address it. She worried the edge of her skirt with a nail.

'What's my kind of art then, Hedy?'

'You paint faces.'

'Not faces. I paint a *face*. The same face, day after day after day. Sometimes making his cheeks a little pinker, his eyes a little darker blue. Flattering him. Touching up his moustache. Shortening his nose. Making him into a matinee idol. A little more hair, a little fewer wrinkles.'

'That's nothing that the old Masters wouldn't do. They had patrons and they needed to please them so they flattered them.'

Herr Fritzl had definitely said this.

'We're not talking about Michelangelo here, Hedy. What I do is hack work. I know Hitler's face better than I know my own. I've painted it on plates and dishes and canvases and candle-holders and beer steins. Sometimes I wonder how he can bear it, seeing his face everywhere. It's on everything except the money and that's only because he remembers the inflation and thinks he had better keep his head off the banknotes in case it happens again.'

Fortunately, their conversation was interrupted at this point by a cheer and a round of applause from the far side of the restaurant. The Führer's brother had emerged and was standing, incongruously, beneath the portrait of his sibling, a cigar in one hand and a beaming smile across his face. At the sight of him, Jochen seemed to forget their argument instantly.

'As a matter of fact . . .'

He was scratching at the surface of the table with his finger.

'I'm going to ask you something.'

Hedwig was bathed in relief.

'Anything, you know that.'

She was rewarded with one of his true smiles, a tender beam which lit up his face, and made his hazel eyes shine. It was the smile that had first made her love him. It opened up a chink in his cynicism and revealed the gentle and protective man that other people would never have believed possible. That was what love did, she supposed. It made you see below the surface of a person, to the soul beneath.

'Is it to do with a book?'

She guessed it would be something to do with literature. Jochen was a fervent reader. He was like Lotti in that. Always quoting little snippets of poetry and talking about writers she had never heard of. Hedwig suspected that he kept a stash of banned books somewhere in his home, too. Perhaps he wanted to borrow something from the library at the Ahnenerbe.

'Not exactly.'

'What is it then? Don't keep me in suspense!'

'I can't tell you quite yet.'

'How mysterious.'

'It is. Shall we meet the usual time next week?'

'Any time. I can tell Mutti I'm needed at work. There's a lot going on at the moment. They're making a film about the Ahnenerbe. Leni Riefenstahl is to direct it.'

He gave a whistle. 'Leni Riefenstahl! Will you be in it?'

'I certainly hope not. I'm going to keep well away.'

'You're far too shy.'

She took off her spectacles and began absently cleaning them on her skirt.

'I'm not exactly film star material.'

'Don't say that.'

He grasped her hand.

'You know? I spend my whole day beautifying the Führer, straightening his nose, giving him a bit of colour in his cheeks, touching up his hair. So it's nice to come out in the evening with someone who doesn't need any beautifying.'

He reached a hand up to brush a curl from her eyes.

'You're perfect, Hedy. You know I think that.'

Chapter Sixteen

Erich Carow's Laugh In was a celebrated comedy act staged at the Valhalla Theatre in an appropriately cavernous cellar on Weinbergsweg, north of Rosenthalerplatz. Just a few years ago Berlin had been the nightclub capital of the world, a neon-lit, champagne-fuelled extravaganza of singing, dancing, and most of all sex. Sex à la carte or off the menu, sex for every taste, no matter how specialized or how depraved, could be found in dimly lit caverns off the Friedrichstrasse and openly in the rooms above. For two decades straight, night-time Berlin was a dazzling, decadent, non-stop party, played out at the Wintergarten, the Admiralspalast and the Residence Casino. But the party stopped abruptly in 1933; the Nazis knocked the needle from the gramophone and most of Berlin's cabarets closed down. The risqué acts were replaced with musicals and the only variety on offer was the choice between folk singing or operetta. Jazz was degenerate – *entartete Musik* – and Goebbels issued all musicians with instructions on how to hold their instruments so they didn't resemble Africans. All the dangerous glamour had been swept up by the broom of National Socialism and the only traces of it were left in a few dark corners, one of them being the Valhalla. Everyone went there – actors, journalists, artists, politicians – and while the comedy survived, the laughter was darker and more bitter. At a time when blackout paper and black material were everywhere, black humour was the only kind in vogue.

Navigating her way down the stairs, past an enamel plate reading *Jazz Dancing Forbidden*, Clara made her way into the shabby cellar and looked around for her friends. Immediately in front of her a table of young soldiers were amusing themselves by trying to shove ice cubes down the cleavages of a pair of buxom waitresses. The waitresses, struggling with large trays of beer and trapped amid the knot of young men, were laughing, but Clara glimpsed the alarm behind their eyes. The soldiers' faces were lean and savage, as though they were already inured to cruelty. Anyone of their age had already spent years in the Hitler Youth being trained to ridicule, taunt and bully, and their sport with the barmaids was no different from cats playing with a mouse. These women existed for entertainment, and their distress was simply part of the fun.

Clara prayed that the same did not happen to Erich.

The foreign correspondents were up by the bar. She detected the lanky frame of Charles Cavendish towering over an animated Bill Shirer, who was jabbing a point for emphasis with his pipe. Further along, Hugh Lindsey, a Burberry coat slung across his shoulders, was deep in conversation with Mary. As she approached he caught her eye and winked, but Clara had no intention of interrupting, so she approached Charles Cavendish, who swivelled towards her, sweeping an oiled hank of hair from his eyes and baring his tombstone teeth in a patronizing smile.

'The lovely Clara Vine.'

She guessed that he disliked her, and that was to be expected, given what he must assume. What else should he make of an Anglo-German actress who mingled in the top circles of the Nazi Party and whose father had been one of Britain's most prominent Nazi sympathizers? When you came to look at it like that, it was a wonder that he was even prepared to welcome her as a drinking companion.

'How are you, Charles?'

'As well as can be expected for a man who has sat through two press conferences and an interview with Robert Ley.'

Robert Ley, head of the German Labour Front, was a notorious drunkard who rarely saw the need to waste good manners on members of the press.

'You've come to the right place, Cavendish,' said Shirer. 'Apparently Himmler has decreed that an evening at the cabaret counts as therapy. He's recommended it for any German soldiers suffering trauma inflicted during their role in Czechoslovakia.'

'Really? Maybe he should suggest it for some of his colleagues, then. They're a dreadfully unhealthy bunch. The Führer's said to be suffering from appalling digestive problems. Goering's diabetic, has sciatica and is always exhausted. Von Ribbentrop is in constant pain because he has only one kidney and Himmler suffers from the most agonizing abdominal attacks and lives in fear of stomach cancer.'

'Even Goebbels is fresh out of a clinic,' added Shirer.

'Well, one thinks one knows what caused that. Or rather *who*,' said Cavendish knowingly, and following his eyes Clara saw a figure she recognized.

Joseph Goebbels might have censored all the cabarets in the city and even dictated which dances could be performed in them, but there was one thing in the Third Reich he could not control: his wife. Magda Goebbels, thirty-eight-year-old mother of six, was seated at a table in the centre of the club in full, embarrassing view. Around her, a circle of dazzled young men clustered, topping up her glass, lighting her cigarettes and hanging slavishly on her words.

'Apparently Goebbels was forced to spend Christmas in the guest house,' said Shirer. 'She won't have him in the house.'

Since her husband's affair with a Czech actress the previous year, Magda had resorted to her own style of revenge. It involved the conventional combination of a makeover, an affair and an awful lot of alcohol. Her wheat-blonde hair was now ashy and stiffly strained into rolls against her head. Her slinky plum dress – an elegant design by Paul Kuhnen – was ostentatiously modern, though its slender silhouette did her bulky form no favours. And the Elizabeth Arden foundation she had always favoured was now painted as thickly as a Van Gogh sunflower.

'She's in nightclubs several nights a week around town,' murmured Cavendish waspishly. 'She likes to invite young men to share her bar stool. She even asks sailors home.'

There was a malicious gleam in his eye at Magda Goebbels' predicament – a malice that was, thought Clara, not too far from the savage laughter of the SA youths with the barmaids. She thought back over the years she had known the Propaganda Minister's wife, a brittle, nerve-wracked, unsympathetic figure, locked into the gilded cage of a Nazi wife by her own disastrous choices. So what if Magda chose to play out her misery on the public stage? Who could blame her, given the horror of her marriage and the remorseless barbarity that her husband's regime perpetrated? She was about to reply when Magda Goebbels turned in her direction and lurched to her feet.

'Bad luck,' said Cavendish. 'Looks like she's seen you.'

Magda, it was immediately clear, was drunk. Very drunk. Drifts of powder had collected in the crevices of her face and her lipstick might have been applied by one of her own little girls. The depths of her cleavage glistened with sweat. Yet beneath the blowsy exterior she was more agitated than Clara had ever seen her. The gold-tipped Sobranie trembled in her hand and her address was far more familiar than she would allow herself in daylight hours.

'Fräulein Vine. Our own little actress. Fancy seeing you here.' She swayed to a stop. 'I wouldn't have thought this was the kind of place you frequented. They tell jokes against Party leaders here, didn't you know? I always had you down as a loyal member of the Chamber of Culture.'

'As I am.'

'Not so loyal as to sleep with my husband, I hope.'

'Certainly not.'

'Well you can always join the queue,' she said with a harsh laugh, which brought a sour gust of schnapps and tobacco. 'Though there's quite a waiting list.'

A hush had descended. Faces turned in their direction, agog with expectation, if not surprise. Magda Goebbels had, in recent months, become an alternative cabaret. She was a living, breathing one-woman stand-up, firing off unspeakable quips about the Nazi leaders. An act like that from anyone else would be closed down instantly, and the performer sent to a camp the same evening, but who would dare denounce the Propaganda Minister's wife? In what newspaper or magazine could the allegation be printed and what court would hear the accusations? Besides, why denounce her, when you could laugh at her instead?

'I've been told to think of that girl as a hiccup in our marriage,' Magda continued, as though her husband's recent affair with a Czech actress was common knowledge, as indeed it was. 'I say, not so much a hiccup, more of a belch.'

Clara felt a wave of sympathy.

'Why don't we sit down? There's a seat over there. In that alcove.'

'Don't let me take you away from your friends. Especially not that handsome young man,' commented Magda, eyeing Hugh Lindsey.

'They're not really my friends,' said Clara hastily. 'Just some journalists.'

She hoped the mention of journalists would be enough. Surely Magda was not so reckless she would get drunk in front of the cream of the foreign press? God forbid she should ask to be introduced to Hugh, or perhaps even invite him back to the Goebbels' villa for a drink.

'I barely know them,' she added.

But Magda's interest had flagged, and all her attention turned inwards again, to her own troubles. She plumped herself down on the banquette with a sigh.

'I have a terrible headache. You have no idea how much I suffer, Fräulein Vine.'

'I have aspirin—' Clara began to fumble in her bag, but Magda waved her away.

'It's a spiritual suffering. There's no pill for that, no matter how much my husband keeps booking me into clinics and sending the frightful Doktor Morell around with his prescriptions.'

Theo Morell was Hitler's own doctor, who had been slavishly taken up by all the senior Nazis and as a consequence enjoyed lavish premises on the Kurfürstendamm and a country villa on the Wannsee. The contents of his pills were top secret, but generally thought to be amphetamines, designed to combat the sleepless nights of the top men.

'God knows what he has in those tablets. I wouldn't be at all surprised if I ended up poisoned one day. At least Joseph would be pleased.'

So they had reached the heart of the matter, in one easy step.

'How is the Herr Doktor?'

'How should I know? He's barely speaking to me. The Führer might have ordered him to break up with that marriage-wrecker, but you wouldn't know it. He went on a grand tour of Europe to "soothe his wounded heart" but when he came back it was just as bad. Do you know what he's done now?'

Clara could only imagine.

'He's commissioned a film from Veit Harlan to tell the story of his affair.'

'I heard a little about that.'

It was, of course, the talk of the studios. Veit Harlan, a former actor turned successful director, had been allocated an eye-popping budget for his latest project, *Die Reise nach Tilsen*. It told the story of an honourable man, torn between his exquisitely beautiful mistress and his dumpy wife, struggling to resolve the conflict between head and heart. The lovelorn Goebbels was constantly popping in to watch the action or examine the rushes with manic attention to detail.

'Joseph denies it's about himself of course. And he refuses to discuss our marriage. Whenever I complain he stuffs his ears and shouts, "*It's the same old song! Even Bormann is allowed a mistress!*" Apparently Bormann has taken up with one of your little actress friends. I expect you know her.'

Clara did, slightly. Manja Behrens was a dental assistant whose aspirations to a film and stage career had undergone a meteoric rise since she had come under the eye of Hitler's enforcer, the vicious, bull-necked Martin Bormann. In a grotesque parallel of Magda Goebbels' own plight the previous year, it was rumoured that Bormann was planning to move Manja under his own roof. Only the browbeaten Gerda Bormann might prove more amenable than Magda, who had tolerated the ménage à trois precisely one week before storming off to Hitler and demanding a divorce.

'Joseph may have a broken heart, but it hasn't stopped him, of course. He's built a new villa for his whores, out at Lanke. It cost three million marks and it's supposed to be the property of the German Film Industry. Though I suppose that makes sense, given the number of German actresses who are put up there.' Her face hardened. 'In a few weeks it's our annual trip to Salzburg for the Wagner. I can see it already. All that operatic passion, and Joseph snuffling away next to me, moaning about his wounded heart.'

Magda sniffed, blinking away the tears of alcohol and self-pity in her eyes. Despite a prickle of sympathy, Clara knew she must not pass up the opportunity of this confessional mood.

'Have you heard much of Frau von Ribbentrop?'

'Unfortunately, I never hear the end of her.'

Since their first encounter in 1933, Magda Goebbels had not bothered to conceal her view of Annelies von Ribbentrop as a nouveau riche social climber and despite the fact that she had now achieved the dizzy heights of Wilhelmstrasse, Magda saw little reason to revise her opinion.

'I went on tour to Italy with Albert Speer. I was desperately in need of a break and we went all round the Doric temples of Sicily and southern Italy. It should have been so fascinating but all anyone could talk about was the von Ribbentrops. He's bordering on insanity, they say, and Annelies is goading him on to all sorts of rash decisions.'

She leaned forward confidentially.

'In fact they worry that von Ribbentrop's advice is badly misleading the Führer in his military planning. Some of the senior men have been consulting a psychic to find out if the auspices are right for what Hitler has planned.'

Clara could barely believe it.

'They're asking a fortune teller?'

'A good one. Her name is Annie Krauss. She has a place up in Wilmersdorf. She read my hand once actually and it was completely accurate. Every bit of it. She said if I stay with Joseph I'll be dead by the age of forty-five. I can well believe it. I feel half dead already.'

The clatter of percussion and a roar from the audience alerted them to the beginning of the cabaret. As the performers made their entrance on stage, Magda rose unsteadily to her feet.

'My friends will be wondering where I've got to.'

Clara picked up her bag.

'Of course. Mine too.'

'I thought you said they weren't your friends.'

Magda lurched forward and gripped Clara's wrist so hard that she flinched. Flushed and sweating, she loomed in Clara's face.

'What is it about you, Fräulein Vine? I've known you on and off for what is it, six years, and I don't think I have ever seen you with a proper boyfriend. Not even my husband, which is quite an achievement, given his penchant for brunettes. And I've never heard scandal attached to your name until now.'

Clara felt the blood freeze inside her, but on the surface she was merely cool.

'Scandal?'

'You want to watch out . . .' Magda smiled cruelly. 'People are keeping an eye on you. Somebody has been saying some very unkind things about you.'

'I wonder who?'

'I can't tell you. And I'd be lying if I said I cared. But for the sake of our long acquaintance, I'd advise you to be careful. Unless you want to spend more time enjoying your own company.'

At the bar Mary was still deeply ensconced with Hugh Lindsey and he had taken her arm to emphasize some point, making her flush with unexpected pleasure. Clara's encounter, however, had not escaped her notice.

'I didn't realize you and Magda Goebbels were so close.'

'It was just a friendly chat.'

'I've seen friendlier Alsatians.'

'She says some of the regime are consulting a fortune teller about their military plans.'

'Astonishing,' said Hugh.

'You'd better believe it,' said Mary. 'Most of them are intensely superstitious. Even Hitler had his own astrologer until the SA discovered the man was Jewish and shot him in a field outside Berlin. Goebbels was joking about it for years afterwards.'

'Our Minister enjoys jokes, doesn't he?' said Hugh drily. 'I heard today he's appointed his own joke-writer in the Ministry.'

'He certainly needs something to improve those speeches.'

'It's not for the speeches. It's rather more ingenious than that. The idea is to create jokes about the senior men and then track their spread across the country. Apparently it's an effective way of monitoring dissent.'

'Aren't these people incredible?' said Mary. 'They're more of a joke than any cabaret act.'

'If the Nazis are a joke,' said Hugh, 'I'd hate to hear the punchline.'

The rest of the evening passed in a blur. As Clara laughed along with the cabaret, her mind was scrolling through the conversation with Magda Goebbels, analysing her parting words from every angle. *Somebody has been saying some very unkind things about you.* To be the subject of gossip was never a surprise in Nazi Germany, but a warning from the Propaganda Minister's wife was far more worrying.

As she made her way back through the shadowed streets, she distracted herself with thoughts of the fortune teller, Annie Krauss. Berliners were famously superstitious. The city was thick with psychics and hand readers. Their advertisements peppered every newspaper and advertising column. Nor was a tendency to superstition limited to the general populace. Not only Hitler but Himmler firmly believed that psychic forces controlled his destiny. How perilous that the future of Europe might hinge on the prognostications of a palm reader or astrologer.

And yet, thought Clara, as she boarded the last S-Bahn and sat in the warm, rumbling darkness, was she not herself in thrall to a kind of superstition? Wasn't she also longing to believe her own personal faith? That unexplained sixth sense, like a quiet flame in her heart, that told her that while Leo Quinn was missing, while he had disappeared without trace, he might yet not be dead?

Chapter Seventeen

Hedwig was sitting in the cramped front room of the apartment with her five brothers, quizzing Reiner on Air Raids. It was Reiner's homework, but all the boys were listening – all except one-year-old Kurt, who was drifting off to sleep on her lap. Kurt was too young to understand about bombs or fire or death, and when he had been given a picture book about air raids, he had torn it up and cheerfully stuffed the pieces into his mouth. Hedwig wished she could do the same with Reiner's quiz.

As she ran through the list of questions, she was trying to keep order as the three others attempted to compete. Wolfgang, who at eleven was younger than Reiner, but brighter, kept butting in. The oldest, Peter, bent over his schoolwork, contributing answers in a tone of bored superiority that infuriated his younger brother. Even little Ludi, who at five was too small even for the Pimpf, the junior section of the Hitler Youth, but had regular air-raid lessons at kindergarten, kept jumping up and trying to interrupt.

'Stop it, Ludi. It's my homework!' shouted Reiner, with a mounting flush on his cheeks. 'I need to get it right because there's a big drill coming up!'

Reiner always found himself left behind by his cleverer brothers. He was hopeless at school. Perhaps that was why the HJ meant so much to him. It played to his strengths, which were running, fighting and swimming. Placing a soothing hand on Ludi's head, Hedwig continued.

'What do you do if you see a fire, Reiner? Who would be the right person to tell? What do you do if someone's injured? How would you deal with poison gas?'

War was by far the boys' favourite subject. It occupied their every thought. Even when they weren't studying it, they were playing it in a variety of military board games: *Tanks Forward*, *Without a Propeller*, *We Sail Against England* – a new one involving U–Boats – and *Bombs Over England*, a game where Heinkel bombers attacked London Bridge. That was Wolfgang's favourite and when Hedwig told him she had seen London Bridge and hoped it wouldn't be bombed, he stared at her in disbelief.

But who needed board games now that the whole of the city had turned into one big practice site? Mock air raids and blackouts went on all the time in Berlin. In a recent drill, soldiers trussed up in decontamination suits had hosed down the streets as if clearing poison gas. The Luftwaffe had been co-opted to drop smoke bombs for a more realistic effect and fire engines raised their ladders up the side of buildings to stage rescues. The Hitler Youth dedicated a couple of evenings every week to air-raid drill and Reiner's battalion had a large-scale exercise coming up. When war came, it would be the HJ that the city relied on to coordinate the air-raid precautions, check the blackouts and sirens and cope with the casualties. That was why Reiner's homework mattered so much, and why Hedwig needed to drum the answers into his head.

She was devoted to her brood of brothers. Sometimes she felt she was never happier than when ensconced in this drab and cramped apartment, parrying their backchat and adjudicating over their arguments. There was Peter, at seventeen serious and ambitious, Reiner and Wolfgang always fighting, Ludi, a burly miniature of their father, and tiny, boisterous Kurt, who called for Hedwig before his mother and whose care Mutti seemed quite happy to delegate.

Perhaps that was why she loved Kurt with a special passion. With his little jutting chin and his air of absolute confidence, it was clear that he would not stay a baby for long. The way he slammed his palms on the table of his high chair, demanding attention, he might have been commanding a battalion of soldiers, rather than a single harried sister. Yet although he was fast leaving infancy behind, his nails were still tiny pink shells and his hair soft as feathers. He watched his brothers constantly, observing their playing and their fights, clamouring to be included. He rarely cried and Hedwig's possessive pride manifested itself in small acts of preferential treatment. She saved the lumps of sugar that were provided with tea for staff at the Ahnenerbe and crumbled them up for Kurt when his brothers were not looking.

In the evenings when she was not taking Faith and Beauty classes, Hedwig cooked and washed the plates, and after her father departed for the nearest Kneipe, divided her time between homework, storytelling and keeping order. Not to mention patching Kurt's clothes, which had been shed by four brothers before him like the skins of a snake. This humdrum existence could not be less like the gracious, elegant life that the Faith and Beauty Society was preparing her for. Here in Moabit there was no art, or dancing, or conversation to speak of, unless you counted their father bellowing at the children or Mutti moaning about the amount of washing she had to do. There was no music, apart from the light dance music on the radio that Mutti used to drown out the squabbling of the boys. And yet it could not suit Hedwig better.

Ploughing through the pages of questions on Reiner's list Hedwig felt a pang of sympathy for him. It had been the same for her in the BDM – endless lists of questions that she could still reel off like some leaden poetry imprinted forever in her mind. *What is the date and place of the birth of the Führer? What are the clauses of* the Treaty of Versailles? What is the date of the Beer Hall Putsch? What is the significance of 10th November? – the answer to that was Martin Luther's birthday, rather than Kristallnacht, which had raged through the city last year.

At times it seemed that citizens of the Reich spent their entire time answering questionnaires. The girls at the Faith and Beauty Society marvelled at the form issued by the office responsible for maintaining the racial purity of the SS for women hoping to marry. It was seven pages long and spelt out cumbersome requirements for the hopeful girl, including the precise date that she learned to walk, and photographs of herself in a bathing suit taken from three angles. Some of the queries seemed as daunting as a university examination.

'*Is the woman positively addicted to housework?*' was one. How did you answer that?

'*Does she hold fast to the values of German womanhood?*'

And the one that had particularly floored Hedwig: '*Does she cherish the high ideals of German philosophy?*'

God knows how she would ever answer them, yet with any luck there would be no need. The only question she was interested in just then was the one that Jochen had mentioned the other evening in the restaurant. *I'm going to ask you something.* If Jochen's request was what she suspected, it would be both thrilling and terrifying in equal measure.

Chapter Eighteen

Paris in late Springtime had a reputation to live up to. The air was soft as a peach. The sunshine had obliged, and the smart ladies at the Auteuil races showed off that season's striped silk suits. Hats were worn with flowers. Eau de Nil, sorbet, champagne and sky blue were the colours of the moment. The bateaux mouches slid beneath the bridges of the Seine, the used book sellers set up their stalls on the parapets, and artists in broad-brimmed hats propped their easels as ever beneath the façade of Notre Dame. The chestnuts were blooming in the broad boulevards and in the exquisite Spring light the elegantly peeling façades of soft mushroom stone and the bleached shutters with their window boxes of tumbling scarlet geraniums seemed almost impossibly beautiful.

Paris, above all cities, was good at putting on a show.

If the French were preparing for war, it was with all the elegance and nonchalance that only Parisians could muster. Young men at café tables still whistled and tried to catch the glances of passing girls in imitation silk dresses, who stalked the pavements as haughtily as fashion models, and policemen still wore brass-buttoned jackets, flat-topped caps and white cotton gloves to conduct the traffic round the Place de l'Opéra. Even the air-raid precautions were undertaken with a view to appearances, and the statues and monuments were fringed with a spotless line of sandbags. Perhaps the French thought the great Maginot Line would protect them from anything the Germans could attempt, or perhaps they trusted that no one, not even Hitler, would dare sully the splendour of their most elegant city.

Clara was wearing a silk day dress – white zigzags on a dark pink background – and a second-hand Chanel scarf which her godson Erich had given her the previous year knotted casually round her throat. She rarely risked bright colours in Berlin. The ideal demeanour for a spy was nondescript, which translated as workday, inconspicuous clothing or at the very least muted shades, but here in Paris she felt more relaxed and besides, it made sense to look as glamorous as possible when you were expecting, or at least hoping, to feature in the pages of French *Vogue*.

At the Gare du Nord she had parted with seven francs for the latest edition of the magazine. *Vogue* was celebrating the fiftieth anniversary of the Eiffel Tower and featured a startling photograph of a model called Lisa Fonssagrives wearing a Lucien Lelong dress, balancing on the very summit, the city spread beneath her like a glorious map. Flicking through, it was clear that the shadow of war had not been permitted to darken the magazine's pages. The chief international crisis of the day was the fact that Greta Garbo, Marlene Dietrich and Joan Crawford were now being dressed by American designers. And a forthcoming movie called *Gone with the Wind* was to bring back the fashions of the American South. Was New York about to inherit Paris's crown? France was fighting back with a Tyrolean style from Mainbocher and blue tulle veils from Jeanne Lanvin. The only inkling that anything more serious might be on the horizon was the news that Schiaparelli was calling her latest vivid shade 'Maginot Line blue'.

Clara stuffed the magazine into her bag and made her way across town. It had been a long train journey, and the narrow bunk in the sleeping car had allowed only minimal rest, but she wanted to walk. She was longing for the brief respite from Berlin and the chance to savour a different city. She wanted to drink in the sight of ladies taking coffee at marble tables and peer through shutters the colour of verdigris into courtyards with ivy-covered fountains. To hear the church bells, with their charming lack of synchronicity, sound out across the rooftops and wander into the shadowy mediaeval spaces glimmering with candles and thick with incense. She wanted to absorb everything from the roosting birds to the sun piercing the wrought-iron balustrade of the Pont Alexander III, lacing the pavement with a dark tracery of shadow.

The Rue Léopold-Robert lay in Paris's 14th arrondissement, between the Boulevard Raspail and the Boulevard du Montparnasse. The list of artists who frequented this district might have been specially composed to enrage the Führer. Picasso, Cocteau, Duchamp, Ferdinand Léger, Modigliani and Dali were locals, arguing all day in Le Dôme, La Rotonde or La Coupole and carousing in the bars all night. Above the streets, rickety apartments were packed with artists' studios, and beneath them lay the bone-stacked catacombs. It was as though Death stretched beneath the feet while Life danced above it.

Clara was early, so she stopped at a café called La Closerie des Lilas and sat inside, beside a dark wood and button-leather bar beneath a picture of Lenin. She ordered an apple tart, revelling in the rich, flaky pastry that melted in her mouth while observing the tiny vignettes of Left Bank life all around. An elderly woman was passing with a baby carriage containing a minuscule dog with a ribbon in its hair. A flock of nuns, wimples lifting in the wind like solemn grey wings, prayer books in hand, were on their way to mass. A toddler with bright eyes stretched out her hands at a falling leaf. Clara's eye was caught by a girl a few seats away who casually took out her compact and applied lip rouge from a pot with her little finger. It was a startling sight – no woman in Berlin would dare apply cosmetics in public.

She tried and failed to read a report in *Paris-Soir* about the imminent trial of Herschel Grynszpan, the young Jewish boy who had shot Ernst vom Rath, a German cultural attaché in Paris the previous year, but it was hard to focus. Despite the reason for her visit, being away from Berlin and its daily fears and dangers was intensely soothing. The French language, with its slick warp and weft and softly undulating vowels, flowed like silk around her and bit by bit tension fell away as she relaxed into the sensations of Paris.

She finished her coffee, paid and walked the short distance to the Rue Léopold-Robert.

Number Eleven Rue Léopold-Robert was a dingy stucco, wooden-shuttered building with ornate balconies of latticed iron and a set of bells beside a peeling green door. Pushing the outer door open she walked up three flights of a stone staircase with a twisted iron banister. The hall stank of urine and fish and somewhere behind several doors a couple were carrying on a heated, uninhibited argument. When she reached apartment four she found the door wide open, revealing a man half a head shorter than her wearing a stained white blouse, horn-rimmed glasses and red spotted cravat. He had a mass of gleaming dark hair, a beaky nose and alert, intelligent eyes. His face was a composition of lines and angular smiles, like a Braque portrait. He removed the Gitane from his mouth long enough to say, 'Mademoiselle Vine. I felt sure you would come. And so prompt. Would that all my models were so punctual.'

Clara stepped into an atelier filled with a pure northern light that poured through the long windows and glanced off the parquet floor. A few pieces of furniture were assembled randomly like some avant-garde art show – a chaise longue, a table, various lamp stands and a bed, beside which stood a glass ashtray overflowing with stubs. A white screen lit by four spot-lights covered one wall and the others were filled with giant blow-ups of Epstein's work – bodies striped with light and bisected by operatic shadows. A lifesize torso draped in wet silk. Through a doorway she glimpsed a bidet and a basin with nickel taps, on the side of which a single woman's stocking hung. A Siamese cat on the windowsill stared at her with indifferent grandeur.

Epstein opened the shutters with a rattle, prompting the cat to bolt, and switched from French to German.

'I hope you don't mind coming here. I could use the *Vogue* studios on the Champs-Elysées, but this place is miraculously cheap. A hundred francs a month and the only catch is I vacate it between five and seven every day so the landlord can sublet for amorous purposes. Please. Sit down.'

He gestured to the grubby chaise longue and Clara sat uncertainly, still unsure what this meeting entailed. She knew Epstein would convey her message to Major Grand, but was the fashion feature in *Vogue* magazine genuine, or simply an elaborate façade?

'Are we actually going to do a photograph?'

'But of course! I love to shoot beautiful women. I live for elegance. It is a religion to me. The more elegance we have in the world, the less horror.'

He picked up a piece of silk and draped it experimentally over her face, then removed it, muttered to himself and disappeared for a moment behind a Chinese screen, reappearing with a piece of material trailing dark ribbons.

'Here, Miss Vine, is your costume.'

She gave an audible intake of breath.

It was a corset. A piece of blush-pink silk, with inky black ribboned laces and stiff bones. The only corsets Clara had ever seen came from the Ufa costume department and were generally stained with old make-up and sweat from repeated use in historical epics, but this one was exquisitely stitched, like a piece of haute couture, and the silk had a pearly sheen to it which shimmered in her hands.

'Just this?'

'Certainly. It will be subtle, of course. I like to strike a balance between modesty and eroticism. To both reveal and conceal. And this is not just any corset. Mainbocher showed it in this year's collections. Please.'

He motioned Clara behind the Chinese screen where she took off her dress, folded it carefully and wriggled into the corset. It was a sensation she had never had before, to be so transformed by a single piece of clothing, to feel the material enfold her, cool and liquid against her skin.

When she emerged Epstein fussed about, leaving the top of the corset unlaced, and then positioned Clara with her back towards him, her face inclined slightly away.

'You mean you're going to take a picture of my back?'

'Precisely. We don't want to see your face, delightful though it is. We only want a glimpse, half in shadow and half in the light. That seems appropriate, doesn't it? In the circumstances? And please don't move. Hold that position. I want you emerging from that corset like a rose from its bud.'

Not for the first time, Clara wondered how Angela had ever managed a career as a fashion mannequin. Acting came instinctively to her, but modelling seemed so much less natural. She could practically feel her limbs seize up in self-conscious stiffness. Epstein fiddled with his camera and tripod, muttering to himself all the while, the cigarette perched permanently in the corner of his mouth.

Yet while Clara's body was rigid, her mind was in perpetual motion. She had arrived here with an important decision – to stay in Germany in the event of war – yet Thomas Epstein seemed not the least bit curious. How long would it be before he got to the substance of their meeting, rather than merely requiring her to sit still and not fidget?

Epstein continued photographing, issuing brief instructions to turn slightly or raise her shoulder, and occasionally darting out from behind the tripod to twirl at the corset's laces, or reposition Clara's arm.

'The corset is a miraculous garment, don't you think? There is something so enticing about it. It implies at once revelation and concealment. Freedom and restraint.'

Not to Joseph Goebbels, it wouldn't. God knows what he would make of the picture if he ever came to see it. The idea of a Reich actress, the representative of the Reich Chamber of Culture, posing for a French magazine dressed only in a corset, could probably land her in jail. Only the previous year he had unleashed a clampdown on actresses who portrayed themselves as 'vamps'. Women like that were a poison to the German nation. Goebbels' favourite costume for an actress was an apron.

Clara consoled herself with the thought that the picture was only a ruse. It would probably never appear in *Vogue* at all. After all, what had Leni Riefenstahl said? *The September issue! That's ambitious. Who knows what will be happening when September comes?*

To divert herself, she asked, 'You're a Berliner too, aren't you, Herr Epstein?'

'My accent, of course. That part of the identity is impossible to erase. You're right, I was born in Dahlem. A wonderful artistic family. They gave me my first camera at the age of ten – a nine by twelve with an ultra-rapid anastigmatic lens, since you ask – and I began my career at sixteen working as an assistant to Yva. The illustrious photographer, you know? She was a superb teacher. She encouraged me to follow my instincts, wherever they led me. Not to be crushed by the narrow morality of the brown plague. Unfortunately, that was almost my undoing.'

'How so?'

'I had been working for seven years. I was a confident young man, almost cocky you might say, and I thought no subject was beyond me, no matter what the Nazis might say. I had taken a portrait of a woman embracing a black man. Very sexy, you know? But it came to the attention of some Nazi, and I received a very unpleasant visit. I would have to leave. Fortunately a doctor friend of mine had a clinic in Paris and agreed to exhibit some of my pictures on his wall with the result that I received a call from *Vogue*. So I joined the exodus. I hope for the sake of her future Yva will do the same.'

He paused and peered around the camera, eyebrow raised.

'But it's *your* future, Miss Vine, that concerns us now. And whether you may be able to help our mutual friends.'

'I'm not sure . . . I hope I can.'

'Good.'

He put down his camera abruptly and motioned her to dress.

'But have you finished? Did you get the photographs you want?'

'I did. Let's talk.'

The flirtatious jollity had gone, to be replaced with a deadly seriousness. Suddenly, Clara could see what made British Intelligence trust a person like Epstein with its secrets.

'You're familiar with the terms live and dead letter boxes?'

She nodded. Live letter boxes were places agents met to pass on messages. Stations, cafés and tourist traps were popular, because it was easier to meet there without attracting undue attention. Dead letterboxes, on the other hand, were locations known to both parties where messages could be left.

'We have a number of dead letter boxes in Berlin, but in this instance you will use a live letter box. When you have something to communicate to us, you can take it there. Have you ever learned a book code?'

'Afraid not.'

'Give me the name of a book you like.'

'Any book?'

'Your favourite novel, perhaps. All that matters is that you must have a copy in your possession. And we must have one precisely the same. Do you have a book with you?'

Clara's hand went to her bag and she couldn't suppress a wry laugh as she found the copy of *The Thirty-Nine Steps*.

'A comedy, is it? Something by your Mr P.G. Wodehouse?'

'No, it's not that. You see, this book couldn't be more appropriate. I've had this novel for a long time, but it's not mine. Years ago, I was invited to the von Ribbentrops' home. They were ardent Anglophiles at the time and they kept a large library of English books. Frau von Ribbentrop invited me to borrow one and I chose this, but somehow I've never had the opportunity to return it.'

She held it out to him.

'It's a first edition. Published by Blackwoods.'

He gave it a peremptory glance.

'Good. Now listen carefully. When you have a message to convey, find the words you want to use, select the page number, followed by the line, followed by the place that word occurs in the line. That way your message will be condensed into a set of figures and the figures operate as a code that can only be decrypted by someone using precisely the same book.'

Clara murmured these instructions to herself the way she learned her lines.

'It should delay any attempt at encryption should our message fall into the wrong hands. It is fairly simplistic, but it's all we have time for right now.'

'So where is this live letter box?'

'The Ritz.'

He laughed at her puzzlement.

'The *Berlin* Ritz. It's a bar in Mulackstrasse. In the Scheunenviertel. Do you know it?'

'I've been there once or twice.'

'There's a bartender there. His name is Benno Kurtz.'

'How will I recognize him?'

'He's in his sixties, has a grey moustache. He was a good-looking fellow in his time and he still thinks a lot of himself.

You'll understand when you see him.' Epstein grinned. 'Benno's very useful to us. When you find him, ask for a gin and tonic made in the English way.'

'I'm not sure what that is.'

'Something diabolical no doubt, knowing the English and their drinks. But no matter. Benno will understand. In the meantime,' he turned casually, and hunted for something in a drawer, 'Major Grand asked me to give you this. It's a Derringer.'

It was a silver pistol, less than five inches long, gleaming treacherously in her hand as if it belonged there. The handle was made of smooth, burled wood, its silver inlay decorated with elaborate swirls of engraving. It looked as beautiful as an elegant, finely worked piece of jewellery. Simply the feel of it made her shudder. How strange that something so deadly should possess such dangerous glamour.

'We call it a stocking gun.'

'It's tiny.'

'It needs to be if you're going to conceal it. But the size means it can only be deadly at short range. There's no room for an automatic mechanism – that would only increase its weight – so you carry it loaded with the hammer at half cock. When you want to use it you move the hammer back to full cock position and pull the trigger. If you misfire, you can pull the hammer back and try again, but it only holds two bullets so there's only the chance for two shots. You can only make one mistake.'

It had such a tactile quality. Clara traced her fingers over the whorled wood and the cool swirls of silver engraving, trying to imagine what went through the mind of the man who fashioned it.

'That pistol has an illustrious history. It was a Derringer that killed Abraham Lincoln.'

'Not so illustrious then.'

He laughed. 'Here's the holster. I suppose you don't want me to show you how to attach it?'

She examined the piece of silky calfskin attached to an elasticated garter.

'I think I can work it out. But Herr Epstein . . . I don't need a gun. I can't imagine that I ever would.'

The smile vanished from Epstein's eyes.

'Only an amateur is unprepared. Keep it with you at all times.'

He watched as she buried it in her bag.

'Our friend in London reminds you that time is pressing. He wants you to contact him within four weeks with whatever information you have obtained.'

'Four weeks is far too soon.'

'On the contrary. Let's hope it's not too late.'

Epstein went over and leaned out of the window, watching the people in the café across the road.

'Look at them down there. Do they have any idea what's coming towards them?'

'Do you?'

'I hear the Germans are planning to mass their tanks on the Polish border by the beginning of September. But Hitler won't stop there. He will certainly look to the west. Belgium, Holland, France. They'll all collapse like a pack of cards. None of them has a chance against a rearmed Germany.'

He lit another Gitane and blew it into the wind.

'Have they any idea of the cruelty, the efficiency, of these Nazis? I have. I tried to leave the fear of it behind, but I suspect I haven't left it far enough. Perhaps it will never leave me. Perhaps it lives inside me.'

'What will you do?'

'I'll be all right. I have my camera and besides, I'm off to America very soon. I've had enough of *Vogue*. The editor, Michel de Brunhoff, swears he would not publish the magazine if the Nazis turn up, but most of the *Vogue* lot are frightful snobs. They're only interested in you if you have a title or a perversion and I suspect they'll be perfectly happy when a bunch of high-born Nazis arrive to occupy their city. Just so long as they're immaculately dressed.'

'So you really believe that the Nazis will occupy Paris?'

'For sure. My concierge friend tells me that some German officers have already made reservations at the Ritz.'

The Ritz. That cocoon of velvet opulence, where women still sat taking tea in Limoges china and choosing between mille-feuilles and éclairs. Where the Duke and Duchess of Windsor kept a suite and Noël Coward regularly dropped in. Clara thought of her brief visit to Coco Chanel's mirrored salon the previous year and wondered if her powder-blue Rolls Royce was still parked outside.

'Does Chanel still live there?'

He laughed. 'She has room 302. Chanel may have liberated women's bodies from corsets but she can't liberate herself from the Nazis. You know about her German boyfriend, of course.'

Chanel's association with Spatz Dincklage was the talk of Paris.

'But surely . . . if it came to an occupation? A famous Frenchwoman like Chanel?'

'Nothing would change. Chanel says she doesn't believe in anything. She only believes in fashion.'

He spun around, all traces of gloom vanished and his lively face transformed.

'You're staying the night, I hope?'

'Just one night. I wish it was more.'

'Then you must come to a party.'

'What kind of party?'

'Does it matter? There are parties every night now. We're making the most of it. It's a reception at the Dingo Bar. There will be all kinds of faces there. Will you come?'

'Why not?'

'In that case I have something for you.'

He went behind the screen and returned again with an armful of shimmering silk which he shook out to reveal a halter-neck evening gown, a fluid drape of deep blue satin, with a backless plunge that culminated in a bow and fell from the waist in sleek Grecian pleats. Clara's eyes widened.

'It's by Alix. Madame Grès. She dresses Marlene Dietrich and Greta Garbo. This frock is one of a kind. You won't find anyone else wearing it.'

Clara couldn't stop herself from touching it, feeling the slippery flow of the satin between her fingers, marvelling at its colour, the blue of a deep summer sea.

'I'm sorry,' she said decisively. 'I can't take it.'

'That's a shame. It's not my size.'

'I mean it's too generous.'

'Miss Vine. You mistake my motivation. I'm off to New York any day now. Do you really think I want to weigh myself down with ladies' gowns?'

Bundling the dress into a bag, Epstein handed it to her with a smile and said, 'Wear it tonight. I'll meet you there. The party will be fun, but be careful please. Don't say anything that could compromise you. The Gestapo are already everywhere. They're deciding who to arrest if war comes.'

It was strange to stroll through the streets of Paris again. Everything about the city sharpened Clara's senses, making her surroundings appear in immense clarity, the details finely set like jewels. In St Germain, people in cafés were eating ice cream from little silver bowls and the scent of frying onions wafting out of an upstairs window made her mouth water. Pungent herbs floated from the door of a spice shop and the intoxicating yeasty aroma of baking bread issuing from a boulangerie was so potent she could barely walk past. She passed galleries and shops full of bric-a-brac, elegant little bookstores and a parfumier whose aromatic floral haze drifted seductively into the street.

Crossing the Seine she reached the first arrondissement, the heart of French fashion. The little streets around the Place

Vendôme and the Rue Cambon were full of milliners and fashion salons and the perfect place for window shopping. On the ground floor were the mirrored cocoons of the haute couturiers with their gilt fittings and silk drapes while above them ateliers of seamstresses bent, patiently stitching the latest creations of Worth and Chanel and Balenciaga. For a moment Clara dallied in front of a blue Schiaparelli jacket, with gold buttons and a rich scarlet lining, before turning away.

In the end she bought some Gauloises – good tobacco was like gold dust in Berlin and people had resorted to stretching it with rose petals and grass – and several bars of Menier chocolate. Then she made her way to the Hotel d'Angleterre.

Chapter Nineteen

The Hotel d'Angleterre in the Rue Jacob was a long way from the Ritz, both in geography and décor. The chandeliers in the gloomy hallway wore a slight coat of dust, the stone steps with their twisty wrought-iron banisters smelled of cleaning fluid and the gilded chairs in the reception area were showing their age. But Clara's room, at the back, overlooking the courtyard, was clean enough, papered in faded *toile de jouy*, with a heavy wooden armoire, a basin prettily tiled with flowered designs and even a bar of soap. She picked it up and sniffed it greedily. It had a fragrance of lemon and cream, so unlike the soap at home that was mostly a rank combination of animal fat overlaid with detergent. After a speculative moment, Clara parcelled the little tablet away in her bag.

She travelled light – she always had – right from her days in repertory theatre in London, so there was not much to unpack. Once she had removed her clean underwear from the suitcase and hung her fresh blouse in the armoire, she washed, then pulled on dark stockings and a pair of lizard-skin T-straps with a peep toe, and reached for the Madame Grès evening dress.

It was beautiful enough laid out on the bed, but when she put it on it came alive. It fitted perfectly and the material, far from being heavy, moved like gossamer. It looked timeless, as a classic dress should, and it possessed a kind of purity that meant it would never date. The glimmering satin clung to her body, flattering her curves at the bodice and flowing in Grecian folds from the waist.

Next she put on Steffi's pearl necklace, feeling its unfamiliar weight heavy against her neck, took out a bottle labelled *Soir de Paris* and touched a dab behind her ears. As the perfume, with its voluptuous notes of vanilla and violet, rose and mingled with the Paris air, it reminded her of Leo, who had loved it, and suddenly it was as though he was standing right there beside her, in the room.

She felt his presence so powerfully that she turned instinctively and stared around her. She felt his smile, his touch, his ironic humour. The shards of gold in his green eyes, the warmth of his arms encircling her. It was as though the whole of his personality had been distilled into an intense and visceral reality.

Was this Leo, or had the force of her longing conjured a phantom out of empty air? Her mind went back to the precious weeks they had spent last year and for the first time she realized that it no longer mattered that she had refused his proposal of marriage. She didn't require any ring from him. Her commitment was deep inside. A band of longing that tightened round her heart when she thought of him. Despite everything she had been told, she held on to the belief she would see him again.

The Dingo Bar was at 10, Rue Delambre, a small street leading south from the Carrefour Vavin. The key to its success was the barman, Jimmie Charters, a one-time boxer from Liverpool, whose jovial presence drew a loyal crowd of wealthy American and British expatriates. Steps led down from the side of the bar to a nightclub crammed with people, as though all the tension and energy of the streets was somehow contained in this crowded arena full of smoke and heat. The dance floor was surrounded by tiny tables and on the dais, a chanteuse was singing Noël

Coward's *Night and Day*. It was one of Clara's favourites, the rhythm tapped out like a heartbeat, its words coiled into her brain:

Whether near to me or far,
No matter, darling, where you are,
I think of you, night and day.

It was almost impossible to move amid the crush of bodies. As her eyes adjusted to the dim light, her gaze snagged on Thomas Epstein at the bar, drinking a Negroni. Beside him, the barman was pouring champagne into a glass containing a slice of peach, a sugar cube and brandy and offering it to a rangily beautiful woman with a clear brow and a loud laugh.

'Who's that?' asked Clara, standing next to Epstein at the bar.

'Lee Miller. Another American. Paris is crammed with them.'

A glance around the bar, at the Brooks Brothers suits and healthy tans, seemed to confirm it.

'Americans are always more optimistic than the rest of us. They won't let any war get in the way of their fun. There's a gossip columnist here, Elsa Maxwell, who has taken to replacing RSVP on her invitations with ICNW. It stands for In Case No War. Amusing, eh?'

'What about the British? Are they still coming to Paris?'

'Sure. They don't dare go to Berlin any more, but Paris is just a hop across the Channel.'

As if on cue, from behind them came a high English voice, strident with self-assurance and too much champagne. Clara turned to see a young woman, her body encased in a metallic silver and jet gown as tight as a bicycle inner tube. There was an empty bottle of champagne at her elbow and she was haranguing an earnest young man, who was braced against the bar, unable to escape. He flinched as she waved her glass in his face.

'Don't tell me there's going to be a war, Jack! What a doom monger you are. Nothing will happen. France lost a million and a half men in the war, can you imagine they will go through that again? For the French, simply having to drink chicory coffee constitutes a major sacrifice.'

'I recognize that woman,' said Clara quietly. 'It's Dolly Capel. She's a friend of our family.'

The Capels were a wealthy landowning dynasty, who had been generous donors to the Anglo-German Fellowship. Their support was heartfelt. They were said to keep a Meissen porcelain statuette of a Nazi stormtrooper on their mantelpiece – a present from von Ribbentrop.

As if sensing she was being watched, Dolly wheeled round, double-took and enveloped Clara in a hot embrace, smelling of sweat and Guerlain's *Mitsouko*.

'Clara! Darling! Fancy finding you here! Where's Angela?'

'My sister? Certainly not here.'

'Aren't you with her? I thought you were with her?'

'She's not in Paris, as far as I know.'

'Isn't she? Well tell her to come. I'm having a simply glorious time. At least here people refuse to let this war talk cramp their style. There's a shop window near me where all the mannequins have gas masks over their shoulders with little coloured bows on. Isn't that just like the French? So elegant. In London it's all Kirby grips and cardigans. The first hint of war and everyone gets out the sackcloth and ashes.'

'Are you on holiday here?' asked Clara, mildly incredulous.

'Absolutely, darling. And I'm making the most of it. I was booked onto a slimming course at a spa but the staff said war was coming and we would all starve so I thought why bother to do the Germans' work for them? Besides, everyone's here. D'you know the Mitfords? I saw Nancy just yesterday. She's been down in Perpignan in the south with that husband of hers, helping Spanish refugees. They're in camps there apparently, on the border, and Nancy had to drive a Ford van full of supplies. Can you imagine? I think it's tired her out because when I bumped into her in the lift of my hotel she was frightfully short with me.'

Sharing a lift with Dolly Capel would reduce anyone to silence, Clara thought.

'She said she's writing a new novel. The pursuit of something. I forget. What's Nancy pursuing, do you think?'

Peace, probably. But Dolly did not stop for an answer.

'Anyhow, I'd just been shopping and bought this adorable frock. I thought it was frightfully slimming but Nancy said I looked like I had been swallowed by a boa constrictor. What do you think?'

'It's very striking.'

'Thank you, sweetie. Oh . . .' As though in an afterthought, Dolly turned to the man beside her and said, 'Have you met Jack? Perhaps I should introduce you two. Clara Vine, this is Jack Kennedy. His father's the American ambassador.'

The young man standing before Clara was exceptionally thin, with a square-jawed, pale face and a broad smile that revealed flawless American teeth. A row of dazzling ivory as regular as piano keys, the kind you never saw in European mouths, filtering black tea and rough tobacco. His expression, too, had an earnest optimism about it that seemed unique to his nation. The family of Joe Kennedy, the American ambassador to London, had cut a swathe through English society and Angela had frequently relayed how glamorous they were and how good at tennis.

He looked at Clara gratefully, scenting escape.

'We haven't met,' she said, taking his hand, 'but you've met my sister Angela Mortimer.'

His skinny frame belied his strength. His handshake was strong enough to crack a safe.

'So you're Angela Mortimer's sister! Are you just over from England too?'

He pulled over a bar stool, took out a pack of Gauloises, leaned forward and flipped a lighter.

'Berlin actually.'

'A tourist?'

'I live there.'

He was instantly focused.

'As it happens, I'm just back from Danzig and Warsaw.'

'What did you make of it?'

'The Poles were dreading a Nazi attack, but I'm not sure. And even if it came, would the Poles really fight over Danzig?'

'Everything's politics with Jack,' said Dolly, bored already. 'Don't expect any chat, Clara. He doesn't make small talk.' She turned to leave, doodling a finger on Clara's shoulder.

'If you do run into Angela, ask her to look me up. I'm at the Montalembert.'

As Dolly disappeared, Clara turned back to the young man with his wide smile and quiet intensity. She guessed that as an ambassador's son, Jack Kennedy might be privy to more information than a regular tourist. Softly she said, 'Yes. I think the Poles will fight. And they'll lose.'

Kennedy sighed, and rubbed his lower back. Perhaps the complexities of what he had witnessed in his tour of Europe had taken a physical toll.

'You know, Miss Vine, at one time I genuinely believed that Fascism was right for Germany and Italy. Their freeways were so impressive. The societies were orderly. I thought their evils were nothing compared with Communism. Now, I'm not so sure. I'm still trying to understand the fascination that surrounds Hitler. Do you understand it?'

Clara thought of the cheering birthday crowd that she had stood in so recently, and the Führer shrine in the home of Lotti Franke.

'A little.'

Something about the expression on Kennedy's face, the earnestness in his eyes, roused in Clara a passionate desire to explain. Here was an American, the son of a very influential figure, who had, until recently, believed that Fascism was the right answer for Europe. Now he was asking her opinion. She must do everything in her power to let him know what the Nazi regime was really like. And yet . . . how much could she tell him, without compromising herself? Even here in Paris, even in the depths of a backstreet bar in Montparnasse, the Gestapo were entrenched. She recalled Epstein's warning. *Don't say anything that could compromise you here. The Gestapo are everywhere already. They're deciding who to arrest if war comes.*

She couldn't stop herself.

'If you'd seen Hitler's birthday parade you would know the extent of his ambitions. He's mobilized two million men. He won't hesitate to attack Poland, if he thinks he can get away without the Soviet Union, Britain or France intervening.'

'But that's precisely what will stop him, isn't it? The Soviet Union.'

'I'm not so sure. We're far too complacent about that. There's speculation about a pact between Germany and Russia.'

'Coming from a family like mine that's always jawing about politics, I know that some people will speculate about anything. Doesn't mean it's going to happen.'

'It might. And if it did, it would allow Hitler to continue his aggression towards the rest of Europe.'

'The French seem very confident about their Maginot Line.'

'Only because they underestimate the National Socialists. Don't let yourself do the same, Mr Kennedy.'

Her mind went back to the document she had seen the previous year. A document which gave first-hand evidence that the leader of Germany did not intend to stop at achieving further Lebensraum for his people. That revealed in unambiguous terms Hitler's ambitions to exterminate the entire Jewish race.

'Their plans for the Jews go beyond anything you can imagine.'

She felt her voice rising, in her effort to persuade him.

'Your father's so influential. Please, go back to London, and beg him not to be deceived about the Nazis. Their ambitions are horrifying, and their efficiency is astonishing. It's a savage, monstrous regime which poses a danger to the whole world.'

She picked up a beer mat and scribbled a name on the underside.

'There's an American journalist you must speak to. Her name is Mary Harker.'

'Where would I find her?'

'She stays at the Adlon in Berlin. She interviewed Goering just the other day. She'll tell you how it is.'

At that point both of Kennedy's arms were seized from behind and he was half-lifted into the air. His captors were a pair of young women who dragged him from his bar stool, laughing and beseeching him to join their table. Apologetically, Kennedy gave Clara a swift wave, and disappeared.

'Bright lad.' Epstein materialized at Clara's side. 'His father uses him as an unofficial diplomat. Probably the only diplomatic thing ever found at the Dingo.'

Already Clara was cursing herself for having spoken out.

'I hope I didn't talk too freely.'

Epstein regarded her closely.

'I'm sure he was listening, whatever you said.'

'He seemed quite relieved to escape.'

'He's probably a little wary of German actresses right now. His father Joe's been having an affair for months with Marlene Dietrich at the Grand Hotel du Cap down on the Côte d'Azur. In fact, you're lucky you met the son and not the father. Joe's unstoppable. They say he sleeps with the friends of his daughters and the daughters of his friends, and just about every Hollywood starlet he can get his hands on.'

Suddenly Clara felt dizzy with the music, the colours and the press of people. Speaking English, not to mention speaking her mind, had been intoxicating, but ditching her normally cautious persona, even for a few minutes, had left her feeling exposed and disorientated. Bidding goodnight to Epstein she made her way up the narrow stairs and went to collect her coat.

The coat check girl had a sharp face, with kohl-lined eyes and heavily lacquered lips. She was wearing a modest little outfit with white collar and cuffs, but the modesty only extended as far as the briefest of skirts and a pair of fishnet stockings. As she handed over the coat she gave Clara a conspiratorial wink.

'You have an admirer, mademoiselle.'

'I shouldn't think so.'

After the talk of Joe Kennedy, Clara was in no mood for admirers.

'He was certainly very interested in you.'

'Who was?'

The girl gave a slow, crimson smile.

'A gentleman. He left just now. You'll catch him if you hurry. If you want to catch him, that is.'

'I'm pretty sure I don't.'

'Shame. He looked nice.'

Was this how all Parisiennes behaved, thought Clara? As though they were duty bound to establish an assignation? Sex, and the possibility of it, was never far from their thoughts. Perhaps that was the unspoken code of Paris.

The girl leaned over the counter, with a surge of sweat and perfume. Her breath smelled of French tobacco and garlic.

'I didn't hear him speak but he was foreign, I think.'

A sudden spark of excitement leapt in her. A foreign man had been looking at her. Could it possibly be Leo? Was that sense of him in the hotel a premonition? Some kind of subliminal awareness that he was near?

'If he didn't speak, how could you tell he was foreign?'

The girl pursed her lips into a magnificent pout at her expertise being called into question and gave a shrug that expressed her absolute conviction.

'I know a Frenchman when I see one and this man was certainly not French.'

It had to be him! Surely this was why Major Grand had set up a meeting in Paris. He wanted to direct her to the place where Leo could be found.

'What did he look like?'

'He was wearing a Loden coat. No Frenchman wears a coat like that.'

But Leo did.

'There was a look about him,' the girl added. 'He was interested in you. A woman can tell.'

Her pulse quickening, Clara bundled on her jacket and dropped a *pourboire* into the saucer.

'Which way did he go?'

'He turned left at the top of the stairs. Heading towards the Boulevard du Montparnasse. It was a few minutes ago. You'll have to hurry if you want to catch him.'

As Clara emerged from the narrow stairway, the breath of raw night air hit her face. She looked the length of the street but there was no familiar figure of Leo waiting on the corner. Even from a distance, she felt sure she would recognize that brush of red-gold hair, and lean, sinewy frame, the hands, as always, plunged deep in his pockets. Decisively, she turned towards the Boulevard du Montparnasse and onto the Boulevard Raspail.

Paris at night, without a map to guide her and only the memory of a single previous visit to orientate herself, was a chiaroscuro world. The city of lights was unrecognizable in darkness. Restaurants were beginning to close, and shadows piled on shadows, deepening like layers of indigo gauze. Lamps cast pools of light on the pavements but between the high-sided buildings, narrow alleyways receded into blackness. Clara had memorized the route back to the Rue Jacob, but how, in this darkened city, amid unfamiliar streets, did she even begin to look for a single man in a Loden overcoat? Should she turn left, or right? Her only thought was to head in the direction of her hotel. If Leo had found her at the bar, perhaps he also knew where she was staying.

In the Latin Quarter faint traces of jazz leaked out of the basement bars and the bright neon of La Coupole hung in the still night air. She passed the vast shadows of the Luxembourg gardens, scanning the streets around her constantly. The ghost of Leo was around every corner. Memory played tricks and sleights of hand, so that several times she thought she saw a familiar building, only to discover when she came closer that she had taken entirely the wrong turn.

At last she saw him. A figure in a Loden coat and hat, striding swiftly, a hundred metres away. Too far to hear her if she called. But almost as soon as she had glimpsed him, he was swallowed behind a passing van. She hurried on, her heart bursting with excitement. It was odd to be the pursuer rather than the pursued. She was so accustomed to the idea of surveillance that she had often thought herself into the shadow's mind. How to hang back when approaching the quarry. Never get too close, yet never lose sight of the target. But this chase was different. Clara actually wanted to catch up, but the figure ahead of her seemed determined to evade her pursuit.

Towards St Germain, as the severe geometry of the mellow stone buildings gave way to a labyrinth of cobbled streets, following became trickier. Clara had lied when she told Goebbels that she didn't need spectacles. In truth, it was getting harder to see distant objects at night. In the darkness the faces of passers-by loomed dim and indistinct like figures in a painting by Edvard Munch. A drunk stumbled into a doorway. She turned her ankle on the cobbles – her heels were too high – and wished passionately that she had not chosen to wear the silk dress, which was now damp and flecked with dirt at the hem. Still she ploughed on, turning back once or twice to re-orientate herself until, eventually, she drew to a halt beside the shuttered grill of a shop.

It was plain that the man she was following was lost from sight, and what was more, she had no idea where she was. She decided to retrace her steps to the nightclub. At the very least, there she could find a taxi and return to the hotel in the Rue Jacob.

Just then, out of the corner of her eye she caught it. The whisk of a coat around a corner. She glanced down a thin alleyway, no wider than an arm's stretch, and saw him again, slipping like a blade of shadow until, at the end, the view opened up to the broad span of the Seine and the man before her had vanished.

He must have crossed the river. Clara walked swiftly across the Pont des Arts towards the classical façade of the Louvre and into the Cour Carrée, the magnificent cobbled courtyard in the western wing. Then, at last, she saw him. Leaning against the pillar, his exaggerated shadow lying diagonal along the ground, his overcoat slung elegantly like a cloak over his shoulders. As he cupped his hand to light a cigarette, the flame leapt up to his face and she realized that it wasn't Leo at all.

'Fräulein Vine. What a surprise to see you here.'

It was the handsome, sardonic face of Conrad Adler.

Chapter Twenty

The surprise was enough to stun her for a moment. The breath tore at her lungs from the speed of her long pursuit, and the blood was still pounding in her ears. Shock, and disappointment that the man she had pursued was so different from the one she longed to see, robbed her of speech. For a second the image of Leo still imprinted itself on her vision, so that she had to shake her head to dismiss it, before focusing on the man who genuinely stood in front of her. Obersturmbannführer Conrad Adler.

He was wearing a smart navy suit, rather than uniform, and the rigid perfection she had observed in him before was exaggerated in the lamplight, making the curve of his jaw and the perfectly carved planes of his face stand out in sharp relief. She slowed her pace as she approached him.

'What are you doing here?'

Even to her own ears, it sounded curt, and although the urbane smile remained in place, she sensed that she had caught him unawares. Both of them were dissembling.

'I might ask the same of you. When we met you didn't mention that you were going to be in Paris. We could have shared the journey.'

She ignored the invitation to explain herself.

'I asked why you're here.'

'I'm visiting the Louvre.'

'It's closed at night.'

He took a draw of his cigarette and exhaled a slow jet of smoke into the night air.

'As a matter of fact you're wrong. It appears to be open for business.'

He pointed to a truck, its back doors open and a ramp leading up. An arc light illuminated a path where large wooden boxes were being wheeled. A team of workmen moved swiftly, silently, stacking a succession of enormous crates. It was not hard to discern their contents. The Louvre was removing its treasured paintings, steadily and methodically, under cover of darkness.

'Anyway, it's fortuitous that I should run into you just now.' Adler's tone was mild and conversational, as though they had bumped into each other on the Ku'damm, rather than engaged in a close pursuit through a maze of Paris streets. 'Because I've been finding out all about you. Researching you.'

'Researching?' she said mildly, attempting to suppress her alarm. 'I can't imagine why.'

'But it was your idea! I was following your advice. You suggested that I might be out of touch with popular culture, so I decided to watch all of your films. *Black Roses*, *The Pilot's Wife*, *Es leuchten die Sterne*. Now I've seen everything you've appeared in, I feel I know you so much better.'

'You've actually been watching my films?' she echoed, relieved.

'Every one. Ask me anything. In fact—' he drew closer, 'why don't we talk about it over dinner? You're certainly dressed for it.' His eyes trawled the length of her blue silk gown. 'There's a place I know. I think you might like it.'

In one way, there was nothing Clara wanted less than dinner with this Nazi official and his sharp, derisive sense of humour, yet having her hopes of finding Leo so rapidly dashed, a crushing emotional exhaustion had descended on her. She hadn't eaten since the café that afternoon, and her senses piqued treacherously at what would no doubt be a fine French restaurant. And the words of Major Grand rang again in her ears.

'*Any way we have into the Foreign Ministry. It's urgent, I don't need to remind you.*'

Conversation with a Foreign Ministry official, a man close to von Ribbentrop, who might be expected to know his mind and the chances of any Nazi-Soviet negotiations, might be the perfect opportunity.

And yet . . . what did Adler want? Was it her company or something more? If he was watching her in the Dingo Bar, did he overhear her incautious comments to Jack Kennedy?

She summoned a cheerful smile.

'Well I *am* awfully hungry. And it's not too late. Where's this place you know?'

'It's called Lapérouse. It's just across the river. Along the Quai des Grands-Augustins.'

She had fully expected Adler to frequent the Ritz, Maxim's or Fouquet's, one of the big statement places that Nazi officers favoured, the kind of place that spelt out Paris in neon letters to the wide-eyed foreigner, with a trip afterwards to the Folies-Bergères. Yet Lapérouse was clearly a place for the cognoscenti. The walls and ceilings were painted with eigthteenth-century pastorals of gods and shepherds. Through a swing door she glimpsed a floor-to-ceiling rack of bottles, their dusty bottoms gleaming like blackberries. Ancient gas lamps hung over tables laid with starched napkins. It was packed with diners.

As if reading her thoughts, he said, 'Most Germans who come to Paris make for the obvious destinations, but I like this place. It was created by a man called Lefèvre who kept wines for Louis XIV. Flaubert, Zola, Victor Hugo, George Sand, all came here. Escoffier used to run the kitchen. In the back there are private rooms with couches where French aristocrats take their mistresses. A charming idea, don't you think?'

He helped her with her jacket, lingering a fraction too long as he did and letting his hand slip down the silk of her dress. As the waiter showed them to a table in a small alcove, she glanced at her reflection in an ancient, mottled mirror and adjusted the clip in her hair, before chiding herself for her vanity. Why was she bothering to look her best?

Although Adler spoke flawless French, he inspired the same chilly deference in restaurant staff that Clara had seen directed at Germans throughout the city. Beneath a surface of unctuous servility, the familiar French superiority remained. The manager brought a bottle with a sepia label and Adler gestured for him to pour it for Clara. She took a sip, astonished at the mellow warmth that slipped down her throat, redolent of chocolate and spice.

He smiled at her reaction.

'It's a good burgundy. See the way it has legs?' He pointed to the drip of wine, slowly funnelling its way down the glass. 'A single drop is probably worth more than a month of most people's salaries.'

'Please don't spend money on my account.'

'Why not? If it gives me pleasure.'

She wondered how old Adler was. Mid-forties, she guessed. The steeliness of his Aryan looks and silvered hair marked him out from the more sallow complexions of the French around him. His grey, metallic eyes reminded her of the surface of a lake, sometimes flat and impersonal, occasionally bottomless. He looked so different from the other Nazis she knew. Unlike Goebbels with his endless sessions beneath the sun lamp, or Goering's futile efforts on an exercise machine, Adler glowed with health and self-assurance.

'That's a beautiful dress you're wearing. I hope the occasion was worth it.'

'It was, thank you.'

'My favourite colour. Prussian blue.'

'I didn't realize you were an expert on haute couture.'

'I'm not. Prussian blue is famous. It was created by a Berlin chemist in 1706 and because we know the exact date it means we can use it to authenticate paintings. There are numerous apparently genuine Old Masters that have been betrayed by the presence of Prussian blue. Painters love it. Picasso could not have managed his Blue period without it. You can see it in Van Gogh's *Starry Night*. As it happens, I can also see it in your eyes.'

She couldn't help a wry smile at this flirtation. Perhaps it was the fact that they were not in Germany, or the delicious aromas of the cooking rising around them, but she relaxed.

'That's a first. No one has ever described my eyes as Prussian blue before.'

'With a few small flaws.'

'You spoilt it.'

'Not at all. Everything's more beautiful for having flaws.'

The waiter appeared and Adler gestured towards her.

'Duck with olives? Would you like lobster? I haven't had lobster for such a long time. The Führer hates to think of them suffering.'

She shook her head. The scale of this hypocrisy seemed too great, just then, to merit comment.

Once he had ordered, he surveyed her, deadpan.

'I've been longing to know. What news of *Love Strictly Forbidden*?'

There was a curl of soft sarcasm in his voice, and despite herself, Clara was nettled.

'Actually, I'm starting work on a new film with Leni Riefenstahl.'

'Now that lady even I have heard of.'

'It's about the Ahnenerbe.'

His eyes widened at this information.

'Himmler's organization?'

'Yes.'

'I wouldn't have thought that was a fit subject for entertainment.'

'Fräulein Riefenstahl thinks otherwise.'

'And what do you think?'

Privately, Clara had to agree. Memories of the rows of skulls and the fusty old books in the Ahnenerbe library came back to her. The preoccupations of the Ahnenerbe didn't seem at all the right subject to ignite the enthusiasm of a nation, let alone to showcase the dubious glories of Nazi Germany. But if anyone could make an epic out of it, it was Leni Riefenstahl. She had, after all, managed to transform the Nuremberg Party rally into two hours' compulsive viewing.

'I'm sure Leni Riefenstahl knows what she's doing.'

The food was astounding. It was a long time since Clara had tasted rich creamy dishes that didn't have the telltale tang of petrol about them. Between courses a sorbet was brought to cleanse the palate. She had to remind herself to stick to her task.

'You didn't explain. I mean really explain, what you're doing here.'

'Nor did you.'

'That's easy. I was being photographed for *Vogue*.'

Adler cupped his face in one hand, a cigarette poised between his fingers, and scrutinized her.

'Were you? I hope they've done you justice. It would be hard to capture a face like yours.'

She laughed. 'Actually, this photographer didn't want to photograph my face at all.'

'Shame. Now I've watched some of your films I see how it responds to light. It changes entirely. I'm almost sorry they invented talking pictures. Your face would have done so well in silent films.'

'Are you saying, Herr Adler, that I'd look better if I kept quiet?'

He laughed. 'That applies to most women, but perhaps not you.' He stroked a pensive finger down his wine glass.

'I'd like to feel your face beneath my fingers. At least, I would start with your face and proceed downwards.'

She stared at him. The urbanity of his manner was entirely at odds with the audacity of the remark. Despite herself, her pulse quickened.

'Don't mistake me. All I mean is that beauty can't be fully appreciated through the eyes. It takes the other senses too, the sense of touch, taste, smell, to experience another person. And you have a particular glamour about you. A dangerous glamour.'

'I don't see why glamour has to be dangerous.'

He leaned forward.

'Glamour is dangerous, because it distracts the eye. It's like a jewel. It sparkles and dazzles and prevents us from seeing what is really there. Even the word itself has associations of enchantment and magic. *Glanz*. It means illusion. It implies radiance or lustre, flashiness designed to distract. Ask Herr Doktor Goebbels. He knows all about it. It's not by chance that his newspapers season every line of soldiers with pictures of actresses.'

'If I did have any glamour, which I dispute, I'm sure you'd see through it.'

'I would certainly hope so. I pride myself on seeing through things.'

He reached over and touched the pearls at her throat with a fingertip.

'These are good quality. I like women wearing pearls.'

The unexpected contact caused Clara to flinch.

'A pearl has a character. It starts with a tiny piece of grit, deep in the heart of the oyster. The oyster is troubled by this, yet gradually it learns how to resist. It builds up its armour, layer upon layer, until at last, in the secret darkness, a pearl is produced. An object of total beauty, with a piece of grit at its heart. Perhaps that's what I like: the thought that beneath all that beauty lies a tough, unglamorous little piece of grit.'

What was he saying? Clara ducked her head to avoid his eyes and watched the candlelight flickering in the bowl of her glass.

He asked, 'Do you collect jewellery?'

She laughed. 'Hardly.'

'I'm surprised. Most women I know are dripping in jewels and furs.'

'Then I'm obviously not like most women you know.'

'That much is plain.' His eyes swept over her with forensic precision, as though monitoring her for any further deviations from the norm.

'I think, perhaps, you remind me of a Vermeer painting. Vermeer loved women in pearls, though of course the pearls he painted weren't real at all, they were made of glass, because the price of pearls was too high.'

'They look so convincing.'

'That's because Vermeer understood light. As well as any Ufa cameraman. Better, no doubt. He saw how light fell on a face and the fold of a gown. How it sometimes sparkles, and sometimes glimmers or gleams. He was skilled at perspective, too. Some Vermeer canvases have tiny holes in them where he has stuck a pin so that he could attach strings to help the line of perspective.'

'You know a lot about him.'

He refilled her glass and handed it to her, his fingertips skimming hers deliberately.

'Vermeer was my speciality. The subject of my doctorate. He left us only thirty-five paintings, yet such a great legacy. The Führer loves him too, above all others. He believes the tradition of Northern Renaissance realism will be the building block of the new Germanic empire. He has already bought Vermeer's *Art of Painting* for his museum in Linz and he paid more for it than he has paid for any painting ever.'

Adler paused as the waiter brought a dish of desserts and he pushed them towards her. It was an assiette – a miniature version of every dessert on the menu – wild strawberries sprinkled with white wine, tiny diamonds of marzipan shaped into jewel-like petit fours and fruit tarts with scalloped edges. Clara picked a truffle and felt her head swim as the unaccustomed rich chocolate swirled in her mouth.

'You were saying . . . what you're really doing in Paris?'

'I'm advising on a collection.'

That was no surprise. All Germans were collectors now. From Himmler's grisly skulls, to the cigarette cards collected by the children and the jars of coffee hoarded by the housewives. Their collections were like flimsy bulwarks, shored up against the fear of what was to come.

'Paintings?'

'Various things.'

His eyes flickered with amusement at the cautious tango of their conversation. The wine was dancing in her veins, and the thought occurred to her that perhaps she had misjudged Conrad Adler. Perhaps he was nothing more than he said – an art lover who found himself co-opted into the Foreign Ministry and was bored with the daily detail of politics.

Adler called for the bill and stood while the waiter helped her on with her jacket. But as they walked outside, he gripped her arm.

'Walk with me a while, if you would. It's a full moon and, after all, moonlight is how Paris is meant to be seen.'

He slung his coat over his shoulder and Clara felt the warmth of his arm through his jacket. Moonlight slid over the cobble-stones and turned the Seine beside them into a flat metallic gleam.

'If war comes, that river will be a guide for bombers,' she commented.

'I wouldn't worry. Hitler will never bomb Paris.'

'You sound very sure.'

'The Führer says that Paris is his favourite city in the world, despite the fact that he's never even seen it.'

'How can he know?'

'Because he has studied every architectural monument, every building, every map and street. He spends his evenings poring over pictures and street plans. You have no idea of Hitler's attention to detail.'

Clara did. And she was beginning to understand it enough to know that when Hitler paid attention, others should watch out.

'How do you know all this?'

'I was present once, when he wanted advice on a matter of architectural history.'

They continued walking, for a while, in silence. Clara found herself relaxing, even enjoying their meandering path, and she had to force herself to return to Major Grand's request.

'Do you miss the Foreign Ministry? It must be annoying to leave at such a busy time.'

'Busy?'

'I mean with the diplomatic moves being made. Danzig and everything.' She hesitated a moment, then added, 'I've heard talk that Ribbentrop is making overtures towards Russia.'

He looked at her sharply.

'And where would you hear talk like that, I wonder?'

'People at the studios were discussing it.'

'And there was I thinking that actresses spent their time talking about make-up and partying. But now I see that between scenes in *Love Strictly Forbidden* the cast is fiercely debating the intricacies of foreign diplomacy.'

Clara could not help the flush rising to her face.

'Your prejudices about people you have never met astonish me.'

He stopped and looked down at her, a slow smile spreading across his face.

'I'm glad I astonish you. It wouldn't do to be dull.'

His gaze was unflinching, and she felt as though she had never been so closely scrutinized by anyone. For a second, she felt a sharp, reciprocal tug of attraction. The closeness of Adler, the clean, fresh smell of him, undercut with hot, masculine musk, and that smile, as though the two of them shared some private knowledge. He was attractive, there was no denying it, but she jerked away so that he would not divine it.

He leaned even closer, cupping her head as if to kiss her, but instead he bent and whispered in her ear.

'There's something wild about you, Clara Vine. Something secret. Which I intend to uncover.'

She jerked away. The arrogance, the sheer presumption of that remark! It was clear the kind of man he was. Presumably Adler thought all his flaws, his vanity and sense of superiority, were in fact strengths.

'I doubt you'll get the chance.'

'Let's wait and see.'

'You'll be waiting a long time.'

'I'm a patient man.'

They walked for a little in silence, until Clara forced herself to return to the matter in hand.

'So we're wrong, are we? About Russia?'

A weariness entered his tone.

'As I said, I haven't been into the Foreign Ministry recently. And as a matter of fact, I'm glad to be out of it.'

'What did you actually do for von Ribbentrop in London?'

He shrugged. 'The usual diplomatic rounds. I met people. Eased the diplomatic channels.'

'Did you enjoy Britain?'

'Immensely. I enjoyed London society but I admired British culture even more. The museums, the concerts, the theatre. The National Gallery was a few minutes from my office at Carlton House Terrace and I used to go in my lunch hour and look at the paintings. It was such a pleasure. Unfortunately art doesn't seem enough for most people. They seem to need drums, flag-waving parades. Films. Cheap sentimentality.'

Ignoring the slight, she continued.

'And did you enjoy the work?'

He grunted. 'Unfortunately, working so closely with our Foreign Minister was not so civilized. Von Ribbentrop sees conspiracies everywhere. He thinks Goering and Goebbels are plotting to have him assassinated, or they're hand in glove with British Intelligence. The Embassy was bristling with concealed listening devices. We used to amuse ourselves by holding conversations for his benefit. *Do you think Ribbentrop is as great as Bismarck? No, I think he's greater.* Schoolboy stuff, but a sense of humour was essential in that place.'

Clara steeled herself not to look around, to check who might be listening. She was astonished at the freedom with which he was speaking his mind in public, yet the last thing she wanted was for Adler to stop talking.

'Hitler used to say von Ribbentrop seems to know everyone, but Goering said the problem was that everyone also knew von Ribbentrop,' he continued. 'The man's a buffoon. He has convinced the Führer that the British are ruled by a decayed and privileged clique who will never allow their country to go to war. His wife's even worse. She may be a stickler for correct behaviour, but she hated curtseying to royalty. Her influence on Hitler is strong and believe me . . .' he glanced at her thoughtfully, 'she utterly detests the British.'

'I heard.'

'It was her time in London that did it. When the Führer came to power he favoured a partnership with the British – he saw the British Empire as a template for his own plans for expansion. But they laughed at Frau von Ribbentrop and now she has a very different agenda. In fact, if she has her way . . .'

He stopped to guide Clara across the road to the ancient white Pont-Neuf, arching over the black mirror of the Seine to the Ile de la Cité, with the looming mediaeval bulk of Notre Dame beyond. The pale stone was punctuated by iron lamps that cast pools of soft light in the darkness, and Adler paused in one of the alcoves, leaning on the balustrade, gazing into the ink-black water below.

'How is it you're so familiar with Frau von Ribbentrop's thoughts?'

'She took a shine to me.'

'Can't think why.'

Adler acknowledged Clara's implication with a dip of his head.

'True. I was a single man, away from home, with no ties. Extremely rich and of more than adequate social rank. She is infinitely more intelligent than that husband of hers, and besides, Annelies was bitterly jealous that he was sending carnations to Wallis Simpson, the English King's lover, at the time. And of course, we shared a passion.'

He laughed at Clara's puzzlement.

'Nothing as exciting as you imagine. She studied Art History in Munich. She liked to swap professional expertise with me. I think she felt it might lead to something more, but I preferred to keep to the subject of painting. She owns several important pieces herself – Courbet and Manet and even a Madonna by Fra Angelico. She brought it to London with her and rigged it up to a burglar alarm. Unfortunately the thing kept going off, causing a complete evacuation of the Embassy every time.'

Clara laughed. The earlier tensions of her chase through the streets had dissipated and she found herself enjoying Adler's company. There were far worse situations than to be here in Paris, enclosed in the ivory circle of lamplight, with only the comforting rumble of the city around them, the occasional hoot of traffic and the laughing murmur of a group of men walking beneath them on the banks of the Seine.

'Did you work in the art world professionally? Before going into politics?'

'For years. I lectured first, then did a little dealing, and advised on authenticity. Funnily enough, Art was not my first love. Philosophy was. When I was a student I thought I might make a future in that, but eventually I chose Art. Philosophy is a stricter mistress. It requires a mind as hard as diamond. That's what I admire the Jews for. They cherish the intellect. You should appreciate that, Clara,' he added, 'being Jewish yourself.'

His words went through her like a knife. Clara froze. The relaxation she had felt until that moment, the pleasure in his company, evaporated instantly. The warmth of his manner, the conversation about art, had encouraged her to relax and let down her guard, yet here was a senior Nazi officer, casually dismissing her carefully constructed persona. At once the sounds of the city, the murmur of traffic, fell away, and it was just herself and Adler, looking at each other eye to eye.

'That's not true,' she protested, quietly.

'Isn't it? Let's see your documents then.'

Everyone in Germany was accustomed to showing their ID. In Berlin it happened all the time and both of Clara's documents had always passed scrutiny. She kept them together, in a small calfskin wallet in her bag. The Deutsches Reich Kennkarte, the compulsory grey identity card complete with photograph and fingerprints, and together with it, the red cardboard document with an eagle on the cover containing an Aryan certificate, the *Ariernachweis,* confirming that Fräulein Clara Vine was a member of the German race, possessing birth and baptismal records of her parents and grandparents and a genealogy table going back to 1850. It was the document required for all members of the Reich Chamber of Culture and it had been procured for her six years ago by Leo, the Jewish ancestry of her mother and grandmother expertly replaced with Christian blood. For a second she contemplated telling Adler that she had come out without her papers, but no German would risk being without them, even in a foreign country. Even here in Paris.

She handed them to him.

Adler took a brief look.

'Impressive.'

'What do you mean?' A chill went through her.

'An obvious forgery.'

'Don't joke.'

'You forget, my dear, in my business I have plenty of experience in spotting fakes. And this is a fake. It's a good one, I admit, but it has certain elements that mark it out instantly to a trained eye. The colour of the eagle – that imperial purple – is not quite precise, for example.'

Clara was rooted to the spot, fighting the urge to flee. What was she to make of his nonchalant dismissal of the document that had served her so well for the past six years?

'I don't know what you're talking about.'

'Don't you?' he asked boredly, lighting a cigarette. 'I'm surprised. You seem such an intelligent woman.'

Clara forced herself not to look around and check if their conversation was being overheard. What else did Adler know about her, that she had so confidently believed was concealed?

He scrutinized the cards closer, squinting in the lamplight.

'A specialist, you see, is trained to tell the genuine article through the minutest scrape in the paint or the pattern of brush-strokes. I can see a forgery in a patch the size of a thumbnail. My eye is honed to authenticity in the same way as a piano tuner can tell if an instrument is tuned. I know all about provenance. So I know yours.'

Clara did not trust herself to speak. The man next to her held her entire future, her work as a member of the Reich Chamber of Culture, her credibility with the senior Nazis, her freedom itself, in the palm of his hand.

'You should get a new one made. Tell your man to pay more attention to the colour. And the bleeding of the ink at the edge of the stamp. Just there. That kind of definition can be hard to replicate with cork stamps.'

'Please give it back to me.'

He was enjoying himself.

'In a minute. You see, it's interesting to mark how they've made the forgery. This stamp here . . .'

'Give it to me. Now!'

Clara reached to snatch the documents from his hand but as she did, he jerked them up out of her reach and she stumbled and collided with his chest. Adler put out an arm to steady her, clasping her to him, and in the process lost hold of the cards, which spiralled upwards, into the air, then pirouetted lazily down behind them into the shifting, sliding waters twenty metres below. Instantly, they both reached over the balustrade and stared as the pale flash of Clara's cards flickered a second on the surface before being engulfed in the vast, swirling water of the Seine.

'Forgive me . . .'

At that moment the rumble of a well-tuned engine caused them to turn. A black Mercedes, shiny as a jackboot, pulled up on the bridge alongside them and a man climbed out of the back. He was in his forties, balding and thuggish, dressed in a clearly expensive evening suit, and he leant against the car, lazily snapping a pair of calfskin gloves as he regarded them. In a second Adler's deportment changed.

'Herr Adler. I've been looking for you. But as so often you've found yourself a more appealing diversion.'

Adler stiffened. His eyes lost their flash and became flinty and unreadable. His face was formal again, sculpted into official disinterest. He was transformed into the sober Obersturmbannführer.

'I'm afraid I must leave you.'

Clara was still too dumbstruck by the loss of her documents to make a proper reply. She gazed at him in desperation.

'Please don't let me hurry you, Herr Obersturmbannführer.' The man had a lascivious gleam in his eye. 'I wouldn't want to interfere with private . . . *affairs*. But if you have finished with this young lady I would remind you that we do have some pressing business.'

Adler bowed and gave Clara a swift hand-kiss, leaving her only with the rough brush of his cheek against her skin and a sense of utter desolation as he turned abruptly and climbed into the car.

Chapter Twenty-one

Hedwig loved the library at the Ahnenerbe. It was her secret domain. Other people assumed she enjoyed her workplace because it was in an upmarket part of the city, amid leafy, pine-scented streets where expensive cars stood in the driveways, but it wasn't anything to do with that. When she was in here the outside world dissolved away, and she was alone in an exotic space, smelling of floor wax and the concentrated must of ancient wisdom. She loved the idea of History; that things had been going on for thousands of years and would continue long after they were all gone. Everyone kept telling her they were living in historic times, by which they meant the Führer's birthday and the expansion of the Reich, but that wasn't the kind of history Hedwig liked. For her, History was about an ancient world and most of all it was about books. At home they hardly had any books – only a couple of children's fairy stories and Goebbels' autobiography *From the Kaiserhof to the Reich Chancellery*. And a big picture book called *The Growth, Struggle and Victory of the NSDAP*, which her parents had collected from coupons in their cigarette packets and exchanged for real snapshots of the Führer, to be stuck in like an actual family album. But the books here were different.

The books at the Ahnenerbe were fragile manuscripts with strange scents of spice and leather. Some were so old their leaves furled up like tobacco and their ink was clotted and dark as if they had been written in blood. She imagined them preserved on their shelves like fossils, their wisdom gradually hardening and solidifying, compressed between the pages like dirt turning into diamonds. Some books had photographs in them of natives, looking into the camera with alien, thousand-yard stares. When Lotti used to come and visit the Ahnenerbe – no one ever minded Lotti visiting – Hedwig would guide her proudly around the library and Herr Doktor Kraus would join in, explaining to Lotti how the Tibetans and Mongolians, with their exotic faces like crinkled autumn leaves, were really part of the Aryan tribe. 'Why do they want to be Aryans?' Lotti demanded. 'Why couldn't they stay being themselves?' Secretly, Hedwig agreed. It was hard to believe that all those flat-faced tribesmen could possibly come from the same Aryan family as her. Then again, it was often hard to believe that her own parents came from the same family as her.

Her mother had started again last night.

'I hope you haven't been seeing that boy.'

They were in the kitchen, preparing dinner on the scarred oak table. The kitchen, with its dark brown papered walls, was the warmest room in the apartment, courtesy of the coke stove from which clouds of steam were unfurling. The damp, urinous smell of boiling laundry mingled with a bone broth on the stove. Kurt was perched in a high chair for Hedwig to feed him, looking around with a bright excitement as if everything they did was a game.

Trussed in an apron, chopping potatoes, Mutti looked hot and fat. Six babies may have earned her a silver Mother's Cross, made of blue enamel with the motto *Der Deutschen Mutter* and displayed in a proud frame on the parlour wall, but six pregnancies had left layers of flesh around her middle like the rings around a tree.

'Jochen's not a boy. He's twenty-one,' Hedwig protested, not actually denying their meeting. She offered a spoonful of porridge to Kurt and he turned his head just before it reached his mouth, so the spoon collided with his cheek and he laughed.

Mutti tossed the potatoes into her stew and gave it a savage poke, then began decapitating the green fronds from the carrots.

'He looks like a Bolshevik.'

Hedwig knew for a fact that Mutti didn't know what a Bolshevik looked like. Reiner and Wolfgang came in and began wrestling on the floor, tumbling like puppies until their mother smacked them on the back of their heads. Kurt observed proceedings with a lordly air.

'How could he possibly be a Bolshevik when he spends all day painting the Führer? You liked that painting he gave you.'

Mutti allowed the truth of this with a grudging tilt of her head. She began peeling carrots and Kurt reached out for the bright festive ribbons that curled onto the tabletop.

'He wasn't in the HJ though.'

'So what? He'll still be called up if there's a war.'

'There's something about him I don't trust.'

'There's nothing wrong with him!'

Mutti turned round and nodded savagely towards Kurt.

'So if he's going to be called up, why throw yourself away, Hedwig? You want to be a widow before the age of twenty-two stuck with some screaming brat in an apartment the rough end of Pankow?'

Oblivious to the bad press he was getting, Kurt slapped his hands into the bowl, spattering porridge everywhere, then wiped them on his hair. Hedwig often wondered if Kurt owed his existence to the enticing prospect of the silver Mother's Cross, which qualified her mother for all sorts of privileges and better treatment on public transport. No one with a silver Mother's Cross would ever find herself standing on a tram or at the back of the bread queue. Then she chided herself. Mutti loved children, even if it didn't seem like it most of the time and perhaps Kurt's difficult birth, or his playfulness, accounted for the fact that she never seemed to show him much affection. Secretly Hedwig had vowed to make up for that. As she took a cloth to his chubby face, Kurt chuckled and reached his sticky fingers out to catch her braids.

'You met Vati when you were eighteen.'

Mentioning that was a mistake. It was no doubt her own experience that led Frau Holz to warn her daughter off any hasty decisions. That was why Hedwig was at the Faith and Beauty Society, trying to be something she was not.

'Vati's not a Communist.'

'Nor is Jochen.'

'What is he then?'

'He's an artist.'

Mutti started on a turnip, slicing off its sprout with surgical precision and reducing it to dice.

'You'll waste everything, Hedwig. Everything your parents have given you. All your heritage.'

Heritage. That word again. The word that seemed to obsess everyone. The word that she heard every day at the Ahnenerbe. Your Aryan Heritage. As though everything in life was about pretending you were a certain kind of person – pure and uncomplicated – when in fact everyone, not just Hedwig, was a glorious mixture of contradictions. Who cared who her grandparents were, that Jochen's mother was Polish or that Jochen's grandfather had been a farm labourer?

'Did you meet him through Lotti?'

Hedwig glared at her mother. Lotti might be responsible for many things, but Jochen was not one of them.

'No.'

Hedwig wished Mutti could see Jochen for what he really was. She knew at heart that her mother's true disappointment was in her own life and her chief hope was that her only daughter would do better for herself. Valiantly, Hedwig tried a rapprochement.

'It's Irna Wolter's wedding this Saturday.'

This sparked an interest.

'It's going to be a classy affair,' Hedwig added, presenting the details up like a peace offering, to allay the focus on her own, unsatisfactory romance. 'It's at a castle that belongs to the SS.'

'That sounds lovely.'

The glow in her mother's eyes was almost enough to make up for her previous disappointment. But not quite.

'So where were you, then, yesterday evening? If not seeing that boy?'

'I was visiting Frau Franke.'

It was true. Udo Franke was still drowning his sorrows at the bar down the street, so Marlene was all alone in the stuffy apartment. Hedwig had forced herself to stay an hour, trying to breathe through her mouth so as not to inhale the stink of fried onions and enduring repeated, sweaty hugs from Marlene, who clutched Hedwig to her pillowy bosom as though for a few moments she was able to retrieve her own child. Marlene was so different from her elegant daughter. Lotti had been cool as ice cream but Marlene was blowsy and bulging out of her apron, her face a blotchy mess. She wanted to talk endlessly about the girls' childhood, their first day at school, their holidays in the little cottage by the lake, and Hedwig didn't mind that – she wanted to talk about Lotti too – but it was hard when there was so much that Frau Franke must not know.

'Poor soul,' said Mutti, wiping her hands on her apron and coming over to scoop Hedwig into her arms. 'You were good to go.'

Her eyes were bright with tears. Her only daughter might be involved with a Bolshevik, but at least she wasn't dead.

Hedwig's visit had not, however, been one of sheer compassion. She might have made a promise to Lotti, but Lotti was dead now and past caring, so after enduring Marlene's odorous hugs, she had asked to visit Lotti's bedroom. *Just to be alone with her.*

The bedroom had been preserved exactly as Lotti left it. Utterly tidy, unlike the rest of the apartment, and decorated with the kind of quirky personal touches that gave it style. Her collection of antique perfume bottles on the mantelpiece. A gemstone necklace hanging from the mirror. Five peacock feathers they had found on Pfaueninsel in a jar. In some ways, the room was like a shrine to Lotti, with her notebook laid out on the desk at the page of her last completed sketch. Hedwig ran her hand along the bookshelf, rummaged in a stack of fashion magazines then felt beneath the mattress and behind the bedhead. She leafed through Lotti's notebook and investigated the drawers of the desk. But it was useless. She found nothing.

Now, standing in the Ahnenerbe library, she came to a decision.

If you remember anything that might be useful, just call me.

She didn't need to remember anything because there was not a second when the matter was not running through her mind like some dreadful newsreel devoted to a single subject. Several times she had taken out the page from Clara Vine's leather notebook and looked at the autograph – a tendril of black ink with loops like the petals of a flower – before folding it carefully up again.

Hedwig had made Lotti a solemn promise, but Lotti was dead now so what did it matter? Clara Vine was the only person who had ever shown the slightest interest in her feelings about Lotti's death, so perhaps she deserved to know. Hedwig decided to call her.

Chapter Twenty-two

For a second, as Clara awoke and stretched out luxuriously on Ursula's white linen sheets, the day ahead lay sunlit and full of possibilities. Outside, it was an exquisite morning. Wild birds were calling, pale columns of birch trees shimmered around the languorous expanse of the Griebnitzsee and clumps of reeds rose like slender green blades from its depths. The air was studded with pollen and glinting insects were coasting on the warm currents. Then she remembered. She was a Jew, in Nazi Germany, without an ID.

The train journey back from the Gare du Nord had been fraught with anxiety. The possibility of being caught without her documents, not to mention the gun in her suitcase, played constantly on Clara's mind and she had needed to maintain a careful synchronicity of movement between carriages to avoid the scrutiny of the guards. Shortly after the train left Paris she informed the other passengers that she had a bad headache, necessitating several trips to the corridor for 'fresh air'. It worked well until they crossed the border into Germany, when she had been obliged to lock herself in the lavatory as a pair of guards came through. But she had underestimated their Nazi thoroughness, and emerged only to run slap into the second of the guards, who

was systematically checking the passengers in the final compartment. He was a young lad, not much more than nineteen she
reckoned, with a complexion that didn't need shaving and fair
hair cut savagely short. Yet his youth was an advantage, Clara
realized at once. He was flustered by their unintended physical
contact and he flushed.

'Documents,' he snapped, automatically, then looked up
with a flash of awed recognition in his eyes. Perhaps he had sat
through romantic comedies under pressure from a girlfriend, or
maybe he had seen Clara's war film, *The Pilot's Wife*, in which
she had been married to a lost Luftwaffe pilot, played by the
real-life air ace Ernst Udet. Whichever it was, finding himself
face to face with an actress from the big screen was overwhelm-
ing. For the first time in her career, Clara was relieved to be
recognized.

'My apologies, F-F-Fräulein.' He had a very slight stammer.
'Is it . . .?'

'Clara Vine, yes.'

'So sorry. Your identity documents please?'

She smiled sweetly, glad that she had just reapplied her lipstick
in the train's narrow mirror and was wearing Steffi's pearls.

'I'm afraid I've left them in my compartment. And it's all the
way back down the corridor.'

'I'll need to see them,' he insisted, in a starstruck mumble.

She tilted her head, coquettishly.

'Do you? Really? Even if I promise I am who I say I am?'

The guard gave a nervous laugh, which turned into a cough.
Far ahead in the corridor his colleague shouted at him to hurry
up.

'You could come back with me to my compartment. It's quite
a way.'

The young man cast an anxious glance up the corridor at his
companion, who was making impatient gestures in the distance.
God forbid the older man should return to help his colleague

out. Clara moved fractionally closer and lowered her voice to a seductive whisper.

'Perhaps you want to search me instead? Is that what you'd prefer?'

He leapt away as if electrified, a puce blush suffusing his entire complexion.

'Fräulein, forgive me! Not at all. It's just we have to . . .'

'How about I give you an autograph instead? That should prove my identity. Do you have a pen?'

Hastily the guard reached for his top pocket and brought out a pen and notebook.

'I've seen your movies,' he stammered, confirming her suspicions.

'Do you have a favourite?'

'*The Pilot's Wife.*'

'I guessed you'd say that!'

'With Ernst Udet.'

Everyone loved Ernst Udet. The fact that Clara had starred alongside him was as good as a golden Party badge in most people's eyes.

'Well it's lovely to meet you, Herr . . .'

'Herr Wolmann. Ludwig Wolmann.'

'To Ludwig . . .'

Clara scrawled her name, hoping that he would not notice the tremble in her hand, gave him her most dazzling smile and tucked the book back in his top pocket. Then she strolled back down the corridor as slowly as her legs could manage it.

It had taken hours for the shock of the encounter to wear off and she sat staring out of the window, barely able to focus on the countryside as it passed. Rooks sat like musical notes on the electricity lines, and in between the fields gun emplacements had sprung up on city borders. But once the train arrived at the Anhalter Bahnhof and the passengers flowed onto the platform there were no more requests for documents and she felt the tension that had been holding her body rigid suddenly ease, her shoulders slumping like a puppet whose strings have been released.

While she may have escaped inspection of her papers, however, Clara's inspection of herself was merciless. How could she have been so careless with Conrad Adler in Paris? Why had she relaxed her guard? What impulse made her snatch the documents from his hand, with the result that they ended up in the Seine? The answer, she knew, was that she had allowed Paris to get under her skin. The atmosphere, the food, the alcohol and the sheer foreign beauty of the place had intoxicated her. And perhaps the jousting conversation and bitter, ironic humour of Conrad Adler, too.

Yet the questions about Conrad Adler, the ones she needed to answer, remained. Why was he watching her at the Dingo Bar? And what did he want with her? Above all, how had he known she was not all she seemed?

Climbing out of bed, she pulled a wrap around her, entered the bathroom, looked into the lightbulb-fringed mirror, and switched on the wireless to drown out the thoughts crowding her head.

The smooth voice of the continuity announcer came on.

'And now, it is with great pleasure that we bring you the Hamburg City Orchestra with Franz Schubert's *Winter Journey* song cycle.'

The Hamburg City Orchestra. Where her mother had once played as a concert pianist. If life had been different – if the dashing Ronald Vine had not sat in that audience and fallen in love with the young Helene Neumann as she played a Brahms concerto, and she had not followed him back to England – then it might have been her mother on the radio that day. Except, of course, it wouldn't, because as the daughter of a Jew, Helene would have been banned from any orchestra in the Reich. She would have been excluded from the Reich Chamber of Culture because she could not show an Ariernachweis. And now her daughter was facing precisely the same predicament.

After applying a light coat of Elizabeth Arden foundation, Clara finished her make-up with a dusting of powder, sprinkled a little salt on her toothbrush in lieu of toothpaste, and pondered her options.

Archie Dyson, her contact at the British Embassy, had been relocated to Rome, a plum promotion that must have thrilled his ambitious wife, Lettie, but left Clara without any direct contact with British Intelligence in Berlin. Even if she got a message to Major Grand through Benno Kurtz of the Ritz bar, and he was able to organize another ID for her, how long would that take? For a second she considered asking Mary Harker if she had any contacts, but such a request could compromise Mary too, and that was a risk Clara refused to contemplate.

A memory flickered. Something Steffi Schaeffer had said.

We have a young man who produces passports and identity papers for us. He turns his hand to anything. His work is superb.

She felt a rush of pure relief, like sun streaking across the lake, and her heart lightened. She made a quick cup of coffee, pulled on a jacket and took up her bag. She needed to find Steffi without delay.

Within an hour she was on a bus, heading down the Königsallee. Thankfully Berlin's big cream buses, like London's scarlet ones, had an open platform at the back, making it easy to get on and off in a hurry. Clara sat, as always, at the back, which meant that she could observe whoever got on from behind. The bus reeked of stale clothes and unwashed bodies. The windows were mottled with condensation. Beside her, at eye level, the standard notice had been fixed: *The fare-dodger's profit is the Berliner's loss!* Underneath was a line to report to the authorities anyone not paying the twenty-pfennig fare.

The bus was held up periodically by workmen installing the new air-raid shelters. A vast honeycomb of tunnels and shelters was being created beneath Berlin, a dark mirror to the new city rising above it. A rabbit warren of tunnels, cellars and giant concrete vaults with soundproof walls several metres thick as though, if any bombing happened, there was the faintest chance people would be able to sleep through it.

She found Steffi sitting in the back room of Herr Fromm's shop with a pair of pince nez perched on her nose, almost buried behind a length of field-grey serge.

'Hold on a moment. I'm just finishing the buttonhole.'

She unwound a length of thread expertly from the spool, and matched it to the material, then continued sewing, her fingers slipping, dipping, tucking and weaving, marrying needle and cloth in a balletic rhythm that was soothing to watch.

'The Wehrmacht is very particular about its buttonholes. They insist they're hand-stitched a certain way and they always check. The stitches need be to a certain length and made from the correct thread. There are very precise regulations. Herr Fromm says no one knows as much about the details of a Wehrmacht uniform as me.'

'So you're as particular with your Wehrmacht uniforms as you are with your Chanel frocks?' Clara smiled.

Steffi would run up exquisite copies of designer outfits at prices even actresses could afford. Chanel, Worth, Lanvin, Patou; there was nothing she would not turn her hand to. She studied the originals and reproduced them down to the finest details so that it was impossible to tell the difference between Steffi's creations and the real thing.

Now she frowned, and bit off a length of thread.

'More, if possible. I've done so many now it's become my new speciality.'

'Some speciality.'

Steffi looked up at Clara over her pince nez. Her face was alive with suppressed meaning.

'Oh, but it is, Clara,' she said softly. 'Did you know there are more than thirty SS cuff-bands and sleeve diamonds? Could you tell me what colour stitching to use for a Death's Head collar tab and how that differs from the silver flat wire on the SS-Gruppenführer's collar tab? How the diamond insignia on an SS-Obersturmbannführer's collar tab should line up relative to the tresse? There may come a day when that kind of knowledge proves very useful.'

She returned to her stitching.

'Fortunately for me, most officers have their uniforms tailor made, so I've had plenty of time to learn.'

Clara felt in her bag for the bars of Menier chocolate.

'I brought these for Esther. How is she?'

'Not here, I'm afraid.'

Catching Clara's alarm she took off her spectacles and lowered her voice.

'We had to move her.'

'Where?'

'There's a Konditorei – the Konditorei Herschel, do you know it?'

Clara started in surprise.

'Of course. It's in Winterfeldtplatz. At the end of my street. I've been there with my godson several times.'

It was a typical Berlin place with a finely scrolled ceiling and delicately tiled floor, filled with a fluctuating population of women chatting and men looking for a quiet moment of relaxation with a newspaper. Its cakes, displayed proudly beneath a glass counter at the front of the shop, were true works of art. In the past one might have found Turks' Heads, sweet, flaky Pigs' Ears, towering piles of profiteroles, Spritzkuchen and Nusstörtchen. Soft sponge that melted in the mouth and pastries oozing cream and cherries. Now the flour was low grade and the butter was whale blubber, but there was always something on display. The nation's sweet tooth demanded cakes.

'That explains it.'

Clara had noticed that certain visitors would enter the café and linger at the glass case, chatting to Frau Herschel, glancing around them at the clientele happily consuming their coffee and then leaving without buying anything. For a close observer like Clara, it wasn't hard to deduce that the Konditorei Herschel had a second, more secretive line of business.

Steffi stood up and stretched.

'The proprietor there, Frau Herschel, has helped us in the past. She's a good woman, but we can't rely on her for long. We still need to get Esther to England.'

Clara glanced behind her to check the door was closed and said,

'As a matter of fact, I didn't just come to bring the chocolate. There's something I need to ask you. You mentioned you knew someone who could do documents.'

A wary glance.

'Who is this for?'

'Me.'

'You?'

'I need a new Kennkarte. And an Ariernachweis. Mine have been destroyed and . . . I don't think it would be possible to get new ones.'

'Why's that?'

'The genealogy records would be lacking. Do you think your man could help me?'

Clara was used to Steffi's sharp scrutiny. The dispassionate look that came over her face whenever Clara tried on a new dress – arms crossed, lips pursed, eyes raking ruthlessly up and down, taking in all her defects and not sparing honest comment if a line didn't flatter or a style made her hips too large. But this was one aspect of Clara that Steffi had never seen or suspected. Jewish blood.

Nonetheless she absorbed it swiftly.

'Go to the zoo. Next Thursday lunchtime. Bring two photographs of yourself.'

'Thursday! That's six days away. I have no identity documents at all. What if I'm stopped before then?'

'I'm sorry. It's the soonest our friend can manage. Go precisely at one o'clock and you will see a man there.'

'Where? The zoo's a big place. How will I recognize him?'

'He'll recognize you. When he sees you he will leave immediately and you must follow him. He will take you a few streets away. When he enters a building, wait, and then knock on the door twice. If anyone but him answers, say you were looking for a Herr Vogel.'

'Herr Vogel? Is that his name?'

'That's no one. If our friend is alone, and certain that you were not followed, he will let you in.'

'Is it safe in daylight? Shouldn't we meet later?'

'Our man believes he is far less conspicuous in daytime. Innocent people don't go scurrying around at night. And Clara . . .'

There was a clang of the bell, and from behind the velvet curtain came the sound of someone entering the shop followed by the unctuous, indistinct tone of Herr Fromm's voice and the curt male bark of a customer.

Both women stiffened.

'You should leave,' said Steffi. 'By the way, I have something for you.'

She crossed the room and reached into a wardrobe, bringing out a slate-blue jacket on a hanger. It was three quarter length, with gold buttons and a rich scarlet lining. Clara recognized it at once. It was the same jacket she had seen hanging in the window of the Paris store.

'A Schiaparelli jacket!'

'I saw it in *Vogue* and I had to try it.'

'But where did you get the materials?'

'That's the thing. You can't get the textiles, but I thought, that shade is awfully familiar, and I realized it was close to Luftwaffe blue. And there was a bolt here that we had to reject on the grounds that it was not precisely the right shade. It wouldn't pass inspection. The Luftwaffe is very strict like that.'

'You shouldn't have!'

'Perhaps. But if war comes, clothes are sure to be rationed and you won't be able to get hold of a thing. Try it on.'

Clara pulled the jacket on, sank her hands into the deep pockets, and did a little twirl. Steffi stood back, arms crossed.

'Well, I'll say this for you. You certainly look like the real thing.'

Chapter Twenty-three

Schwannecke's wine bar on Rankestrasse was a popular hangout for actresses and theatrical types. In the old days photographers would gather outside, hoping to catch a shot of Marlene Dietrich as she came out, and the actress would favour them with one of her trademark hundred-watt smiles, but Marlene Dietrich was an ocean away now, beaming at Hollywood photographers, and the press had other things than actresses on their minds.

There was a sign on the counter.

Do Not Ask for Coffee. We Hate to Disappoint.

Clara was nursing a cup of watery tea. She had, as always, paid up front so that she could leave quickly if necessary. From her position at the back of the café she had every customer in sight by profile, as well as an eye on potential observation points across the street, as she leafed through a copy of the *BZ am Mittag*.

Already the euphoria of the Führer's birthday had faded and the paper had returned to its customary fail-safe formula of propaganda, threats and atrocities. In the top right-hand corner was a list of people who had refused to contribute to the Winter Relief fund. Naming and shaming was a way of life in Germany. Anything from homosexual love affairs to hoarding food, reading banned books or the catchall crime of 'attitudes negative to National Socialism'. Often the only way to escape denunciation was to denounce the accuser. Recently, however, police were beginning to buckle under the weight of accusations coming in from one citizen against another, with the result that a new scheme had been dreamt up. Now you could win a reward for denouncing anyone making false denunciations.

That day's centre pages, however, did contain something fresh. A double page spread devoted to the scale model of the Welthauptstadt, the new world capital that Albert Speer had created for the Führer's recent birthday. It was a marvel of its kind – far more impressive than the models Clara used to buy for Erich from Märklin's toyshop in Charlottenburg. Every house in Speer's city was rendered in bone-white balsa wood, the windows glinting, streets gleaming, the great dome like an upturned ostrich egg and the replica cathedral cleansed of its grimy façade. It was a pearl-white paradise, delicate and shimmering as a heavenly city – except this was a city that existed only in Hitler's mind. Clara imagined his fingers dawdling along the façades, poking into doors and windows, marching down Unter den Linden, caressing the curve of the giant dome. Every detail was perfect and exact, except for the fact that there were no people. It was as if the world had been tipped and all the untidy, inconvenient inhabitants had slid off the edge.

People are keeping an eye on you. Somebody has been saying some very unkind things about you.

Ever since the evening at the Valhalla, Magda Goebbels' comments had been sounding at the back of Clara's mind. What had she meant? Was it just the usual whispers that swirled around actresses, who were always the target of gossip and innuendo, or was it another scrap of the feverish speculation and spin that obtained in the upper circles of the Nazi Party? Was Clara genuinely being watched? With no call for filming that morning, she had steeled herself to find out.

All spies, Leo told her, must learn to read. Not newspapers, but voices, body language and faces. As a man entered the café and came to sit beside her, Clara thought of the first rule on Leo's list. *Look out for the unobtrusive.* Beneath the fedora his worn, creased face had a hangdog expression and this anonymity, coupled with the fact that he made no eye contact or subtle acknowledgement of her, instantly aroused Clara's suspicions. That was until his roll and hot tea arrived and he began to wolf it down with feverish haste. She realized instinctively that the man must be a non-Aryan, no longer allowed in cafés or restaurants, and that he was savouring a pleasure he might not experience again.

A speech came on the radio, and the owner reached over to turn it up. As the harsh jackal's shriek of Joseph Goebbels rang out, all conversation hushed immediately – it was the law – and most people even stopped chewing, as if eating and drinking were disrespectful when the Propaganda Minister was holding forth. They weren't far wrong. No element of normal life was too trifling to avoid Goebbels' scrutiny and this issue had, in fact, been covered in a recent pamphlet, *Instructions to the Catering Trade on Restaurant Etiquette in the Case of Political Pronouncements.* Clara, like everyone else, lowered her cup and allowed her face to go blank. In more zealous districts, customers would stand and salute the radio, but in this upmarket area a respectful silence was thought to suffice. It was not an easy listen. Hitler's yell was bad enough – it must hurt his throat as much as it hurt the listeners' ears – yet it had a mesmerizing quality. There was nothing whatever seductive about Joseph Goebbels. But his voice reminded Clara of something he had said. *You look totally unrecognizable with those spectacles.* By chance the spectacles she wore for her film part were still in her bag. Fishing them out, she waited for the speech to finish, and left the café.

She walked down the Kurfürstendamm, past the great stuccoed apartment blocks whose baroque decoration was now topped with the ultra-modern addition of anti-aircraft guns pointing into the porcelain-blue sky. Stopping at Harry Lehmann's perfume store she lingered and spent a few minutes testing her favourites – Tulip, Violet and Rose. The flasks of perfume were ranked along a shelf, a mirror at their back, spangled with iridescent reflections from the sun. A leisurely parade of sniffing, dabbing and testing enabled Clara to keep an eye on the street outside but no figure shuffled to a stop, or loitered against the green Litfass advertising column to light a cigarette.

Turning into Fasanenstrasse she passed the remains of the synagogue, burned to the ground the previous November. When the fire was at its height the synagogue cantor had appealed to the fire crews who drew up outside to save them, but the firemen held back, explaining they had only come to protect the neighbouring buildings.

Clara's eyes scanned the road. It was the least likely people you watched for. The elderly gentleman in grey homburg, kid gloves, shiny boots and spats, an umbrella over his arm, proceeding at a leisurely pace along the other side of the road. The woman queuing outside the fishmonger's for a fresh consignment of herring. The newspaper seller, calling out a friendly greeting from his cast-iron kiosk.

There was a man she noticed, with a sallow, forgettable face, proceeding at a steady pace behind her. She stopped where a salesgirl was rattling a Winter Relief box, fumbled for her purse and extracted some coins.

'Here.'

'All in a good cause.' The girl winked. 'Our soldiers need their guns.'

Cynicism was everywhere on the streets now, like a black market brandy that passed from one person to another and warmed the secret places of the soul. It was what made Goebbels' joke-writer such an inspired idea. Clara deliberately dropped a few pfennigs on the ground, but when she dipped to the pavement to collect them, the sallow man overtook her and vanished from sight.

All the same, she descended into the U-Bahn, past the sign that said Jews and dogs were barred from the escalator, and let the first train leave without her. When the next train arrived she waited until every other passenger had boarded before slipping on just as the doors closed. Two stops later she got off and caught a train in the opposite direction, then left the U-Bahn and jumped on a bus as it was moving off and disembarked at Alexanderplatz.

Eventually she came to the Marienkirche. The thirteenth-century church, with its red brick and green spire, could not seem more of a contrast to the granite monumentalism of Albert Speer. Although churchgoing was frowned on now, and most places of worship were deserted, a visit to the Marienkirche counted as a cultural outing because of its most famous artefact – the Totentanz, the dance of death.

The fresco had been lost for centuries until it was glimpsed under a layer of whitewash and painstakingly brought back into the light. How like life that was, Clara thought. Death hovered out of the corner of the eye until it came suddenly, drastically into view. The theme was a German tradition. Death danced, holding the hands of cardinals and popes, saints, kings and fools. Looking at the saints with their eroded features, softened by time and devotion, she wondered if Hitler's own features might one day become dulled and worn away with familiarity, until, like a dreadful saint, the sight of him no longer had the power to surprise.

Emerging into the bright sunshine, she ran straight into Hugh Lindsey.

'How lovely to see you,' he remarked, as though they had bumped into each other on Oxford Street, or at a cocktail party in Mayfair. 'I was miles away.'

She almost laughed with relief. In his Burberry coat, tie slightly askew, and hat pushed back on his head, Hugh was like a great breath of Englishness. It was just like she had felt on the bus in the King's Road, surrounded by the staid, understated British citizens. Everything about him made her feel safe.

'Were you, Hugh? What were you thinking about?'

'You don't want to know.'

'I do.'

'All right. I was thinking about England's batting averages. At the last count . . .'

Clara held up a hand and laughed.

'You're right. I don't want to know. I know absolutely nothing about cricket, and I'm not sure I'll ever learn.'

'As a matter of fact I was heading back to the Adlon. Care to walk with me?'

The two of them progressed companionably through Alexanderplatz, past the circular lawn in one corner of the square.

'You know, in 1918 there was shooting going on in this square. Fighting between the Reds and the Freikorps,' remarked Hugh. 'But even though crossing this lawn was the shortest distance across the square, and the obvious way to escape the bullets, Berliners still refused to walk on the grass. Isn't that extraordinary? Lenin said he realized at that moment that the revolution was lost. He said you can't hold a revolution in a city where people obey the "keep off the grass" signs.'

In the Schlossplatz, arcs of water spurting from the Neptune Fountain turned into rainbows in the air, and Hugh brought out a packet of cigarettes. He lit one then almost immediately chucked it into the water.

'I can't smoke these things. I've run out of Benson and Hedges but these are like a hand grenade going off in your chest.'

'Have one of mine.'

'A Gauloise? Lucky girl.'

'I got them the other day, in Paris.'

'Paris? What were you doing there.'

'A fashion shoot for *Vogue*.'

'How refreshing to find a British girl who loves fashion. Most women I know don't give a hoot about it. Their favourite shade is porridge and they like their tweeds hard as a board.'

It was a relief to be with Hugh. He had a way of speaking that was midway between joking and serious. Englishmen were often like that. It helped them cope with feelings – that was what Rupert Allingham used to tell her. Irony was the first lesson Englishmen learned at public school. Even Hugh's manner, and his way of swiping away his forelock, reminded her of her brother Kenneth, a City stockbroker now, but just as obsessed with the fortunes of the English cricket team.

Hugh inhaled the Gauloise greedily.

'You need these things to take the edge off the appetite. Don't you find yourself getting frightfully hungry nowadays? I have a recurring dream that I'm at Rules, on one of the back banquettes, being served smoked salmon, potted shrimps, Dover sole and jugged hare. Followed by crumpets and buttered anchovy toast.'

He hesitated.

'I'm not making you feel sick, am I?'

Being with Hugh Lindsey, talking about England, had brought on a compelling urge to confide.

'I think I'm being followed.'

'Is that all? I shouldn't worry. Mary says we're all being followed. I imagine my chap is having a jolly dull time of it.'

'Not like that. That's just the regulation minders from the Propaganda Ministry. I think this is something different.'

His smile dropped and he regarded her more seriously.

'Could it possibly be to do with that man we saw the other evening? Herr Adler?'

'I'm not sure . . .'

'I don't mind telling you, there's something about him I didn't like, Clara. I think you should keep away from him.'

'I will. I can't imagine I would see Adler again. It's nothing to do with him.'

'Do you know what? I think I can guess what's really bothering you.' His eyes were kindly, with an Englishman's repressed emotion. 'It's that business about the Faith and Beauty girl. You knew her, didn't you, and you said you were living close to where it happened.'

'Yes.'

'The whole affair must have been a tremendous shock.'

'It was, but . . .'

'They think the man's still around, don't they?'

'Apparently.'

'That decides it then. I'm giving you a lift home. My car's right outside the Adlon. It's a Mercedes Sport Roadster. Burgundy red and a real thoroughbred. Runs like a dream. I'm pathetically proud of it.'

'Thank you, I'd like that.'

Once they were in the car, and driving out towards the west of the city, Hugh lifted a silver Dunhill hipflask from the side pocket and tipped it towards her.

'Can I tempt you? I always keep a little something and having managed to get hold of a half decent bottle of Glenmorangie it would be a shame not to share it.'

Clara sipped, grateful for its slow, reviving fire.

As they entered the fringes of Griebnitzsee they passed a couple of police cars. Since the murder, there were police cars all around the area. The newspapers said there was to be 'no expense spared' to catch the killer. It was as if Lotti Franke had come to symbolize everything that was good and pure about German womanhood, and her hideous murder was an outrage that threatened to sully the whole of the Aryan race.

Hugh parked his car outside Ursula's home and peered enviously through the screen of trees. He gave a low whistle of admiration.

'Some place.'

'It's only temporary.'

'Bet it looks right out on the lake.'

'It does.'

'Want me to come in? See you're all right?'

She knew she should invite him in. Hugh had, after all, gone out of his way to drive her home in his smart new car. The very least she could do was to brew up some of Ursula's stash of coffee. But she was suddenly desperate to be alone.

'Really, I'm fine,' she said, getting out of the car. 'Another time?'

'Absolutely.' He gave a broad smile and drove off.

She did want to be alone, but the sight of the police had brought Lotti Franke to the forefront of her thoughts. She had promised the girl's parents that she would see if there was anything she could discover about their daughter's death. That was weeks ago, and in the time since, the tearful hysteria of Marlene Franke and the quiet desperation of her husband had been playing at the back of her mind, yet she had been far too busy to give it any attention. Now she was reminded that Hedwig Holz had left a message the previous day at the studio, asking if she would mind calling in at the Faith and Beauty home. She had been sure that there was something Hedwig was not telling her.

She decided to visit the next day.

Chapter Twenty-four

It was smart, as all the villas were out in the affluent suburbs west of Berlin: Schlachtensee, Nikolassee, Wannsee, Griebnitzsee. Groups of large, turn-of-the-century villas with gravel drives and high gates that allowed only a glimpse of a world framed by curly wrought iron, of sunlit lawns screened by abundant pines. It was the heartland of Berlin's aristocracy. Back in their heyday, in the 1900s, there would have been carriages in the drives and families photographed on the front steps, plump men in swallowtail coats and ladies in wide hats, flanked by their servants. There would be dances that went on until dawn, with fairy lights strung in the trees and views across the lakes. All the big house owners were rich industrialists, lawyers and bankers; patriarchs with wide moustaches who were a picture of confident prosperity. Many of them were Jewish, and they had plenty of good taste to go with their money. They hung their halls with fine art and their gardens were garnished with statuary. But in 1933 everything changed. Most of the owners were moved out of their villas as fast as it took to pack a suitcase. Some of the new residents reported find-ing the coffee pots still warm.

The Faith and Beauty home was an ornately decorated house whose builder had, in common with many around here, regarded the Austrian Tyrol as the apogee of architectural sophistication.

Stained-glass windows and Jugendstil decoration were garnished with a pair of antlers affixed above the doorway. Little gables and cross timbers gave it the air of a hunting lodge plucked from the Bavarian countryside and transported intact to the plush districts that edged up against the Grunewald's dark heart.

Inside, sun swirled up to the icing sugar cornices of the high ceiling, filling the room with a wash of pale gold. An early bee butted softly on the window, like an inaccurate bomber failing to reach its target. An opened window carried the smell of grass on the breeze and as she waited Clara glimpsed a group of girls practising gymnastics on the lawn, shiny braids swaying in unison. From somewhere in the distance came the sound of clear girls' voices singing a marching hymn to the Führer.

> *Uns're Fahne flattert uns voran.*
> *Uns're Fahne ist die neue Zeit.*
> *Und die Fahne führt uns in die Ewigkeit!*
> *Ja! Die Fahne ist mehr als der Tod!*

> *Our banner flutters before us.*
> *Our banner represents the new time.*
> *Our banner leads us to eternity!*
> *Yes! Our banner means more to us than death!*

Their singing unfurled into the air, rising and falling in uncertain counterpoint, a tapestry of sound that occasionally achieved harmony but then frayed and fell apart. Every now and then it was interrupted by the staccato of the singing instructor. 'Enough! Again! I remind you, ladies, the Führer requires perfection!'

Clara had deliberately arrived a few minutes early to allow for a look around. As she stood in the hall, she felt the glance of passing girls sweep over her. It might have been recognition, but it felt different, as prickling and hostile as stinging nettles, as though her intrusion in their domain was some kind of threat. But a threat to what? To their privacy, their togetherness, their beliefs? Or was it merely the natural distrust that any stranger inspired after the recent trauma that had taken place in their midst?

Hedwig Holz came hurrying down the stairs, apologizing as she went. She had changed since the last time Clara had seen her. Her face was taut with misery and her eyes grey and hooded. She stood before Clara, pushing the sleeves of her smock up and then pulling them down again.

'Shall we go in the garden?' Clara suggested.

They navigated the path past the gymnasts towards a bed where a display of tulips stood to attention at the end of the lawn. Even the grass was of a higher quality here, soft and springy, its fragrance floating in the air. As the two women passed, the crunch of their feet on the gravel turned curious probing eyes on them.

'Thank you for your call, Hedwig. Can I call you Hedwig?'

'Please.' A quick smile that lifted her features. 'Though I hate my name actually. There's only one person who doesn't call me Hedwig and he calls me Hedy.'

'I've just been in France. There they would call you Edwige.'

'Would they? That sounds so much better. *Edwige*. It's beautiful. I'd love to visit France. Lotti promised that if we joined the Faith and Beauty we would end up visiting all sorts of foreign places.'

'Was that why she wanted you to join?'

'I suppose. She said she wasn't going to be some old hausfrau, shuffling around in slippers with a load of brats at her ankles. She was going to travel. She wanted to live somewhere glamorous. She had expectations.'

Hedwig used this word reverently, as if it conjured all the magic of foreign places, of haute couture and a life where she would never again wear her hair in braids or sit around with a hundred identical girls sharing the greasy contents of an Eintopf stew.

They walked past the flowerbeds and through an arch of budding roses, towards the dapple of sun and blur of shadow at the end of the lawn. Beyond it lay the fringe of forest separating the order of the garden from the wild and unknown. Conrad Adler's comment came into Clara's head. *There's a narrow boundary that separates the savage from the civilized.* Here, in this temple to female purity, that boundary had grown thin and permeable and savagery had seeped in.

'That's where they found her.'

At the edge of the trees Clara could see a flutter of tape marking off an area of the ground.

'We're not allowed to go near.'

Clara wanted more details, and thought about asking Hedwig outright, but she seemed like the kind of girl who would clam up at a direct question. She was the kind who let her twisting hands and involuntary glances do the talking.

'Did she often go into the woods?'

Hedwig was kicking at the gravel with her foot, scuffing it and turning over the stones.

'She used to say that solitude was essential for the development of character. She was quite a private person.' Clara remembered the composed and secretive smile that Lotti gave. 'She said that was what was wrong with our country – I'm sorry, Fräulein Vine – that people were never alone. She felt it was impossible to be a creative person if you didn't have solitude.'

'But why could she not be alone?'

'You don't know what it's like here. All the women in one group stay together throughout their membership. In that time we're encouraged to share everything – we eat together and learn together and sing together. It's hard to feel different. They don't want you to. But other people don't realize that.'

Clara did. She had felt it standing there in the hall. A silent sense, like pheromones in a hive. She could feel the emotion in the place pressing up against the walls, all eyes alert, hearts beating as one, the sense that everyone there was part of something bigger than themselves. That was a powerful emotion. It was the emotion that the Third Reich relied on. It was the kind of emotion that could move mountains.

'Most of the people here have known each other since they were girls, anyway. All their parents know each other too. Lotti and I were the only ones who came from the east of Berlin. That's good, I suppose. They always used to point Lotti out to visitors, to prove that there was nothing stopping a girl from an ordinary background being special in the Reich.'

They stared together, into the blurred shadows.

'So was there a reason that you asked to see me?'

'I should have told you this before. I think . . .' An instinctive glance behind her. 'I might have a thought about why Lotti was killed.'

Her voice had layers of secrecy in it. She was concealing something.

'You said there was a boyfriend, and that she was frightened of him?'

'That's true. But it's about something that happened, just before she died. It was a Saturday like this, and Lotti came into the house. She had make-up on but her face was dirty and you could see the tear stains on her cheeks. She laughed a little when she saw me – she always laughed – but I could see something was wrong. She was late to the art class and I know she had spent the night with him. She was flustered, which was so unlike her, Lotti was always perfectly turned out. Anyway, after the class was finished, she came out here and told me a secret. She said she'd stolen something.'

Her words hung in the air, glinting with meaning.

'I had to promise not to tell anyone else about it. She was very aggressive. She frightened me. She made me swear on my life.'

'What was it?'

'I don't know.'

'And where is it now?'

'I'm not sure.'

'Didn't you ask her?'

'I would have done. But that was the last day I saw her. The next thing I knew, they found her body.'

Hedwig swallowed, reliving the horror of the moment.

'I've tried so hard to think what she stole and where it might be. I visited her parents and went into her bedroom, saying I wanted to spend a last moment alone with Lotti, and I searched everywhere but there was no sign of anything.'

As they walked back to the house the high clear voices of the girls were finally rising in harmony, coming together in clear, pleasing unison in their hymn to the Führer.

'The only thing she said was, "*It's precious, Hedwig. It's more precious than you can imagine. There are a lot of big people in Germany who would kill for this.*"'

Clara had a sudden, spiky sense of dread. Perhaps the murder of Lotti Franke was not, after all, the random act of a lone madman. Perhaps it had roots that went deeper. Roots that stretched and touched and entangled others, and ultimately reached out to the darkest places of the Reich.

Chapter Twenty-five

'I'm afraid I'm not to be trusted.'

Conrad Adler was holding the reins of a dappled grey horse, saddled up and ready for a ride. He was dressed in a finely tailored riding jacket, breeches and high boots, his slick hair shining and a sharp edge of amusement in his eyes. To his side stood a groom with a larger chestnut horse, already snuffing the air impatiently and tossing his head against the reins.

The Reitclub Grunewald, the city's smartest riding stables, enjoyed an idyllic location directly next to the Grunewaldsee. Though the water and the woodland gave it the feel of deep countryside, the club was near enough to the S-Bahn that one could travel from Ku'damm to stable door in twenty minutes flat. Berliners loved horses and the city was full of bronzed beasts, sculptures of horses rearing in battle, their manes blowing in the winds. Even the famously unsporty Hitler liked to carry a riding whip in his hand. But there was no substitute for the real thing.

That morning the place was humming with activity, grooms polishing harnesses, cleaning out stables and loading wheelbarrows with old straw, darting in and out of the tack room and hanging saddles on the doors. And two dozen shining, well-fed horses were clattering their hooves on the cobbles, thumping against the stable doors as they waited for their ride or being rubbed down, their coats steaming in the morning air.

'Why can't I trust you?'

'I told you I wanted you to accompany me to the cinema but now it comes to it I can think of nothing worse than wasting an evening with you watching drivel. I would far prefer to take a ride and talk to you. And we're lucky to have countryside like this so close to the heart of the Reich.'

Clara had found Adler's postcard when she returned home the previous day. Vermeer's *A Young Woman Seated at a Virginal*. A sweet-faced girl in a blue dress, dreamily poised with her fingers on the keys, the sunlight dazzling off the blue of her silk gown, a choker of pearls around her neck. She snatched up the card with apprehension, wondering how Adler had managed to find her address, before turning it over and reading his invitation.

The Reitclub Grunewald. 12pm tomorrow?

The invitation threw her into an agony of indecision. Since that evening more than a week ago in Paris, Adler had a terrifying hold over her. He knew the truth about her, yet she had no idea what he intended to do with it.

The horse assigned to Clara tossed his head fretfully and Adler rubbed its velvety nose, easing a place where the bridle was tight.

'D'you think you can handle him? Perhaps he's too large for you.'

'I used to have a horse back in England. Inkerman. This one's about the same size.'

'Then this will remind you of happy times.'

She took the reins from Adler and swung herself up into the saddle and Adler's groom helped him onto his own horse.

'Thank you, Karl.'

They made their way along the bridle path, out of the sunshine and into a tunnel of shadow where the density of the darkness was layered with the low gurgle of wood pigeons. Once or twice the flash of a coppery squirrel crossed their path. The horses picked their way expertly along a route they knew by heart, their hooves padding softly over the leaf mould. It was just as Adler had said. The sight of the conker-brown horse in front of her and the rising scent of warm horsehair, oiled harness and burnished leather provoked a sharp stab of nostalgia. In truth, he was right – the horse was larger than she was used to – but he seemed calm, and she loved the sensation of him moving beneath her, the instinctive communication between animal and rider. It had been years since Clara had been on horseback, and then it was down lanes in the Surrey countryside, fringed by hawthorn hedgerows. Here in the Grunewald the air was fresher, with an edge of pine, and unlike the deciduous English wood-land, the densely packed pine trees were dark and impenetrable.

Apart from the occasional command to his horse, or a sugges-tion of right or left, Adler progressed without speaking, follow-ing a route deeper into the wood. From time to time Clara glanced across, but could tell nothing of his thoughts other than he was apparently absorbed in his ride. Leaning down to slap the horse's neck he said, 'What do you think of Flieger? He has the most wonderful pedigree, but I don't care about any of that. I bought him because he is such an intelligent animal. The moment I saw him I had to have him.'

There was a tenderness in his voice she had not heard before and her heart warmed to him in response. She had never met a man who loved horses the way she did. The men she knew liked a hard competitive gallop, or a morning's hunting on the South Downs, but they rarely spoke about their mounts with the same undertow of attachment.

'Karl looks after him wonderfully. I've told him to make the most of it while he can.'

'Why's that?'

'He's a Jew,' he said, matter-of-factly. 'The Führer's shortly to ban Jews from caring for animals so Karl won't be able to work at the stables any more. He's going to be looking around for a new occupation.'

After a while they emerged from the forest trail to a clearing where a timbered biergarten stood, complete with a cobbled yard dotted with scarlet geraniums where drinkers were sitting in the sun. A man in lederhosen and a short Bavarian hat was playing Mozart on the violin, and sparrows hopped and pecked between the tables. A stag's head hung above the door, and glancing into the dim interior Clara saw a collection of other animals – birds, badgers and pine martens in glass cases. Foxes' heads snarled at each other across the room and a moulting hare, inexpertly stuffed, cocked a glassy eye. At the entrance a stuffed bear with the fur rubbed away at the snout stood, paw extended like a maître d' welcoming new customers.

'This place has been here for centuries. Shall we stop?'

They tethered the horses on the fence and sat in the dappled shade. Adler ordered beer for both of them.

'So. Did the ride bring back pleasant memories?'

'I'd almost forgotten how much I loved it. I haven't ridden for so long. It reminded me of being a child.'

'What were you like as a child?'

His question brought her up short. Her childhood seemed locked off from her now. A vanished dream of gardens and lessons, of intense, intimate adventures with Angela and Kenneth. Yet also, she realized with hindsight, a time of secrets. Of concealed diaries, repressed feelings and hidden emotion.

'I suppose I was a typical middle child. Self-reliant. Very reserved.'

'Yes.' His keen eyes seemed to penetrate her. 'I can see that. Though from my time in London I would say that's something of a national trait. The English are very skilled at concealing their emotions.'

She smiled briefly, but did not trust herself to reply. Since Adler's discovery of her forged document she was determined to guard every detail. She had no idea of his intentions towards her, or what he planned to do with her secret. She wondered if he would raise the matter, or if he expected her to throw herself on his mercy. She would not bring it up herself. She decided to wait and see.

'Why were you reserved? Were your parents unhappy?'

He could not have dissected her more accurately if he had been armed with a scalpel. Towards the end of her mother's life the marriage was over in all but name. She had found herself going between her parents like a double agent, translating and embroidering their comments for each other, shoring up the glaring cracks in their façade of family life. Her father retreated to his study with its bay window overlooking the rose garden and her mother to hours of practice on the grand piano.

'I think they were mismatched. They had a whirlwind romance – I suppose that's what you'd call it – and once it died down they discovered they were very different.'

'There's nothing worse than a romance that has gone sour. It's why I have always preferred my solitude. What was your first memory?'

'The Titanic sinking. I remember my parents sitting at the breakfast table – our breakfast room had high walls with a pattern of dark green leaves like wreaths and I was counting them. My father was reading the newspaper and he said, "*All those people dead.*" I tried to allot a wreath in my mind to each dead person. It filled me with fear.'

'Why? It wasn't your tragedy.'

'The idea that death could come quite suddenly, out of nowhere. And then of course it did. My mother died when I was sixteen. I thought as time went by I would miss her less, but in fact I miss her more.'

'What was her name?'

'Helene. Helene Neumann.'

Not the name on the gravestone in the Surrey churchyard of St Michael and All Angels, softly eroding as the rain dripped down its runnels. But her mother's absence was chiselled into Clara's life in a way that could not be erased. It had brought home to her the telescoping of Time. The way it felt tangible, curdled, the minutes growing thick. Gradually running out.

'I miss my sister too. We were so close at one time, you would never believe. We just grew apart.'

'Do you see her much?'

She had a sudden, passionate desire to talk about Angela. It had been so long since anyone asked her questions like this. Yet she refused to let herself relax.

'Not really. And I haven't seen my father for years.'

'Would you like to?'

'I suppose.'

'Why stay in Germany then?'

'For my work.'

'Can your work be so important?'

'I think so.'

She took a deep draught of the beer. It was a Berlin Weiss, with a shot of fruit syrup – unexpectedly refreshing. Adler's questions disconcerted her. Maybe that was the point. She shifted beneath his forensic gaze.

'Enough of me. What about you. Were you born in Berlin?'

'No. My family comes from Weimar.' He leaned back in his seat, languidly stretching his jodhpured legs. 'I'm a count, actually. Von Adler. The decoration was bought a few generations back. I'm not proud of it, that's just how things are. I had every blessing I could ask. A perfect heritage, a bloodline, money, and land in the finest city in Germany.'

'I've never been to Weimar.'

'You should. It's the home of the Reformation and of Goethe, of course. Have you read *Faust*?'

'Afraid not.'

'You must know the story. The man who made a pact with the devil.'

'He sold his soul in return for anything he wanted on earth.'

'That's the one. Don't go reading anything into that, though.'

Adler tilted his glass towards her and took a sip of foamy beer. The sun caught his glass and made it sparkle.

'I often think of my life back in Weimar. The place was enormous. You can't imagine the upkeep, but as a boy one never thought of those things. We had horses, of course, stables of our own, magnificent gardens. A lake and a chapel. Even an ice palace. My mother was much younger than my father and neither of them had any idea about children. I was the only one they had and they treated me as a type of miniature adult. Or rather . . .'

He paused with his head tilted, as though this was the first time he had ever considered it.

'Like a dinner guest. They were always utterly courteous. Polite. They talked about politics, or history, or art, as though I would understand, which of course, being intelligent, I did.'

Clara looked into Adler's impenetrable eyes and tried to see in him the young boy, isolated and awkward. Polite.

'In the winter we would go hunting. There's a hare there that learns to camouflage itself perfectly against the land. It has a deep grey coat but in winter it undergoes a moult and turns entirely white. I admire that. The skill of camouflage. You can't be a good hunter unless you've studied camouflage. This little hare turns white so expertly that only the best hunters can see it against the snow.'

'Sounds like you miss it.'

'I do. I often wish I'd made my life back there, managing the estate, living quietly. Keeping out of politics.'

'So why did you?' She kept her voice low but her words flared with passion. 'Why get involved in all this . . . brutality? If you didn't have to?'

Adler observed her change of expression, then gave a cool shrug. 'It was necessary to join the Party if I was to pursue my work as an art specialist. Once the Reich Chamber of Culture was instated, it was mandatory.'

'You didn't have to enter *politics*.'

'I didn't think of it as politics. When von Ribbentrop was made ambassador to England, he invited me along as his aide, and I liked the idea. I've always enjoyed foreign travel.' He leaned in confidentially. 'Though I would have liked it a lot more if it hadn't been for the attentions of his wife.'

'Can it really have been so bad?'

'She never let me alone. She liked my wealth. My aristocratic heritage. Probably the same reasons you like me.'

Clara smiled.

'Who said I like you?'

He laughed, delightedly.

'But of course. You came here this morning solely for the exercise. And you accepted my dinner invitation in Paris out of a desire to discuss international affairs.'

She fought the urge to tell him how accurate he was.

'Talking of Paris, I was wondering. Who was that man you met?'

Adler's face shuttered instantly, the way it had on the bridge.

'It doesn't matter.'

'Is it something I shouldn't know?'

He sighed.

'His name is Alfred Rosenberg. You've heard of him, I take it?'

Alfred Rosenberg was the mad philosopher seer of the Party, one of the earliest members to demonize Jews, freemasons and Communists.

'There are a lot of Jews selling their stuff right now, trying to raise money to leave France, and there's desperate competition for it, from the highest places. Paris is crawling with art experts, art restorers, art packers, cataloguers.'

'So how does that involve Alfred Rosenberg?'

'He's overseeing it all. It's a joke really. Rosenberg likes art about as much as he likes Jews. To have a man like that in charge is quite ridiculous.'

'So he's in charge of paintings being sold?'

'Not just that.' A dry laugh. 'He's masterminding the cultural audit of Paris.'

'What does that mean?'

'All these questions, Clara Vine. Your curiosity is extraordinary.'

'I'm interested.'

'Fair enough. I'll tell you. We're bureaucrats, we Nazis, you see. That's where we excel. Some of the best works in the world are in Jewish hands – all the rich families, the Rothschilds, the Wildensteins, the Seligmanns. Rosenberg's scouts are finding where the Jews live and marking down their addresses. Inventories are being made of every important object of artistic and cultural value. Not just paintings, but sculptures, furniture, tapestries, bronzes, carpets, antiques, jewels.'

'Jewels?'

He's hunting for a jewel. He's looking for it high and low. God help anyone who gets in his way.

Adler shrugged. 'Everything. It will all be noted and entered in a ledger just in case the Reich needs to acquire it.'

'Just in case.'

'As you say. Just in case.'

'So the people at the Louvre . . .?'

'They were trying to outwit Rosenberg. The French are working overtime sending all their museum works to châteaux and other hiding places in the countryside. They think they can hide things, but it's futile. Rosenberg's spies know precisely where the valuable things can be found.'

Clara could scarcely believe she was hearing this. She tried valiantly not to look around her, to see if they were being overheard, until she realized that these comfortable burghers, with their great steins of frothing beer and their plates of Heaven and Earth – clouds of mashed potato with black pudding – probably agreed with Adler. The riches of a foreign country would sit far better in the Reich.

'So France will be relieved of her art if the country is invaded.'

Adler gave a casual shrug.

'Is it any different from what Napoleon did? He was the greatest art thief in history. And what about your Elgin Marbles? The glories of the Parthenon carried off to London. Beautiful objects will always be desired by the powerful. They will be well treated, appreciated. Loved, even.'

'And you're one of Rosenberg's spies.'

'God, no!' His eyes flashed with steel and Clara saw that a savage anger lay beneath Adler's urbane exterior. An anger he generally managed to suppress.

'I'm sorry. What else should I assume? He seemed to want to speak to you pretty urgently that night.'

'As I told you, I was advising on a collection.'

There was silence between them for a moment, and Adler stared sightlessly out into the forest before recovering his composure. Then his eyes became mellow again, dancing with amusement as though everything that had passed between them was a game.

'On the subject of Paris . . . I mentioned I was there to see beautiful things, and as it happens,' he reached to his side, 'I did come across something beautiful.'

He brought a minute parcel from his pocket. It was a burgundy coloured box, with the name Cartier tooled in gold. Adler flicked the catch to display its glinting contents sitting snugly on snow-white linen and pushed it across the table towards her. Two sparkling diamond earrings set in bright, buttery gold. A large diamond at each centre and a cluster of smaller ones around it. A shaft of sun lit the stones like a lick of flames at their core.

'Like fire behind ice. They reminded me of you.'

'I can't possibly.'

He swept a nonchalant hand.

'I was inspired by those pearls you wore the other evening. You seemed a woman who suits fine jewellery.'

'I couldn't accept them.'

'I hoped you might see them as by way of apology. For inconveniencing you. On the bridge.'

Clara couldn't take her eyes off the diamonds. They were lovelier than any jewellery she had ever possessed. Before she could help it, an image flashed through her mind of Conrad Adler fastening the studs to her naked ears.

Quietly, she said, 'I don't think diamonds are the answer to that.'

'It's a gift, but if you find it inappropriate then really, no matter.'

'I'm sorry.' She slid the box back across the table.

'As you wish.' He picked it up and replaced it in his pocket.

At once Clara worried that she had acted too hastily. Would the rebuff anger him? She had no desire to encourage Adler's romantic interest, but he was a valuable contact if she was to learn anything about the inner thinking of the Foreign Ministry.

'Shall we go?' He was rising from the table and reaching for his crop. 'There's something I'd like to show you.'

Adler strode ahead of her, out of the biergarten, remounted and led the way further into the wood.

It was darker here. The pale sky was lanced with branches and in the complicated shadows, deer skittered away through the brushwood. They carried on further as the bridleway narrowed, forcing them to duck beneath low-hanging trees with fists of fungus protruding from their trunks. The air tasted of dusk and decay. The claustrophobic gloom was freighted with the dank aroma of moss and soft, rotten mulch underfoot. Clara could not help thinking of Lotti Franke, and how, just a few miles from here, her body had been found.

Suddenly, the trees cleared and an expanse of lake lay ahead. On the far bank it was possible to see a large white villa, modelled in old Tyrolean style with red roofs and formal, well-cultivated gardens. Adler dismounted, tethered his horse to a low-hanging branch and Clara followed suit.

'That's my home.'

'It's beautiful. And very isolated.'

'There's no one there apart from my housekeeper and my dogs.'

'Were you ever married?'

'More questions, Clara.'

'You're quite happy to question me.'

'No, then.'

'Don't you get lonely?'

'I like it that way.'

He turned towards her and reached out.

'Perhaps you'd like to see it someday.'

He leaned to kiss her but she averted her face so that his lips merely brushed her cheek. Undeterred, he put his hands round her waist, pulled her roughly towards him and tipped her face up to his.

'Don't tell me some part of you doesn't desire this.'

Shock made her laugh, but there was a bubble of fear beneath.

'I can't imagine why you would think that.'

'Can't you? I thought you were different from the others. Do you want me to play some complicated game, to court you with flowers and violins?'

'Not at all.'

'Good. Because I'm not like that. If something pleases me, if it gives me pleasure to look at, then I say so. If I like it, I make that clear. I may be much older than you, but I sense we're both realists. We're both capable of taking what we want.'

'This is not what I want.'

He frowned, as if her refusal was some ancient philosophical problem that he was determined to solve.

'There must be someone else then. But he's not in evidence. Let me think. He must be married to another woman. Are you one of those actresses who have to make do with the scraps of a married man's attention? Or delude themselves that he will ever leave his Frau and his kleine Kinder. Who live out their lives waiting for the telephone to ring, losing out on their own hopes of happiness? Take a lesson from Frau Goebbels. You've heard the gossip. A woman is capable of making her own romantic decisions.'

'This man isn't married.'

'But he's not here, is he?'

'No.'

'And nor, I assume, is he married to you?'

Clara passionately did not want to tell him any more. She was mad to give away any information about her personal life. She felt a ripple of nerves. Any scrap of information was enough for the Gestapo to work on. Like a single drop of blood to a hungry predator, the smallest detail was enough for them to work with.

Adler was staring down at her, arms crossed, eyes drilling into hers.

'I'm not sure I believe in this phantom lover of yours. I don't believe in ghosts.'

'He does exist.'

'What's his name then?'

Leo. His name leapt into her mouth but she could not give it breath.

'It doesn't matter.'

'You don't swallow that nonsense about there only being one person, one soul mate, do you? It's a delusion, you know.'

'Not to me.'

'You're far too intelligent. That kind of thing is only fit for the script of *Love Strictly Forbidden*. You know as well as I do that's not for adults. Human emotions are entirely untrustworthy. I, for one, have never been in love and I don't intend to start now.'

He was smiling, yet she could see from the bruised eyes and the way his fingers flicked, that her refusal had bothered him.

As if struck by a sudden thought, he took her hand.

'Perhaps I could think of a bargain,' he said lightly. 'If you become my mistress, no one would need to know that you were Jewish.'

Suddenly all Clara's fear was turned to a churning anger. Any attraction he had ever roused in her evaporated. She wrenched her hand away.

'If that's what you think I am, why would you want a Jewish mistress?'

He looked at her impatiently.

'I told you. I don't care about race. Pedigree. I thought you realized.'

'What would that relationship be worth, if you bought it at a price?'

'Everything comes at a price. Even the greatest art is traded in the marketplace like bread or eggs.'

'And you think human beings have a price?'

'Don't be a fool, Clara. Of course they do. I'm proposing a bargain. We all make bargains in our lives. I'm not a savage. I don't want to force you into something against your will. That would be beneath my dignity.'

'So is making threats against me.'

He lifted a hand to touch her cheek and she jerked away.

'You can't want a woman under these circumstances. What about love, or affection?'

He shrugged. 'Just words.'

An image flickered through her mind. Something old,

something she had not thought of for years. Her brother Kenneth's collection of butterflies. Ken was mad about butterflies. He collected them all through one summer in Cornwall; Red Admiral, Cabbage White, Purple Emperor, and once they had expired he stuck them with a pin into a frame. As a girl Clara had hated to see those tiny fragments of beauty, designed to be seen only in a transitory flutter, fixed forever. The dust scalloped on their intricate wings offered up to any passing gaze. That was what she meant to the bored, cultured Conrad Adler. A pretty specimen to be studied and admired, imprisoned by compromise and circumstance.

Ducking out of his arms, she sprang back onto her horse, turned his head sharply and spurred him to a canter. The horse responded willingly, flying much too fast through the difficult forest terrain until a bird whirring up from the brushwood caused him to startle, and he shied forcefully to one side, throwing Clara out of the saddle and pitching her painfully into the undergrowth.

Instantly Adler was at her side. He hauled her up with one hand and held her shoulder. The sardonic, jousting manner was gone. His eyes were serious and concerned.

'Are you all right?'

'Yes. I think so.'

He caught her horse's reins and slung them across a branch, then came down to squat beside her.

'Rest a minute. Lean against my arm. You need a moment to recover.'

He was right. The shock of the fall had momentarily dazed her. She leant back against him and when he touched a tentative hand to her forehead, she did not resist.

He had lean hands, the hands of a pianist or an artist or a surgeon. Hardly the hands of a member of Himmler's élite. But then, what were the hands of an Obersturmbannführer supposed to look like? Once the blood had returned to Clara's head, she sprang up, brushed herself down, and patted her hair back into place.

Adler helped her back into the saddle, the old, sardonic smile back in place.

'You should think about it, Clara. After all, I'm not a ghost. I do have the great advantage of being flesh and blood.'

Chapter Twenty-six

She had lived all her life in Berlin, yet Hedwig had never set foot in the Admiralspalast, even though it was everything she loved. With its scrolly, Expressionist façade, it was the biggest and brashest of the fantasy palaces which lit up Friedrichstrasse's theatre land. The Admiralspalast was a great, baroque barn of a place seating twenty thousand people for a repertoire that included dance acts, operetta, magicians, and every aspect of light entertainment. It was probably the last place on earth that Jochen would want to visit, so it was with a mixture of astonishment and delight that she heard he had tickets for the Saturday evening show.

That night an eager queue wound along the street. Theatre audiences were up this summer. Everyone was trying to escape the worries of the present – the continual daily niggles of what the next meal might resemble, and after they'd eaten it, how to look presentable enough to go out. And once they'd got there, whether the gaudy signs and blinking neon billboards of the theatre might be plunged into darkness when war arrived in a few months' time. Just then, all anyone wanted was to lose themselves in a few hours of romantic nonsense and that evening's variety performance perfectly fitted the bill.

Standing beneath the pillared entrance, her face dappled emerald and ruby in the flashing light, Hedwig shuffled her feet and hoped Jochen would not be much longer. Her legs ached. All day they had been practising waltzes for Minister Goering's ball. Their own ball dresses – white taffeta and silk with blue sashes – were not yet finished, so they were wearing gym kit, which only seemed to make the waltz practice more ridiculous, and the routine was being supervised by Fräulein von Essen, whose hefty form was more at home on an alpine hike than pirouetting around a dance floor.

Waltzes were what the Führer loved best, due to his Austrian heritage, and not only would the Führer actually be present, there was a chance that one of the Faith and Beauty girls would be asked to dance with him. Even the thought of that made Hedwig rigid with horror. If the Führer's gaze fell on her, would she have the courage to go through with it, or would her legs simply give way beneath her? She consoled herself with the knowledge that Fräulein von Essen would regard the partnering of Hedwig and Hitler with precisely the same horror, and would ensure that if there was any line of female partners for the Führer, Hedwig would be at the back of it.

Especially after that morning's practice. Hedwig had been partnering Hilde, one of the prettiest and most graceful of the Faith and Beauty girls, with a doll's delicate, creamy complexion and a glossy crown of braids. It was bad enough that Hedwig had two left feet, but Hilde's skill made everything worse. A couple of Kripo detectives, part of the investigation team for Lotti's murder, loitered at the doorway, ogling and making ribald remarks, and the sensation of the policemen's eyes on her made Hedwig trip on Hilde's feet and even from the other side of the room she could hear their snorts of laughter.

She gazed anxiously up the street. Friedrichstrasse was thronged with people. The crowds flowed seamlessly between those returning from work and others setting out for an evening's entertainment. Trams screeched, people jostled and neon dazzled all around them. The show was due to start in less than five minutes and Jochen was nowhere to be seen.

I was going to ask you something.

Every night since he had said that, she had lain awake, puzzling over it, cherishing it like some delicious secret, wondering what it might be. Or, more precisely, what her decision would be, because she had guessed already what Jochen was going to ask.

He was planning for them to elope. The idea sent a thrill through her, even as she mentally shied away from the daring it would entail. How would she pluck up the courage to leave the home she had known all her life? There would be more work for her mother without help in the kitchen, let alone with all the boys. Yet also there would be one less mouth to feed, and with the apartment so crowded, they could use the extra space. But how could she leave the children? How would darling Kurt, with his sleepy smile and milky breath, cope without her? Kurt was more like her own child than her brother. What would it do to him if she suddenly disappeared?

Despite these dilemmas, Jochen's proposition had come as a welcome distraction. It was the only thing diverting her from endless brooding about Lotti's death.

'Sorry I'm late, Hedy. Work.'

He broke into her dreams with a gust of cold air and a rough kiss on the cheek. He had his briefcase in one hand, and with the other he took hers and tugged her through the throng. 'We have precisely two minutes.'

They edged their way in through the crowds and settled in a row at the front of the stalls, waiting for the luxurious swags of purple velvet to rise and reveal the stage.

'What have you been doing?' he whispered.

'Practising for Reichsminister Goering's ball.'

'Sounds interesting.'

He was being polite. That was another change. Jochen had been in a difficult mood lately and much as she tended to attribute all problems to her own deficiencies, she knew it was more likely down to the stress of work. His company had been working overtime making anniversary editions of *Mein Kampf* and Jochen was an important part of that, crafting the elaborate, mediaeval-style frontispiece for each edition in Gothic writing, replete with swirls of black ink, oak leaf swags and fat little cherubs at the margins.

'It's not just dancing. We're having to practise conversation. They say it's important that the Prince of Yugoslavia gets a good impression of Germany.'

Most girls could barely lift their thoughts above their families and their favourite movies, but Faith and Beauty girls needed to understand the currents that motivated world affairs.

'Apparently Russia holds a Bolshevik dagger at Germany's throat but Prince Paul can help the Führer restore balance to Europe.'

'And how exactly will he manage that?'

'I can't remember.'

Hedwig was sketchy on the details because she had lost all ability to concentrate. Every visit to the Faith and Beauty home these days filled her with apprehension. Everything had changed. The place was buzzing with policemen, shouldering their way through the corridors, building a picture of Lotti's last hours. A pair of detectives had even come into the art class and hauled Herr Fritzl out for questioning. Hedwig couldn't help thinking that his face, chalky with fright, had resembled one of the pieces of Degenerate Art he was so keen to condemn.

'They read out an address from Reichsführer Himmler. He says he wants us to be Hohe Frauen, Sublime Women. We're going to be trained in several languages, as well as debating and chess.'

'So I'm taking out a sublime woman, eh? I don't need Heini Himmler to tell me that.'

She could feel the undercurrent of laughter in Jochen's voice. Not derisive mockery, like the Kripo men, but affectionate amusement.

The lights darkened and she shuffled down in her seat as the chorus line came on. A variety show always started with the chorus, before the individual acts got going. The orchestra struck up *Dein ist mein ganzes Herz*, the song that Richard Tauber had sung to Marlene Dietrich in *The Land of Smiles*. You Are My Heart's Delight. It could hardly be more perfect. She reached across to Jochen and felt his warm fingers stroke the back of her hand.

Even though they were dressed in feathers and tulle, the girls performed with as much military discipline as any stormtrooper on the Führer's birthday parade. When they goose-stepped, turned, bent and regarded the audience through their parted legs, Hedwig expected to feel Jochen stiffen with distaste, but instead he was transfixed. It was a revelation to her that he might like dancing. She hoped he never wanted to dance with her.

The girls changed costumes and returned dressed as Red Indians with strategically placed feathers preserving what little modesty they possessed. Watching Jochen more closely out of the corner of her eye, Hedwig realized that despite their shapely legs and high kicks, it was not the dancers that had captured his attention but the orchestra. And in particular, one member of the orchestra. Following his gaze, she saw a stunningly lovely brunette playing lead violin, her instrument clenched beneath her chin and her bow sawing the air with febrile energy. She must have been in her early twenties, her thick chestnut hair bundled up like ballerina's from a face that acted as a mirror to the passions of the music, by turns grave and joyful. Jochen seemed entirely captivated by her, as though all the dancers, musicians, the theatre audience and even Hedwig herself simply did not exist.

A blind surge of jealousy rose in her. Early in their relationship she had coaxed out of Jochen the dismaying news that he preferred brunettes to blondes, except in her case. Now, she guessed, he was reverting to type.

It had rained again during the show and when they emerged from the theatre two hours later Friedrichstrasse was glinting with a thin sheen of water, the puddles rippling with speckled light. People jostled for cabs and flung up their umbrellas. Others huddled into their fur collars and turned down the brim of their hats. To her surprise Jochen seized her hand and ushered her around the corner down the dank alley to the theatre's stage door.

'I just need to see someone for a moment. Don't mind, do you? It's work.'

'Work?'

His face shuttered in the way that brooked no argument.

'I'll be out in a moment.'

Hedwig stood mutely beneath the misty light of the stage door, trying to keep out of the rain and to prevent herself being engulfed in a wave of misery and outrage. How could Jochen bring her to the theatre if his true interest was a brunette who played the violin? Did he imagine she wouldn't notice, or did he think she was the kind of doormat to tolerate some amorous adventure when he was supposed to be on a date with her? She heard her mother's voice again, with its knowing, cynical ring.

That boy is not to be trusted.

Less than two minutes later Jochen was back, briefcase under one arm.

Hedwig walked stiffly, trying to transmit her unhappiness through silence, but Jochen actually preferred walking without conversation, so eventually she said, 'What was all that about?'

'All what?'

His mouth was a tight line and his jaw was set like rock. As they dodged the crowds pouring out of theatres and cinemas, he increased his stride.

'The girl in the orchestra. I saw you watching her. Then you went to meet her, didn't you?'

He gave a little humourless laugh.

'You're not jealous, surely.'

He was walking fast. Hedwig had to do a little skip to keep up.

'Why did you see her?'

There was an even longer silence so that she feared he was furious, and part of her longed to abandon the matter entirely, though another part insisted that she discover everything. After a while he said, fiercely, 'You don't want to ask these questions. You won't like the answers.'

'Just tell me!'

They had proceeded as far as the Gendarmenmarkt, where the grey stone Concert House was flanked by two matching cathedrals, the French and the German. The plinth where the bust of Schiller, Germany's Shakespeare, had stood for generations was still empty, having been removed a few years previously on account of his new-found degenerate status.

Still Jochen stared ahead, saying nothing. Something intense and dangerous loomed between them. Hedwig didn't care any more about the rain that blurred her spectacles and mingled with her tears. She didn't know where they were heading, or why the man she loved was behaving in this cruel and unfamiliar fashion. Her voice choked in her throat.

'Jochen?'

Eventually he replied.

'Are you sure you want to hear?'

She nodded weakly. She didn't trust herself to talk.

'All right. I'll tell you. Her name is Sofie. We meet every Tuesday.'

'Do you love her?' she said, in a small, stricken voice.

'Sofie has nothing to do with you and me.'

'I asked if you loved her.'

'I admire her, certainly.'

'How long have you known her?'

'Some time.'

'And where do you meet?'

'Her father has a villa in Dahlem.'

It was everything Hedwig feared. Her beloved Jochen was in love with a clever, rich, beautiful woman. A woman whose family lived in Dahlem, which was so far from Moabit in its social status, it might as well have been Timbuktu. No social graces Hedwig could ever learn at the Faith and Beauty Society – no amount of ballroom dancing, or flower arranging or chess – could match the social status of a girl called Sofie who lived in a villa in Dahlem.

'And does she take you there?'

'Yes. For dinner. Her family know all kinds of artists, politicians and priests. Important people. They talk about literature; Brecht, Schiller. Other people I've not heard of.'

A conflict of emotions warred in his face.

'A lot of them are aristocrats, bohemians. Not my sort. But their hearts are in the right place. And the main thing is . . .'

He stopped, turned to her and moved his face very close.

'They all hate the Nazis.'

His words floated quietly on the night air, like a hiss.

'Some of them hate National Socialist politics but others just consider the Nazis ill bred. Rich people think like that, you know, but being smart works in these people's favour. No one believes a family like Sofie's could have money and still belong to the KPD.'

The KPD. The banned German Communist Party. Hedwig's heart sank like lead. Mutti had been right.

'Are you a Communist?'

It was not a word she ever used. It felt as bitter in her mouth as a lump of shrapnel. Communists were never mentioned at home, except as a curse. Bolsheviks were Germany's worst fate, it said on the radio. The Jew devil.

'No. I'm a good German. But we do have Communists. And Conservatives, Social Democrats, Catholics, Lutherans, Jews. Doctors, military officers, academics. One of them is a playwright who works in the Propaganda Ministry. There's a guy called Helmut who's the official dentist to the Ufa studios. He does all the stars' teeth. He gets us typewriter ribbons and ink for our newspaper.'

'Why would he do that?'

'Same reason as any of us.'

Hedwig was floundering. Grappling with her coordinates the way she tried to work her compass in the forest. Trying to reset everything she had believed with this new information.

'They're not all smart types. There's a waiter at the Kaiserhof who reads all the foreign newspapers for us, everything – French, English, Danish, Dutch, Russian – so we get an idea of opinion beyond Goebbels' lies.'

Her whole world was shifting on its axis. Everything she knew had turned upside down as though an enormous wrecking ball had taken aim and was reducing her life to rubble.

'But why? What do you want to do, Jochen?'

'I wanted some way of resisting what was going on, and it wasn't going to be killing Hitler. I was never going to be able to manage something like that.'

Killing Hitler? Hedwig's knees almost buckled beneath her and she craned her head round in the quick instinctive glance that was known as *der deutsche Blick*. The German look.

'How did you . . . how did you meet these people then?'

'Through a friend. He thought I would be useful because I'm a graphic artist, but he still screened me first, to check my leanings. He gave me a cigarette packet and when I opened it I found a message asking me to make a flyer denouncing the occupation of the Sudetenland.'

The Sudetenland. Then this must have been last year, Hedwig thought, making mental calculations and trying her hardest to recall the current affairs that generally passed her by.

'And did you? Do what he asked?'

'I did. I designed the pamphlet and someone else in the group printed them. Then another member, who is a Persil washing powder distributor, packed them in Persil boxes, and topped them up with detergent.'

'What happened to them after that?'

'I don't know. The idea is that we don't know too much. So we can't reveal anything if we're caught.'

The frankness with which he alluded to this terrifying possibility astonished her. Yet although alarm and horror were churning through her, there remained a residual sense of jealousy.

'And that girl at the theatre? Sofie. What about her?'

'Sofie's a professional musician. She's extremely talented. She studied under a student of Mendelssohn's.'

'Oh.' This information did nothing to alleviate Hedwig's jealousy.

'At the moment she performs in the orchestra at the Admiralspalast every night, then after the show she takes our pamphlets out in her sheet music portfolio. No one ever suspects sheet music.'

It was dark, now that all the streetlamps had been dimmed to save money, and they had reached the point in Französische Strasse where an arch supported by giant caryatids flung a pool of deeper shadow. Jochen halted and drew her towards him.

'What we do is important, Hedy. One of our members has a brother in the army who supplies him with details of Jews who are scheduled for arrest, so we can warn them in time.'

'Are these friends of yours *Jews* then?' The word almost choked in her throat. Whenever Hedwig thought of Jews she imagined the leering figures you saw on the front of *Der Stürmer*, like crooked shadows with their long black coats and yellow eyes.

'Some are. Some have been in camps, but we have to be extra careful with those because sometimes people are only released from camps on the condition that they find their former friends and lead the Gestapo to them. They call the people we help U-Boats. Submarines. You must have heard of them.'

Now that he was speaking, it was as though he couldn't stop. But Hedwig wanted to stick her fingers in her ears. The delight-ful evening had taken a terrible wrong direction. She wanted everything she had heard to disappear.

'Why are you telling me all this?'

'You asked me.'

'I had no choice.'

He stopped and turned towards her, taking her face in his hands. His eyes burned into her like acid, so fierce she almost flinched.

'And now, my darling, you *do* have a choice. You can denounce me, or you can help me. If you denounce me then I will be hauled off to be shot and maybe you too. Perhaps even your dear Mutti and Vati will come under suspicion.'

Her tears began to stream and Jochen took her in his arms.

'Don't cry. I can't bear that. I never intended to involve you. I had every intention of keeping you out of this. But you're going to need to choose. Just like we all have.'

After a pause, she said, 'I could never denounce you.'

'I knew that, Hedy.'

He kissed her. A tender, lingering kiss.

'Remember that question? The one I was going to ask you? You haven't forgotten about it?'

The question that had fuelled her fantasies and kept her miser-ies at bay night after night. Might it still be the question she had imagined? Hedwig shook her head mutely.

'Good. There's no time to talk about it now. It can wait for later. We'll meet next Thursday, shall we, like always? At the usual place?'

Chapter Twenty-seven

A lone hawk hung in the sky. Clara watched as it hovered on a blade of air, then dropped like a stone and slammed through the mist into the leather glove of the falconer below. Beyond it lay the horizon of the Westphalian plane bisected by the River Alme, damp and grey as a photograph slightly out of focus. Stone houses and dairy farms hunkered beneath a low drizzle that was rolling across the sky. Looming on a hill above them all stood a hulking castle, as brooding, implacable and ominous as anything from the Ufa studios' own horror movies.

Wewelsburg. The spiritual heart of the SS.

Himmler had discovered the derelict castle of Wewelsburg in 1933, close to the site where an ancient Germanic chief had defeated the Roman army of occupation. With a provenance like that, it couldn't appeal more to the Gestapo chief and without hesitation he bought the lease and set about establishing a Reichsführerschule to train the élite ranks of his SS. Yet although Wewelsburg combined German pre-history and mystical significance in one implacable, blank-walled monument, the castle was far more than an officers' leadership school. It was to be Himmler's Camelot, the place where he would raise up a new order of Teutonic knights, a blood brotherhood of the racially pure.

For that reason, much to Clara's relief, no women would ever be permitted to stay the night.

They had travelled in Leni Riefenstahl's Mercedes convertible, past undulating fields ploughed in corduroy rows with a film of spring green hovering over the turned earth and isolated half-timbered houses with casement windows and geraniums at the sills. South of Paderborn they passed a gang of ragged workers, who from their stubbled faces, starved frames and striped uniforms must have been drafted in from a concentration camp. Some were digging trenches in the earth and others were hacking at piles of rocks, cleaving them into smaller pieces. None turned to sneak a glance at the sleek maroon car, with its gleaming brunette at the wheel. Were they afraid, or were they simply used to processions of shiny vehicles whose passengers seemed to look out at them, and yet look through them at the same time?

'What are those workers doing?'

'They're building an SS village,' said Leni. 'Himmler has bought up a lot of the land around here to provide homes for the wives and children of SS men. Those workers come from a KZ.'

'I didn't know there was a camp near here.'

'There wasn't. Himmler built one, especially for the building work. The only problem is, they keep unearthing old pottery beakers and cup handles and every time they find a fragment Himmler orders a halt on account of it being part of our ancient Germanic heritage.' She gave a gravelly laugh. 'It will take them years at this rate.'

She turned off the road at a small, timbered lodge with a carved wooden exterior and a sharp triangular gable called Ottens Hof.

'Let's stop. I don't think I can manage this without a drink.'

A glimpse inside Ottens Hof, however, and it almost required a stiff schnapps to get over the threshold. The tavern might have been plucked straight out of the sixteenth century, complete with hunting gear, harnesses and mediaeval torture implements fixed to the walls. Axes, spears and animal traps were suspended beneath a high timbered ceiling from where candles in elaborate wrought-iron holders only dimly pierced the gloom. Sturdy oak tables, set for dinner, stretched the length of the hall, yet at this time of the day the place was almost deserted, with only a single barmaid mopping the floor. She straightened up as they entered and resumed her place behind the bar.

'This is Himmler's private dining club. All the senior SS men come here to relax after summits at the castle. Look at the benches.'

Peering down Clara saw strange symbols carved into the wood and looking closer saw that the intricate letters were runes, worked all around the seats, and along the legs of the tables. Identical markings appeared on a frieze at the top of the wall, and carved into jutting timbers between the alcoves. Although the wording was indecipherable, the message from the emblazoned SS symbol was all too clear. No place was too obscure to escape the influence of Himmler's enthusiasms.

Leni returned with two glasses of beer, pounced on Clara's French cigarettes and leaned back against the Totenkopf skull carved on the pew.

'What a journey! Why does Himmler have to choose Westphalia of all places? Wewelsburg may be the centre of the world, but it would help if it was a little more . . . *central*.'

'In what way is *this* the centre of the world?'

'Oh, it has ancestral energy, apparently. Himmler says it will be the centre of the rebirth of the Germanic nation. You know how he is about superstitions. Some astrologer told him an old Westphalian legend says an army from the East will on this very spot be beaten by an army of the West. He adores that kind of thing. You've met him, haven't you?'

'Once. Last year.'

At five foot eleven, short-sighted and with surprisingly delicate fingers, Himmler represented the precise opposite of his Nordic ideal. To look at he might have been an accountant or a lawyer or a clerk, anything rather than the head of a fifty-thousand-strong terror outfit. Though he probably knew more about the atrocities being visited on people in the Reich than even Hitler himself, Himmler was an ardent family man, devoted to his daughter Püppi and his scrub-faced wife Marga – a dour woman seven years his senior who obstinately refused the siren call of Berlin and all its glamour, preferring to stay home on their rural farm. Though Clara hoped passionately that Himmler would not remember her, it was said he never forgot a face. He himself barely needed the rotating file index of fifty thousand names that had been installed at Gestapo headquarters in Berlin.

Leni narrowed her eyes.

'The way he's behaving you'd think the castle was under siege already. His office has been impossible about the filming. I told him I needed a crew of a hundred and he said no more than thirty. What's more, we won't be able to film inside anywhere except a single room where a wedding consecration is taking place. That's the only thing he actually wanted me to film. Himmler's keen on weddings.'

She rolled her eyes.

'He's going to allow outstanding SS men to marry two wives. He calls it a reward for heroes. Apparently there was some ancient custom in the early Germanic tribes, where men of elevated social position were exempted from monogamy.'

'It's not that ancient. I know plenty of men who think the same.'

Leni grinned. 'I've met those men too. So we'll start with you, up on the battlements, the wind in your hair, symbolizing the legion of German ancestors who have repelled the enemy from the East. A tight shot on your face then we pan out to reveal the entire landscape of Germania spread before you. You saw the costume?'

Leni's costume idea for the Spirit of *Germania* translated to a modified dirndl, a deep green dress with a laced bodice and

square neckline, but thankfully without the frill of lace or the
spill of cleavage that the true Bavarian costume would demand.

Clara nodded.

'Lovely,' said Leni, stubbing out her cigarette and rising to her
feet. 'Shall we get on with it then?'

Up close, Wewelsburg looked more like a prison than a castle, its
ranks of narrow windows gazing blankly out across the valley and
turrets silhouetted starkly against the lowering sky. It had a striking triangular design, with massive stone walls orientated in a
north–south axis and twin domes garnished with the fluttering
black and white lightning flash flag of the SS.

As they crossed the drawbridge, Clara could hardly stop herself
from trembling. She kept her hands folded in her lap and her
gaze fixed, but her stomach was as clenched as a fist and she
could barely swallow. This was the moment of truth. It was
inconceivable that she would be allowed to enter Himmler's
most precious domain without an identity check. Her plan was
to say that her identity document was 'lost' – a situation that
counted as a misdemeanour in itself.

At the gatehouse there was the sound of dogs barking and a
harsh command of silence as two soldiers with helmets and rifles,
wearing waterproof capes against the first spattering of rain,
approached the car.

'Don't look so gloomy, Clara. It's a tremendous privilege to be
here. Himmler is obsessed with secrecy. A big part of him doesn't
want anyone to know that this place even exists – but he recognized that our film would be incomplete without it.' Leni gave a
slow, crimson smile.

'Well, hello, young man.'

The guard's chiselled features and hard eyes broke into a grin
of surprise when he recognized her. His expression said it all.
The Führer's film director! So that was who the cameramen and
lighting operatives and production crew were waiting for.

'Fräulein Riefenstahl. Welcome to Wewelsburg!'

'I'm honoured.' Her voice was huskily seductive. 'I hear you don't often get female visitors.'

'Only for wedding consecrations. Today is a special day.'

'We shall have to make the most of it then.'

The guard peered closer into the car, towards the passenger seat. Beside him, his dog was broad and muscular, with dense black fur like the canine equivalent of an SS dress uniform. Clara focused on its flat, uncomprehending eyes.

'And your companion?'

Clara remained impassive. Of course the solider would want to know who she was. Wewelsburg of all places in the Reich would employ dedicated guards with the most scrupulous attention to duty. How could she possibly have hoped that her lack of identity documents would be overlooked?

'My star, you mean?'

'Of course!' he registered half-recognition, but not enough to deter him from his duty. 'I wonder if . . .'

At that moment there was an almighty crash, the sound of splintering glass and a volley of shouts arose from across the courtyard. Furious voices called for help. The guard glanced behind him in confusion and waved them through. Leni drove the Mercedes into the courtyard and the gate clanged behind them.

Once inside, the forbidding, mediaeval-style exterior gave way to a triangular courtyard that contained an unexpected bustle of activity. The crash they had heard was a steel ladder falling from a truck containing lighting equipment being unloaded down a ramp into one door of the castle. It appeared the ladder had narrowly avoided decapitating a camera operator. Other production staff scurried around, trailing wires and carrying megaphones. Standing arc lights, lenses and a number of aluminium boxes were being ferried into the building. Against an opposite wall, the drivers leaned, killing time with a cigarette break. A

couple of SS officers in leather coats skirted the truck with unmistakable irritation at the intrusion of the film world into their
private domain, but Clara was glad for these tokens of normality.
Wewelsburg castle was under siege that day, and she didn't care
if the movie world laid waste to it.

Leni parked up, adjusted the rear-view mirror, touched up her
mascara and gave herself a quick dab of powder.

'If this is the only time women are allowed to set foot in the
castle, a girl has to be her best. I'm not looking bedraggled with
the cream of SS honour guards standing around me.'

Yet again Clara was astonished at Leni's coquettishness. She
was the greatest female director in the world, she had the ear of
Hitler himself – yet still she cared about her complexion in front
of a bunch of SS leadership trainees.

Leni stowed the make-up away and grabbed her bag.

'Right. The crew have had plenty of time to set up. I need you
in position straight away. You're up on the north tower. We
open with a leaflet fluttering along the battlements. Its headline
says *Germania*. The camera will pan up towards your face. You
look towards the East. You are solemn, but transfixed. Your face
glows with optimism for the future and faith in the Führer. And
remember, you represent your country.'

It was chilly on the battlements and needles of rain were carried
on a sharp wind. Clara spent an hour gazing into the distance
with Leni and a cameraman lying on a trolleyboard at her feet.
Though she tried her best to summon a look of optimism for the
future, the sight of an SS guard marshalling in the courtyard
beneath with parade ground precision made it quite a challenge.

After five takes Leni was satisfied and the crew began to
dismantle their equipment.

'It's the wedding next.' A sardonic grimace. 'Irna Wolter's
special day. We don't need you in this scene, Clara, but you're
welcome to watch.'

Clara followed her down the stone steps.

For a wedding, it would be hard to imagine a venue more funereal. With its spartan brick floor, exposed timbers and windowless walls, the oppressive gloom of the consecration hall was barely penetrated by the greasy light of a gas lamp hanging from a wrought-iron fitting. At the front, a wooden table was furnished with a pair of völkisch candlesticks and oak leaves, and as a gesture to the essentially joyful nature of the occasion a picture of their host, Himmler. The groom was in place already, fiddling with his belt and cap and trying valiantly to ignore the bevy of lighting men, sound men, cameramen around him, not to mention the figure of Leni Riefenstahl, crouching at knee level. He looked scarcely out of his teens, rigid with tension and bearing a bubble of blood on his cheek where he had cut himself shaving. All around him black-uniformed officers engaged in the same awkward chat that occupies any wedding party, as they await the entrance of the bride.

Irna Wolter looked younger than her twenty years. She had procured a long white dress and had been furnished with an armful of creamy roses whose weak fragrance wavered faintly across the chilly space. Her expression was strained, as well it might be, considering the amount of preparation she had devoted to this moment in the previous six weeks. Apart from her time at Bride School, essential to gain the document of marriage consent, Irna must also have compiled a sheaf of further certificates – proof of her ancestry and physical health, of the measurement of her facial features and her blood type, not to mention medical certificates to ensure that no one in her family suffered from any mental or congenital illness. There was more paperwork in a Third Reich wedding than any amount of confetti.

The prospect of being filmed for posterity did nothing to ease Irna's nerves. Directly in front of her Leni had mounted a step ladder and was softly instructing the camera operator to focus on the bride's face. As the officiating officer began his talk – a lengthy drone centring on the responsibilities of SS marriage, including at least four children and entering their names in the clan bible of the SS Sippenbuch – Irna was as pale as a ghost. Her hand visibly trembled during the exchange of silver rings engraved with runes, but she managed not to drop the gifts of bread and salt, nor the specially inscribed copy of *Mein Kampf* that was presented to all happy couples.

What must Irna feel? Had she winced at the chill steel of the calliper, measuring the distance between her nose and upper lip? Had she trembled at the prospect of tainted blood or disease being detected deep in her ancestry? Did she fret at swapping one set of regulations at the Faith and Beauty Society for the fresh constraints of married life? Or was anything bearable, if it meant being with the man you loved?

For a brief second the proceedings in front of Clara faded and it was she herself in the white dress, standing at a church altar in England somewhere with Leo beside her smiling into her eyes. The image hovered only a moment in her mind before she blinked, and brushed it away.

Suddenly the oppressive air of the wedding chamber was more than she could bear. The tension of being in Wewelsburg was making it hard to breathe. Turning tail, she slipped softly out of the door and headed off down the corridor, trying to remember the route back to the north tower.

It was more complicated than she had imagined. After two wrong turns she found herself in a long brick corridor studded with doors that appeared to be offices. Between them were arranged suits of armour and collections of ancestral knives and swords. The passage was narrow and badly lit and the icy walls themselves seemed to exude a sense of menace. Clara hesitated, wondering whether to turn back, when from the far end of the corridor came the crunch of boots and she hurried on, taking the next available turning and descending a flight of treacherous steps into depthless darkness.

It was a crypt of sorts, about fifteen metres wide, and as her eyes adjusted she saw that the blackness was penetrated by spears of light lancing down through narrow apertures onto twelve seats set into the walls. Each had a wall niche set above it, and on the ceiling, a swastika extended its crooked arms. In a circular depression in the centre of the room, an eternal flame flickered, filling the air with smoke and acrid incense. She guessed at once that the twelve seats represented the twelve knights of King Arthur and the round table. A devotion to Wagner was compulsory among the Nazi élite. Hitler would stand on the balcony of the Berghof with the prelude to Parsifal playing on his gramophone. Goering had concocted his own Wagnerian fantasy in the shape of his hunting lodge Carinhall and even Goebbels claimed to love the composer and devotedly attended the annual Bayreuth festival. Himmler – intent on surrounding himself with a band of racially pure blood brothers – had chosen Wagner's Camelot as his personal obsession, but the future occupants of these seats would be no knights in shining armour.

The blood pumping in her ears, Clara felt the air around her contract. She remembered the feeling she had at the Faith and Beauty house of a rapt devotion, a sense of belonging in the women to something greater than themselves. The same claustrophobic feeling existed in this crypt, savage and almost tangible, inspiring a terror as real as if she had plunged down a lift shaft with no chance of escape.

Scanning the crypt, she detected at the opposite side a gap in the wall. It led to a spiral staircase of damp stone and she laboured blindly up countless winding steps until she felt the first breath of fresh air on her face and saw a glimmer of daylight ahead. By her calculation she was close to the battlements once more, but as she reached the top she was distracted by the sound of voices and stopped in her tracks.

Leni Riefenstahl was standing with the falconer they had seen on their arrival. The hawk was hooded now, with a bell tied to its leg, and the falconer was running his finger down the bird's glinting plumage, tenderly stroking the feathers of its neck, as Leni engaged in a lively argument with two men. The men had their backs to Clara, but even from behind, the shaved skull, wide breeches and black cap of the nearest man would be unmistakable to any citizen of the Reich.

SS-Reichsführer Heinrich Himmler.

Clara shrank back against the wall of the staircase as their conversation carried on the wind.

'I thought you understood, Fräulein Riefenstahl. Animals are prohibited in Reich film making. Surely you of all people should know that?'

'I wasn't aware that birds were covered by that edict,' said Leni, with a sweetly furious smile.

'Of course, birds. I, of all people, understand the intelligence of birds. I ran a chicken farm for years. No German under my command will mistreat animals or birds or inflict any unnecessary suffering. I hope I can ensure that you will abide by these restrictions for the remainder of your stay.'

'Whatever you say, Herr Reichsführer.'

Gesturing to the man beside him, Himmler turned on his heel. Clara found Leni cursing softly.

'Damn.'

'What was all that about?'

'I had a beautiful shot lined up with that hawk. It was to be the final image of the entire film. The brooding ancient walls, the sheer perfection of the lines of young men, then I pull focus to find a single hawk climbing upwards, eastwards, until it disappears into a rent in the clouds. The hawk symbolizes ambition, the future, the eternal quest of the Reich. But Himmler, of course, disapproves. He understands nothing about art. He says filming his damn hawk constitutes illegal exploitation of animals.'

'Who was that man with him?'

'Oh, his masseur.'

She rolled her eyes.

'I know. Hard to imagine, isn't it?'

More than hard, the image of a prone Himmler, relaxing for a tender muscle rub, was inconceivable.

'Himmler was unbearable because he was in constant pain and no one could help him. His staff were beside themselves, until eventually someone discovered this man, Felix Kersten, who had studied Tibetan skills under a Llama. Himmler was persuaded to try it and fortunately for Herr Kersten, the treatment actually worked. Himmler was an instant convert, but the thing is, Kersten has to stay a big secret. That's why Himmler meets him here. He does everything he can to keep Kersten out of sight.'

'Is he embarrassed?'

'Are you joking? Nothing could embarrass Himmler. No, he's terrified that Heydrich will find out and get hold of his medical details.'

'But Heydrich is his own deputy.'

'That means nothing. In Heydrich's mind, information is power. He has a locked safe that he refers to as his "poison cabinet" where he keeps all his files on the senior men.'

Looking at Clara's face Leni laughed, and added, 'Sounds crazy, doesn't it? But the fact is, all the top men are at each other's throats. Their true war is with each other. Goering hates Goebbels far more than he could possibly hate Poland, and you know how much Goebbels despises Himmler. Himmler is rivals with all of them. I never told you why I chose you for this part, did I?'

'You said I had the right face.'

'Of course, darling.' A smile of malicious pleasure. 'But I could have chosen any number of actresses. It's not a difficult part, after all. No, the real reason I chose you was not to annoy Goebbels but Himmler.'

The wind was battering their words away, so there was no danger of being overheard, but all the same Clara lowered her voice.

'Why on earth would choosing me annoy Himmler?'

Leni chuckled like a girl revealing a conjuring trick. 'Oh, he was terribly interested in you. I've overheard him asking about you and I was curious because Himmler doesn't go for actresses as you know. That's Goebbels' speciality. And despite all his windbaggery about Wagner, Himmler doesn't really have a cultural bone in his body. I despise him actually.'

Clara looked down the battlements to the field below, where the hawk was swooping again, its pewter plumage gilded in the sun. It rose high, then dropped like an arrow onto its prey.

'But . . . you said it would *annoy* him if I had the part?'

'I certainly hope so.'

'Why? What was he saying, when you overheard him?'

'Just enquiring about the rumours.'

'What rumours?'

A moment of pity softened Leni's sardonic features. As if explaining to a child, she said, 'That you were in some way non-Aryan.'

Clara was frozen with shock. It explained everything. Magda's remark. *Someone has been saying some very unkind things about you.*

'I wouldn't worry too much. There's nothing new about it. They're always discovering that someone might have Jewish roots. Goebbels set up that rumour about me, only he reckoned without my blessed Führer. He made his photographer, Hoffmann, take a photoshoot of Goebbels and me walking together in my garden to scotch the rumours.' Leni's face brightened at the memory. 'Anyway, the fact is I can't stand Himmler or his wretched Ahnenerbe, so choosing you was ideal. It's mischievous of me really, but I thought what a laugh it would be to cast Clara Vine as the symbol of Germany. Himmler couldn't object because the Führer has given me absolutely free rein, and besides . . .'

'Besides what?'

'They have nothing on you, do they? They must have gone over your background with a fine toothcomb. If there was a drop of Jewish blood in you it would have leaked out by now.'

Tension was holding Clara's limbs together like steel cords, tighter than the most expert masseur could relax.

'When you overheard him discussing me, who was he talking to?'

'It was at Prinz-Albrecht-Strasse. I try to keep away from that place, but I was called in a while ago so that Himmler could discuss this film with me. We were in Heydrich's office and Himmler and Heydrich were talking together and there was someone else there – that Obersturmbannführer, Conrad Adler.'

'Adler?'

'D'you know him? Frightfully good-looking, but a bit of a mystery. I can't get on with him, to tell the truth, though they say he's a loyal member of the Party and he's worked for the Foreign Ministry for years.'

'He's at the Propaganda Ministry now.'

'With Goebbels? No. Adler's been seconded to Heydrich. That's why he was there. He's working on some special project. I've got no idea what it is, but it's terrifically hush-hush. I shouldn't even have mentioned it.'

Two hours later they had loaded up the trucks and Leni's Mercedes was making its way down the cobbled road out of Wewelsburg. The effort of trying to appear normal as she processed Leni's revelation was almost beyond Clara. Conrad Adler, the man who had approached her, who had asked such tender questions about her childhood, had taken her riding and propositioned her, was an acolyte of the head of the SD security service. Reinhard Heydrich, with his long equine face and hair shaved a savage three inches above his ears, was a sadist, pure and simple. Clara racked her brain to recall what Adler had specifically told her about his secondment and realized that, in fact, she had simply assumed he was working for Goebbels. *I'm on loan. Like a painting in a museum.* But if Adler was working for Heydrich, what was his interest in her?

The drive back would be long, but Leni was in high good humour. She leant her arm out of the window, trailing a thin scarf of cigarette smoke in her wake.

'I've just had a message from the Führer. He's told me that Albert Speer is to set aside thirty thousand square yards in the new capital for the Riefenstahl Studios. All funded by the state! He's going to announce it next week. In fact . . .'

She glanced across, beaming.

'He's invited me to a film evening at the Chancellery. I have to go, so you might as well come with me. I'll put your name on the guest list. It's next week. Brace yourself though. Goebbels may well be there, along with that ghastly wife of his. But the event will be useful. While we're there I can think about how to shoot the Führer.'

Clara gave a start and Leni looked at her curiously.

'On film, of course.'

Chapter Twenty-eight

Berlin was alive with rumours. The British Prime Minister had resigned. The Poles were about to attack. An illegal radio network called the Freedom Station had emerged, moving its transmitter around Berlin to avoid detection. An atmosphere of nervous anticipation stalked the city like a living thing. The proximity of war made every goodbye more intimate, every kiss more intense, every friendship more important. At tram stops, in the bread queues and amid the momentary knots of customers that coalesced round coffee stalls, conversation flowed between strangers. Rumours rose and faded like echoes of sound through static. Yet while the talk was of foreboding, there was also excitement in the air. It eddied down the quiet residential streets of Schöneberg, rippled through the smart boulevards of Wilmersdorf and Charlottenburg, swirled round the dank tenements of Moabit and Wedding and Prenzlauer Berg. People felt part of something, even if it was not something they desired.

At times over the preceding days Clara had felt as though Thursday would never come, but at last it dawned, heavy, the sky stippled with cloud. She had invented an appointment at the Charité hospital to escape her filming commitments for a few hours and even thrown in the name of her former neighbour,

Doktor Engel, for good measure. By ten to one she was standing on Budapester Strasse outside the outlandish, spectacular Elephant Gate of Berlin Zoo. The gate, with its green turrets, red and gold arch and kneeling sandstone elephants, could not be more of a contrast to the sombre street architecture around it. It stood freakishly proud, a splash of oriental colour that jarred against the orderly greys and browns. It suggested that merely by entering, citizens could escape the gloom of Berlin for a more joyful, exotic world.

Clara felt it too; the zoo was special to her. It was the place that Leo had first taken her to teach her the art of espionage; when she was a nervous ingénue and he a brusque passport control officer. And anxious, as he later confided, to be inducting a naïve young actress into a peril she could barely comprehend. Since then she had visited numerous times with Erich, who would always head for the Grosses Raubtierhaus, eager to see the elegantly pacing lions and tigers, to marvel at the sleek jaguars and panthers. That was until he announced that he couldn't bear to see such magnificent animals caged and would never go again.

She bought a ticket and made her way along the meticulously planted beds of begonias and roses towards the animal enclosures. The zoo was a haven of peace in the city's heart and now, in early summer, it was at its most beautiful. The traffic fumes were replaced by a sweet mingled aroma of straw and dung. Two boys in lederhosen flashed past on scooters, threatening to scrape the shins of anyone foolish enough to get too close. A dog in a little overcoat waddled along importantly. A pair of excitable matrons were being hoisted onto an elephant idly flicking his trunk as he waited to give his hourly ride. Clara threaded through the crowds, wondering what would happen to these animals if bombing came. Were shelters being built for them too?

He will find you.

Clara hadn't questioned Steffi's suggestion at the time, but now it seemed absurdly ambitious. Even on a weekday lunchtime, the zoo was busy, and the visitor numbers were further swelled by the arrival of a gargantuan sea lion called Roland, whose appearance on the Ufa Tonwoche newsreel had granted him celebrity status. How could she begin to find a complete stranger here, especially if he was purposefully anonymous? Could she be sure he would recognize her?

Her first thought was to head for one of the more distant animal houses. Surely the elephant house on the furthest edges, or the elegant ostrich enclosure, styled like an Egyptian temple, would be better suited to an assignation. And yet, if he had been seeking privacy, why had the man she was to meet chosen such a public place? Was it, perhaps, precisely because of the crowds? After a moment's deliberation she gravitated towards the milling throng that had gathered to watch the sea lion being fed.

It was a spectacle of high entertainment. Every time the keeper, armed with a bucket of sprats, dangled a tiny, silvery flicker above the water, the sleek grey mass would rise abruptly, water sheeting from his sides, to a volley of delighted shrieks. The sea lion would then heave his three-ton bulk onto a rock and open his mouth. Predictably he had already been nicknamed Goering.

As Clara focused on the feeding ritual, wondering what to do, a flicker of movement wrenched her eyes upward. A man leaning with his elbows on the far side of the rail, dressed in wide-legged trousers and a nondescript checked jacket, had glanced in her direction and adjusted his hat. He had a sharp-edged face, but the trilby's deep brim shaded his eyes as he stared, apparently absorbed, into the enclosure below.

At the back of her mind a memory stirred. There was something about that half-shaded profile she had seen before, but where? The image remained frustratingly unknown, floating free, without context, evoking only an uncomfortable frisson of unease.

Then she looked again and recognition electrified her.

When she was a child she had adored puzzle books. Each Christmas her parents would give her a story album that was interspersed with games, crosswords and picture puzzles. As she grew, she progressed to entire books of them and one of her favourites was called Spot The Difference. It featured two scenes with minute changes that forced the eye to focus on fine detail. A Sunny Day, On The Beach, At The Fair. Two versions of Trafalgar Square but in one a man was carrying an umbrella and in the other he was empty handed. Two identical jungles with a missing monkey in the second. You knew if you looked closely, really closely, you would uncover aspects that had not at first revealed themselves. Comparing the man at the railing over and over with the image in her mind, she realized, with a jolt of horror, what was bothering her. That lean face, the eyes which deliberately avoided hers. It was the man she had found standing in the lobby of her apartment block in Winterfeldtstrasse. The man who, she was convinced, was not sheltering from the rain.

Hovering at the back of the crowd, she fought the urge to walk away as fast as possible. Was this the man she was supposed to meet? If so, either the Gestapo had somehow discovered their plans, and replaced Steffi's accomplice with their own person, or the figure before her was genuine, and her assumption about him was wrong.

Even as she hesitated the man threw his cigarette stub down on the ground and peeled languidly away, as if motivated by nothing more than a casual desire for lunch. As he moved slowly towards the gate, Clara made up her mind to follow him.

Immediately outside, he made for a dark green bicycle leant against the railings, mounted it, and proceeded slowly eastwards, along Budapester Strasse and across the Landwehrkanal, turning right towards Lützowplatz. Almost immediately he turned right again into Keithstrasse. Although the bicycle was proceeding slowly, Clara was forced to walk as fast as she could to keep up and by the time he stopped outside a tall, brick-faced residential block, she was gasping for breath.

She lingered in a porch on the opposite side of the road, assessing the situation. The building was the type of multi-use block that could be found all over Berlin. An office on the ground floor, apartments above. A floating population that afforded a certain amount of privacy from prying eyes, and where unfamiliar visitors would raise no eyebrows. The man dismounted and disappeared inside.

Clara glanced around her. The street was empty and there were no parked cars close by. A burst of laughter spattered out of an upper window, and a radio buzzed further off. Eventually, she knocked twice, preparing to ask for Herr Vogel if any other face answered the door. But it was the same man.

'You took your time. I was beginning to give up on you.'

He was young, now she saw him close up, and spoke with a rough accent, but his demeanour was shrewd and intelligent.

'It's hard following a cyclist.'

'It's safer than buses or trams. No one looking you up and down. You'd better come in.'

He led her down a dim, tiled corridor through a door to a back room containing only a couple of cheap wooden chairs and a table.

Clara looked around her.

'You know what I'm here for?' she asked.

'A Kennkarte and an Ariernachweis.'

'My documents fell into the Seine in Paris.'

He gave a dry laugh. 'Use that as an excuse and it might get you points for originality.'

'It's true, as it happens.'

'It's of no concern to me, Fräulein, where you lost them. I'm here to replace them. I've got the cards ready. All I need are photographs of you.'

She fished in her bag for the contact sheet shots that had been taken for the publicity for *Love Strictly Forbidden*. He surveyed them critically.

'Ideally we'd want one with no smile.'

'It's the best I can do.'

'They're not too bad.'

She recalled Leni's words. *Your face has a useful quality. It's a blank canvas. It's like I can project anything I want.*

The young man switched on the desk lamp and bent over a piece of card. An Ariernachweis, on which Clara's details had already been filled in. He took the photograph and placed it in the corner of the card then fixed it to the pass with brass eyelets.

'It took ages to get these looking right. Eventually I found a cobbler who supplied me with the tool he uses to fix eyelets for bootlaces. It was perfect.'

He reached for a fine brush and a jar of purple dye and began painting on a separate piece of card.

'There are twelve long and twenty-four short feathers on the German imperial eagle, did you know? The hardest thing is to get the correct colour and shape.'

He continued working intently, his movements as tender and delicate as if he were creating a Renaissance Madonna and Child, rather than an eagle and swastika. His face was closed, intent, inscrutable in the dim light. When he had copied the eagle he took a piece of newspaper, dampened it with spittle and pressed it down on the newly painted symbol, creating a mirror image on the newspaper. He then took the paper and pressed it onto the photograph of Clara.

'The stamp needs to project across the photograph. Now we'll need to give it a few minutes to dry.'

He sat motionless, as if expecting that she too would sit in silence beside him. But Clara had too many questions.

'Where do you get the passes to copy?'

'One of our supporters is a church pastor. Some of his congregation drop their expired ID passes into the collection box instead of money. They know how valuable they'll be. I've had all kinds, even Wehrmacht passes. The equipment I get from work. There's no shortage of brushes or paint there.'

'You make it sound simple.'

'That's only the beginning. Once we've given someone a new identity, we advise them to join a lending library and get a card with their new name on it. As many extra pieces of ID as possible.'

'So you can make anyone into anything?'

'Not at all. You need to match the face with the occupation. If I have a card which gives the occupation as kitchen cleaner, I can't hand that out to some smart lady whose husband owned a department store.'

'Are you busy?'

'It's constant. But time's running out. People are going to need more than ID documents. Jews here are trapped in a net. They need places to hide.'

'Or they need to leave Berlin.'

'No. Berlin's the best place to hide. Did you know almost half of the city is underground? There are a thousand bunkers in Berlin. Speer has built a tunnel running all the way from Mitte to Tempelhof so Goering can ride the whole four miles in his car. The customers of the Adlon Hotel have their own shelter under Pariser Platz. Not so grand for the rest, of course. They'll mostly be using the U-Bahns. They've just finished a new shelter at Alexanderplatz.'

'I was there just the other day. I didn't see anything.'

'You wouldn't. It's entirely inconspicuous. You walk along the tunnel to the U5 line and you pass a green steel door. You'd miss it if you didn't know it was there.'

So that was where they would huddle. Waiting for the explosions. Listening to the muffled boom and the lick of flames as above them the dark blast of bombs flowered into the night sky.

The young man put out his half-smoked cigarette and tucked the stump in his pocket.

'The Nazis may be driving people underground now, but one day soon they'll be driven underground themselves.'

He jumped up and checked the card.

'There. You're no longer a Jew. But don't go dropping it into any French rivers again. Don't allow it to get wet at all. Even a drop of rain might dissolve the watercolour.'

She placed it in her bag and looked at him soberly.

'Thank you. I'm sorry. I don't know your name.'

'I'd be a fool to tell you. If anyone thought this was a forgery, they'd ask where it came from and who forged it. There aren't many people who can resist answering when they're having a chat with the Gestapo.'

She made her way to the door.

'ID forgery is punishable by death, isn't it?'

'You ask a lot of questions, Fräulein. Most of my clients are too frightened to do anything but sit in silence.'

'Just because I ask questions, doesn't mean I'm not frightened too . . . I do have another question, though. When I first saw you, I knew I'd seen you before. In the lobby of my apartment building in Winterfeldtstrasse. You remember, don't you?'

'You're an observant lady.'

'What were you doing there?'

He smiled; a quick smile that utterly transformed his features.

'As a matter of fact I had just posted a flyer on the wall opposite. I had my leaflets and the paste bottle in a suitcase. But a policeman appeared and I needed to leave in a hurry.'

Clara left the apartment as swiftly as she could and got on the first bus she found. As she travelled, the bus rocking under her, she thought how her whole life was like the young man's painstaking work. The least inconsistency, the tiniest slip, and her entire, carefully constructed identity would unravel, like the silk spooling from a beautiful gown. Yet in a few days' time the existence that she had crafted for herself over the past six years was facing its greatest test. And whatever happened, she would not be the same person afterwards.

Chapter Twenty-nine

Their meeting place was the bridge over the Spree just before Museum Island. It was, according to their Heritage Studies teacher, the place where the first settlers in Berlin, who were fishermen, had erected their wooden huts. Hedwig leaned for a moment, watching the canal as it glittered in bright rings beneath the setting sun, stirred into lazy arrows by the coal-heaped barges making their slow progress westwards. Above, the sky was as luminous and mottled as an oyster shell and faint traces of Linden blossom were carried on the breeze. It was a lovely summer evening, but Hedwig was sick with nerves.

She had barely slept since the evening of Jochen's revelations. Tonight was their regular meeting but she had no idea what they might do or where they would go. Everything had changed now. She had hurried home after work and pulled on a flowered dress that Lotti had made up from one of her own designs. It clung to her curves a little too obviously for her taste, and Hedwig was only wearing it because Jochen had once said casually that he liked girls in flowered dresses. And because the memory of the beautiful Sofie, whom Jochen admired, burned in her mind.

A hand on her shoulder made her jump, but the sight of him brought the reflex rush of excitement.

'So where are we going?'

'Somewhere interesting. Up west.'

'Where exactly?'

'I'll tell you when we get there.'

'Is it . . . to do with what you told me? The other night?'

He grinned.

'Patience, Hedy! It's a secret.'

On the tram Jochen seemed lost in contemplation so she stared out of the window at the glimmering shop windows and the commuters in their office outfits hurrying home from work and thought how foolish she had been to assume that Jochen was planning to propose. Perhaps it was for the best. Hedwig thought of her mother savagely scrubbing, her father looking her up and down in that way he had. They already thought badly enough of Jochen; God knows what they would think if they knew what he was really doing. Since Lotti's death her life seemed to be spinning out of control, with one terrible shock following on another. She desperately hoped the next surprise was not about to arrive.

She waited until the tram had reached the smart boulevards of Wilmersdorf, and they had disembarked, before she spoke again. Jochen walked fast, hands jammed in his pockets, as if propelled by some urgent inner force.

'I still don't know where we're going.'

'Actually, we're going to see a fortune teller.'

She so wanted to believe him. It was such a wonderful, imaginative idea and it might have been planned expressly to delight her. Numerous friends had visited fortune tellers to investigate their romantic futures. Hand reading and Tarot cards were all the rage. Irna Wolter had visited a psychic with her fiancé before they married and had learned they would enjoy a long, happy marriage, blessed with five children. Hedwig had not consulted a psychic herself, but she never missed her horoscope and she kept a Winterhilfswerk donation pin in the shape of her star sign – Pisces – in her lapel. She had bought one for Jochen, too – Aries – but she had never seen him wear it.

'I thought you didn't believe in fortune tellers.'

She couldn't keep the excitement out of her voice. Her stars in that month's edition of *Der Zenit* promised dramatic developments in her love life.

'I believe in this one. Her forecasts are impressively accurate.'

After a few minutes they reached a building in Pariser Strasse, the kind that Hedwig sometimes fantasized about inhabiting but had never set foot in. It was a five-storey stucco block with fancy scrollwork round a doorframe. A lot of smart houses were having swastikas set into their lintels, but here the plaster was moulded into an elaborate confection of leaves and squirrels. Next to it a buffed brass plaque read '*Psychic consultations. First floor.*'

The door was opened by a maid who ushered them into a front room with a vaguely eastern air bestowed by drawn tasselled curtains, fringed red lamps and rich Turkish carpets. Around the room low tables were clustered with the accessories of the trade – crystal balls, Tarot cards and a porcelain phrenological head segmented into areas with labels like Caution, Secrecy, Eloquence and Artistry. A pungent odour hung in the air. Hedwig was quite used to homes that smelt strongly, but unlike the cabbage intercut with rancid fat that perfumed her family's apartment, this scent was exotic and mysterious. Nutmeg, cinnamon and frankincense, perhaps. Like the incense in a Catholic church or the ancient smells that emanated from the library at the Ahnenerbe.

The door opened and a short, commanding figure swept in, wearing a cerise kimono-style silk jacket and a beaded cap. She must have been in her late sixties, with a crooked nose and kinked hair, her dark caramel eyes heavily lined in kohl, and her makeup thickly applied. Exactly like a fortune teller was supposed to look, thought Hedwig, enthralled.

'This is Hedwig,' said Jochen shortly. 'Hedwig, this is Frau Annie Krauss.'

The Annie Krauss! Everyone had heard of her. All the top people, film actors and singers and sports people, were said to consult her. There had been a feature on her work in *Der Zenit*, *Madame Krauss Prognosticates*, with a picture of her craning over a crystal ball wearing a fringed headband, and reports of some of her predictions, mostly picking winners at the Hoppegarten race course. This was so thoughtful of Jochen. It was impossible to get an appointment with her unless you booked months in advance.

Frau Krauss approached Hedwig and seized her hand. There was an unexpected strength in her stringy claw and Hedwig wondered if the old lady could discern her future merely from the faint impressions of lines on her palm. She squinted at Hedwig, as if reading the secrets of her soul.

'Good evening, my dear. I've heard about you. I'm so glad to meet you.'

A beady glance up and down. Yet again Hedwig regretted wearing the clingy dress.

'I'm honoured to meet you too, Frau Krauss. I've always wanted to.'

'Hmm.' She turned away slightly, allowing Hedwig to whisper to Jochen, 'Are we going to learn our futures?'

He shrugged enigmatically.

'In a manner of speaking.'

Chapter Thirty

From the pavement tables of the Café Kranzler it was possible to see a line of people stretching most of the way round Pariser Platz to the doors of the American Embassy. The queue for visas began before dawn and would still be there at dusk. Not that there was anything interesting about a queue in Berlin. Waiting was a way of life. Along with the ordinary queues for bread and meat and vegetables, there were long, snaking queues for train tickets and visas, and foreigners crammed the stations like walkers desperate to get home before the first drops of a storm arrived. A pair of hard-faced soldiers had been deputed to guard the American Embassy queue, but no one seemed remotely likely to step out of line. Disorder was not something they could afford. Occasionally a secretary bearing a tray of tea and sandwiches moved along, pouring cups and asking people if they required sugar. Their faces registered astonishment at the young American's request. It had been so long since they were considered not just names and numbers, but humans, with preferences and opinions, even about how much sugar they took in their tea.

A few hundred yards away, Clara was waiting for Mary Harker. She had no idea why Mary had asked to meet, but she was glad of the diversion. Even if only for a few hours, it would take her mind off the task she was about to undertake.

Mary arrived late, wrenching off her battered felt hat and running her hand through her hair so that bits of it stood up vertically in a tangle of straw.

'I'm trying to calm down.'

She threw herself dramatically on a seat, lit a cigarette and inhaled furiously.

'I've just been expelled from a press conference.'

'Not another one.'

'I know. There are two press conferences a day now, so I have twice as much opportunity to get ejected. I wouldn't bother, but with everything moving so fast, you can't afford to miss one in case they let slip anything important.'

'And did they?'

'No such luck. It was "Good News About Employment". The usual mixture of boasts and lies. They said full employment has finally been achieved in Germany.'

'And I'd guess that's not true?'

'I felt obliged to point out that if there was full employment, it was only because all the workers are now producing arma-ments. Before I knew it, two thugs had frogmarched me out of the door.'

'And you let this upset you?' asked Clara incredulously.

'Don't be silly. I've been thrown out of more press confer-ences than I've had hot Wurst. No, that's not why I wanted to see you. It's about your Faith and Beauty girl. Take a look at this.'

She pushed across the table the latest edition of the *Völkischer Beobachter*, the ultra-loyal Nazi newspaper. Clara glanced at the headline. *Investigation Continues into Slain Girl*. There was noth-ing new in the report except that it was accompanied by a fresh photograph of Lotti Franke. All the previous shots had shown her wearing her regulation Faith and Beauty outfit but this was a large, glamorous image of Lotti dressed in a provocatively low-cut dress, eyes smouldering at the camera, one leg propped vampishly on a chair. In the upper right-hand corner was the photographer credit: Yva.

'What does this photograph say?' demanded Mary.

'That she modelled her own designs. She was artistic.'

'Nope.' Mary thrust the paper away, as if disgusted.

'A picture says a thousand words, right? And I know how newspaper picture desks work. If they have a choice of photographs to illustrate a piece – and there seem to have been a hundred pictures of Lotti Franke – then they'll choose the one that transmits the correct message. Most of the *Völkischer Beobachter* might have been dictated by Goebbels himself and this photograph is not an accident. It says Lotti was not the archetypal German maiden. She was not the pure Faith and Beauty girl everyone imagines. She was different, original, a little out of the ordinary. In other words, she got what was coming to her.'

'She deserved to die?'

'Pretty much.'

'But why?'

Mary frowned. 'That's what I don't understand. For some reason the investigation is changing course. Did I mention that they have a suspect now?'

Clara clattered her cup back into the saucer. 'Mary! You left it until now to tell me?'

'When I was leaving the Propaganda Ministry this afternoon I ran into one of the few sane press deputies and he told me they've arrested a man. They're announcing it tomorrow.'

'That changes everything.'

'No it doesn't. Because it's a Pole. If you believe the police department – which of course I don't – Poles have been responsible for most of the crimes in the Reich for the past three months. Whoever this man is, he didn't do it. But it shows that they're tired of the story now. The police are no longer trying to solve the murder. If they can't tar Lotti as a promiscuous eccentric, then they'll pin her murder on a Pole. I'm afraid, Clara, it means they can no longer be bothered to find the right man.'

'Or they don't want to.'

She felt again that intuition that had dawned at the Faith and Beauty home, that Lotti's murder was not the act of a lone madman. That it had roots in something far beyond the opportunistic sexual murder of a girl in the wrong place at the wrong time. But it was impossible to explain, and besides, Mary was rushing impatiently on.

'Also Clara, I wanted to say goodbye. I'm leaving town for a while.'

'Just because you were expelled from a press conference?'

'Much better reason than that.' Mary grinned. 'I'm making a trip to England because I've had the strangest request. Jack Kennedy, the son of the American ambassador in London, wants to meet me. He thinks I might be able to give his father a better idea of what the Nazis are like up close.'

Clara smiled. 'I met Jack Kennedy when I was in Paris. But I never thought he'd ask you to lecture his father.'

Mary reached over and gripped her arm. 'I might have guessed it was you. Thank you, Clara. It's an incredible opportunity. And believe me, I won't hold back. I owe you.'

Clara hesitated. 'In that case, there is something you can do, something for me. There's a little girl, Esther Goldblatt. She's fourteen. Jewish. She reminds me of myself at that age and she's in a bit of trouble. She desperately needs to get out of Germany and she has a visa for America, but it will take years before her number comes up. She could get an exit visa to travel to England, but only if she has a sponsor there who is prepared to adopt her.'

'That's quite a hurdle.'

'I think I know the right person.'

Clara reached for her notebook.

'Here's her address and telephone number.'

Mary looked down at the paper.

'Angela Mortimer? Are you serious? I would have thought your sister was the last person on earth to contemplate adopting a little Jewish girl.'

'That was my first instinct, but there's more to Angela than you think. Her views may be reprehensible, but she's a decent person at heart. She was very motherly to me when I was a truculent teenager. And she has no children to mother, so it's perfect. Tell her I'll write and explain but she needs to register as a sponsor as soon as possible. She must contact Bloomsbury House in Great Russell Street. It's the headquarters of the Jewish refugee committee. Oh, and something else.' Clara reached up to her neck and unclasped Steffi's pearls, then handed them to Mary.

'Take these, sell them for the best price you can, and give Angela the money. Tell her it's for Esther.'

She watched as Mary stowed the pearls carefully in her bag.

'And good luck.'

'Thanks.'

But Clara knew if anyone was going to need luck, it would be her.

Chapter Thirty-one

The Kaiserhof Hotel was a dingy building the colour of bad teeth. It stood out in the Wilhelmstrasse because all the other buildings in the government area had undergone a makeover of impressive expense. The new Reich Chancellery, directly opposite, had been finally completed that January, a quarter of a mile of yellow stucco and grey stone stretching down Voss Strasse, its monumental proportions designed to quash any lingering concessions to the human scale. Goebbels' Propaganda Ministry, originally housed in an old, Empire-style palace opposite, had been given a total revamp, with an extension that was architecturally severe and modern, in line with Goebbels' modernist taste. The Kaiserhof, however, Hitler's first home in Berlin, lingered on like a widow in dowdy lace, steadfastly resisting cosmetic enhancement.

Clara had arrived early and installed herself in the bar of the hotel. What the Kaiserhof's proprietors had saved on exterior renovation they put towards securing the best of the city's available food, making it one of the finest places to eat, but Clara had no interest in food. She had brought her copy of *The Thirty-Nine Steps* to distract herself and sat with it open in front of her, the sour, gritty taste of fear washing round her mouth like grains of Ersatz coffee. Occasionally she stole glances across the road to where security police known as Schupos, in their green uniforms and black leather hats, manned the Chancellery gates.

If the opportunity arose, we would not want you, Miss Vine, to be hindered by fears of 'unsportsmanlike' behaviour.

All day she had questioned herself. Would she ever have the courage to do it? Could she shoot Hitler? Sitting in the garden at Griebnitzsee, with her eyes closed and the sun flaring scarlet against her eyelids, she felt so intensely alive. Her limbs tingled with vitality, every fibre of her body wanting to live, even if her lover was missing and her family estranged.

Never before had she come so close to Hitler, yet it would also be the closest she had come to death herself. Shooting Hitler would, almost certainly, mean death, but without him Germany would be free. There would be no fighting and thousands of young men would no longer be required to go to war. Erich would be safe.

Yet all the time, seductive counter-arguments whispered sweetly. What if war didn't have to happen? If there could be a way to negotiate? Might the Third Reich continue as barbarously without Hitler at the helm? What if the Derringer failed to fire? And besides, what right did she have to kill another human being? Even when the questions receded, the hideous images remained. What special tortures would be reserved for the assassin of the Führer?

When Clara looked back on her life, so much of what she had done had been impulsive, actions taken on the spur of the moment. Her decision to become an actress had been spurred by the disapproval of her parents. She moved to Berlin to escape an unwanted fiancé. She began spying at the request of Leo Quinn. She had put herself at the service of others – people whose motives she strongly believed in – but never at her own instigation. This time it was different. This audacious, deadly plan was hers alone. Its planning and execution owed nothing to anyone except herself. It required her to summon every ounce of moral courage and to quash every doubt. She remembered what a

Luftwaffe officer had once told her – that to be a truly successful pilot meant losing the last shred of fear. Then she thought of all the people she had known in her six years in Berlin, the brave men and women who had tried to resist the Nazis. They had all made their own choices, but this decision, so hard and difficult, was hers alone.

Eventually, the murmuring arguments died down and she felt the fear inside her harden into resolve.

In the afternoon she had returned to Winterfeldtstrasse to go through the belongings in her old apartment. Rudi, the Blockwart, who carried out his duties from a chair in the corner of the hall, seemed almost pleased to see her. Despite his advanced age and crooked spine, he sprang up to block her path. He had always been a staunch Nazi and it surprised Clara that it had taken him so many years to cultivate the little postage stamp moustache that he now sported proudly in emulation of his hero.

'Heil Hitler, Fräulein Vine! Are you back for good?'

It was almost as though he was missing her, though the old fraud had never shown an iota of fond feeling in his life. More likely, he was calculating how the landlord might raise the rent if she chose to end her lease.

'Not sure yet, Rudi. How's everything?'

'Busy. We're converting the cellar into a shelter. We have directives from the Air Protection League.

'Of course.'

She tried to scurry away up the stairs but Rudi was well prac-tised in forestalling escapes. Edging forward, he barricaded her way as effectively as a squad of riot police. His breath smelt of the kind of alcohol not found in high-end Berlin clubs. He signalled a confidence.

'A gentleman was calling for you yesterday.'

'What kind of gentleman?'

'Ah, that's not for me to say, Fräulein. I'm a simple man. I can't judge. Perhaps it was a fan.'

'I doubt it.'

It was almost certainly a collector. Barely an hour went by some days without a charity official knocking on the door and rattling their tin, demanding funds for the Hitler Youth or the BDM. For the orphans or the poor or the Luftwaffe or the rebuilding of Berlin.

Rudi gave a smile of greasy complicity.

'I told him I had no idea where you were. That was right, wasn't it?'

'Yes. Thank you, Rudi.'

'I know you actresses need protection. That's what I'm here for.'

Sidestepping him, Clara fled up the stairs and shut the door securely behind her. Then she made a rapid inventory of her apartment. If she was arrested she needed to ensure that there was no trace of Erich. No books with his name in, no photographs or school reports, none of the birthday cards he had given her and she had kept. God forbid that his name should be linked with hers. She dreaded the thought of the Gestapo raiding the tenement in Neukölln, shaking the bewildered old Frau Schmidt out of her bed and hustling Erich to some frightening basement where he would be questioned about the woman he had known since he was ten until his tired mind made a mistake and somehow incriminated him too.

She wandered round the apartment, touching her possessions. She pulled the fox fur coat that her mother had left her out of the wardrobe and buried her face in it, inhaling the ghost of violets that she once wore. The fur was chill in her hands, but when she pulled the coat on its warmth enveloped her. Finally, she picked up a book of Latin verse Leo had given her and kissed it, the way Italians might kiss a prayer book; the way she wanted to kiss him. She thought of that sensation she had in the Paris hotel room and tried to bring it back, but she felt nothing.

*   *   *

Towards evening, the adrenaline began to exhaust her. She had dressed methodically, assessing every item with careful scrutiny. Around the top of her thigh she fastened the calfskin holder with the stocking gun inside. It fitted snugly against her leg and, wearing her most sturdy evening shoes – black leather T-bars, she marched up and down the room to ensure it did not slip as she walked. When she donned the Madame Grès dress, it was exactly as she had guessed, the flowing Grecian folds giving no hint of the metallic bulge beneath. The dress also went perfectly with her new Schiaparelli jacket. She brushed her hair until it gleamed and fastened a diamanté clip in it, rejecting her Elizabeth Arden Velvet Red in favour of a lipstick that was almost nude. The Führer had been known to confront lipstick-wearing women and subject them to a rant on how cosmetics were made of human waste and poisoning the entire health of German womanhood.

Her leather jewellery box was battered now, its oval mirror spotted and cloudy, like a blurred portal into the past. She touched the silver locket her mother had given to her at the age of sixteen, with pictures of them both inside, but after a moment's reflection, picked a diamond brooch in the shape of a swastika. It came from Jaeger's in Unter den Linden and had been given to her six years previously by Joseph Goebbels himself. She remembered him pinning it to her dress at a fashion show in full view of the press – a deliberate act to mark her out and compromise her in everyone's eyes. Back then Goebbels had trusted her as his go-between – a secret weapon in the ongoing war with his wife – but now, who knew what he thought?

Her hand hovered over her perfume bottles until she chose one called *Scent of Secrets*. It was sweet and floral – bergamot, jasmine, Turkish rose and violet iris, with a powdery base of vanilla. The scent reminded her of her childhood garden in England and her mother's favourite rose, the amnesia rose, with its unusual blooms that looked almost grey at first, before shading into lilac. She inhaled the scent deeply, as if for strength. If the evening was to end as she feared, she wanted the memory of her mother to accompany her.

The Führer's film evening at the Reich Chancellery was the hottest ticket in town. It was the invitation everyone wanted and no one expected to enjoy. Each night when he was in Berlin, Hitler would invite a select group of high-ranking Nazis and actors for a private screening in the Chancellery Music Room. The advantage was that visitors got to see films denied to ordinary Germans. Goebbels' latest blacklist of sixty American actors did not extend to the Führer's private parties and all the latest Hollywood releases, from *Tarzan*, *Tip-Off Girls*, *The Lives of a Bengal Lancer*, to *Captain Courageous* with Spencer Tracy, were firm favourites. Walt Disney was held in special esteem, thanks to his public reception of Leni Riefenstahl the previous year when other Hollywood producers had pointedly turned her down. The disadvantages of the evening were self-evident. Everyone was on their best behaviour, no one could smoke and it was impossible to relax. Relaxation, like coffee, eggs and chocolate, was now a luxury that not even VIPs could afford.

The reception hall of the Reich Chancellery was done out in contrasting coloured marble like an ugly cathedral. The walls were black slabs splintered with quartz, interset with veined, bloody red Saalburger stone, with yet more marble underfoot. As she followed an SS orderly dressed in the short white jacket that all Hitler's domestic staff wore, Clara was overwhelmingly conscious of the gun against her thigh. She had guessed that no one on Hitler's guest list would be subjected to the indignity of a body search, yet she was intensely aware that she must not slip on the highly polished surface and send the gun skittering beneath her. Even in her sturdy T-bars, the floor beneath her was as treacherous as a skating rink, deliberately waxed to a dazzling shine. It was a private joke for Hitler, who refused all requests to

lay a carpet because diplomats needed practice moving on a slippery surface.

At the far end of the hall a door was flanked by two of the
Leibstandarte, Hitler's personal bodyguards. Selected for their
above-average height and unquestioned fidelity to the Führer,
they formed an invincible barricade against his enemies, but at
Clara's approach they moved simultaneously sideways, opening
the doors as though to Aladdin's cave to reveal a dazzle of sound
and light.

The party was already in full swing and studded with VIPs,
most of them stars of stage and screen. Leni Riefenstahl and
Heinz Rühmann were talking to Gustaf Gründgens, another
favourite actor of the regime. The actress Jenny Jugo, in magno-
lia satin, was air-kissing Zarah Leander. The good-looking celebrities were a festive sprinkling to leaven the dark mass of politicians. Rudolf Hess and his wife. The Goebbels and the Speers.
Youth Leader Baldur von Schirach and Reich Labour Minister
Robert Ley. Everyone was there. The entire upper echelon of
the Third Reich was assembled to watch Mickey Mouse.

To Clara's relief, Hitler had not arrived. She was desperate not
to meet him. She had heard of the effect he had: *Führer Kontakt*,
it was called, an intense magnetic hold that made the person with
him believe, just for that moment, that they were the only one
in the room. A hypnotic force that dazzled, empowered and
enslaved.

Instead, one of the first faces she saw was Conrad Adler. He
was standing in the corner nearest the door, inclining his head
close to Henriette von Schirach, the Youth Leader's pretty
blonde wife. Her face was tipped adoringly upwards towards
him, and she was smiling merrily. Although he barely turned his
head, Clara knew Adler had seen her and she registered a spark
of alarm in his eyes. She sensed that he was about to break off and
approach her until something deterred him, and turning she saw
Joseph Goebbels looming behind her.

'Fräulein Vine. What a surprise. And may I say what a charming choice of brooch. For a charming woman.'

He reached out to brush the spot where it was pinned, letting his fingers trail her breast, and then, for the first time in their acquaintance, he moved to kiss her. As his hand travelled round her waist and downwards, Clara's flesh turned to ice. If he strayed any further, he could not miss the stocking gun attached to her left thigh. Her entire body was rigid with alarm, yet even as she froze, she realized her reaction would arouse no suspicion at all. Goebbels must be well used to women flinching at his touch. Barely suppressed distaste was the natural response to the Propaganda Minister. How else should any woman react to a man who had persecuted so many and sent thousands to their deaths? Whose bigotry had goaded an entire nation into a spiral of coruscating hatred?

'I've not seen you here before. Remind me who invited you?'

'Leni Riefenstahl,' said Clara, stepping backward and looking hastily around. 'She thought I might enjoy it so she put my name on the guest list.'

'She's like that. She likes to take liberties with other people's invitations. Still. It's always a pleasure. The last time I was here was with your English friend, Unity Mitford. We watched *Cavalcade*.'

'She mentioned that.' According to Unity, Hitler had declared Noël Coward's film about three generations of an upper-class British family his favourite movie.

'I thought it very poor,' said Goebbels.

'It won Best Picture, didn't it?'

A snort. 'Perhaps in one sense that film is what Britain does best. An extended wallow in a rose-tinted version of her past. We in Germany prefer to focus on our future. But then . . .'

He broke off mid-sentence and Clara became aware of an intense, hostile glare. She looked round to see Magda Goebbels approaching, causing her husband to move swiftly in the opposite direction, like one in a pair of repelling magnets. Magda was dressed in high-necked, monkish black and wore the tragic expression of someone invited to her own funeral.

'Don't let me interrupt. I can see you and my husband were deep in conversation.'

'Not really. We were discussing films.'

'That's what he always calls it. Discussing films. You take me for a fool, Fräulein Vine. Especially considering the way you're sporting his brooch.'

Clara cursed herself for choosing Goebbels' swastika. She had thought of it as a useful accessory, part of her disguise, and instead it had parachuted her into unforeseen difficulties.

'I have one exactly like it. But then, so do half the women in Berlin. He has his jeweller make them. Some men – Goering for example – take a real interest in jewellery, but my husband lacks that imagination. He orders precisely the same trinket every time. Usually when he wants to reward an actress for "discussing films".'

What misfortune to encounter a paranoid Magda Goebbels on a night like this. Clara was just summoning conciliatory words when the Minister's wife lifted a glass from a passing tray and shrugged.

'Don't bother to deny it. I don't care anyway. I just want this evening to be over. Let's hope the Führer's tired.'

'Why's that?'

'Because when he's not he watches two films, back to back. I've been here so many times and it's always the same routine. Cartoon first, then a newsreel, then the movie. Or two. Then he stays up talking until four in the morning and it's always the same subjects. Vegetarianism, Wagner, History, dogs. I'm praying it's not a two-movie evening.'

Clara glimpsed her escape in the adjacent room, where a vast marble table was piled with diverse objects, like a grand church jumble sale.

'Are those the Führer's birthday gifts?'

'Haven't you seen them yet? You should. You wouldn't believe some of the junk the poor man has been given. In my opinion most of it should go straight to the Winterhilfswerk.'

Magda was right. The display was exactly like something one might find at a wedding, only far larger and more vulgar. Instead of wine glasses, fish knives and toasters, the Führer's beloved nation had produced an extravagant and frankly kitsch selection of gifts. A bust of Goethe rubbed shoulders with an ivory hunting horn. Dull landscapes were propped against oils of ancient military figures. A garish gold model of the Führer's art gallery in Munich, the *Haus der Deutschen Kunst*, jostled for the bad taste prize with a handcrafted castle studded with precious stones. One citizen with a vivid imagination had supplied a pair of baby bootees and a knitted bonnet, which had been deftly concealed behind a vase of striking ugliness containing a yellowed skeleton of dried flowers.

Clara stared at the gifts without seeing them, focusing on what the next hour would bring. She wanted to choreograph her movements precisely, minute by minute. She saw herself as if from above, unstoppable, like a character in a film, except that there was no rehearsal that could prepare her for an attempt like this. No prompt to help her. No possibility of a retake. This task had to be carried out perfectly, and she had only one chance.

'Aren't they wonderful? The people love their Führer very much.'

The speaker was a young woman in her twenties with frizzy, dark hair and a deferential expression. Compared to the Nazi wives, her clothes were dowdy and her manner restrained. She extended a polite hand.

'I'm Christa Schroeder, the Führer's secretary.'

'Clara Vine.'

'Yes. I mean, I recognize you, Fräulein Vine. I know who you are. I was admiring your dress. Is it French?'

It was a mistake to wear Parisian fashion in Hitler's presence. Not only did he hate the French, but he believed the slender Gallic silhouette was the last thing likely to encourage the fecundity he wanted for his Reich.

'It was a gift,' she replied noncommittally.

'Such a lovely one. And look at all the Führer's gifts! We've been working round the clock to catalogue them. People have been so generous. He's had a Titian portrait, and the most marvellous Meissen porcelain and a sailing ship made entirely from flowers. Captain Bauer, his pilot, gave him a model Condor aeroplane. Just over there. And Herr Porsche gave him a model car as well as a real one.' A little confidential smile. 'To tell the truth, it's the models the Führer loves best. He's like a kid with them.'

The secretary sighed fondly. 'But the birthday was so tiring for our poor chief. All those receptions went on for days . . . I'm sorry, Fräulein, are you cold in here?'

'No.' Clara rubbed the goose bumps on her arms. 'I'm fine.'

'It's nerves, isn't it?'

'Nerves?'

'Please forgive me saying, but it's quite normal. That's how everyone is when they meet the Führer. If only they knew how important the film evenings are to him. He loves being with people, and being entertained. He used to adore going to operettas and variety shows at the Wintergarten or the Admiralspalast but he can't go any more because his presence disrupts the performance. So he sends his steward instead and the man brings a programme back for the chief to look at. But that's no substitute. It's sad really. This is the nearest he gets to an evening of pleasure.'

Suddenly, from the room behind them, the click of heels rang out like pistol shots, followed by a volley of Heil Hitlers, and a large dog, fur plush and shiny and claws skittering on the marble floor, padded into the Music Room. As it stood with its long, pink tongue hanging out, absorbing the gazes of the guests, it was as if, for a freakish moment, the dog itself was the object of their adulation. Then, a heartbeat later, its master arrived.

When Hitler entered, it was as though all the air had been emptied out of the room and replaced with something sharper and more electric. Every eye was drawn to him as if on a wire, every expression one of bright, jewel-like intensity. Here was the face that had launched a thousand placards, that hung in every shop window, and featured on almost every stamp. The face that appeared to some women in their dreams and others in their nightmares.

Hitler's eyes were very dark blue. His hair had a stark side parting and one lock, like a scribble of charcoal, sliced diagonally across his brow. He was wearing a plain grey suit, and under it a white shirt and spotted tie. His expression, which generally looked long-suffering and aggrieved, as though he was enduring some intolerable injustice, was now relaxed and he was smiling broadly. After all, aside from military manoeuvres, movies were his favourite thing.

Several rows of red plush seats had been arranged in front of the screen, much like the gilt chairs Clara had shunned in the VIP enclosure at the birthday parade, and as soon as Hitler arrived, there was an undignified jostling for position, as if the whole company were engaged in a party game of musical chairs, and if they didn't hurry they might find themselves with nowhere to sit. Clara looked around in confusion. She had not anticipated this. For a second, as the seats filled up, she hoped she might be reprieved – perhaps she would find nowhere to sit, and like a child at a party, be forced to leave the game – until Christa Schroeder came to her aid. She had taken two seats in the row directly behind the Führer.

'Won't you sit with me, Fräulein?'

The chairs were arranged so that viewers could see between the heads of the people in front. Clara's chair was behind and to the right of Hitler, out of his peripheral vision and close enough to see the bull neck with the beginnings of a roll of fat above the collar and the comb marks in his oiled hair, tightly shaven at the back and sides. Everything appeared to her in extraordinary clarity, as through binoculars. She saw the patch of stubble on the pallid skin that the razor had missed, and the place where a boil was forming on one side of his neck. She heard the snuffle and grunt of the dog lying, head on paws, at its master's feet.

She let her hand drop to her thigh and felt again the apprehension she remembered as a child during a sermon at church, worrying that she might lose all power of inhibition and shout Major Grand's words out loud.

I hope if you were ever in the same room as him, you would have no qualms.

Now she *was* in the same room as him. She was sitting no more than two feet behind him. She could even detect the edge of his famous halitosis, mingled with Kölnisch Wasser, his favourite scent, and see him chewing a fingernail. She removed her jacket and laid it over her lap and then she let her hand cover the shape of the Derringer beneath her dress. Its warm steel burned against her thigh. She practised the movement in her imagination. Her previous nerves vanished and she felt strangely calm.

As the lights dimmed Hitler fished out the pair of gold spectacles that he hated people to see him wearing, and Christa Schroeder leant back with a sigh. This must surely be the most pleasurable part of her job.

It would be best to wait until after the newsreel.

It's always the same routine. Cartoon first, then a newsreel, then the movie.

It made sense to act when the audience were deeply engaged and all attention was immersed in the action on screen. How long would the cartoon last? Ten minutes perhaps? Ufa Tonwoche newsreels were longer – typically up to twenty minutes. That meant half an hour, at the outside, before the main feature and

then another ten minutes until the opening credits had rolled and
the story properly begun. Forty minutes then. Clara couldn't
stop herself glancing at the Leibstandarte, the ones who would
shortly arrest her, standing impassively at the door. Then at the
shadowy form of Conrad Adler, to her left on the end of the first
row, sandwiched between Goebbels and the pretty Frau von
Schirach. Adler did not glance back, but the fixity of his posture
told her that he was well aware of her. She felt intensely alert, her
head throbbing with tension. Everyone flinched as the projector
issued a high-pitched squeal and then, with a splash of frenzied
Technicolor, Mickey Mouse in *Society Dog Show* burst onto the
screen.

The softness and warmth of the cartoon shapes could not be
more out of place in the Reich Chancellery's marble tomb. As
Mickey's falsetto, dubbed into German, chattered brightly
through the action, Clara tried to keep her eyes rigidly ahead.
Everything about the cartoon's vibrant jollity and rubbery invin-
cibility was dramatically at odds with the chill formality of the
assembled audience. The dog-loving Hitler gave himself up to
loud, delighted laughter, but the reaction of the others was less
fulsome. Robert Ley yawned. Goebbels wore a little sneering
grin and his wife a stony glare. Rudolf Hess's face was a study in
blank incomprehension.

The cartoon lasted nine minutes. Slightly shorter than her esti-
mate. It was followed seamlessly by the trumpet fanfare and black
and white spinning globe of the newsreel. The Ufa Tonwoche
would contain, by Clara's reckoning, at least five items. It was
narrated in the usual tone of high-pitched, hectoring excitability
– both pessimism and reflection were frowned on in news reports
– and began with footage of military exercises taking place near
the Polish border. Row on row of marching men and tanks were
followed by a camera panning towards a stack of newspapers
pegged to a kiosk. '*Warsaw Threatens Bombardment of Danzig*',
'*Three German Passenger Planes Shot at by Poles*', '*German Families*

Flee Polish Monsters', *'Why is Germany Waiting?'* The customary crowd appeared, cheering and saluting. A country coaxing itself into a frenzy of adrenaline.

The next item was about the Ahnenerbe. A group of men in civilian dress were seen loading equipment into large trunks and the screen filled with a map of the world, marked by arrows pointing towards South America. Following the Ahnenerbe's success in Tibet, another, even more expensive jaunt was under-way to Bolivia, on the assumption that Nordic colonists had sailed there a million years earlier. The face of Doktor Kraus loomed on screen, explaining that through a series of expedi-tions, explorers would probe every corner of the earth to uncover music, folk tales, even paintings, that testified to the ancient pre-eminence of the German race. Hitler removed his glasses and took out a handkerchief to clean them. Others shifted in their seats. The adventures of the Ahnenerbe might have captured Himmler's imagination, but nobody else was quite so enthralled.

Eight minutes into the newsreel. Clara's hand beneath her jacket edged up the side of her dress with her fingers, eased the Derringer from its holster and slipped it into her palm. It was small enough to remain entirely hidden beneath her hand. *When you want to use it you move the hammer back to full cock position and pull the trigger. If you misfire, you can pull the hammer back and try again. But there's only the chance for two shots. You can only make one mistake.*

Another twelve minutes to go.

The compilers of the newsreel always liked to mix in trivial items with the heavy news. It was a journalistic technique, Clara knew, called 'light and shade'. The next item concerned a Hitler Youth marching band in Bremen that had won a national compe-tition. The players were all gleaming tubas and knobbly white knees, toting their instruments like rifles, notes clashing like swords in the air. The youngest were still in the Pimpf and could not have been more than ten years old. At the sight of the smooth, clean faces, shining with ardent pride, Hitler replaced his glasses and peered closely. Clara thought of Erich and wondered what he would say to see her here, so close to his beloved Führer, and what he would think of her tomorrow. If he would ever forgive her.

A glance at her watch. Fifteen minutes in. Hitler belched and not a head turned.

The final item concerned Stalin reviewing his troops in Moscow. He stood on the viewing dais on the top of the Lenin Mausoleum alongside a row of Soviet top brass – Molotov, Andreyev and the rest of the Politburo, breath frosting as they inspected a march past in Red Square. Every cinema-goer in Germany was accustomed to regular news of Russia. And even those who never visited the cinema could not escape it in newspapers and endless political speeches. The Russians were Bolsheviks. Slavs dominated by Jew devils. Stalin was controlled by the Jewish world parasite. This report, however, was different. Startlingly different. The script was conspicuously neutral. The customary snide remarks were absent and the cameras, usually angled to portray the podgy Stalin's least flattering aspect, provided a more appealing perspective. The smiling Soviet leader with his bristling moustache appeared reasonable, if not benevolent. Strong but fair.

In front of her, Hitler shifted in the gloom, smoothed his hair with the side of his hand and leant forward. Instinctively Clara tightened her grip on the gun beneath her palm, and inserted her finger into the trigger. Hitler was speaking – far too softly for most to hear – but she caught his words.

'That man has a good face. One should be able to negotiate with him.'

Then he rose abruptly and marched away without warning, prompting a scrape of chairs and a scramble of officers to their feet, a hurried clicking of heels and a raising of right arms as the Leibstandarte seamlessly opened the door and Hitler left the room.

For a second, a startled silence reigned, and then loud general chatter broke out. The relaxation at being out of the Führer's presence, mingled with relief at being spared another film, prompted a feverish jollity. The lights went up. People pushed back their chairs and began to mingle. Others pulled out cigarettes and lit up greedily, the film forgotten.

Only Clara sat in silence. The significance of what she had just heard was dawning in her mind, drowning out the shock of her assassination attempt so narrowly averted.

One should be able to negotiate with him.

Why was Hitler talking about negotiating with Stalin unless the rumours of a Nazi-Soviet pact were not rumours at all? Unless an alliance between the Third Reich and Stalin was already underway?

In which case Major Grand was wrong and British Intelligence needed to know without delay.

Chapter Thirty-two

It was now nine fifteen. Dropping the gun into her beaded evening bag, Clara slipped discreetly out of the Music Room and retraced her steps through the reception hall of the Reich Chancellery, across the road to the Kaiserhof Hotel. She made for one of the polished telephone cubicles at the back of the lobby, its bottom half enclosed and the top half glassed, closed the door and pulled out the copy of *The Thirty-Nine Steps*, repeating to herself Thomas Epstein's instructions.

When you have a message to convey, find the words you want to use, then select the page number, followed by the line, followed by the place that word occurs in the line.

She bent over the telephone directories, as though searching for a number. Then tearing out a page from her gilt-edged notebook and leafing quickly through the novel, she transcribed the words she needed.

Russia – page four, line seven and seven words along
Germany – page four, line seven and nine words along
Alliance – page four, line five, six words along
Very – page three, line three, two words along
Soon – page eight, line nine, first word along
477, 479, 456, 332, 891

Russia Germany Alliance Very Soon

She rolled the scrap of paper up to the size of a matchstick and inserted it horizontally deep in the bottom seam of her jacket pocket. Then she bundled the novel back into her bag, left the hotel and turned right, to make her way swiftly along the Wilhelmstrasse.

Berlin at night was the photographic negative of Albert Speer's pearl-white city. The pavements were drowned in a crepuscular gloom, interspersed with pools of dense shadow. Barely any light issued from the office blocks that ran the length of the government sector. The Air Ministry was a looming cliff of darkness and blackout gauze had already been erected on the Propaganda Ministry's windows. A few lights, however, were still visible in von Ribbentrop's Foreign Ministry. Plainly its staff were working overtime.

Clara progressed north up Luisenstrasse, past the jagged shadow of the Charité hospital where Erich's grandmother worked. In the courtyard she noticed one of the metal collection points – a pile of twisted saucepans and old tin cans destined for the Luftwaffe – and propping one foot against the wall she snatched off the calfskin holster and tossed it and the Derringer inside.

She hurried on as swiftly and inconspicuously as possible until a right turn along Torstrasse brought her to the Scheunenviertel, the Jewish quarter.

Fingering the matchstick of paper containing her code, she wondered if she would recognize Benno Kurtz when she saw him. *He's in his sixties, has a grey moustache. He was a good-looking fellow in his time and he still thinks a lot of himself.* She would ask for a gin and tonic made in the English way – presumably nine-tenths gin to one-tenth tonic – and pay him with a banknote, the paper concealed beneath.

As she went she tried to remember what she could about the Ritz bar. It was, from what she could recall, as far from its Paris namesake as was possible to imagine. Its wallpaper, lit by a series of gas sconces, was mottled and peeling, and its hospitality extended to cheap chairs grouped round deal tables on a scuffed wooden floor. Yet the place was a Berlin institution, famed for its ancestry and the diversity of its celebrity clientele.

You didn't need to be rich to drink there – the glass 'hunger tower' on the bar contained only humble delicacies like meat in aspic, bread dumplings, salted eggs, gherkins and pickled herrings – yet it attracted celebrities as diverse as Bertolt Brecht and the cabaret singer Claire Waldoff, to the less salubrious stars of the Berlin underworld. Its reputation had been formed in the Weimar era when Berlin was a sexual Wild West and that spirit lingered on in a variety of humorous signs taped behind the bar.

'Prostitution is strictly forbidden. At least according to the police!'

With a customer base like the Ritz's, no wonder it stayed open most of the night.

Five minutes later Clara turned into Mulackstrasse and glimpsed the hanging iron lantern at the far end of the street illuminating the entrance of number 15. But as she did, she became aware of a car behind her, its headlamps glittering on the cobbles.

Look out for a car travelling either too fast or too slow.

There was no other vehicle in the street. No jam up ahead. No parked cars to overtake. Yet the car behind her was moving at walking speed. It was not even driving as such, but cruising. When she slowed slightly, to allow it to overtake her, the car slowed too. She quickened, and like some devilish ballroom dance, it matched her pace. By now, Clara was just yards away from the hanging lantern of the bar. She guessed there were another twenty steps to go. Giving into the urge to glance behind her, she saw the car come to a halt at the kerb. It was a black Mercedes 260D with low-visibility headlights. Regulation Gestapo transport. She abandoned caution and began to move faster, the rapid thud of her heels on the paving echoing the beat of her own heart. Three feet from the door of the Ritz she moved across the pavement to allow a man coming from the opposite direction to pass. Then, with a slow horror that seemed to freeze time, she sensed two people approach from behind, and the man in front of her came to a stop, all closing ranks to form a trio that enclosed her entirely. Fear winded her like a fist in the stomach.

The two officers behind slipped their arms through hers, as politely as if they had been rivals competing for a waltz, and led her towards the waiting car.

Chapter Thirty-three

'I hope you won't mind if I don't accompany you.' Annie Krauss gestured slightly towards the velvet-covered table. 'I require a period of quiet meditation before my next customer.'

Baffled, Hedwig looked at Jochen but he was already moving towards the far end of the house. He had obviously been here before, because he led the way through a kitchen to a cellar door and then down two flights of narrow steps to a low-ceilinged room with bare walls. A single weak bulb illuminated a table on which stood a machine, several jars and stacks of paper.

'What's going on? I thought we were going to have our fortunes told?'

Jochen was sorting through a pile of papers on the table with his back to her.

'I think mine's already decided.'

Reality was dawning on Hedwig. Hard, unhappy reality.

'This is to do with the people you were talking about, isn't it? Are you going to tell me who they are?'

'I can't. None of us must know too much. They tell us to think of a stone thrown into a lake. The stone causes circles and then more circles that ripple out to the edge of the lake. We are in one of those circles.'

We? How happy she would have been a week ago, whenever she heard Jochen use that word. How she longed to go back to that time, when her only worry was whether he preferred brunettes or blondes.

'And is Frau Krauss part of this?' she said, incredulously.

'Annie is a very valuable member of our group. She's well respected in her profession.'

'Everyone knows that.'

'Precisely.'

His eyes were shining.

'Everyone knows Annie Krauss, and that includes a lot of military men. Hard to believe, isn't it? But the fact is, they flock to her. They like to think Germany's destiny is dictated by the planets. Remember that quote from Shakespeare? They do teach you Shakespeare at that place?'

She nodded dumbly.

'*The fault, dear Brutus, lies not in our stars, but in ourselves.* These military men prefer to believe the fault for the Fatherland's problems lies in the stars, rather than in themselves. Or in that ugly dictator in Wilhelmstrasse. Well, I'll tell you something. Recently they've been consulting her about Hitler's plans. They say he's fully intending to invade Poland. They ask, what should they do?'

Hedwig fought the impulse to turn tail and run up the stairs out of the house.

'And what does she tell them?'

'She tells them an invasion is a bad idea. The heavens are against them. But she doesn't say too much because she wants them to keep coming back. Every snippet of military detail they give away gets straight back to us.'

Hedwig picked up one of the leaflets on the table. It took the form of a newspaper front page except that it was much smaller, six inches by ten, and printed on rough, mimeographed paper. A headline read, *Germany awake! We are Sleepwalking into War! Resist*

Hitler! and underneath was the sub-heading: *Working for a New Free Germany*.

'Where do you leave these?'

'Public places: phone books, cafés, doctors' waiting rooms. We deliver them at night. We make flyers too. And documents. One of our people has a daughter in the Bund Deutscher Mädel, who takes them around wearing her uniform. It just looks like she's delivering copies of the BDM newspaper.'

Jochen gestured at the mantelpiece where a bottle of cleaning fluid stood alongside a box of matches.

'We keep these ready so we can burn them at a moment's notice if we get an unannounced visit.'

Hedwig's mind was a blur, the words collapsing before her eyes into tiny heaps of soot.

Germany awake! We are Sleepwalking into War!

'So why did you bring me here?'

'I was coming to that.'

He put the stack of papers down and perched on the edge of the table, arms folded.

'That ball you're going to.'

'The dance for the Prince?'

'The whole idea of the evening is to persuade the Prince of Yugoslavia to stand by while Hitler carves up Europe. There will be guests there from all over the world. Influential people from every country. They need to know that there's some kind of resistance in Germany – that we're not all on Hitler's side – and that if he's given carte blanche to invade Poland, he won't stop there. The ball is a perfect chance. I have a friend there.'

The way he said 'friend' told her everything. There was an undercurrent of admiration. A whisper of enchantment.

'It's Sofie, isn't it? From the orchestra?'

'She plays in a string quartet that has been hired to perform at the ball. She will distribute the pamphlets.'

'So what does that have to do with me?'

'You have access. You need do nothing more than take the pamphlets in. I'd do it myself but there's no way they'd let me into the Schloss Bellevue.'

Hoping against hope, she raised a protest.

'What's the point? What good can reading a pamphlet do? It's just a piece of paper.'

She seemed to have hit on an important issue. Jochen was suddenly excited, impassioned.

'Quite the opposite, Hedy! Reading is everything, Goebbels knows that. It's why he controls everything we Germans can read. He burns books and censors the newspapers, so people can't find any voices except his. We Germans have always been great readers. Literature is our lifeblood. But Goebbels would rather people sat and watched variety shows or romantic films than lose themselves in books. He knows that if you control what a nation reads, you control their souls.'

A terrible realization came upon her. Had Jochen only met her, had he only ever told her he loved her, because of what she might do for him? Had everything, from their first kiss onwards, been leading up to this?

Hedwig looked at him, a bright sheen of tears in her eyes, and summoned all her courage.

'Tell me truthfully. Is this why you were interested in me? Because of what I could do for you?'

He ducked his head to evade her gaze, running his finger up and down the table as if the grain of the wood might spell out an answer. Then he stood up fully and put his hands on her shoulders, his gaze frank and unflinching.

'It's true. Robert wanted me to get to know you.'

'Robert Schultz?'

Her childhood friend. A local boy who would scuffle in the schoolyard with a football and whose tawny hair and good looks had sometimes earned him an admiring glance from Lotti Franke.

'Robert thought you might be useful to us.'

'In that case . . .'

'Stop!'

Misery and hurt pride welled in her throat, but Jochen pressed his hands into her shoulders so hard that it hurt and shook her a little.

'That may be why he introduced us, but that doesn't change how I feel. I love you, Hedy.'

A sudden ferocity, a mixture of anger and fear, rose in her. She had always been the one longing for his affection, cravenly seeking his love, but now she felt a new strength, born of bitterness.

'Do you? Really? I'd say if you loved a person, you wouldn't ask them to do something as dangerous as this.'

'I used to think the same. But now I think it's *because* I love you that I want you to do it.'

Was this what love meant? Being brave, taking risks? Living in fear? She remembered Lotti's face on the last day she had seen her. Lotti was in love, and love had made her frightened too.

'Have you gone mad, Jochen?'

'No. I think we're the only ones who are sane.'

Chapter Thirty-four

The Barminstrasse women's prison in Friedrichshain was generally crammed to the rafters, but following an amnesty to celebrate the Führer's birthday a large number of prisoners had been released in a spirit of joyful reconciliation, with the result that the place was emptier than usual and Clara had a cell to herself. The single bulb was kept on at all times, presumably for the purpose of sleep deprivation, but the light was failing miserably at its job, stuttering and blinking fitfully and casting only a purgatorial gloom around the narrow space. The window looked out onto a courtyard ten foot below. Previous prisoners had left their marks on the brickwork, a selection of clumsily scratched initials all that remained of their individual identities. Attached to one wall was a single wooden bench worn smooth. How many women had sat there before her, wondering what came next?

If the prison guards were surprised at the sight of a woman wearing a couture evening gown and diamond swastika brooch arriving in their cells, they did not betray it. Nor had the men who arrested her been rough, but instead icily polite. There was no shoving or wrenching of hair, yet her wrists had been cuffed, making it impossible to remove the code paper from her pocket, and as soon as she arrived both jacket and bag had been taken away.

Clara was desperately tired. Her eyes were gritty and exhaustion seeped upwards in her limbs, like a draught of sedative, and although she did everything she could to keep her mind alert, it was hard. From time to time she drifted into a light sleep, but was jarred awake when her head hit the wall or by sounds of shouts and crying from the other cells. A deep unflagging terror settled in her guts, yet still she tried to focus through the fog of shock that engulfed her. She dropped her head to her knees, hoping that the blood coursing round her brain would help her to concentrate. It was as though she was solving some dreadful cryptic crossword puzzle, whose clues and half-formed suppositions spun around, split apart and refused to come together in her brain.

How long had she been followed?

She knew now that the young man in the lobby of Winterfeldtstrasse was not a police tail, but an illegal fly poster, who also forged documents for Steffi's resistance group. Yet the instinct that she was under surveillance had continued for weeks, even on the day she had spent walking through the city. Had the Gestapo been shadowing her all this time? Had they followed her to Paris? And if so, what exactly did they suspect?

Someone has been saying some very unkind things about you.

Leni Riefenstahl told her Himmler had suspicions about Clara's Aryan status. That meant right now they would be scrutinizing her identity documents. Despite the forger's skill, who was to say that the fake Ariernachweis would not be just as easily spotted as the one demolished by Conrad Adler? After all, the Gestapo had a string of fine art experts on their books, precisely for the task of examining documents. And yet . . .

To be apprehended for false identity was so much less grave than being arrested as a spy. The penalty for false identity was imprisonment, a camp perhaps. Please God, that they suspected her only of being a Jew. Because to be convicted as a spy was far worse.

But nothing so bad as if they suspected her of an attempt to kill the Führer. There was only one penalty for that.

She turned the problem over and over in her head, looking at it from different perspectives, examining it like a jewel of many facets. Questions revolved in a dizzy, sickening whirr. Would they have actually found the tiny scrap of paper that she had so precisely, carefully concealed deep in her jacket pocket? She remembered Steffi telling her that the Gestapo had become adept at ripping the linings of coats and jackets, running their fingers along the seams in the hunt for hidden valuables. If they found it, what importance might they place on it? Would they suspect Benno Kurtz? She was glad she had not actually had the chance to contact him before they took her away; if he was anything like as resourceful as he sounded, he would be able to bluff his way out. But what would it mean for Erich, and his hopes of SS leadership school, if his godmother was arrested as a spy?

Eventually, she gave up and ran through the store of images that, like a series of glittering stones, lit the path back to her own childhood. Her early theatrical career, the films she had acted in, coming to Berlin and meeting Helga Schmidt and Erich. Loving Leo. In her head she played the adagio of Mozart's Clarinet Concerto, the one that Leo so cherished. He said it was the closest that music came to prayer. She teased out each note in her memory, forcing her limbs to relax into its yearning. She thought of the first time she had seen Erich, on an outing to the funfair at Luna Park, and the following years, his voice breaking, his shoulders broadening, his life opening out before him.

Everything hung in the balance now. Her whole existence might soon be unstrung, like a necklace snipped and its pearls sent spiralling over the ground.

The table in the interrogation room was pocked with burns, sending the ominous message that the interrogators were far from cautious about where they stubbed their cigarettes. A low cloud of tobacco smoke, acrid in the mouth like petrol, hung in the air, barely troubled by the draught from an open window. The officer slouched in a chair with his legs crossed had an unhealthy, jaundiced look to him, as though he spent his life in the artificial glare of a Gestapo spotlight. His face might have been plucked straight from one of the cabinets at Himmler's Ahnenerbe, with skin stretched taut over the cadaverous cheekbones, pale scalp beneath his freshly shaved skull and a yellowish tint of ivory to the eyes. One of his ears was cabbaged, suggesting that physical violence was a familiar medium for him.

He rocked back in the chair when he saw her, and twisted his cigarette to join the others in the ashtray on his desk.

'Sit down, Fräulein Vine.'

She wondered how senior he was. Not very, or he would have been at home asleep, rather than doing an interrogation night shift. The look of brute malice in his eyes seemed to confirm that.

'My name is Kriminalsekretär Riesbach.'

Her guess was correct. He was relatively low-ranking, which made it all the more important that she gauge her response carefully. There had been a rash of Ufa performers arrested recently, hauled in for questioning about activities detrimental to National Socialism, and their brash, actorly manner, their namedropping and threats, only served to irritate the rank and file policemen, who treated them more harshly as a result.

'Perhaps you can explain why I'm here,' she said quietly.

'I was rather hoping that you would explain that to me. But maybe you will need some encouragement.'

'Could you tell me why I was arrested?'

Riesbach made a clumsy play of reasonableness, as though he had decided that because she was an actress, a degree of play-acting was appropriate. He spread his hands.

'Why not? A loyal patriot advised us that we should keep a watch on you, Fräulein Vine. From your file I see it's not the first time you have come to the attention of the authorities.'

'That was a mistake. I was released immediately and without charge.'

A frown descended on Riesbach's brutish features. He was pretending puzzlement.

'Have you ever heard of the saying *No smoke without fire?*'

'Yes. It's a common cliché.'

'So what are we to make of this? Another arrest. Another patriot who believes you are engaged in actions against the well-being of the Reich.'

'Actions?'

'Espionage, woman!' His face flushed and his voice rose to an angry bark. 'This patriot believed you may not be loyal to the Reich. That you may in fact be an English spy.'

Stay calm. Don't react instinctively.

'That's an outrageous accusation.'

Indignation and fear was the only correct response. The response of the innocent.

'I'm glad you see it like that. I feel the same. But then we found this.'

With a flourish, he reached beneath the desk and pulled out a book, light blue with darker blue lettering, that Clara recognized as her copy of *The Thirty-Nine Steps*. Her lips blanched with fear and reflexively she bit them to force the colour back into them.

Riesbach opened the book carefully at the frontispiece, as though examining some precious, ancient manuscript.

'You can imagine my colleagues' excitement when they found an English novel which appears to belong to the library of the Foreign Minister. Unfortunately, when they telephoned the Herr Minister's home, only Frau von Ribbentrop could be found and she was not pleased to be contacted in the middle of the night.'

The figure of Frau von Ribbentrop in a dressing gown, summoned to the telephone to explain why an actress should be carrying one of her husband's books, would indeed be formidable. Clara could only imagine her response.

'My men decided to postpone their questions, for the time being at least.'

So she had been saved. Saved by the foul temper of Annelies von Ribbentrop.

'But please don't think that our enquiries have ended there.'

A twist of pure pleasure spread across Riesbach's face as, like an amateur magician, he produced an envelope and tipped it out on the table. It was Clara's tiny matchstick of paper, carefully unrolled to reveal the line of numbers. How foolish to underestimate their efficiency.

He poked at the paper with an extended finger.

'I wonder what this might be?'

'I have no idea.'

'Strange, when it was found in the pocket of your own jacket.'

'I'm sorry. I'm very tired. I can't remember.'

This was inadequate, but the only answer Clara could summon while her brain moved at lightning speed to explain away the code.

'A list of numbers. What should we deduce from that?'

'It's probably a telephone number. Fans pass me their numbers all the time. They push notes into my pockets.'

'Good try, Fräulein. We rang it already. Or tried to. That doesn't work.'

'Then, I'm afraid . . .'

'Perhaps you need to take a closer look?'

As Clara bent to examine it, Riesbach moved abruptly forward, reached over and swatted her upwards, across the face. The impact of the ring on his knuckle sliced the skin on her cheek. The blow took her by surprise and she reeled backwards.

'Perhaps that will refresh your memory.'

'It hasn't.'

'You're an actress, Fräulein. You're supposed to remember things. Another one might help.'

A second blow, this time on the side of the head, making her ear ring and forcing her to clench her teeth.

'That's not a helpful technique.'

'What innocent person walks around with a list of numbers in their pocket?'

She decided to keep her head very still, as though facing an aggressive dog, in an attempt to forestall another attack. They had taken away her watch but the clock on the wall opposite told her it was five am.

'As I said, Herr Kriminalsekretär, people put things in my pocket all the time.'

The door clanged and another man entered the room. Although Clara did not turn, she could tell that he was senior, by the way that Riesbach half rose, before the newcomer jerked his head abruptly and leaned against the wall, arms folded.

'Carry on, Dieter.'

Riesbach's tone modified, marginally, and took on an air of aggrieved bureaucracy.

'I was asking the prisoner the significance of a list of numbers found on a piece of paper in her jacket.'

The newcomer interrupted.

'The charges before you are very serious, Fräulein.'

Clara did not look round. From the corner of her eye, she could make out that the senior man had a hard face and a tooth-brush moustache. His voice was more educated than Riesbach's, exuding the deep tedium of the early hours.

'Charges?'

'Allegations, precisely. The charges will come later. You need to talk to us. One way or another, we are going to require some answers.'

Clara continued staring rigidly at the clock. She was cold, in her sleeveless evening dress, and her flesh rose in goose bumps, but shivering would look like fear. She wrapped her arms round her in an attempt to keep warm.

'Not cooperating is not going to help you, Fräulein Vine.'

The senior man's tone said he was bored, his civility in short supply.

'Playing dumb might work at the Ufa studios, but it won't work here.'

'I have cooperated in every way.'

'Fine.' He scraped a chair by its legs across the room and brought it right next to her, his face so close that she could feel his breath on her cheek. He smelt of tobacco and good aftershave.

'Perhaps you think I'm a little slow.'

'Not at all.'

'Only, as Kriminalsekretär Riesbach says, we are puzzled by this piece of paper that was found in the pocket of your evening jacket. Dieter, can you fetch the jacket?'

'No need. The paper's right there.'

'I said fetch the Fräulein's jacket.'

With sullen menace, Riesbach got reluctantly to his feet and left the room. As he did, the tall officer rose swiftly and moved to the door. He pulled it shut, came back to Clara and put his face even closer. Forcing herself to look at him, she saw two different eyes. One brown, one blue.

Such a distinguishing feature would make undercover work impossible.

That was what she had thought when she passed a man in the corridor of D Section in London. Could it be possible that the same man, with his narrow tawny moustache and mismatched eyes, was standing right in front of her? Could a man trained in the depths of British Intelligence have been transplanted to the Gestapo in Berlin?

As if to confirm it, he spoke in English, very quietly.

'I'm going to let you out. Go quickly. Find somewhere to stay out of sight. If my senior officers object there's every chance you will be picked up again.'

Clara could barely move. She was paralysed with fear.

'Who informed on me?'

His voice was so low she could barely catch it.

'It must have been someone close to you. I heard Dieter say it was the last person he would have suspected. Now go.'

As she rose, the door clanged open and Riesbach returned, Clara's evening bag in one hand and her jacket suspended like a rag from his other fist. Springing to his feet, the senior officer snatched it from him, tossed it across the desk to her and turned to his colleague with an expression of barely suppressed fury.

'For Christ's sake, Dieter! All your talk of codes. One look at this and I can tell the lady is plainly innocent. Did you even bother to examine this nonsense?' He picked up the piece of paper, held it tauntingly in front of his baffled colleague, before screwing it into a ball and tossing it out of the window.

'Have you never in your life seen a line of Reichslotterie numbers?'

Chapter Thirty-five

Dawn had broken as Clara hurried through the east of the city. A sheet of clouds was pulled across the sky, lanced with sunlight that left their vapour pearlescent. Early workers were beginning to arrive at the textile factories and hooters were sounding. A horse-drawn milk cart was making its rounds, awaited by hausfraus touting capacious blue cans for their deliveries, and the first queues for bread and groceries were beginning to form. Here in the east, Albert Speer's construction work was well underway and blocks of houses were being razed, the dust blooming into the air. Twisted metal and hunks of mortar lay alongside pathetic domestic debris – a stray kitchen sink, a banister, a wardrobe mirror, a cot. Everywhere, it seemed, life had been turned inside out and what was previously concealed was now on full display.

Clara wiped the place on her cheek where Riesbach had hit her and tasted metallic blood on her finger, but she barely registered the injury. Her mind was racing with the question of who might have betrayed her.

I heard Dieter say it was the last person he would have suspected.

Was that because the informant was the wife of a senior Government minister? Had Magda Goebbels reported her, out of a mistaken paranoia that Clara had slept with her husband? Or, more likely, had Conrad Adler decided to punish her, merely because she refused to become his mistress?

Although the Gestapo officer had told her to stay out of sight, she had no idea where to go. She had no desire to return to Griebnitzsee, nor would she dream of seeking shelter with Erich and his grandmother in Neukölln. For a moment she contemplated visiting the Adlon and finding refuge in Mary's room before remembering that Mary would be far away by now, on her way to London. And that she badly needed a change of clothes. She decided to return to her old apartment in Winterfeldtstrasse and seek at least temporary sanctuary while she worked out what to do next.

In Nollendorfplatz, early morning commuters were already streaming into the station with its high glass dome, the red and yellow trains clanking along the elevated section. Clara walked swiftly along Potsdamerstrasse, but as she turned the corner into Winterfeldtstrasse, a figure stepped out of the shadow of a recessed doorway.

'Do you have a death wish?'

Conrad Adler was still in the suit he had worn the previous evening at the Führer's film screening. His coat was draped over his shoulders and, by the look of it, he had not slept all night. He appeared far older than before. His face was shadowed with stubble and his eyes bloodshot.

He gripped her roughly by the arm and pushed her back into the porch, away from the road.

'You're a fool, coming back here.'

Anger rose in her. Fury at the treacherous sexual attraction she had felt for this man who, if her suspicions were correct, was prepared to dispose of her at a moment's notice and consign her to a horrible fate.

'I'm a fool ever to have listened to a word you said. I expect you're wondering why I'm walking the street considering you handed my name to the Gestapo. You were hoping I'd be sitting in Prinz-Albrecht-Strasse by now.'

As if on cue a car proceeded slowly up the street and pulled to a stop further down the road opposite Clara's apartment building. The engine died, but no one got out. Adler pulled Clara closer into his arms. In their evening clothes they resembled a pair of lovers who could barely bring themselves to separate after dancing until dawn. His face was just inches from hers and she detected his shock at the purpling cut on her cheek.

'You don't know what you're talking about.'

'I was informed on and arrested. I know the informer was you.'

'That's ridiculous. Why would I have you arrested?'

'There's no telling what someone like you would do.'

'Someone like me?'

'Magda Goebbels told me someone was spreading rumours about me. You must think I'm naïve. Listening to your talk, having dinner with you, riding with you, when all the time you're working for Heydrich.'

'What makes you say that?'

'Leni Riefenstahl overheard you and Heydrich discussing me.'

Adler's grip on Clara loosened slightly. Outwardly, he was composed, but his eyes were alive, calculating.

'I can't deny that I have undertaken some work for Heydrich. But I promise you, Clara, for what it's worth, I have not informed on you. I knew nothing whatever about you until we met on the night of the Führer's birthday.'

'So how did you know where to find me now?'

'Goebbels insisted I attend that goddamned film evening. He had the nerve to suggest I might find it educational. When you left the Chancellery in a hurry I followed you, and saw you being picked up. Later I enquired at the police station and was surprised to discover you had been released. I guessed you might head for your old apartment.'

'And how did you know this address?'

'I'm a bureaucrat, Clara, remember? I told you. I did my researches.'

He reached his coat round so that it draped over both their shoulders, and arm in arm they turned back down the street.

'My car is parked round the corner. It would seem you might need a change of plan.'

Adler's lakeside villa was the epitome of good taste. It was painted a buttery yellow and framed by magnificent Blutbuchen – blood-red beech trees that flamed against the sky. At eight in the morning the air was fresh and still. As she climbed out of Adler's car, Clara would not have been surprised to find a servant at the porticoed entrance, but it was Adler himself who pushed open the door and ushered her inside.

Even from the outside, she could never have guessed at the sumptuousness revealed within. Everything spoke of long, deep-established wealth. The thick carpet and the carved, mahogany banister. The walls lined with ivory silk and the table bearing a bowl of white roses and a platter of fruit. Even the light felt expensive here, pale lemony sun gilding the burnished wood, glancing off the oak panelling and illuminating the paintings, row on row of them, hung in frames of clotted gold. The air smelt of citrus oils and sandalwood.

A dog came to greet them, a silvery Weimaraner with a coat like polished steel, his body highly sprung, lithe and muscular like the precise canine equivalent of its owner. The dog's eyes were piercingly pale and amber-coloured, his spine undulating beneath the pelt. When he came to a stop next to his master, the tendons on his legs stood out like strings on a bow and Adler placed a tender, proprietorial hand on him.

'Most hunting dogs have an unrivalled instinct for prey, but this one is an exception. He doesn't like to run with the pack. He's a very individual animal. He goes where he pleases.'

As if in demonstration, the dog trotted off again.

'Wait here.'

He disappeared down a corridor and Clara heard the distant clink of china. In his absence she looked around her. There was a roll-top desk in the corner on which stood an SS-issue Olympia typewriter, specially fitted with its SS double lightning flash key. There was a stack of official-looking papers beside it, a tortoise-shell inkstand and a brass reading lamp. A glass paperweight like a teardrop, inside which a flower was imprisoned. And the tooled Cartier box containing the diamond earrings she had refused.

She drifted across to the paintings, gleaming like gems in their polished setting, their pigments almost alive. They were portraits mostly, ordinary seventeenth-century citizens gazing out at the painter with inscrutable eyes, enclosed in a soft glow of shining domesticity. The men were playing cards or the lute, and the women were immersed in the simplest of tasks – stitching, pouring milk, reading letters.

'The Dutch Golden Age,' said Adler, over her shoulder. He was carrying a tray bearing coffee, rolls and a bottle of cognac. He proceeded to pour a glass and handed it to her.

'Northern European realism is my greatest love. It was a time when artists moved away from religious painting to the detail of their own lives. Vermeer, of course, is the master.'

He swirled the cognac around in his glass and then swallowed it.

'It troubles me that Hitler should love Vermeer. Does it devalue the art, do you think, when evil people love it?'

Clara looked up sharply. She had no idea where this was heading.

'Perhaps Hitler approves of seeing women in a domestic setting,' he mused. 'Maybe he thinks the paintings express some time-honoured concept of Germanic tradition. Whatever his notion, he obviously has no real idea of what Vermeer is about. Nor have any of them.'

Adler continued to fix her with an odd, speculative look.

'I ask myself, is Wagner's music less ravishing because it is adored by a sadist like Himmler? Is a Vivaldi concerto as beautiful when it is played by a psychopath like Heydrich? Does a vicious thug like Goering sully the Titians and Rubens he professes to adore?'

Adler's eyes were intently on her own, as though his life depended on her answer.

'What do you think? Tell me, Clara. It's a question that torments me.'

'Of course not. An object can't be accountable for who loves it, any more than a person can.'

'I'm glad you think that. Because that's their crime as far as I'm concerned. It matters far more to me than their politics or their ambitions. I'm not a political man. In my opinion Germany is the greatest nation on earth, and she deserves her empire. No empire is achieved without the spilling of blood. But these men have committed a crime against civilization. They have no respect for art, no true understanding of it. It's a commodity to them, like iron or steel. The masterpieces they squabble over are pearls before swine. Goering, that fat sentimentalist, may profess some scintilla of cultivation, but he's no better than a child running his fingers through a jewellery box, picking out the biggest, most glittering stones. Hitler is a peasant, and has a peasant's appreciation of art. Goebbels may have the wit to perceive, dimly, the value of some work, but he has become a vandal. You heard about the bonfire? Four thousand artworks? Irreplaceable. All in an attempt to impress the Führer.'

'And how do you propose to stop them? By advising Rosenberg on which works are the most valuable?'

If this barb struck home, Adler barely flinched. He seemed distracted, as if some long suppressed confidence was now tumbling unstoppably out of him. He refilled her glass.

'I've never spoken about this before. Or only once, and that was during my stay in London. I was with a man from British Intelligence, as it happens.'

A tremor went through her, and she hoped that his sharp eyes had not detected it.

'Why would you meet with British Intelligence?'

'It wasn't my idea. A chap called Erich Kordt, one of Von Ribbentrop's entourage, had put feelers out. Kordt's an Oxford man and a convinced Anglophile, and he engineered a meeting. The fellow I met seemed to think I would want to work with them. He told me I was too intelligent not to.'

'And what did you say?'

'He was right, of course, about my intelligence. It's impossible to avoid the fact that the National Socialists are by and large a group of ignorant thugs. There's no real intellect among them. Cunning perhaps, in the case of Goebbels, but a notable lack of brain cells elsewhere. That's why Frau von Ribbentrop is so dangerous. She has all the intelligence her husband lacks. I often wonder what she suspects of me.'

It was very still in the villa. Only the distant ripple of birdsong pierced the air.

'So . . . did you accept his offer?'

'Of course not.'

The anguish left his face and he gave a dazzling smile. 'What a suggestion, Clara. Can you imagine the penalties for that kind of thing? In fact, Kordt must be a quivering wreck now, imagining that I will report him, but so far I've not felt the need to tell anyone.'

He cast his evening jacket aside and wrenched off his tie.

'Eat something, won't you?'

She took a roll, helping herself to the thick pat of butter and wondering where it came from.

He scrutinized her as she ate.

'Are you tired?'

'I think the nerves are keeping me awake.'

He came in front of her, touched the abrasion on her cheek left by Riesbach's knuckles and turned over her wrists where the handcuffs had left a sore red bracelet of skin. Then he bent and kissed them.

'I can't imagine what they did to you in that prison. I would like to kill the brutes who put their clumsy hands on you. Do you want to sleep?'

'I'm not sure if I could.'

'In that case, we shall have to decide what to do with you.'

She gazed at him directly. The air between them seemed to shimmer with expectation.

'Do with me? What do you mean?'

A small smile lifted up the corner of his mouth.

'There's something you should see.'

He pulled her towards a door. Inside was a small, windowless, wood-panelled room, like the chapter house of some mediaeval castle. The burnished walls were hung floor to ceiling with paintings, every surface covered and canvases stacked two or three deep. Yet it was not the number of canvases that surprised her, but the paintings themselves. They were portraits mostly, almost all of them women. An ochre nude of a woman reclining in a posture of luxuriant abandon. Another woman, the neck sharply turned away, the skin pale and luminous as a pearl. A couple, clinging to each other in the wreckage of a world, unsettled and utterly alone, both fascinating and repelling. The figures were spiky and angry and their quality intense and stunning, unlike anything she had seen before. Adler's personality flared out of them savagely, in bold brushstrokes and angular lines.

'I come in here when I need to escape. Whenever I have attended meetings with Heydrich or wasted my time with von Ribbentrop, I know that I can return here and shut myself away. I find it useful to immerse myself in art. It cuts me off from the ugliness of everyday existence.'

In one portrait she recognized something. A pose from a film she had made called *The Pilot's Wife*. The girl in the picture was Clara, but as she had never seen herself, caught in a few deft strokes, a figure whose stark lines and angular intensity reminded her of Egon Schiele. There was a sadness in her eyes, as if she was mourning something, and a defiance too.

'Why keep these pictures secret?'

'Isn't it plain? Mine's a dangerous art. It's what those barbarians would call degenerate. Hitler fears us, and I understand why. Modernists are angry and self-loathing. We paint our own crisis of spirit. Our work emits the scent of our unconscious. The Nazis want art that's full of sunlight and pure maidens, whereas we see man how he is. Flawed, miserable, ignoble, compromised.'

'You didn't tell me you were an artist.'

'I was at the Berlin School of Arts when the Gestapo moved in in 1933. I remember staring out of an upper window when they took all the Modernist work down to the courtyard and destroyed it. Do you know what happens when paintings burn? You see flashes of colour as the pigments ignite – peacock blue, emerald green, violet, rose, all glowing like liquid jewels. It's the chemicals, you see. For a moment there are these gorgeous flickering embers, as the paint bubbles and sizzles, then in an instant it's all soot and dust. When they trashed the art school I knew I had two choices – I could be like Emil Nolde: change my style, stick to insipid watercolours and pastorals. I could be like Otto Dix and agree to paint family portraits of the von Ribbentrops and their children. Or I could hide in plain sight. I think that's what they call it. I could wear their colours, like that little hare I told you about in the fields back home. I would focus on the Old Masters and allow everyone to believe I had abandoned my own work.'

'There was another alternative.'

He frowned.

'And what would that be?'

'If you thought they were barbarians, why get involved with them? Nobody forced you to advise them on which masterpieces to steal.'

'I told you. I'm not political.'

'You didn't have to work with them. You didn't have to stand by while they ride roughshod over every law and civil right. While they arrest and murder thousands of their own citizens. You could have left the country.'

'You think I should have run away?'

'You're already running away. You're hiding from everything the Nazis represent. You shut yourself in here and pretend the world outside doesn't exist. That you don't bear some responsibility for it.'

'But my dear Clara, it was my responsibilities that kept me here. There was the estate to look after. That's my patrimony, you understand. The von Adlers have lived in Weimar for generations. It was unthinkable. No, I knew my passion must be concealed. You see,' he gave her a quick, sharp glance, brimming with meaning, 'concealed passions are nothing new for me.'

, He moved towards her, easing his fingers through her hair, pulling it away from her head so that it kindled against the light and revealing the side of her neck.

'I love the place where the skin is translucent and you see the blood beneath,' he murmured. 'It's like seeing through you.'

She felt desire quicken in him, his breath hot on her skin.

'You don't want me, Conrad.'

He drew back, his perfect face clouded with incomprehension.

'Why not? That would be particularly irrational and whatever else you know about me, I am a rational man. Besides, I like you.'

'You said human emotions were entirely untrustworthy.'

'Perhaps I'm coming round to them.'

There was barely any room to move in the close, contained space. Running his hands down her shoulders, he eased the straps of the evening dress from her shoulders, so that it fell from her and lay in a puddle of silk at her feet. Then he drew her towards him and kissed her.

Just for a moment she responded, then she pulled herself free. He laughed and spread his hands.

'Very well then. First things first. I also want to paint you.'

She sat for him in the drawing room beside a wall of Delft tiles, bathed in the pure light coming in from the lake. As his hands moved over the paper, Clara felt his eyes sweep over her, taking in every detail of her colouring and complexion, right down to the dusting of freckles on her nose and the flecks of darker blue in the iris of her eye. It was the type of close attention that would serve a policeman well, but in Adler the appraisal seemed entirely non-judgemental, as though he was simply evaluating her living flesh, assessing her proportions.

'I still want to know. Why you were in Paris, if you were not following me?'

A distracted shrug.

'I told you. I was advising on a collection.'

'For Goering or for Hitler?'

'Clara Vine, this persistent line of questioning does not suit you. Especially when you should be grateful to me.'

'Grateful to you? Why?'

He sighed, and dashed down his pencil.

'All right. I'll tell you.'

Reaching behind him he found an old shirt, daubed with paint, which he tossed towards her. Instantly, she covered herself up.

'It's true, Goering and Hitler are engaged in a race. Their intention is to carry off every piece of art they desire to the Reich. But my business in Paris was something different. You see, when I first met you I recognized your name.'

'That's not entirely unusual for me, though it might be hard for you to understand.'

'Be patient, woman. Let me explain. When you asked me what I was doing in Paris, I told you I was advising on a collection. I have allowed you to think that collection was one of paintings. But it wasn't. It was names. And when I first met you, it wasn't your Christian name I recognized.'

'You'd heard of my father? That's no surprise.'

'Perhaps I should explain what I was advising on and why. Shortly after I returned from England, Reinhard Heydrich contacted me. To say it was a surprise is an understatement. A call from Heydrich is not the kind of invitation you put on the mantelpiece. But I went along to his office in Prinz-Albrecht-Strasse and saw to my dismay that he had my file open before him on the desk. Always a bad sign.'

What had Leni Riefenstahl said? *In Heydrich's mind, information is power. He has a locked safe that he refers to as his 'poison cabinet' where he keeps all his files on the senior men.*

'But contrary to my expectations, he began to compliment me on my memory.'

'Do you have a good memory?'

'Exceptional, actually. I'm a freak of Nature. As a child it was called an eidetic memory because I could recall images and objects with high precision. Even the minutest details. It's declined a little with age, but it is a talent all the same, and it was that talent Heydrich wanted. He knew I'd spent two years mingling with British society, reading British newspapers, meeting British aristocrats, politicians and writers. He pointed out that my enthusiasm for that country was flagged in my file as a warning. There had been fears that I intended to make London my home. Suggestions I preferred the British way to life in the Reich.' A gruff chuckle. 'I was able to reassure him on that score.'

He glanced out of the window at the splendour of the gardens beyond, the manicured lawns, clipped hedges and sculpted trees.

'Who would forsake somewhere like this in a hurry?'

'So what did Heydrich want?'

'He told me something in deep confidence. It wasn't a confidence I wanted, but once I had it, I was bound by it. Heydrich knew he had me captive simply by telling me his plans. That's how it works with secrets. Once you know them, you're trapped.'

His eyes shifted as if passing over private thoughts.

'Heydrich is creating what he calls his Black Book. A collection of all the most significant enemies of National Socialism in Great Britain.'

'You mean, in case of invasion?'

'Should his plans go ahead. Ultimately his deputy, Walter Schellenberg, will be in charge of this operation. Schellenberg is Chief of Amt VI – that's the Foreign Intelligence branch of the Security Service, but in the meantime Heydrich wanted my advice. I'd spent two years immersed in British society so I was perfectly placed.'

His gaze was distant, as though he was seeing far beyond the boundaries of the Reich to England, and all the people and parties and places he had once enjoyed.

'Take your film about the Ahnenerbe, Clara. Germans travelling the globe, studying different societies. Well, what Heydrich wanted from me wasn't so different. He has compiled a picture of British society, made up not of old bones and skulls, but names. On that day in his office he gave me his Black Book and asked me to provide notes on which of the names inside it were friendly to the National Socialist government and who might prove hostile.'

'How many names?'

'Two thousand, eight hundred, to be precise. Both British subjects and European exiles, who are to be arrested or taken into protective custody in the event of a successful German invasion. The people deemed enemies will be arrested immediately. Churchill. Eden. Duff Cooper. They'll be seized within days. Churchill will be placed in the hands of Foreign Intelligence and the rest turned over to the Gestapo for imprisonment. The others, lower down, will merely be placed on trial.'

'Who are they?'

'I recognized most of them immediately. H.G. Wells, Virginia Woolf, Noël Coward, E.M. Forster, Aldous Huxley, Stephen Spender, Sigmund Freud, Rebecca West. And when I heard your name I recognized it too.'

'But my father has been a fervent supporter of the National Socialists for years. It's well known. He was a Nazi sympathizer right from the beginning. It would be absurd to arrest my father.'

'I'm not talking about your father.'

Adler walked across to the roll-top desk and felt in the top drawer. He retrieved a photograph of a woman, cut from the pages of a magazine – *The Tatler*, it looked like. She was in evening clothes with a mink stole around her shoulders. Her hair was neatly pinned in a chignon, her eyebrows lifting slightly, as if in surprise.

'This is your sister, I believe.'

Angela.

Chapter Thirty-six

'I heard your sister was in Paris, so I made a quick visit. That was why I was there that night at the Dingo Bar. I was keen to see if what I had been told about her was true.'

Clara gave a sharp laugh of disgust.

'If Heydrich has my sister's name in his Black Book, then that's proof he has absolutely no idea about English society. My sister was a founder member of the Anglo-German Fellowship. She and my father held the earliest meetings at our family home. Her entire life is devoted to fundraising in support of closer ties between Germany and Britain. You couldn't find a more devoted admirer of the Nazi cause than Angela.'

'Or a more deceptive one.'

She stared at Adler. Tiny fragments of thought were glinting in her mind, like diamonds in rubble. The image of the maid at the door of Elizabeth Street. *She's visiting her sister.* Dolly Capel in the Dingo Bar. *I thought she was here.* What reason could Angela have for visiting Paris? Unless it was true that Angela concealed as great a secret as Clara herself.

Turning to the roll-top desk again, Adler took a piece of paper from a sheaf and read aloud.

'*My enquiries in London, and later, confirm my view that Angela Vine is an agent of the British Intelligence Service, working undercover to infiltrate German-sympathizing factions within the British establishment.'*

'That's impossible.'

He continued reading. '*She has held these views from the early days of the Reich. She reports on the activities of National Socialist sympathizers to the British government. More recently she has been liaising with agents in Paris to assist resistance in the event of a German invasion.'*

'But I . . .'

'You what? You never suspected that your sister had a talent to deceive?'

'If it's true, why did I never guess?'

'Presumably that's the idea.'

'I should have, though. I've known her all my life.'

'That's probably the point. You were too close. You could never get perspective.'

'I can't believe you would give my sister's name to the Gestapo.'

'I didn't produce these names. The Gestapo collected them. I was merely asked for my opinion. What these men and women stand for. Who they are and what they believe in.'

'Your opinion will be their death warrant.'

'I haven't yet submitted my opinions. But they are known opponents of the Reich and in the event of invasion their fate is unavoidable.'

'So you'd happily line them up for a firing squad.'

'Not happily.'

He walked over to the window and surveyed the patterned box hedges dividing the flower garden and the crystalline purity of the lake beyond. A man was raking the lawn and Clara saw that it was Karl, the groom from the Reitclub Grunewald.

'Happiness is not something I expect. I never have. I always assumed that one needs to learn happiness early, like a foreign language, if it is to come at all. Too late, and you can never properly be fluent. You'll never understand its inflections. I don't think I'll ever know what it is to be happy.'

Adler turned round.

'Does he make you happy? This unmarried man who is so intriguingly absent from your life?'

'Yes.'

'Is he coming back to you?'

'I choose to believe so.'

'So Love gives you faith, does it? Faith's a pretty poor substitute for real life, Clara. Look at that picture there.' He pointed to a painting of Venus being pursued by Adonis, prettily depicted in glinting oils. 'They're imprisoned like that for ever. They never fade, but they never kiss. They exist in an eternity of yearning. Is that what you want?'

'Who cares what I want? What does it matter?'

'You're right, of course. But it matters to me because I have a proposition for you.'

'I already said . . .'

'Hush.' He put his fingers to her lips, then drew them down across her face. He smoothed the hair from her temples and rubbed a strand of it between his fingers, as though it was silk. The way he was looking at her had changed now. He was no longer the painter, examining his subject, but a man savouring something precious, like a jewel.

'War is coming soon between our two countries. Hitler has already breached the terms of the Munich Agreement. I've read documents demonstrating the enormous superiority of Germany's airforce over those of Britain and France. I've played a small part in the preparations myself, so I can scarcely claim innocence. But you, Clara, will be in a difficult position. A woman who is half-English, and hiding her Jewish identity. You've just spent the night in a prison cell. What could be safer than marriage to a senior member of the Party?'

'Marriage?'

'You'd have to go through the selection procedure, of course, for marrying into the SS. There's a questionnaire, with preposterous queries about whether you like cosmetics and perfume. Whether you smoke.'

'As you've already noticed, I would hardly pass the Aryanization tests.'

'I'm sure that can be arranged. You have blue eyes, which is good, even if they're flawed with something darker. And besides, we Nazis are not the only ones who are good at faking our identity. If we can invent a cultural heritage, why shouldn't you?'

Still, she was staring at him in astonishment.

'Don't look at me like that. It's as though no one has ever asked you to marry them before.'

'And you look like no one's ever refused you. I don't love you, Conrad. That must be obvious.'

'I'm not asking you to love me. I wouldn't presume to think that affection was involved. On your side at least. I merely suggest it as a strategy you might find useful. An alliance, if you like, between interested parties.'

'You deserve more.'

'I'll be the judge of what I deserve.'

He turned his attention to a Dutch interior on the wall. It was of a young girl sewing, with a dreamy look on her face and light from a window filtering through the glossy web of her hair.

'Vermeer's wife was Catholic, did you know? That was illegal in seventeenth-century Holland. So by marrying her Vermeer was making a secretive alliance. I like the idea of that. Making our own alliance. You would be safe under my protection and I wouldn't deny you your freedom. You could come and go as you choose, but I would suggest that, at least for a while, we move to my estate at Weimar. It is, my darling, one of the loveliest parts of Germany. Not only the home of Goethe and Schiller, but it also boasts the most beautiful woodland, the lovely forest of Ettersberg.'

The way he was discussing it, it was as though she had already agreed. For a moment, the exhaustion of a night without sleep overcame her and Clara allowed herself to contemplate his proposal. Would it be so bad, this loveless marriage? Reporting for her Rasse Merkmale, her racial characteristics assessment, where she would be examined, weighed and have her upper lip measured? It need only be a temporary measure. It would mean she could stay in Germany with a safe cover for her work. More importantly, she could stay close to Erich.

Adler watched these thoughts travel across her face and his voice dipped.

'Don't you ever get lonely, in that house out at Griebnitzsee, eating your solitary dinner? Don't you ever long for some intellectual companionship as barbarity descends?'

'Are you seriously suggesting that you would marry me just to keep me from arrest?'

'That wouldn't be my only motivation, but it might be yours.'

'So a short-term marriage of convenience?'

'I think that's the phrase. That's one thing I've always admired the French for – their approach to affairs of the heart. They have none of the dull Protestant rigidity that afflicts us Germans, and the British too. The French understand that human passions come in many forms.'

She shook her head. 'It would be living a lie.'

'Aren't we all living a lie? You have, I assume, sworn an oath to the Führer as a condition of your employment at Ufa?'

He was right. Whatever Goebbels said about big lies being needed to convince people, life in Nazi Germany was full of little, everyday lies. What would one more matter?

Adler smiled down at her, a rare trace of tenderness softening the perfect lines of his face like a statue momentarily blurred by rain.

'Besides, there would be honesty between us. Sometimes the most unlikely partners come together for mutually beneficial reasons. That's an idea being actively propounded in my old Foreign Ministry workplace just now.'

She was instantly alert.

'You're talking about the Soviet Union.'

'An alliance between Germany and Russia is coming any day now.'

'How do you know?'

'You'd shown such an interest that I took the opportunity to catch up with Frau von Ribbentrop. She loves to confide in me. Perhaps she thinks, because I share her interest in Old Masters, I must share her other views. I raised the subject with her.'

'And she told you?'

'Something she shouldn't have. But she couldn't resist. She knew I would understand why. It's a personal triumph for her, you see, although the world will never realize it. All those years of hostility, that long-nurtured hatred of the English, has finally born fruit. What is that saying? *Hell hath no fury like a woman scorned.* The way they laughed at her in London. Mocked her pretentions. Ridiculed her husband's infatuations. It hurts, being laughed at. It leaves a lasting legacy. Now Britain will reap the consequences. She showed me something actually. Perhaps you'd like to take a look.'

He picked out a piece of paper and handed it to her casually. At the top it bore the eagle and swastika, the official stamp of the Foreign Ministry, and beneath it, von Ribbentrop's personal seal, bearing his family coat of arms. Clara scanned it, trying to accustom her eyes to the dense gothic script.

Reich Ministry for Foreign Affairs: Top Secret.
Operation White.
Operational Orders for the Invasion of Poland.
Issued by German Military High Command.

'Von Ribbentrop is shortly to fly to Moscow to negotiate a non-aggression pact,' said Adler. 'The Soviet Union and Germany will join arms and carve up Poland between them.'

Clara's eyes raced to the final paragraph of the directive.

Preparations must be made in such a way that the operation can be carried out at any time from 1st September 1939 onwards.
By command of the Führer.
Heil Hitler!

Adler watched as she absorbed it. Musingly he said, 'Curious, isn't it, how important a scrap of paper can be? We Germans place such childish faith in what is written. We surround ourselves with minutes, directives, cultural audits, requisition orders. Invasion plans. We document everything. It's as though, once something is committed to paper, everything that follows is legitimate.'

'First of September? So they've set a date.'

'And now you're wondering when you can alert your sister.' He plucked the paper out of her hands. 'But you mustn't. If they find out that I've shown you this, they'll take a very dim view of me. Showing top secret Ministry documents to actresses is probably worse than showing them my portraits.'

Clara looked up at him soberly.

'If I married you would you take Angela's name off your list?'

'Yes.'

'How can I trust you?'

He was entirely unmoving, his face tense and still, his eyes shining with some unexpressed emotion.

'You can't. None of us can trust each other. That's the message of this murderous brigade. They show us the true face of humanity. They may try to stamp out reality by destroying paintings, but who needs paintings when we have ourselves to look at? Besides, if you want to understand human nature, we still have the Old Masters. Brueghel's a good start. I recommend him.'

He drew her towards him and she felt the fight go out of her. His body felt hard and solid, like a pillar, and she was so tired.

'I need time to think.'

'Time, I'm afraid, is one thing we don't have. Let me explain. While I was in Paris, I met an American. That's not unusual – Paris right now is crammed with Americans trawling for any booty on offer – but this man was different. He offered me a job at the Metropolitan Museum of Modern Art. It would be a dream of a job. I would be an expert by day and a painter by night. You mentioned the idea of running away, and I admit I am coming round to it. I'm forty-four, Clara. I'm the last of my line. I have no parents, no wife and no children. Nothing to lose. In a couple of weeks the doors will slam shut and my chances of leaving will be gone. So I need your answer very soon.'

He wrenched her face up by the chin and kissed her, a thick, greedy kiss.

'Accept me, Clara. You'd be mad not to.'

Still that arrogance, that patrician confidence, the disbelief that he might be refused.

She almost loved him for it.

Chapter Thirty-seven

'They built this place when we had our first colonies. The plan was to collect exotic plants from German territory all over the world and bring them back to Berlin. Think about that. The entire German empire in a garden.'

They were walking along a gravel path through the lush borders of the Botanical Gardens, a short ride on the S-Bahn to the south-western borough of Steglitz. The gardens were the city's green jewel; an oasis of greenhouses, intersected by streams crossed by small bridges and stepping stones, with meadow areas and formally laid parterres set behind high, unprepossessing walls. It was a favourite outing for Berliners, and even more for Hedwig and Jochen because it was where they first met.

It had been more than a year ago, on a rare Saturday when Hedwig was not engaged in classes at the Faith and Beauty Society. She had taken a book with her to the Botanical Gardens, but the book was only a prop because what she actually wanted was to sit beside the decorative lake beneath a monkey puzzle tree and imagine that she lived there. She loved the gardens, partly because they were situated as far from Moabit as was possible in Berlin, and partly because being there allowed her to indulge her fantasy of being a Hohenzollern princess living in elegant splendour, rather than a dank tenement with washing hanging in the courtyard.

But that day her fantasy was interrupted by Robert Schultz, an old school friend who, it turned out, was carrying out his *Arbeitsdienst* year as a gardener. He had a friend with him, a wiry, fierce-eyed young man who showed great interest in the book she wasn't reading. Shortly afterwards, Robert left, and she and Jochen had spent an hour in intense conversation before he had leaned over in the shadow of the monkey puzzle tree and kissed her.

They had come here often since then, although their approaches to the outing were entirely different. While Jochen was obsessively interested in botanical detail and would frequently squat down and scrutinize the plants and their Latin names, Hedwig was happy simply to gaze around her. She liked Nature to be orderly, and the sorting of plants into their appropriate categories, the Japanese garden, the Italian Garden, the rose arbour and so on, appealed to her sense of tidiness.

Today, however, the gardens' tranquillity was shattered by the racket of drills. A band of workers at the far end of the garden were constructing yet more air-raid tunnels. A digger was biting straight lines into the ground, slicing through the grass and leaving a frill of earth behind.

'Those tunnels are going to house all the SS files and personnel,' commented Jochen quietly. 'They've decided it's one of the safest places in the city when the air raids come.'

'How would you know a thing like that?'

He didn't answer. Apart from his comments about the colonies, he had scarcely said a word since they met at the S-Bahn and made their way here. There was nothing new about that – Jochen never saw the point of small talk and Hedwig was quite used to his moods – but that day his jaw was clenched more rigidly than ever and his air of tension, like some hunted wild animal, alarmed her. The horror of the past few weeks – of Lotti's death and Jochen's revelations – had filled her with a constant, tremulous anxiety. But the task he had asked of her now – to smuggle illegal pamphlets into the following week's ball – made her feel physically sick. She had barely eaten for days. Even Mutti was casting her suspicious glances.

They came to the biggest greenhouse, the Great Tropical Pavilion, an Art Nouveau triumph of glass and steel that towered at the garden's centre like a glittering, crystalline castle. As they passed from the clear summer air to the sweltering, damp atmosphere inside, the humidity clung to her skin and the lush density of plants seemed to pulse with their own life. This was another world, an enclosed, mossy universe, surprisingly noisy with the screech of birds in the rafters and the rushing of artfully constructed waterfalls into koi carp ponds. Giant vines and bamboos stretched to the highest parts of the roof and glossy leaves, as big as elephants' ears, waved all around. Between the delicate fronds, orchids dangled from hairy vines thick as babies' arms, and at their feet the ubiquitous Berlin sparrows pecked at a tangle of ferns.

They followed the winding path to the deepest part of the glasshouse. This area was reserved for the flesh-eaters: the fly traps with their suggestive lobes and stamens thrusting frankly up from reddened petals. Vivid tubes that persuaded insects to crawl into their pendulous prisons. Hedwig had always hated carnivorous plants. The whole idea of plants eating flesh seemed a dreadful inversion of the natural order.

Jochen sat down on a bench that had been painted yellow to indicate that it was for Jews. Since November Jews were no longer allowed in the Botanical Gardens, so the yellow benches had reverted to Aryan use, but they still bore the instruction *Nur für Juden*, and despite the fact that they were unobserved, Hedwig felt uneasy about disobeying an order. Beside them cacti, cobwebbed with flimsy silk, reared up, their spikes tipped with flowers like hanging drops of blood. She realized Jochen had chosen this spot because the trickle of a stream into a stone grotto behind them drowned out their conversation.

He reached in his bag and brought out a book wrapped in plastic.

The Proper Care of Cactuses.

'Good, isn't it? I made it up at work. Never judge a book by its cover.'

He took off the wrapping and opened it. Between the stiff boards was a wedge of what Hedwig immediately recognized as Flugblätter, a wad of pamphlets tightly packed together. She didn't want to look at them.

'You remember everything I told you?'

'Yes.' Just the thought of it made her feel even sicker.

'When you have the afternoon rehearsal at the Schloss Bellevue, go to the women's washrooms. They're on the ground floor, to one side of the reception hall. You'll have the book with you. Leave it in the cistern of the cubicle on the far end.'

'And Sofie will pick it up?'

'That's all you need do.'

'Why can't she take them herself?'

'The guards check their instrument cases and everything. The orchestra don't arrive until an hour before the ball begins, but the Faith and Beauty girls will be practising all afternoon.'

'What if someone sees me?'

'They won't. Put it away in your bag now.'

'What if the pamphlets drop out of the book?'

'It's simple enough!' he snapped. 'Just do it, Hedy!'

He was sitting with his elbows on his knees, staring ahead.

After a moment's silence she said, 'Why are you being like this?'

Jochen took out cigarette paper and tobacco, rolled it and lit up, even though smoking was not permitted in the pavilion.

'Something's wrong.' His voice was gentler, but grave. 'I think my number's up.'

Her insides churned.

'What happened?'

'There was a woman, the other day. Part Jewish. I was making an identity document for her. Everything seemed straightforward. I did the cards and we waited a while for them to dry. She left quickly and I waited a few minutes before leaving. But when I came out on the street, I realized she was being followed.'

'That's her problem, surely.'

'No. Don't you see? I have no idea how long she had been shadowed. If the man was watching her before we met, he would have tailed her all the way to the building, and then he would have seen me too. That apartment can't be used any more. And they may be onto me too.'

'Oh, Jochen.' Instinctively she looked around her to check for eavesdroppers, but it seemed they had the jungle to themselves. 'What did you do?'

'I evaded him at once. Jumped on a tram, doubled back. There was no sign that he was after me.'

'So you're safe?'

'No. I'm blown, Hedy. I'm sure of it. I've already moved out of home.'

'What did you tell your family?'

'I said I'd been sent away. I'd been specially requested by a manuscript factory in Dresden. They won't find out for a while.'

'But if you're stopped?'

'I'm changing my identity.'

'What about your job?'

He flicked his cigarette into the leaves, where it fizzled out in the damp vegetation, then turned to face her.

'I'll have to leave it and lie low for a while. There's no alternative. I need to disappear completely. There are people who can help me. There's a pastor in the West End who's offered me a place for a while, so please don't worry about me.'

'How do you expect me not to worry about you?'

Her voice was harsh with anxiety.

'If you need to contact me, leave a message with Robert. You know where he lives, don't you? You can trust him.'

Panic was starting to overwhelm her and she began looking wildly around her.

'Of course I'll need to contact you. I need to see you.'

'And you will. I promise. We'll be together after all this is over.'

She had a sinking feeling of desperation, as though they were in trouble with no path back, like a butterfly that has crawled into a fly trap and finds its frail wings stuck to the treacherous nectar. In so far there was no way out.

'Take me with you.'

'Do you mean that, Hedy? You'd leave your family and all those little brothers, would you? You'd leave the Faith and Beauty? Because you couldn't go back, if you went underground with me.'

She thought of everything she had been told her life would be: all the painting and dancing and chess. Then she thought of her real life: Mutti's tired face, and the boys jousting and squabbling. She heard Kurt's laugh. Love was supposed to be uplifting. It was a balm that made your life complete, not a knife slicing your heart into ribbons. Not a constant stream of questions about who you wanted to be. Hedwig or Hedy? Ordinary or exceptional?

She forced herself to focus.

'Yes. Yes I would.'

He smiled. A strange, bitter smile.

'Perhaps. But first, there's one more thing you can do for me.'

She clutched his hand tightly, as though he was proposing to vanish right there and then.

'What? What is it now?'

'I need you to find me a gun.'

Chapter Thirty-eight

Rule Seven: stick to public places.

The spot in the Alte Nationalgalerie where the Titian had hung bore a small label.

On permanent loan to the collection of Hermann Goering.

The Alte Nationalgalerie was one of the first places Clara had ever visited with Leo and in the six years since then it had become a regular outing for her and Erich. Increasingly, however, the more famous of the artworks were notable by their absence. Goering had led the way, favouring paintings of naked women, the more voluptuous the better. Then Goebbels had taken his pick, under the auspices of creating a home of sufficient grandeur for his ministerial rank, and Hess and von Ribbentrop followed suit. Soon the walls were pockmarked with labels alerting the citizens to the fact that its paintings were serving a more important function in the private homes of the Nazis' senior men.

That day the gallery was thronged with summer tourists. A crocodile of Bund Deutscher Mädel girls was being shepherded through a gallery of Austro-Bavarian realism – the type of folksy landscapes the Führer adored, replete with jolly monks and tavern scenes. Art came well below sprinting and long jump in the BDM curriculum, yet the occasional tour round the duller parts of the city galleries, avoiding nudes or foreign painters, was on offer for those who showed an interest. And, judging by the giggling, even those with no interest at all. Clara drifted in the girls' wake, pretending to eavesdrop on the lecture, but all she could hear was a date.

First of September. The date for the invasion. The date for war.

She had stolen back to Winterfeldtstrasse that morning for a change of clothes. She made her way up the familiar stone steps, so worn away by the tread of thousands of feet that they caved in the middle, shut her front door and leant against it, trying to absorb everything that had happened. The suggestion that her own sister was liaising with anti-Nazis in France was astonishing, but whether it was true or not, Angela's name featured in Heydrich's Black Book and accepting Conrad Adler's proposal was the price for her sister's safety.

Clara longed to barricade herself inside, to sit amid her own belongings, brew coffee, to linger and reflect. Yet what if her apartment was no longer a sanctuary but a place of danger? She had no idea if her release had been agreed, or whether the Gestapo were still trailing her. Whether she would hear the cough of an ignition when she left the block, and the slow growl of a Gestapo car following her down the street. There was no point in waiting to find out. She donned a pair of sunglasses, covered up the mark on her cheek as best she could with foundation and closed the door behind her.

Walking through the ground floor of the gallery – Neoclassical and Romantics – she focused on the people around her, checking for repeating faces, or anything that suggested anomaly. An art gallery was the perfect place to disappear. One could linger, staring not at the pictures, but the reflections in the glass, wandering this way and that as taste dictated. Clara found herself gazing blindly at still lives of dead game, spoiled fruit, and rotten, blown flowers. The bloodied fur of a rabbit, posed beside a dying rose. Until a soft voice came in her ear.

'Did you know that the Führer originally wanted to be a painter? He was turned down by the Vienna Academy of Fine Art twice. I wonder if they're regretting that now.'

She turned, astonished. The speaker was a man of middling height with solemn brown eyes and a fedora, which he doffed with an air of old-fashioned gallantry.

'Forgive me. You are, I think, Fräulein Vine?'

Strangely she felt no alarm. There was something benign in the man's expression and his vaguely beseeching air. He looked more like a salesman than a policeman. Besides, what choice did she have?

'That's right.'

'I wonder if I could have a word?'

'Should I know you?'

The man glanced round the gallery, with his grey felt hat clasped in front of him, as if he too was unsure why he was there.

'Not at all. We've never met before. But you might know my brother. My name, you see, is Goering. Albert Goering.'

With his slender frame, thin moustache and sideburns, Albert Goering could not have looked less like his older brother Hermann. His high, arched eyebrows gave him a startled air, and he was dressed with dapper Viennese charm, from the handkerchief sprouting at his jacket pocket, to the fat gold watch suspended by a chain across his waistcoat. He looked more like an assistant in a high-class gentleman's outfitters than a member of Nazi royalty. Instantly Clara recalled Emmy Goering's words.

Hermann's brother is very keen to meet you.

'I have tried to contact you a couple of times. I even visited your apartment. I hoped to find somewhere discreet, but it seems Fate has intervened. Shall we visit the Post-Impressionists?'

Clara shot a glance around her, searching for any police or security services, but there was nothing unusual. Besides, who was going to arrest her in the company of Hermann Goering's brother? He was employed at the film company Tobis-Sascha, Emmy had said. Perhaps he wanted to talk to her about a part.

'Why not?'

The Post-Impressionist gallery was predictably deserted. Those of the exhibits that had not been filched or deemed Degenerate were of dubious quality and mostly French. No schoolchild in Germany was going to waste time learning about French artists. Although there was little to detain them, Clara and Albert Goering strolled slowly along the undistinguished walls.

'Are you here for the ball, Herr Goering?'

'I had a little business to attend to first.'

'Film business?'

'No.' He fished out his handkerchief and gave a quick, fastidious dab at his moustache. 'It was to do with some Jewish friends. I needed a word with my brother about them.'

He acknowledged her astonishment.

'It is a sideline of mine. I escort them personally to the border and provide them with currency.'

'And your brother knows about this?'

'Of course.' He gave a quick, nervous laugh. 'Hermann says he will decide who's Jewish. He tells me he can get anyone he likes redesignated as Aryan. Occasionally it works the other way. It was Hermann who called me about Henny Porten. The actress. You've heard of her, I'm sure.'

Henny Porten had been a legend of the silent movie era, but with the arrival of the Nazis, her star had faded. Although she was Aryan herself, her husband was Jewish, and she had no inclination to divorce him.

'I met her a couple of times.'

'It was my sister-in-law Emmy, I think, who got Hermann to contact me. I was able to secure a contract for Miss Porten at my company so she moved to Vienna.'

There was no way to know how to react to this. That Hermann Goering, a man capable of such extreme viciousness, who had overseen the arrest and murder of so many people, who had personally dreamt up the plan to fine Germany's Jews a billion marks for the damage inflicted on Kristallnacht, should bother himself with sorting out the affairs of an actress and her Jewish husband.

His brother gave a pained grimace.

'You look surprised. But Hermann wouldn't be the first to be flexible in his approach to Jewish affairs. Goebbels was once engaged to a half-Jewish girl, I believe, and his wife was involved with a Zionist. I can't pretend I have anything but abhorrence for Hermann's behaviour. My brother's actions horrify me, but I do what I can to atone for it. It's a very little part, but the Jews have a saying. *He who saves a single person, saves the whole world.* It comforts me.'

'So what exactly did you want with me?'

'It's a bit of a story.' Albert Goering looked around him, but the room remained as deserted as a church. Not a soul had entered or left in the time they were there. All the same, he lowered his voice.

'A few months ago, a friend of mine, Gustav, a former employee of Tobis-Sascha who I had helped escape to England, got in contact with me. He is now working for British Intelligence Services and he said there was someone coming to Vienna that he wanted me to meet. Gustav said the man would be waiting at six o'clock in the musicians' section of the Zentralfriedhof – the big cemetery, you know. He would stand by the Mozart memorial.'

Mozart. The closest that music comes to prayer.

'I went along to the cemetery, and sure enough, the chap was there.'

Her throat constricted.

'Leo.'

'Yes. Mr Quinn knew I was in the habit of making regular trips to Berlin and he begged me to get in contact with you. He gave me your address in Winterfeldtstrasse and made me promise to find you. He said he had needed to leave very suddenly and that you would be worried about him. But you must not be. Does that make sense to you?'

'Yes. Yes, it does!' She was laughing, half mad with delight. In her joy she barely registered that Albert Goering remained sombre. 'Thank you, Herr Goering. Please, tell me, where is he now?'

His kindly eyes dipped.

'That, my dear Fräulein, is the part of the story I am less happy to tell. We arranged to meet the following day at the same time and place, but when I arrived, there was no sign of him.'

'So he missed the meeting. There must have been a hitch. Surely you went back?'

'I did. I returned the following day. And the next. And I asked around, as much as I could.'

Clara reached forward and gripped his wrist unintentionally hard.

'You must have contacts. Couldn't you ask them?'

'Of course. That's exactly what I did. And what I discovered was most unfortunate. A policeman I knew reported that a suspected enemy agent had that day been denounced to the Gestapo. I'm afraid the man who betrayed his predecessor must have betrayed Mr Quinn too.'

'But you don't know.'

'I fear the worst, dear lady. I'm very much afraid that he's gone.'

Gone. The word hit Clara like a piece of shrapnel. It ripped inside and hollowed everything out.

Albert Goering rested a hand on her arm, then replaced his hat and made to leave.

'I'm sorry to bring you this news, Fräulein Vine. If you are ever in Vienna, please come and visit me at the Tobis-Sascha studio. I would be happy to see you again.'

After he had left, Clara stood for a while, clenching and unclenching her fists. To have her hopes raised and dashed in such rapid succession left her unable to move, as if winded. Uncertainty paralysed her. For a moment the thought that Leo was alive had lit up her life like a flame, yet almost immediately that spark was doused. It seemed that Major Grand had been right after all when he advised her to forget Leo. Conrad Adler had been speaking the truth when he said she was in love with a phantom. Did she face years of private mourning, of never being able to tell another soul what her lover had meant to her? Was she doomed to be one of those women she had known in childhood, who lost their fiancés in the war and were dogged with disappointment and silent grief? Would she walk through Berlin, haunting the places they had inhabited like a ghost in her own life?

There was a painting in front of her. It was of a naked woman washing. With a shock she realized that she recognized it as one that Leo had pointed out to her, when they visited the gallery together, all that time ago. It was a small pastel by Manet of a woman in a tin bath, the water silvering her back, looking up at the painter with a frank and open gaze. It had a kind of purity about it. The model was not ashamed of her sexuality, nor was there anything salacious about it. Instead the connection between the woman and the painter seemed to contain a deep, unspoken conversation. She wondered how this portrait had remained in place without being removed. How it had been spared Goering's wholesale pilfering and Alfred Rosenberg's strictures on degeneracy. How it had escaped the attention of Robert Ley, the Labour Minister, famous for his salacious tastes. Perhaps being inconspicuous, or simple or foreign, was what it took to survive.

It was then that she made a deal. A pact with whichever deity might be listening. If Leo was alive she would do whatever he wanted. Go back to England, abandon her work, leave Berlin entirely. Become the woman Leo wanted her to be. If only he was alive. Let him be alive.

Chapter Thirty-nine

In the courtyard of the Schloss Bellevue, a fountain shot a shower of diamonds into the night air. High above, fireworks blistered the sky and inside everything was candlelit; china, crystal and flowers, all captured in an antique golden glow. It could have been a tableau from another era as butlers dressed in knee breeches and powdered wigs welcomed men in eighteenth-century frock coats and women barnacled with jewels in long, sweeping gowns. The great hall was hung with art treasures and perfumed by elaborate sheaths of hothouse orchids, roses and white lilacs. But despite the historical decor, nobody was giving much thought to the past. Not when the future hung so perilously in the balance.

A flurry of attention signalled the arrival of Goering's car, a distinctive, aviation-blue Mercedes 540K cabriolet, dubbed the Blue Goose. Because he liked to drive himself, the vehicle had been modified not only with the standard bulletproof glass and armoured walls, but a specially engineered seat broad enough to squeeze the corpulent Minister behind the wheel.

It was obvious, once he had heaved himself out of the car, that whatever his wife might claim, Hermann Goering's diet was not a success. The Minister's fat fingers were manacled with emeralds and gems of sweat were already glinting as his gargantuan paunch preceded him into the reception hall. His outfit of embroidered mauve frock coat, frilly cravat and tight silk breeches didn't help, nor did the floor-length white fur coat flatter his curves. Emmy, at his side, looked almost svelte in a low eighteenth-century gown, the neckline drawn aside like a pair of theatrical curtains to reveal her powdered bust.

An extensive cast of diplomats, aristocrats, politicians, hangers-on and members of the film and theatre world had been assembled to greet the Yugoslav royals. Tonight was the summit of the state visit and the culmination of Hitler's attempts to flatter and intimidate Yugoslavia into remaining neutral in case of war. Yet alongside this important agenda, a range of lesser ambitions were on display. Joseph Goebbels, in white uniform and medals, was purposefully late. Magda lagged a deliberate few steps behind her husband with a dyspeptic glare. And von Ribbentrop had opted to accessorize his full Foreign Ministry fig with the magnificent diamond-studded collar of the Annunziata, expressly to annoy his host.

Once the guests were gathered, a string quartet struck up a waltz and a host of Faith and Beauty girls, done out in taffeta dresses as white as clouds, began to dance.

Clara skirted the packed reception, the reds and blues and golds unfurling and mingling before her eyes. The sparkle and glitter of the evening reminded her of the line from *Paradise Lost* about 'barbaric peal and gold', yet it was impossible to concentrate fully on the scene when her mind was still in tumult. She was in possession of a secret more valuable than diamonds – the date for war – but there was nothing she could do with it. The month that Major Grand had allotted her was about to elapse. Yet still, she could barely focus on anything. Thoughts of Leo drowned everything out. After the meeting with Albert Goering she had gone to the Ufa studios in a daze, and spent the afternoon buried in the costume department, selecting a dress for the evening ahead.

'You know what they're all gossiping about.'

The voice was icily familiar. Syrup undercut with steel. Clara
turned to find Annelies von Ribbentrop, sheathed in grey lamé
as tight as aircraft fuselage, standing uncomfortably close.

'I don't, I'm afraid.'

'Oh, but I'm sure you do,' she insisted, lips puckering into a
smile. 'All anyone's talking about is the pact.'

The pact. Could it really be this simple? Was the alliance so far
advanced that it was already a topic of casual party conversation?

'Don't tell me you haven't heard?' The malice in Frau von
Ribbentrop's face glittered like the diamonds at her neck. 'I
thought someone who likes gossip as much as you would be
bound to know before the rest of us. You always seem to have
your ear to the ground.'

'Not in this case.'

She shook her head sorrowfully.

'It's the pact between the Goebbels. Joseph has signed a document with Magda agreeing to a year's good behaviour and Hitler
has offered to act as guarantor. It's the only peace treaty Hitler
has ever put his name to.'

Clara looked over at Magda. Though she towered like a chess-
board queen over her husband's pawn, she had evidently
succumbed to checkmate. The pact may be a small victory in her
marital war, but she had plainly been obliged to attend the ball,
and to add to her humiliation she was at that moment being
introduced to Veit Harlan and his wife Kristina Söderbaum, the
director and star of *Die Reise nach Tilsen*, the film that Goebbels
intended to commit his affair to romantic posterity.

'You wonder why Goering has to invite all these actors. I
mean, I know our hostess feels more comfortable surrounded by
fellow . . . *performers*, but really, there must be the entire staff of
Ufa here tonight. Was there some kind of round-robin
invitation?'

'I was asked because the Minister wanted some English
speakers.'

'Oh. Of course.' She took a sip from her glass and winced, as if she had been drinking vinegar rather than the best Sekt. 'The English are all very well, I suppose, but must they endlessly try to butt in on our business? Threatening war over the return of a city like Danzig, which is German already. And when the Poles provoke us in the extreme. Hitler has been in love with England for years, but I tell him, it's unrequited. All these years he has paid court to England, admired her empire, entertained her aristocrats, and what does he get for it? My husband says all we ask of the English is that they recognize the Germans are also a great nation, with our own special sphere.'

Clara was saved from continuing this conversation by the announcement that dinner was to be served. Annelies von Ribbentrop disappeared to take her place on the top table, and Clara drifted towards the grand dining room, where a feast of clear soup, goose with potatoes and lettuce, cheese, fruit, coffee and pastries was waiting. Not forgetting the kilo of Russian caviar which had been delivered that morning from the Soviet Embassy.

They were only on the first course – *crab royale à la mayonnaise* with asparagus – when a muffled cry and a shout caused heads to turn up to the balcony. A beautiful young woman whom Clara recognized as the violinist from the string quartet was leaning over the balcony, screaming something and pulling from her lace-edged yellow jacket a flutter of paper, white and coloured, that came drifting down onto the heads of the crowd. The guests ducked and cowered, as if bombs, rather than leaflets, were being rained on their heads. One drifted to the table beside Clara and the man next to her, a Dutch diplomat, picked it up and studied the headline. *Hitler means war!* Almost immediately he dropped it, as if he had received an electric shock.

Most of the guests politely averted their eyes from the balcony, but Clara watched the girl with her heart in her mouth. For a second she stood poised, as if planning to fly down and join them, before three soldiers arrived and seized her roughly, stretching her arms outwards like a crucified saint. The light shone a gold halo on her hair and the tendons stood out on her slender neck as her terror transmitted itself through the air. As they wrested her away the girl's face was drained of colour but she submitted quickly, walking with dignity between the men, her upright bearing failing entirely to disguise her fear.

At the table waiters leapt forward instantly, sweeping up stray leaflets like embarrassingly spilt milk. Goering's face was puce with fury but for the first time that evening, Goebbels gave a thin, colourless smile.

Conversation started up again and the clatter of cutlery resumed, but Clara's appetite had deserted her. It was impossible to eat with the memory of the violinist's bloodless face in her mind and the thought of what she might now be enduring. The girl looked so young. The fact that she must have known the penalty for such a public protest was no consolation. Suddenly, Clara felt as though all the colours in the room were vibrating and blurring into each other, the candlelight off the chandelier splintering into a thousand stars.

'Please excuse me. I feel a little dizzy.'

She escaped to the terrace overlooking the magnificent garden, lit that evening by a hundred lanterns, and waited for her head to clear. From the shadows beside her, a figure appeared.

'Hello, Clara. I thought it was you.'

Olga Chekhova was wearing a deep, strapless gown with a full-skirted froth of grey tulle studded with roses at the hem.

'Are you all right?'

'I needed some air.'

'I'm not surprised. That poor girl. One dreads to think . . . Breathe deeply, darling, and drink more champagne. It'll settle you.'

She came and leant her arms against the stone parapet with a sigh.

'I had to get away from Goebbels. Do you know, he uses me as an alibi? When he's been seeing that woman, Lída, he tells

Magda that I've invited him for dinner. He does drop by my apartment, but he only stays a few minutes and then he leaves. So every time I see Magda she stares like a witch who has put a curse on me. Tell me, is she watching now? Don't make it obvious.'

Clara peered back into the ballroom.

'I can't see her.'

'Good. I wish I'd never come. I only came because the Yugoslav Princess is half-Russian and she's a fan apparently, but Goering hasn't even bothered to introduce me. He's been utterly boorish towards me, in fact. Quite rude.'

Clara realized there might be no better opportunity than this, in the quiet gloom of the garden, to tell Olga what she knew.

'Actually, I think I understand why.'

A sharp, interrogative look.

'You do?'

'Frau Goering mentioned it to me and I haven't had the chance to tell you. The fact is, Olga, Goering suspects you of spying.'

In the darkness, the actress's expression was hard to read, but she coolly opened her velvet evening bag and drew out a cigarette, lighting up before replying.

'Well I can't say I'm surprised. Why should he be any different? Everyone suspects me of spying. You have no idea what a nightmare it is for me, Clara. I'm both German and Russian. In Moscow, they suspect me because I live in Germany, and here, people assume that I will be leaking secrets to my brother, Lev, because he's close to the Russian government. And I can't say a word. How could I ever denounce Stalin while my relations are living in Moscow?'

'It must be hard.'

'Oh, don't worry about me. The truth is, Clara, it's you I'm worried about.'

The older woman inclined her head. Behind them the blithe precision of a Viennese waltz danced out of the open doors and a hundred pairs of gleaming shoes shuffled on the shining floor.

'The other day in the Adlon, you were talking to a man.'

'I thought you didn't see me. I called and you didn't reply.'

'Forgive me, my darling, I did see you. But I pretended not to hear. The fact was, I couldn't disappear fast enough. You see, I knew that man. The one you were with. He's a friend of my brother Lev's.'

Clara looked out into the darkness. Her fingers were so tight around the stem of her glass, she almost crushed it.

'The man you were talking to is a senior officer in the NKVD. I would recognize him anywhere but I hardly expected to find him standing in the bar of the Hotel Adlon.'

In the second before Clara completely understood, it was as though she was standing in the shadows of the sound stage, look-ing into the dazzle of the set, trying to see a face against the light. Waiting for the face to take shape as her eye adjusted.

And then she knew.

'Be careful, won't you?'

Olga Chekhova touched Clara's shoulder lightly, and walked away.

Chapter Forty

It was late by the time her taxi reached Griebnitzsee. A lustrous moon made the shadows denser, the darkness blacker. Firs crowded in across the narrow road. Silence came sifting down like snow and a fine sheen of rain puckered the glistening surface of the lake.

She guessed now who it was that had given her name to the Gestapo and the knowledge had made the world change shape and close in around her. Her adrenaline was firing like an electrical charge, sparking through her body, yet her mind was focused and determined, rinsed clear.

The big villas with their gates and long drives were draped in darkness. Shutters were closed and curtains drawn. Either the owners were away or they weren't bothering to light the street for the benefit of a rare, late-night passer-by. Yet again Clara regretted moving to this isolated spot. In the city there would be noise and nosiness, but in Griebnitzsee there was only indifferent silence.

As she approached the house, she remembered another point on Leo's list. *Listen to what you don't hear. Pay attention to anything unfamiliar, to the gaps in the environment around.* Any whisper that lay behind the natural stirrings of the forest and the waves thudding against the jetty in the lake. She stopped for a moment, ears strained for any change in the texture of the silence. Anything that might make her senses prickle, the way they did when danger was near.

And it was there. The rattle of the front gate that had been left unlatched. The gate that Clara always closed. Like a bat squeak of menace, it sounded a high note of alarm in her ears.

But it was not until her key turned in the lock that she realized he would be waiting for her.

Hugh Lindsey was standing in the drawing room holding the postcard of the Vermeer painting that Clara had propped on the mantelpiece. The lamps were unlit, but the flood of moonlight washing in through the long windows accentuated his face in unfamiliar chiaroscuro.

'I like this one. *Young Lady seated at a Virginal*. It's from the National Gallery, isn't it?

'What are you talking about, Hugh?'

He carried on, as though she had not spoken.

'Vermeer's ladies look so pure and innocent, don't they, but who's to say they are really? Isn't that what appeals to us about them? The suggestion of corruption underneath? This one here – this little musician – we know that she may have more than music on her mind, because there are erotic paintings behind her. There's Cupid and a procuress.'

Clara snapped the light on, causing him to blink.

'What are you doing in my house?'

'I've been here a couple of times actually, since I drove you that evening. I wish you'd invited me in then, but there was obviously something on your mind. I've been thinking about you. I've watched you.'

'You *watched* me.'

'Don't take it personally, Clara. I like you a lot. I know your family. But ideology means more than pure sentiment.'

'You mean Bolshevik ideology.'

'If you like.'

She remained where she was standing, by the door. Her legs were trembling too much to move.

'You probably don't know but your dear Bolsheviks are planning to team up with the Nazis. There's a pact underway right now. What does that say about them that they're prepared to ditch their principles at a moment's notice?'

He smiled. 'Principles are a luxury that other people pay for. Besides, this pact you're talking about – if it happens – will ultimately advance the cause of Bolshevism.'

'And how is helping Hitler going to advance your cause?'

'I'm no admirer of the Nazis, as you well know. But Stalin needs to protect the world from the expansion of British imperialism.'

'Protect the world? The English are the only ones who will oppose Nazism.'

'Oh, Clara.' He gave an indulgent smile, as though at the foolishness of a child. 'The English are hopeless. They have no idea of the Nazis' methods or intentions.' He looked around him, restlessly. 'I suppose you don't have any more of those Gauloises with you?'

She reached in her bag and withdrew the packet, tossing it to him.

'Thank you.'

Pulling out his Dunhill lighter he inhaled languidly.

'There's something about us English which makes us think that because we all go to the same schools and belong to the same clubs, White's or Brooks's, or the Athenaeum, or at a stretch the Reform, and because we share the same tailors, that we must also share the same mind. King, Country, Class and Club, that's our religion. The effortless English gentleman. Born to rule the waves. The only rules being not to sleep with a colleague's wife and not to light one's cigar before the third glass of port. Our highest test of character is being a good cricket umpire and playing by the rules. Ideological dispute is the stuff of university common rooms. Well I've never been part of that pompous, self-satisfied tribe.'

'So it was better to become a spy?'

He gave a gravelly, cigarette-choked laugh.

'My dear, isn't that rather a case of the pot calling the kettle black? It takes one to know one.'

If Hugh Lindsey knew about her, what others might he be aware of? Despite his outward languor, Clara felt their two minds matching each other, calculating, intensely alert. Trying to compute which of them was the more dangerous.

'As soon as I realized what you were about I informed my friendly local Gestapo, but for some reason they allowed you to slip the net.'

Clara had heard that in extreme situations, fear would turn to anger, and now she felt fury, pure and hot, coursing like fuel through her veins. It was so difficult to equate the handsome, cultured, smiling being before her, with the threat he posed.

'Why not have the courage of your convictions and join the Russians outright?'

'Perhaps. But how much more satisfying to destroy the citadel from within. It's rather a thrill, outwitting others. Hugh St John Lindsey. Just the sort of chap they expect to mingle with them, attending their grand dinners at the Grosvenor House and the Dorchester and Claridge's, listening to their deeply misguided speeches.'

Claridge's.

'It was you, wasn't it? You were the man Lotti Franke met in London. The one she fell in love with.'

'There was a hotel dinner. The Faith and Beauty girls were being paraded like Hitler's little princesses. The pearls of the Reich. Well, a couple of nights in the company of the lovely Lotti was enough to settle that question. Lotti was like one of Vermeer's girls. An exquisite face and the morals of the gutter.

Did you see that photograph of her in the paper the other day – the one by Yva? It captured her perfectly, I thought.'

'But to kill her, Hugh? Why would you need to do that?'

'She was threatening me, I'm afraid. In the most extortionate way. She wasn't a nice person, Clara. She'd stolen from me.'

'I know all about that. She stole a jewel.'

'A jewel? No.'

For a moment he looked baffled and his bloodshot eyes blinked as though Clara was speaking a foreign language. Then he smiled.

'Ah. That's what the Führer's dealer called it. Hildebrand Gurlitt. *A jewel*. I suppose it is, in its way. One of the great gems of Western culture. But it wasn't a real jewel. It was a book.'

'A book? That can't be true.'

'But it is. I had come by a rather lovely manuscript. I knew what it was because, without being immodest, Roman literature of that era is my speciality. And this was a copy of the Tacitus *Germania*.'

'You're lying. I met an expert at the Ahnenerbe who told me it was in Italy.'

'As indeed it was. The Codex Aesinas. Hitler's dearest wish. The one manuscript above all others he would like to possess. But there was another codex. It had spent hundreds of years at a monastery in Austria until it came into the hands of an antiquarian dealer there. Who was unfortunate enough to have his collection thieved by Nazi louts. I'd heard of it years ago, in Vienna, and once my contact described it, I knew exactly what it was. I just had to have it. I went to Austria to find it, but no luck. It had already been carted off back to Berlin. So I followed it, and once I arrived here I discovered I'd come in the nick of time. The stash was being held in a warehouse in Kopernikusstrasse under the auspices of Hildebrand Gurlitt. The riches there were mouth-watering. Paintings, silver candlesticks, porcelain, all sorts. But most importantly the *Germania*.'

The fragments that had been spinning around Clara's mind began to pair and come together.

'So that was what Goering wanted.'

'Goering wanted it passionately because the Führer wanted it too. The competition between them is pitiful. Goering was a regular visitor to the warehouse and when he heard about the *Germania* he was determined to have it. He's engaged in some kind of race with the Führer and knowing how much the Führer desired the Tacitus made it all the more desirable to him. I managed to buy it the day before Goering turned up. It was better in my hands than his, I reckoned.'

Clara felt a choking emotion. Pure rage that this man had dispensed with a life so casually.

'So Lotti had to die for that? Just that?'

'To my astonishment the girl recognized the Codex for what it was. Apparently she'd heard about the Tacitus at the Ahnenerbe. Anyway, because she imagined I was having some affair with another woman, she took it upon herself to steal it. I assume she wanted to teach me a lesson, but I don't need lessons from young ladies. Particularly not on the subject of Latin literature.'

'But to strangle her?'

He dragged a handkerchief from his pocket, dabbed at his brow and gave a faint wince of what might be remorse.

'I didn't want her to die. I wanted her scared in order to get my Codex back. That's what I told the man. But he was a local communist hoodlum and he killed her in an excess of patriotism.'

'Is that what you call murder?'

'The chap assumed she was an enemy of the Soviet Union. Indeed she probably was.'

'And where is this precious Codex now? The one that's worth a woman's life?'

'That's my greatest regret. It's lost. I'm afraid it will have to remain a casualty of war. It's a shame. I must be one of the very few people in the world who could recognize that Codex right off for what it was. I was a Greats scholar at Oxford, you know.

There was only one man above me. He took the Newdigate Prize. Just pipped me to it. And it still rankles, if I'm honest.'

Hugh had entered a kind of reverie. The whites of his eyes were cracked and yellowish, like the glaze on an old painting. Clara realized he must have been drinking all evening. He leaned against the mantelpiece and turned the photograph of Clara's mother around to face him.

'I suppose whether one likes Stalin, or England, Fascism or Communism, it's all a question of taste, isn't it? Like the difference between Vermeer or Klimt . . .'

He took another swig of whisky, then placed the bottle on the mantelpiece with the deliberation of the profoundly drunk.

'I'm not proud of this, Clara. I've been a faithful servant of the Soviet Union since my twenties and if Stalin wants me to dispose of British agents, that is what I must do. No matter how much I might personally like or admire them. I do like you, very much.'

He reached downwards and she saw the sudden glint of metal in his hand.

'But I suppose betrayal is one of those things we English do so well. Like garden parties and well-made gentlemen's shoes.'

'You wouldn't shoot me, Hugh. Think how easily you'd be traced.'

'As a matter of fact everyone imagines I'm in Prague. I was obliged to leave my car in the care of the Adlon and I'll be heading off tonight.'

She looked down at the pistol. It was bigger than the tiny Derringer she had possessed. As Hugh moved the muzzle a fraction, pointing it more directly at her chest, a cold fear clutched at her. She looked over at the pictures of Erich and her mother on the mantelpiece and wished passionately that she had kept a photograph of Leo after all. Yet it was still Leo's face in her mind as the shot rang out.

★   ★   ★

The noise filled the room and blasted out into the darkness. Hugh Lindsey staggered, as if surprised, a dark treacle of blood beginning to stain his suit. As his body jerked sideways and backwards, and then fell awkwardly to the floor, Clara spun around to see Hedwig Holz. Her arm was shaking so much that the muzzle of the gun was a blur. The room smelled of gunpowder and perfume.

'I never thought I could shoot someone.' Hedwig's voice was trembling, but she lifted her chin resolutely. 'All those lessons must have counted for something.'

Clara forced herself to remain calm. She wondered if Hugh might die, and how quickly, but looking at him sprawled awkwardly on his back she saw that his skin was already becoming chalky, and his eyes were open and motionless, as if surprised. She moved swiftly to the front window and looked out.

'Don't worry,' said Hedwig. 'They're always hearing shots round here. They'll think it's the Faith and Beauty girls having night-time pistol practice in the forest. Either that or someone shooting geese.'

Clasping her arms around her chest, as if to protect herself from the trauma, Clara walked off into the kitchen and poured herself a glass of water. She felt a violent nausea at the sight of Hugh Lindsey lying there, and her own surprise at not being dead.

Something he had said, a comment she barely registered in the fear of the moment, now resounded.

I was a Greats scholar at Oxford, you know. There was only one man above me. He took the Newdigate Prize. Just pipped me to it. And it still rankles, if I'm honest.

The Newdigate Prize was Oxford's great honour for poetry. John Buchan had won it in his time, and Matthew Arnold and Oscar Wilde. And, more recently, it had been awarded to another gifted classics student: Leo Quinn.

Hugh Lindsey must have fostered a grudge against Leo. A grudge that had stretched for decades all the way from the golden stone cloisters of Oxford to the other side of Europe. And finally, years later, he had found a way to take his long desired revenge.

Hedwig had followed her mutely to the kitchen and was standing, shivering violently, as shock took hold. Gently Clara removed the gun from the girl's shaking hand and put her arms round her.

'I owe you my life.'

Hedwig leant her head on Clara's shoulder and for a moment the two women stood motionless in the deep silence, aware only of their own beating hearts. Then Clara stepped back and gazed searchingly into Hedwig's unassuming countenance.

'Are you all right?'

'Yes.'

The blood had drained from Hedwig's face, but her voice was steady. Clara hoped she would not be burdened with guilt at the idea of having killed a man.

'I can't ever thank you enough. That was very brave of you.'

'I wasn't brave.' Hedwig's jaw clenched. 'It wasn't courage; it was anger. That man killed my best friend. I shot him for Lotti's sake as much as yours.'

'I'm grateful all the same. More than I can say.'

There was something about this young woman that belied the apologetic posture and the hesitant demeanour, Clara realized. Behind the awkward exterior there was steel in her.

'Why are you here?'

'I had to get a gun for my boyfriend. He's in trouble.'

'I thought you were going to the ball?'

'I was. I went to the afternoon practice but I was terribly nervous. I made quite a hash of it. I kept getting out of time. At the end of it, Fräulein von Essen took me aside and said I stood out too much. I didn't stay in line. If I took part in the dance I would let down not just myself but the entire Faith and Beauty movement and probably the Führer himself. She had been considering making the whole group withdraw because of my laziness, but instead she had decided that I should suffer the shame alone. I would not be able to come to the ball and should just stay quietly at home.'

'So you came here.'

'I went to the Faith and Beauty home. I knew it would be deserted, and it was the ideal opportunity to collect my pistol.'

Clara's head was still spinning, trying to piece together the fragments of information.

'Why does your boyfriend need a pistol?'

'He works as a forger. He makes documents for Jews in hiding. Identity documents. Recently he undertook a job and he thinks he was followed. He was providing a document for a lady . . .'

'A forger, you say?'

'Yes. He had a job and when this lady left, he could tell she was being watched.'

'How could he tell?'

'He saw she was being shadowed.'

Fragments of information were colliding in her head, like shards of a broken vase forming together into a whole.

'But that's not the point,' continued Hedwig. 'If this lady was being tailed, then it's likely that they saw Jochen too, so he's worried now that the Gestapo are on to him as well. He's already left his job. And he wanted me to get him a pistol.'

'But why come here? To my house?'

'I was on my way back to the S-Bahn and I saw a man ahead of me. I recognized him at once.'

'Because you'd met him in London.'

'Lotti was obsessed with him. I told you. They'd become lovers. As soon as I saw him again I realized it must have been him that Lotti had been meeting. That was the man she was terrified of. The man who must have killed her. But I still don't know why.'

A sudden, sharp clarity possessed Clara and she took hold of Hedwig's hands. Circumstance had brought the two women together, but fate had interlaced their lives and the events of that night made a lasting bond between them. Now she wanted to do everything she could to help.

'You were right about the jewel, Hedwig. Lotti died because of it. And I think I can tell you what and where it might be.'

Chapter Forty-one

Elsa Neuländer-Simon's photography studio was in a tall stucco building in Schlüterstrasse, just off the Ku'damm in the west end of the city. For years, Studio Yva had been the most successful studio in Germany until the Nazi regime blacklisted the photographer and obliged her to carry out all work under the auspices of an Aryan studio manager. It would take more than that to stop Yva working, however, and every part of the house, from its pillared entrance, to its grand balconies and winding staircases, continued to be used as backdrop to her legendary shoots. The door was opened by a fey young man in a sleeveless sweater and bow tie who ushered Hedwig into a parquet hall and yelled, 'Yva! Ein Fräulein to see you.'

A reply floated down from several floors above.

'If it's another one of those girls collecting for the Winterhilfswerk, tell them we don't want to buy any more tanks.'

The young man gave a camp little shrug and said, 'Follow me.'

The studio, a sparsely furnished, open space running the length of the house, had a vacant, abandoned air. It was furnished only by a couple of chairs, a cabinet and a pile of dustsheets. In the midst a slight woman was kneeling on the floor dismantling a cumbersome tripod.

'You'll have to wait.'

Awestruck, Hedwig looked around. The girls whose portraits hung on these walls were entirely different from the images of womanhood she had seen anywhere else in Germany. Here were no hearty, fresh-faced mothers, none of the wholesome members of the Faith and Beauty Society or the League of German Girls, but glacial blonde goddesses who emitted a cool artifice that seemed to say although they may be advertising cosmetics, shoes or jewellery, their bodies remained their own. Their limbs were hard as marble, their eyes heavy-lidded, and they had a smouldering erotic charge.

One picture in particular caught Hedwig's attention. It was a young woman, platinum hair rippling in tight waves, fur coat flicked aside to reveal a slash of ivory flesh from the top of her stockinged leg to the snow of her exposed breast. The composition was all geometric lines and oblique perspectives like an old silent movie, its dramatic lighting and edgy glamour breathing a sense of violence and danger. The expression on the girl's face, the poise of her body, and the cigarette dangling from one hand, was at once decadent and rigidly controlled. It was as though all the sex that had been suppressed in Germany was distilled in a single photograph.

The subject was Lotti Franke.

'Everyone loves that one. It was taken by my apprentice, Helmut Newton. He loved big blonde girls in high heels,' said Yva, getting to her feet. 'Especially naked ones. He's left me now, unfortunately. He could have been quite a talent, but he would insist on emigrating. Perhaps he was right. I had an offer from *Life* magazine to go to New York but I turned it down.'

'Why didn't you go?'

'My husband wasn't keen. Only now he has lost his job and been given a new occupation as a street sweeper, he's regretting his decision. But there we are.'

Yva finished folding away the tripod and began meticulously dismantling the camera. Her angular, intelligent face, framed by dark brows, looked in no mood to expend any niceties on Hedwig.

'I'm sorry to disappoint you, but this studio is officially closed. They've given me a new job too, as it happens. A technician in the Jewish hospital, working with X-ray cameras. Is that a joke, do you think?'

'I think they have no sense of humour.'

'You're probably right. Anyhow, if it's photography you're after, I'm unavailable.'

'That's not what I came for.'

'Then . . .' The eyebrows lifted slightly.

Hedwig nodded towards the photograph on the wall.

'Did you know her well? Lotti Franke?'

Yva's voiced hardened with suspicion.

'Who are you exactly?'

'My name is Hedwig Holz. I was her best friend.'

'Ah.' Yva abandoned her business with the camera and rose. She made her way to the solitary cabinet.

'In that case, perhaps you'll share a drink with me.'

She poured two large whiskies into cloudy tumblers and handed one to Hedwig, who gulped it like lemonade, the unfamiliar burn causing her to choke. Yva perched on one of the chairs, extended one long, fishnet-stockinged leg and stroked it thoughtfully.

'I first met your friend Lotti a year ago. Perhaps she mentioned it.'

Hedwig nodded silently.

'She came to me with some sketches for clothes and wondered if I would photograph the finished products. Perhaps I would speed her progress as a designer. But though they were good, it wasn't only the clothes I was interested in. I could see your friend had quite another talent. I said I would only photograph the clothes if she modelled them and she agreed straight away. She had drive, that girl, and a hard ambition. I recognized something of myself in her. I was one of nine children – my mother was a milliner – so I knew what it was to work hard and graft. To use everything God gives you to succeed. Lotti was not ashamed of using her body if it helped her. Helmut Newton loved her. He said Lotti was his ideal woman. But then, with a body like that, I daresay she was a lot of men's ideal woman. Even the Führer's.'

Her needle-sharp glance grazed Hedwig's own legs, causing her to blush fiercely. But she persisted.

'The last time you saw Lotti, did she seem distracted by anything?'

'If she was, I wouldn't have known it. She was far too professional.'

'The fact is . . . the day before she died she told me about something she had. And I wondered if perhaps she left it here.'

For a long moment Yva continued to scrutinize Hedwig, as if trying to decide whether she was worth trusting, then she nodded.

'She asked me to look after it. Just for a few days. She wouldn't say what it was, or why she wanted me to take it, and my first instinct was to refuse. You don't hide other people's possessions without a very good reason nowadays. But your friend had the face of an angel, and I was not about to lose a model that good. Unfortunately the next time I saw that face it was on the front page of the *Berliner Tageblatt.*'

Quietly, so quietly that her voice barely travelled across the narrow distance between them, Hedwig said, 'Where is it now?'

Yva remained motionless for a moment, then she stubbed her cigarette on the floor, ground out its embers with the toe of her shoe and rose decisively. She crossed to the cupboard where she had found the whisky bottle and rummaged behind rows of satin dresses until she retrieved it.

It was a light tan leather briefcase, expensive-looking but slightly scratched and worn at the corner, with brass fittings and the gilt initials H S L indented on the front. A smaller monogram on the clasp said *Asprey of London*. Hedwig's fingers trembled as she unlatched it. The air that escaped smelt of burning, the mustiness of an old fireplace, the ancient molecules of another era. And vacancy.

'There's nothing here.'

'What were you looking for?'

'A book. A manuscript.'

'Oh that. I disposed of it.'

To one accustomed to handling the manuscripts in the Ahnenerbe with white cotton gloves, Yva's casual comment was devastating.

'You can't have any idea what it was.'

'On the contrary, my dear. I knew exactly what it was. No good German can fail to be aware of the importance of the *Germania*. To me, it is the world's most dangerous book.'

'But where is it?'

'As I think I mentioned before, I'm a Jew, Fräulein. I reasoned that the book belonged somewhere far away from the hands of those who would use it for their own purposes. Last Saturday I was taking a picnic out by Krumme Lanke. We go there to sunbathe and swim, though it's still not quite warm enough yet for my tastes. Anyhow, at one point I made my excuses and went into the woods. Your manuscript is there, somewhere. Don't ask me where. I forget.'

In that moment, her shock evaporated and Hedwig laughed out loud at the little woman's ingenuity. She was right; it couldn't be more appropriate. The *Germania*. The work that meant so much to Doktor Kraus and SS-Reichsführer Himmler and everyone at the Faith and Beauty Society. The key to the German people's past. How fitting that old Roman, Tacitus, would have thought it; that his work on the ancient forest tribe should remain where it started, deep beneath the must and mouldering leaves of the Grunewald.

★   ★   ★

An hour later she found Jochen in the place they had arranged, beside the Löwenbrücke in the south-west corner of the Tiergarten. The bridge was suspended by four cast-iron lions with ropes in their mouths, and above it the sun cascaded through the lush summer foliage and flint-necked crows squabbled in the boughs of the sweet chestnuts. Jochen was concealed in shadow at the foot of the bridge, smoking a ragged cigarette with deliberation, savouring each inhalation like a connoisseur enjoying a fine wine.

She had so much to tell, yet the sight of him silenced her. Already, only a few days since he had left home, he looked dramatically different. Feral almost. His entire frame seemed to have shrunk; his cheekbones stuck out cadaverously and he was wearing an ill-fitting, dingy jacket and unfamiliar cap. Hedwig might not even have recognized him were it not for the way that he was surveying the vegetation intently, his eyes fixed on the variety of weeds and the bees that were blundering between the flowers, pollen spinning like jewels in the sunlight.

'Where are you living?'

'Schmidstrasse.'

It was a slum area, north of Kreuzberg.

'Are you sleeping all right?'

'I'll sleep better if you've brought me what I asked for.'

She felt in her bag and brought out one of Kurt's muslin cloths in which she had wrapped the pistol. He took it from her swiftly, almost imperceptibly, and slipped it into his pocket.

'Also, I brought you some food.'

She passed him a lovingly prepared roll of ham and cheese, a piece of white sausage, a packet of tea and a bag of sugar she had purloined from work. These too he transferred wordlessly into his jacket.

'What about your clothes? Do you need me to wash them?'

Still, Jochen didn't move, but his eyes flicked towards her and he gave a sharp smile.

'You think of everything.'

'I'll have to if I'm going to come with you . . .'

'You're not coming with me.'

'You said I could.'

'I've changed my mind.'

Looking into his face, dappled with green shadow reflected from the water under the bridge, she felt he had already receded from her, like an animal into deep camouflage.

'But why?'

He remained slouched against the bridge, staring straight ahead, taking swift, savage drags of his cigarette.

'It won't work. I have no idea how long this will go on. Where I might go. What will happen when war comes.'

'All the more reason for us to be together.'

'I don't need you.'

'You don't *need* me?'

The words almost choked her. Jochen's tone was offhand, as if he was declining a cup of coffee, rather than her life.

'Not exactly. I *do* need you. But if I'm going to survive underground, I need you on the surface. Someone who would never arouse a moment of suspicion. Somebody ordinary.'

'Is that what you think I am, then? Ordinary?'

'No.' He ground out the cigarette impatiently beneath his foot, swivelling his heel in the damp gravel. 'I thought you realized that. You're brave. Just as brave as Sofie. You took a big risk at the ball the other day. And you were willing to leave those brothers you love so much and come with me.'

'Then why . . .?'

At last Jochen's gaze lost its hardness and he turned to look at her full on.

'Don't you see, Hedy? Surely you understand? It's not only food or clothes or guns you can give me. It's the *thought* of you. The thought that there's someone good waiting for me. Someone worth caring about.'

He was staring at her now, as if trying to stamp the impression of her face indelibly in his mind. He lifted a grimy finger to her cheek and touched it briefly.

'Everyone needs something to keep them going. For me, it's you.'

She knew then, as she looked at him, that this gruff, prickly man was her fate – a fate that no fortune teller would ever have predicted. Who at the Faith and Beauty Society, training her up for the black-liveried arm of an SS man, would have paired Hedwig with an angry, independent anti-Nazi instead? Plain Hedwig Holz, who except on the dance floor had never put a foot out of line. What could she possibly have in common with this unpolished character, so indifferent to the social graces and averse to pleasantries or compliments? Yet Jochen had divined something in Hedwig, a potential she had never recognized herself and nor, she was sure, had anyone else.

He noticed her eyes were glinting and burrowed in his pocket. 'Here. I got this a while ago from work and I forgot to give it to you. Dry your eyes. If I'm going to think of you, I don't want to think of you crying.'

He passed her a square of synthetic silk, emblazoned with the words *Our Führer is Fifty* and pictures of Germany's achievements: a People's Car, a Luftwaffe plane, a factory in the Ruhr, and at the centre an image of the Führer. Hedwig blew her nose on it and they stood in silence, shoulders touching, as the wafts of cigarette smoke curled into the brightening air.

Chapter Forty-two

Berlin Mitte had been washed in blood. It was ablaze with crimson pennants, marching troops and the clatter of drums and brass. There was a greasy swirl of gasoline on the wind, and a sea of eagle-topped banners, glinting in the sun, recalled the triumphal march of a Roman emperor. Percussion shivered in the air and the thump of side-drums made the ground quiver. An excited crowd of sightseers had gathered to watch, and every so often the monstrous operetta of boots and belts and guns caused them to break into frenzied applause. If something was that good to look at, who cared if it was fake?

The filming of *Germania*, like every other project in the Reich, was proceeding at an extraordinary pace. No obstacle would be allowed to get in the way and every barrier, no matter how great, would be conquered. Not that many people dared put up obstacles to Leni Riefenstahl, even when it required commandeering half of Unter den Linden and the whole of Pariser Platz and filling it with cameramen, lighting crew, stills photographers and a squad of fifty Faith and Beauty girls.

Several detachments of soldiers from the nearby Lichterfelde barracks had been co-opted – some to march up and down for as long as the director required and others to string up banners, halt traffic, erect barricades and clear the way for cameramen on roller-skates who were filming the troops from street level. The guards participated enthusiastically, agog at the girls, assiduously preventing ordinary citizens from crossing the square lest they collide with extras dressed as ordinary citizens crossing the square. It made a pleasant change from their usual occupation of practising military manoeuvres, endlessly cleaning and reloading their guns.

Leni herself had spent much of the day winched on a minute wooden platform up a ten-metre-high flagpole next to the Brandenburg Gate, squinting up the new East-West axis with a viewing device and defying the inelegance of the situation with a pair of Dior trousers and her glossy hair bundled tightly beneath a director's cap. Around midday the Führer had dropped by for a viewing, accompanied by Goebbels, who was unable to resist the opportunity for an impromptu speech. '*Whoever has seen and experienced the face of the Führer in* Triumph of the Will *will never forget it. It will haunt him through days and dreams and will, like a quiet flame, burn itself into his soul.*' Leni, dressed in her trademark white greatcoat, stood by, smiling, though everyone knew that inwardly she was seething at the waste of precious time.

The previous day Clara had left Griebnitzsee for good. It was impossible to stay in the place where a death had happened; where she had lugged a man's body down the garden like a sack of rotten cabbages and watched it slip, without a trace, into the dark water of the lake. She had made two trips, the first to transport her few possessions back to Winterfeldtstrasse, and the second to bundle Erich's rabbits into their basket and deliver them to his grandmother's apartment. She found her godson tanned and cheerful, full of the excitements of the HJ camp. His entire demeanour was energized through a combination of rigorous exercise, songs and marches. *As agile as a greyhound, as tough as leather and as hard as Krupp's steel.* That was how Hitler described his ideal youth and outwardly Erich, with his newly shaven head and shining eyes, fitted the description perfectly. Yet as he sat there, fondling the rabbits' ears, stroking their pale gold fur and feeding them cabbage scraps, Clara knew he was still the tender-hearted boy he had always been, still excited by a world beyond guns and planes. *Perhaps we could go to the Strandbad Wannsee this Saturday, Clara. I've got so much to tell you. Is there any chance I could meet Leni Riefenstahl?* His sunny optimism warmed her and just for a while the sleepless fog which had descended on Clara since Hugh Lindsey's death lifted, and she was able to think beyond the events of the past few days.

By mid-afternoon, her scenes were finished, and she changed into her own clothes to watch the final shot of the day. It was the scene everyone was waiting for: the technically dazzling feat that would showcase Leni Riefenstahl's trademark choreography. Leni had already explained her plans. The shot would form the opening sequence of the film. Accompanied by a soundtrack of Wagner's Lohengrin, a Luftwaffe plane piloted by the Führer's favourite aviatrix, Hanna Reitsch, would approach and dip down like a divine messenger from the skies. The on-board camera would record the clouds parting to reveal the whole, glorious city of Berlin laid out, and right in the centre, a swastika. As the plane drew closer, the swastika would be revealed as a troupe of perfect Faith and Beauty girls massed in the Tiergarten. In a continuous uninterrupted tracking shot, the camera's eye would come right down to ground level, until the focus was resting on a single girl's face.

Word of the stunt had spread and sightseers had been collecting at the west side of the Brandenburg Gate for the past hour, their gaze oscillating between the celebrity director herself, and the film of low cloud covering the sky. Soldiers linked arms to control the crowds. From a perch on a viewing platform beside the gate, Clara joined them, looking out at the sea of entranced faces below.

They didn't have long to wait. It was just a sound at first, a low rumble from the distance, growing to a roar as the Junkers appeared, a grey gleam in the air, the swastikas on the underside of its wings clearly visible. The faint, buffeting breeze strengthened to a wash of air that flattened the leaves on the trees as the plane lowered, like some monstrous bird of prey, wings tilting slightly on the currents. Every face in the crowd was excited, expectant, enthralled as a crowd of children at a conjurer's trick. Every face was turned upwards.

Every face except one.

She couldn't see his features, because his hat was tilted down over his eyes, but he stood immobile, hands in pockets, pressed into the crowd, staring right at her. Even as she saw him she noticed something else – the only moving figures in the throng, two men shouldering their way fast in his direction. They were wearing long, belted raincoats, the unofficial uniform of the Gestapo, and were making a direct line for him. When Clara looked back at the place he had been standing, he had disappeared.

As swiftly as she could, Clara darted through the crowd, pushing past the dense press of onlookers in the direction of the man she had seen. But it was useless. With so much practice waiting in queues, Berliners had got used to standing their ground. They moved as slowly and obstinately as cattle. No one was giving way, certainly not to anyone without official ID. Once Clara had fought her way through to the spot where the man had been standing he was nowhere to be seen. She stood looking around in frustration.

Was it Leo? Or a figment of her imagination? And if it was Leo, where would he go?

To the west of the Brandenburg Gate lay the Tiergarten, the largest park in Berlin, dense with trees that could provide cover, but at that moment staked out with cameras and arc lights, as the Faith and Beauty troupe held their gymnastic pose in the open ground. To the left was Potsdamer Platz and behind stretched Unter den Linden. Anyone being pursued would surely be more likely to make his way towards the busiest centre of population, where streets and crowds and buildings offered potential escape. Clara turned and pushed her way back through the stolid crowds to Pariser Platz.

Past Wilhelmstrasse she came to the Soviet Embassy, a handsome building with high brass lanterns, and she stopped and changed her bag to her other shoulder, giving her the opportunity to glance casually behind her, before scanning the street ahead. It was filled with pavement cafés and ambling shoppers, but there was no sign of Leo. If he had headed this way, both he and the men following had already been swallowed up in the crowd.

On the corner of Friedrichstrasse two policemen were standing, their eyes travelling over the passing pedestrians with more than usual scrutiny. Were they a second patrol on the lookout for him? And if so, how many others had been posted to join the hunt?

A couple of minutes later she had the answer. Towards the Lustgarten and crossing the bridge, a ribbon of lights on the dancing waters of the Spree, she noticed a car moving slowly, two men in the front seats, their faces sweeping left and right, scanning the crowds on the pavement as they trudged home from work.

At the same moment, far ahead, she caught sight of him. A vague shadow, moving swiftly, dipping in and out of the throng. A flash of red-gold hair. He turned sharp left, up to Museum Island, along the side of the canal where it was impossible for a car to follow, heading for the maze of streets around the courtyard complex of the Hackesche Höfe. Clara turned too, but once she had reached the elevated S-Bahn arches she lost him again.

In this area, Albert Speer's redevelopment of Berlin was at its most advanced. In some places entire streets had been flattened and elsewhere half-demolished homes stood like broken teeth, their debris coated with dust. Cranes and trucks were parked up for the evening. She hastened along Spandauer Strasse, past a restaurant whose glass front was shattered and a board hammered diagonally across the door. Inside, tables and chairs were over-turned, cups and plates abandoned on the tables. A paper was taped to the cracked door.

Closed until further notice. By order of police.

A zealous official had added a handwritten explanation.

I charged extortionate prices and that is why I am now in a concentra-tion camp.

Blood drumming in her ears, Clara looked around her, wondering if she had been wrong, trying to guess where in the maze of streets Leo might go. The streets in this part of the city were narrower, older, more winding than the broad boulevards elsewhere in Berlin. She remembered that Leo had once had an apartment near here, in Oranienburger Strasse, close to the enor-mous, gold-domed Neue Synagoge. That meant he knew the local streets well and he knew where best to disappear.

Amid the jangle of trams, a high-pitched angry shout rang out and faces turned. The police car that Clara had seen earlier had rejoined the street two hundred metres behind her at Dircksenstrasse and was coming in her direction, one man's head craning out from the passenger window. Ahead of her the figure of Leo darted across the road. The occupants of the car had seen him too.

At that moment the air was riven by a clanging bell. A siren wailed like a mournful wraith and a plume of smoke mush-roomed into the street, obscuring the houses on each side. Traffic drew to a halt. Klaxons sounded and people on the street looked hesitantly around until they saw a patch of derelict waste ground where a row of HJ boys was assembled in a line facing their corps leader, a grown man in shorts with a whistle, issuing staccato instructions through a megaphone. Almost immediately surprise mutated into mild irritation. Everyone knew what this was about.

Air-raid drill.

Practices for the bombing raids were happening every day now and they always involved the Hitler Jugend. The HJ, Erich had told her, would play a vital part in air-raid precautions. It would be their job to assist in the clean-up, to get casualties to first aid points and help relocate bombed-out civilians. Some would act as air-raid wardens and others would help put out fires. The really lucky ones, Erich said, would get to help operate the flak guns.

Amid the swirling smoke, a host of boys with Red Cross armbands dashed forward with stretchers. Others threw themselves enthusiastically on the ground, issuing loud, theatrical groans, enacting the aftermath of a bombing. Further recruits spilled from a nearby building and others, outfitted in gas masks and fireproof suits, proceeded to spray the ground with water, dragging wheeled canisters behind them as if removing traces of poison gas.

Immediately a jam formed. Trams slammed on their brakes. Cars bunched up. A cream bus shuddered to a halt, its passengers looking out incuriously. Most pedestrians vanished down side streets, unwilling to be detained by a performance they had seen numerous times before. Behind the bus, the police car revved in frustration and sounded its horn. Inside, the driver banged the steering wheel hard in frustration, but the HJ leader was blocking the road, arms outstretched officiously as his troop stretchered their pretend casualties into an adjacent block decorated with a large red cross. Another boy stood by with a placard that read '*Two dead*'. No one was allowed to interrupt an air-raid drill. The police car reversed, with a screech of gears.

Up ahead Leo was making a U-turn, heading east in the direction of the Schloss.

Clara hurried on breathlessly, pain tearing at her chest, desperate to slow down, yet terrified that she would lose sight of him. She could barely believe the direction he was taking. Of all the

places a fugitive might go, why would anyone being hunted by
the police head for Alexanderplatz?

The windswept square, intersected with yellow trams, was the
home of the Polizeipräsidium, the central police station. The
building known as the Alex rose with its towering dome on one
side of the square, lit up in the dusk like a great liner, with several
hundred policemen inside.

She drew to a halt at the centre of the square, static roaring in
her ears, and made a three hundred and sixty degree turn. From
one side came the clatter of steam trains pulling into the arched
glass vault of the Alexanderplatz Bahnhof. She scanned the shop
fronts. Leiser's shoe shop – the biggest in Berlin. The Mokka-Fix
Café. Then a Ufa movie theatre that she saw, with a shock,
featured her face on a billboard in a poster for *Love Strictly
Forbidden*, due for release in a fortnight. The effect of it was
somehow more startling than any unexpected, unflattering glance
in a mirror. The light-hearted smile, calculated to deceive, the
head thrown back in joyful abandon, told no truth about her
except one. That her life was one long façade of playing a part.

Of Leo there was no sign. As she surveyed her surroundings
her gaze snagged on the tall, limestone arch that announced the
entrance to Alexanderplatz U-Bahn.

Almost half of Berlin lies underground.

Then she understood.

Berlin's U-Bahn stations were the envy of the world. Styled by
the architect Alfred Grenander, they were little palaces of elegant
design with their finely wrought iron fittings, art nouveau lamps
and mosaic inlays. Alexanderplatz was no exception, sleekly
modern with its green glazed tiles and elegant iron banisters,
serving both the U5 and the U8 lines. Clara dashed through the
entrance hall and bought a ticket. She hunted fruitlessly for the
figure of Leo among the flow of commuters, then at random she
followed the signs to the U5 line and arrived onto a steel-arched

platform, the dirty yellow light smelling of dust and stale air. A train appeared, emptied its passengers and moved off.

She was torn between leaving immediately and remaining where she was. The U–Bahn was the obvious place to disappear, but if Leo was being pursued, surely he would have taken the train, rather than stay where he was.

Unless he knew that she had followed him.

She looked down into the darkness of the tunnel. The rails lit up with a dim gleam and the tracks hummed in anticipation of the next train, heading east for Lichtenberg, Frankfurter Tor and Friedrichsfelde. In the flicker before it arrived, the crowd on the opposite platform parted and she glimpsed a figure on a bench, hat pulled down over his face. The train passed before her eyes – the driver in his cabin, face set, and the passengers, exhausted by work and soothed by the jolting motion, blinking sleepily at the seats opposite – but once it had disgorged its set of passengers and moved on, the opposite platform was vacant. Only empty benches remained beneath a poster.

Haribo Makes Children Happy!

Clara was frozen with indecision. Another train burst into the station with an upwash of warm air. The crowds swelled and cleared and the train departed. At that point, a hundred yards away at the end of the same platform she occupied, a figure appeared. This time she could see his face. It was not the face of a phantom, but a living breathing man.

Chapter Forty-three

At precisely the same moment, the police she had seen before arrived on the opposite platform, looked across and shouted.

Springing up, Clara signalled to Leo that he should follow her and ran back up the steps the way she had come, along the exit tunnel, trying to recall what Jochen had told her.

Almost half of Berlin lies underground.

She knew now why she had chosen the U5 line. It was not a random choice, but a subconscious memory.

The green door to the air-raid shelter was entirely inconspicuous, just as Jochen had said. A blank sheet of steel studded with iron rivets and a vast handle, newly set into the wall. She pulled it, and found to her relief it was unlocked. Seconds later, Leo caught up and they slipped through the arched entrance into the darkness, pulled the door to and flattened themselves against the damp brick.

Inside, the air was dank and claustrophobic, but a glimmer of light revealed luminous paint outlining doorways and exits, and a long corridor punctuated by thick steel doors. A honeycomb of cells, waiting for occupation. There were signs for washing rooms and lavatories. Bedrooms. And immediately before them an immense, shadowy space like a station waiting room fitted with wooden benches. An entire underworld hotel with accommodation for hundreds.

Leo looked different in the phosphorescent shadow, at once strange and familiar. The light emphasized his finely cut features. He had grown a moustache, which made him seem older, and a triangle of tanned skin showed at his throat. He leaned against her, enfolding her entirely in his arms, and his hands traced her shoulders and spine as though he was remembering her flesh, inch by inch. She felt his heart slamming against his chest and pressed harder into his body – the body she knew by heart – inhaling the warm, familiar musk, feeling the pull of yearning for him, even now, and the answering surge within him. Not a breath of air separated them. His cheek was rough with stubble as they kissed.

They tensed themselves for the tramp of feet in the corridor outside, listening for the stamp of heavy police boots, the hurrying footsteps to halt outside the door. But amid the regular flow of travellers, nothing stood out.

She whispered, 'How many are following?'

'Three teams, I think. Two pairs on foot and another two in a car. By now, there could be more.' His breath was hot against her ear, his entire body tense and alert. 'I had to come back and find you. I needed to make sure you were safe. I couldn't go back to England without knowing.'

'What do you mean, you're going to England?'

In the darkness she gripped his hand as if to lock him to her, the questions tumbling through her mind.

'My name's a priority on the Gestapo watch list.'

'If you're on a watch list, they would have stopped you at the border . . .'

'They spotted me at Tempelhof. They could have picked me up there but they chose not to. I assume they wanted to see who I was meeting. I've put you in danger, my darling. We need to keep moving. We have to get out of the Underground.'

The S7 line train was full of commuters travelling home to the western suburbs. Past the Zoo, Charlottenburg, Grunewald,

Nikolassee, bodies rocking companionably on the wooden benches to the soothing rhythm of the train. The clattering of the tracks, the stops and starts, the squeal of brakes and the station announcements. Leo insisted that they did not sit or speak together, so Clara chose a spot three rows away and tried to keep herself from looking at him. The tension of being unable to hold or touch him was excruciating and the enforced silence was even worse. There was so much to tell him. About Angela and Hugh Lindsey and the proposed pact between Russia and Germany. But it wasn't until the train approached its final stop that he rose and she followed him up the steps, out into the prettily gabled station of Berlin-Wannsee.

Wannsee Station, with its gothic signs and arched windows, might have been straight out of a Grimm Brothers woodcut of a fantasy Germanic past. Even the air was different here, pure and green, infused with the watery scent of the Havel River that lay to one side, pocked with sailing boats making their slow, scenic way in the summer dusk. On the opposite bank, a path ran through dense woodland all the way to Potsdam. On Sundays the route was thronged with hikers, cyclists and families out for a lakeside walk, but now, on a weekday evening, only the occasional dog walker could be seen trudging along the leaf-strewn path.

They crossed the bridge, but it wasn't until they reached the cover of woodland that Leo allowed himself to speak. They walked, clasped close to each other, the filigree of branches above them framing a darkening sky.

'The night I received that call they told me that two of our agents had disappeared in Vienna. All we knew was that they had arranged a meeting in the Café Louvre with a pair of German officers who were thought to be anti-Nazis.'

'I know the Café Louvre. I made a film in Vienna three years ago. We used to go there.'

Clara recalled the pale spring light streaming through the big windows, the violin-backed chairs and booths finished in dark brocade along one wall. The Schnitzel and creamy Kaffee mit Schlagobers.

'I went there straight away. I became a regular and made friends with the barman. A nice chap. Georg.'

Clara pictured Leo faux-drunk, boozily intimate, leaning against the bar late into the evening.

'Sure enough, Georg told me what had happened. He saw the agents arrive and sit at a table with two other men. And it must have been a set-up because within minutes the door slammed open, there was shouting, and the Gestapo came in with guns and dogs.'

She saw the dogs slavering, pulling against the lead.

'Our men were taken away, almost certainly to be tortured and shot.' Leo swallowed and paused for a moment. 'But Georg had noticed something curious. There was another customer in the bar, not a regular, and he was there as the arrest took place. Georg said to me, "*Something like this happens, everyone tries to hide their face, but they're looking all the same. They can't help themselves. But this man, he didn't turn a hair. Just kept reading his book.*"'

'What does that prove?'

'That he knew the arrest was going to happen. That he was part of the set-up. And Georg was doubly curious because the book this man was reading was in a foreign language. It wasn't English, he said, or French, or Hungarian, any other language he recognized. All he could say was that it was the language you found on tombstones.'

'Latin?'

'Exactly.' Leo stopped and turned to Clara, urgently.

'And there was only one person I could think of who would sit in a café reading a book in Latin. As soon as I realized, I knew you were in grave danger. I had to get to you before he did.'

It was her turn to astonish him.

'Hugh Lindsey is dead.'

Jaggedly, she explained about Hugh, and the woman he had killed, and about how he had tried to kill her too. As she spoke, Leo laced his fingers through hers and gripped her tightly, as if attempting some retrospective protection.

'I should have known,' he said bitterly. 'I should have seen through Hugh much earlier. Good old Hugh. Everyone's best friend. Always the life and soul of the party, even if he did like one too many and was always the last to leave. If anyone had looked more closely they might have sensed a vacancy in him. There was a kind of emptiness, which he filled with drink and liaisons with other people's wives. But nobody did look closely.'

'Why was that?'

'Because Hugh had the most lethal of all qualities. Charm. Charm deflects enquiry. We're taught about those types in train-ing. They're dominant. They imagine they can calculate risks and manage them better than anyone else.'

'You knew him at Oxford, didn't you?'

'Yes. I liked him a lot actually, though we were intellectual rivals. We had some of the same friends, but we lost touch after-wards. Hugh lived a peripatetic existence. After Christ Church he travelled to Vienna, then went back to England and took up a job as journalist. At the same time he began working for the Intelligence Services.'

'Like you.'

'Only in Hugh's case, it was a cover for his work for the Soviet Union. He'd formed Marxist sympathies in Austria and began to spy for the NKVD. They managed to infiltrate him into D Section and that way he had knowledge of our entire European network. Hugh knew I was in Vienna, and he let the police know too. I disappeared just in time.'

Leo stopped for a moment and pulled Clara to him, resting his chin on her head and kissing her hair.

'There was a day a few weeks ago, when I was on the run, that I slipped into a cinema. I had taken to going to matinées because there were hardly any other people there and it meant I could snatch some sleep, but that day the film was one of yours, so I didn't sleep. And as I sat there in the darkness I felt you were right there, in my arms. It was so real I could almost taste your skin and smell that perfume you wear. It was like . . . a vision. When I came out into the foyer I knew I'd been wrong to enforce that vow of silence on you. But it was part of my plan, Clara. I thought I knew best. It was for your safety. I thought it was essential that we stayed completely secret.'

'Have you ever told anyone about us?'

'Never. Or only one person – an old schoolfriend, Ed Russell. I bumped into him back in London, years ago. It was one of those dismal winter evenings when your spirits are low, and I was walking down the Strand, thinking about you, missing you, and I ran slap into him. We went for a drink. He's one of the nicest chaps you could ever meet. He has a way of getting your secrets out of you – we could probably do with him in the Section – but I knew we had no mutual acquaintance, and I'd probably never see him again. And I never have.'

Clara felt a bewildering prickle of jealousy at the idea of Leo's life in England without her and the unknown Ed Russell who was sole witness to their love.

'I've kept our secret, Clara, but I don't want to any more. I want you with me in England. There's no telling when war could break out.'

She stopped in her tracks.

'But there is. That's what I need to communicate. Von Ribbentrop is flying to Moscow imminently to agree a non-aggression pact. The Soviet Union will stand by when Hitler invades Poland. I've seen the memorandum. It's codenamed Operation White. And they've set a date. The first of September.'

His face was a mixture of emotions: astonishment at the news, amazement at her skill in the world he had inducted her into and horror at the risks she must have run.

'Have you told anyone this?'

'Only you.'

It was darker now, the surroundings becoming more mono-chrome. They had emerged at the spot where the elegant grey-green steel arches of the Glienicke Bridge spanned the Havel. To the north the land rose up in densely wooded slopes to the land-scaped park and fairy-tale turrets of the Schloss Babelsberg. To the east, a few fragile points of light signalled the outlying streets of Potsdam. Leo gestured to a car parked on the far end of the bridge, its engine idling.

'There was a man I knew in the German Foreign Ministry. I'd met him years ago in London, and I thought he might be sympa-thetic to us. He was unwilling to cooperate, though I sensed that he was not an ardent Nazi. So I took a chance and called him earlier today. My instinct was right. He agreed to drive me across the border tonight.'

The breath caught in her throat.

'You're leaving?'

'No. *You* are. If we try to leave together we risk attracting attention. You will take my place in the car. I'll follow.'

'How can you follow? You're on a Gestapo watch list. How long could you evade them?'

'I'm not leaving you here.'

'You don't have a hope of escaping them, Leo. This is your best chance.'

He squared his shoulders and wrapped his arms round her waist, closing any distance between them. The movement of his body against hers aroused the old, familiar feelings, the urgency of desire, the recognition that loving each other had become a part of them – the best part perhaps – and that what they possessed was solid and incorruptible. Clara yearned to stay suspended in that moment, for the earth to halt in its orbit and the stars above them to slow.

He said, 'I've spent so much of my life in the shadows. Pretending. Deceiving people. Changing my identity the way other people change their shirt. That's the job, I know, but I don't want to live like that any more. I want the most important part of my life to be open, public, dull even. I used to crave excitement and novelty, but now I want my life to be normal, or as normal as it could be alongside the loveliest woman in the world. I want a row of children with your blue eyes. As many as you like. I want to be able to say, *"Look, everyone, this is Clara Vine, who is not only the most beautiful woman you have met, but is also my wife."*'

She glanced away, down to the river below, remembering her pact with the deity that she would do whatever Leo wanted if only he was alive. That she would be the woman he wanted her to be.

'What good would it do if you were dead? How could we marry then?'

He carried on, almost as if she had not spoken.

'When I came away from that moment in the cinema, I sifted through the whole of my life since I met you and I realized the only precious moments were those I had spent with you. I begrudge every day we're not together. Take my place, Clara.'

He looked at her, as if trying to compress a lifetime's conversation in a single glance.

'I can't leave Germany without saying goodbye to Erich.'

'Erich will understand.' The light in his eyes pierced as sharply as the first time she had met him. That same level gaze, that shivering intensity.

'There are three surveillance teams looking for you. No one's looking for me. I can take the first train out of Berlin. I can leave Germany tomorrow.'

'No.'

'When war comes Erich will be called up and I might never see him again. I have to see him before I leave. And then I will come straight away. You must trust me, Leo. You do trust me, don't you? There's no point in anything if you don't.'

He cupped her face. Although his expression remained controlled, a tremor in his hands betrayed the depth of his emotion.

'I do.'

'And you believe I'm capable?'

'That's one thing about you that I have never doubted.'

She linked her fingers into his, as tightly as if they had been parachute jumpers planning to fling themselves into the cold unknown.

'Go then.'

He walked along the bridge. She could see the soft glow of the car's gauges and the gleam of the leather inside. But whether Conrad Adler saw her, as the door opened and Leo got inside, it was impossible to tell. She stood watching, until the car's lights dimmed into the distance and finally faded from sight.

Author's Note

No event was more central to the outbreak of World War II than the Nazi–Soviet Pact. Signed on August 23rd, 1939, it was an enormous coup for Hitler, turning Germany's greatest foe into an ally overnight and avoiding the danger of a war along the eastern borders of the Reich. Leni Riefenstahl records how she was present at the film evening at the Chancellery when Hitler's remarks about Stalin gave the first inkling of his intentions.

The Sonderfahndungsliste G.B., the Gestapo *'Special Search List for Great Britain*, was designed to be given to every soldier. It was a Who's Who of the British establishment with details of more than two thousand people, complete with photographs, home addresses and private hobbies. It also probed every facet of British life, from political parties, police forces and secret services to newspapers, radio stations and trade unions.

The Rote Kapelle, the Red Orchestra, was a network of seven resistance groups with more than one hundred and fifty members, including the fortune teller Annie Krauss. They sheltered Jews and Communists and provided forged papers for those attempting to flee. More than a hundred and twenty members of the Berlin group were arrested in 1942 and sentenced to death.

Alois, the half brother of Adolf Hitler, ran a restaurant at 3, Wittenbergplatz for many years. He was approached anonymously by the Rote Kapelle with an invitation to join them and circulate a typed flyer denouncing the Nazis' culture of lies. Instead he handed over the note to the Gestapo, and the leaders were ultimately arrested and executed.

Albert Goering, brother of Hermann Goering, took a different approach. The SS kept a file on him and he was declared a 'Public Enemy of the Reich' but Hermann rescinded the arrest warrant. When he was arrested at the end of the war, Albert secured a speedy release by producing a list of thirty-four key figures who would testify to the numerous Jews he had helped. He refused to change his name after the war and died impoverished.

Magda Goebbels' affair with Karl Hanke came to an end when he volunteered for military service. When *The Journey to Tilsen* was launched in November 1939 in Berlin, Magda ostentatiously walked out of the premiere.

A large amount of the 'degenerate art' seized by the Nazis went missing but in 2013 a celebrated haul was discovered in the Munich apartment of Cornelius Gurlitt, whose father Hildebrand Gurlitt had privately amassed more than a thousand works by painters including Matisse, Chagall, Beckmann, Nolde and Picasso while he worked for the Nazis.

Elsa Neuländer-Simon, also known as Yva, was a celebrated fashion photographer in Berlin and gave Helmut Newton his first apprenticeship. She and her husband were deported to the Majdanek concentration camp and murdered in 1942.

Leni Riefenstahl abandoned her film *Germania* on the outbreak of war.

Acknowledgments

Behind the name on the title page, there are many people involved in the appearance of a novel, and I would like to say a huge thank you to them. I am truly grateful to my agent, Caradoc King, for his early encouragement for the adventures of Clara Vine, and to everyone at United Agents. Thank you also to my superb editor, Suzanne Baboneau, and the team at Simon & Schuster UK – Ian Chapman, Clare Hey, Hannah Corbett, Isabel Prodger, Elinor Fewster and Rik Ubhi – to name but a few. I am thankful to many magnificent booksellers I have met around the UK, including all at Hatchards, Wimbledon Books and the energetic Colin Field of Waterstones.

In particular I want to thank John Carey, writer, critic, wit and beloved uncle, for whose inspiration and encouragement I am always grateful.

Black Roses

Jane Thynne

1933 and warning bells ring across Europe as Hitler comes to power

Clara Vine, a young, talented British actress, finds herself in Berlin and, unwittingly, in the midst of an uneasy circle of Nazi wives, among them Magda Goebbels.

There she meets Leo Quinn, an undercover British intelligence agent, and is soon recruited to spy on her new acquaintances.

But when Magda Goebbels reveals to Clara a dramatic secret and entrusts her with an extraordinary mission, Clara feels threatened, compromised and desperately caught between duty and love.

'Superbly atmospheric' Kate Saunders

PB ISBN 978-1-84983-985-3
EBOOK ISBN 978-1-84983-986-0

The Winter Garden

Jane Thynne

Berlin, 1937. The city radiates glamour and ambition. But danger lurks in every shadow...

Clara Vine is an actress at the famous Ufa studios by day and an undercover British Intelligence agent by night. When a young girl is found brutally murdered in the gardens of Berlin's notorious bride school, where young women are schooled on the art of being an SS officer's wife, Clara soon discovers that the murder is linked to a far more ominous secret.

With the newly abdicated Edward VIII and his wife Wallis set to arrive in Berlin, and the Mitford sisters dazzling on the social scene, Clara must work in the darkness to find the truth and send it back to London. It is a dangerous path she treads, and it will take everything she has to survive...

'A thoroughly enjoyable read: fast-paced, atmospheric and genuinely suspenseful'
Mail on Sunday

PB ISBN 978-1-84983-989-1
EBOOK ISBN 978-1-84983-990-7